# THE SECOND ENDGAME

## ORDER'S LAST PLAY BOOK THREE

## E. ARDELL

JovianEmPress.com

The Second Endgame (Order's Last Play, Book III)

Published by Jovian EmPress

San Jose, CA



Edited by Ashley Oliver

Cover Design by AEKCreates and Character Illustration by Yella Arts

Interior Book Design by E. Ardell

Splash Page Illustration by BaileyFawnuhArts



First edition published 2023.

Printed in the United States of America

ISBN: 979-8-9870099-2-5

To my sister Candice, who asked, "When are you going to write about the Ladreths again?"

# Chapter 1

## Lyle

A FLAMING HULA-HOOP FLIES AT my face, then springs upward, spinning over my head as if waiting for my permission to come down. I wave it away, watching it whirl off toward someone else, and glare at my brother across the clearing. I told Evan I don't dance, or hula hoop, or whatever the hell else he wants to call it, but he won't give up.

*How are we related? You have to dance. It's in your blood.*

Evan's thought is a shout echoed by feelings of incredulity and amplified by surges of something I don't understand.

My older brother comes from the same mess of DNA I do, half-human and the other half a conglomerate of multiple breeds of alien fae the Lauduethe side of the family slept with over the centuries. This made me psychic, Devon superman,

Lawrie an elemental, and Evan a fire-breathing magic user who gets sugar highs from being outdoors.

Months of getting used to him keeps me from jumping when Evan is suddenly in my space, grabbing my shoulders and pulling me down to match his shorter height. Once my green eyes are locked onto his identical ones, he shakes me. "This. Is. A. Celebration. Let loose!"

He lets go of my shoulders so I can straighten up but then grips my arm, turning me in a slow circle so that I can see things I've already seen. The back-wood clearing behind The Maiden's castle is a grassy dance floor, the trees providing natural walls and lighting. Their basketball-sized fruit-bulbs flicker white-blue, green, and purple. The deep pounding of multiple drums and the trills of woodwinds from a sunken orchestra pit at the center of the chaos echo into the night. The rave that looks like a RenFaire Gone Wild, the Green Alien Edition, will probably rage until morning.

It's hard to believe that only a few months ago this wood was razed by battle. Some of these carefree, Lenoran partygoers had stood on ground zero, chanting spells to erect and hold barrier wards around the palace. And maybe they're not cavalier at all. The passion in their dancing, the movements acrobatic and fast, could be a way to release pent-up frustration and anger at their home being invaded. They turn and leap, going up on their toes and down on their knees. I'm tired just watching. A few work fiery hula hoops around their hips, unafraid of being burned.

"Where's Lawrie?" I look around for our little brother, feeling guilty for losing track of him about ten minutes into the party. We came together, but since this party is for him, and *he* dances, he was dragged into a routine.

"Having fun." Evan lets me go, pushing me closer to a group of women working hula hoops around their waists. "Lyle, this is our last night together before Lawrie leaves. Don't make him want to end his own party early."

I shut my eyes and take a deep breath. Lenore's permanent smell of cinnamon and sugar, the outdoor scent as normal as the reek of road tar back home in Houston, makes me sick. Lawrie takes off for another planet in the morning, and in a few days, we'll know if his eyesight can be restored. Or if he's going to live life in the dark forever.

I don't think I could do it. Don't know how he manages. He says he sees through his powers. That the atoms around him shape the world, and his other senses are sharpening. But I think he copes because he believes the healers on Bruhje will fix him.

"Let me teach you to dance." The intention behind Evan's words is clear: keep Lyle from depressing himself. In his opinion, I wallow too much. "You should know how. There'll be more flame-dancing for Devon's return party in a little while—and don't tell me he doesn't dance either."

So, I don't, because my twin dances at parties. Hell, he throws them. He was popular in school. Played sports, was nice to people, kept up with trends. And if Devon was here, he'd push me to dance too.

A pang of separation anxiety almost makes my eyes water. I blink rapidly and startle at Evan's sharp whistle. A grass-vine creeps toward his hand. He grabs it, whipping it straight and then blowing on its bottom end. The vine ignites in his hand, the bright flame becoming an eerie spotlight that illuminates his tawny skin and catches the darker undertones in his too long, curly blond hair. He tosses the vine into the air, whistling again, causing it to furl... into a damn hula hoop. It lowers, and he puts his arm through it, spinning it, then moving it to the other arm, over his head, down to his waist, then back up to his neck.

"You don't have to know any steps. Just keep the ring going. The trick is,"—the ring jumps, flying over his head and revolving above mine—"the ring moves itself. If it comes too close to your body, it'll avoid you. So, you'll look good doing virtually nothing."

The ring drops, falling to my waist. And then I'm stuck with a flaming hula hoop. My older brother laughs like someone fresh out of an asylum before vanishing into the crowd. Did I really miss out on anything by not having grown up with him? Jerk.

Bodies brush by me. Voices speaking in foreign languages rush past. The bright colors decorating the clearing make my vision blurry. Weeks ago, I would have been in sensory overload. Collapsed somewhere dark, wishing for brain-numbing drugs to knock me out.

I suppress a smile. Warmth from my Stone seeps into my skin as it emits a soft blue glow. An extra layer of protection drapes itself over my mind like a blanket, my mental shields rock solid in a way they've never been. I stroke the Stone, tracing its smooth edges through my t-shirt. Great leader or not, I will always prefer Earth cotton to alien silk.

A mental proximity alarm thrums, the pulse rippling from the nape of my neck into my scalp. I whip around, fiery hula-hoop swaying, to be face-to-face with Maiden Nialiah. Her solid black eyes gleam as she flutters long lashes and smirks at me with red lips.

I don't know if she wears makeup or if she naturally looks like a green Barbie doll, but she's attractive. I know it, and my girlfriend, Caea Harliel, knows I know it. I step back. "What is it?"

She raises a thin brow. "Perhaps I want a dance." She reaches out, but her hand stops at the flaming hula hoop. I take back any bad thoughts I had about Evan. Nialiah's flirty expression turns serious. "We have had word from several checkpoints and a report concerning Disiez."

Disiez.

The last planet Devon had been on before he left with his Stone. "Did Devon call again? Did he ask for me? Is he okay?" Fear tries to rip the blanket off my mental shields.

No.

Devon will be here soon. He gave an ETA of a few weeks. It's been that.

And Nialiah's not answering me.

"Nialiah, is he okay?" I keep my voice level as new panic gives fear the strength it needs to invade every fiber of my being.

The Maiden frowns. "Not here. Come with me."

The hula hoop stops turning. It falls to the ground with a thump, its fire extinguishing. My lungs can't keep up with my rapid heartbeat. I grab Nialiah's wrists.

Power from the Stone surges through me. The mental blanket that hysteria ripped away is tucked around my mind again. It's a medicated bandage, sealing out excessive emotions and any external thoughts and feelings from the outside world.

Suddenly, I can think, breathe, and continue to function without melting. Because broken psychics burn out. I'm not broken anymore.

I release Nialiah's wrists and put steel in my voice. "Where the hell is my brother?"

Nialiah smiles slowly, seeming impressed. "He has been taken."

TRAVERSING THE TUNNELS BENEATH THE castle will never stop being creepy as hell. Why The Maidens put their secret meeting room in what used to be a dungeon is beyond me. I keep two feet between myself and Nialiah as we approach a set of double doors. Before she can knock, I open them with telekinesis. The wooden frames rebound off the stone walls, and I frown. I only gave it a little push. Or at least I thought I did.

The Stone glows, its power calming me. *Everything will be fine*, it whispers.

Councilors Theorne and Viveen, as well as Nialiah's adopted sister Maiden Hellene already sit around the rectangular table. Their heads snap toward the door, then to me. I scowl at them and make my way to the chair at the head of the table.

I sit and wait for Nialiah to take her seat, then gaze at the faces around me.

Theorne and Viveen meet my eyes. An undercurrent of irritation runs through them both, and I bite back a smirk. They hate not being able to talk down to me anymore.

"Leader Three," Theorne says, voice neutral, "this is your first damage control meeting. No one else in the palace is privy to what we know as of right now. Seeing as you know nothing of these kinds of procedures, I suggest you simply listen."

He doesn't want me to talk, which is fine. I've got nothing to say. But I love that Theorne has to 'suggest' what he thinks I should do instead of barking commands like he could months before I joined Order's inner circle.

Order had let Her secret conspirators know that I'm Her favorite Champion now. Reprimands in the form of magical shocks are dealt to members who openly disrespect me.

I meet Theorne's sharp gaze and hold it. "If you start with what happened to my brother and how we're going to fix it, I don't care."

Theorne's electric blue eyes spark, and I swear his goatee curls.

Maiden Hellene, green-skinned like her adopted sister, clears her throat and glares at me through hard black eyes. "The mainland of Disiez was lost to a tidal wave. There are no survivors."

I lean forward, resting my elbows on the table, brows knitting. That doesn't make sense. Devon's mage built a ward to keep that from happening. That was the agreement the Allegiances struck with the Disi people. Devon would be allowed safely on-planet to retrieve his Stone from their ocean, if the Allegiances provided them with magical protection from their rising waters.

Hellene's tone is cold. "Leader Two's ship never departed from that planet. It was recovered, along with a number of bodies that belong to our Allegiances' military."

My stomach climbs into my throat.

"Missing from the count of recovered bodies are Leader Two and the Harliel king. The message you received from your brother came approximately five *jewels* after the population of Disiez was destroyed."

My lungs shudder, only working when they want to.

"You say this as if the tidal wave was not a force of nature." Nialiah looks up from her manicure. "That planet was a lost cause."

"A lost cause drowned by magic, not nature. Traces of a barrier spell broken by its caster were discovered," Hellene retorts. "There is also evidence of Nazflit occupation. Bodies in Nazflit military uniforms were also found along with take-off rings on the launch site Leader Two and King Xijure Harliel should have departed from. Leader Two left the planet before its demise, yes, but not on one of our ships."

Air filters into my lungs. Devon was gone before the disaster. He's not at the bottom of some ocean. He's not dead. I know this because I talked to him. He... he seemed strange, off. I missed something in the call. Had he tried to send me a signal, anything, to let me know he was in trouble? I was so distracted by the Stone, Order's inner circle, Caea...

The room swims in and out of focus while the conversation continues around me.

"Only key members of the Silver and Gold Allegiances have this information." Viveen's sharp features make her look more vulture than person. I always feel like she's waiting for people to drop dead so she can pick their bones.

"Key members," I murmur, like us. "Do they have deals too?"

"With Lady Kahanna?" Nialiah peers at me under her lashes. "Of course. To win a war, our goddess must have deep pockets."

Order—Kahanna—the goddess with shark-teeth and black holes for eyes, created a prophecy about my brothers and me. Our choices will end hundreds of years of intergalactic war. Everyone on Her side will live happily ever after, and all the bad guys on Her Son's side, the god Pandemonium—Kahine—will go to Hell. Or so the Old Texts written during the Prophetic Cycles are rumored to say. The fact that Order's prophecy is a wild spell She cast and can't control is something only this circle knows.

"I think we should wait until after Leader Four's departure to release this development to the public," Theorne says. "It is imperative that we attempt all measures to have his vision restored. Such news may postpone his journey."

Theorne looks at me.

Lawrie would insist on staying here. And maybe I want him here, so I know where he is, unlike Devon. I'm going to throw up. If I open my mouth to say anything else, I'll... Cool energy flows through my body, and I pull the Stone from under my shirt, fingering its silver chain.

*Breathe*, it says.

"What happens to Devon if we wait?" I ask carefully.

Viveen rests her long-fingered hands on the table. "Our recent discoveries are undoubtedly known by the Nazflit and the Su, so we should anticipate an attempt at negotiation from them soon. If Leader Two and Xijure Harliel are still alive."

*Breathe.*

"We know they are still alive, fool, or else why would the Nazflit bother to have Leader Two send a message?" Hellene sneers at Viveen, who glares back.

I don't know their back story, but none of the people in Order's VIP circle get along inside or outside of class. And I don't care. "So, we'll negotiate. What do you think they'll ask for? We should start getting it together—"

"They will ask for our surrender, or for us to cast aside Order's Gifts." Hellene draws out her words, as if speaking to a toddler who won't listen. "We cannot do that."

Surrender means we cease to exist because Pandemonium wins.

But to give up Order's Gifts: the Harliels' weapons, the Maidens' armbands, the Stones... *my* Stone.

That brings control.

Peace.

Quiet.

"I can't give up my Stone." I can't go back to that loud, painful place that was psychic hell ever again. Guilt from knowing I can't give up the Stone for Devon and grief for my brother grip respective shoulders and pull until I feel something inside tear.

"I will not surrender my Gift either." Hellene touches the silver cuff I know she wears beneath the gauntlet sleeve of her dress.

"Caea and Ramesis might. Lawrie and Evan might," I say. They'd all be weaker in battle. Order's Gifts have saved all of us at least once, Evan twice.

"This is a game of strategy, Leader Three." Theorne steeples his hands under his chin. "You never give up a trump card for a release of materials that are of lesser value."

"Lesser value." I jump up, bringing the heavy stone table up with me. I slam it down, power unstrained, satisfied at the cracks made in the floor. Viveen and Theorne push their chairs back, leaping away. Their eyes are wild as they look at me. Hellene and Nialiah remain seated, unaffected. "What the hell is that supposed to mean?"

I think about getting in Theorne's face, staring him down with only millimeters between us. But...

*Breathe.*

"Lyle." Nialiah's voice is intoxicating, like a singing witch who makes people strip and hand over their cash. "Kahanna has ten Champions. Xijure and Devon are but two. Do we risk endangering our deals, meaning none of us will survive this war, none of your brothers will survive, for the return of two?"

I stare at her.

*Breathe.*

"With all of our weapons gone, we lose." Nialiah's words are soft, purring. "Do you value Devon over the rest of your family and friends? And even then, if he is returned, he will be safe for a limited time. If we lose the war, it is over for us all."

*Breathe.*

I can't.

"C-can't we... We should summon Her. Call Order," I choke.

"Kahanna cannot be bothered with such small matters." Hellene's voice drips with disdain. "This is why She selected us to know Her ultimate vision. We are trusted to deal with the trivialities of war. Our policy is not to negotiate."

"We did not negotiate for Leader One," Viveen says.

I reach for her with my powers, sensing the thrum of her mind. I can't hear her thoughts through her mental shields unless I break them. And I can. I can wring her brain like a sponge. Let's see her say things like 'We planned your brother's funeral before he was dead' after that.

*Breathe.*

I clench my jaw. "I think Order will make an exception."

"For you?" Hellene laughs, but her eyes are on fire. "She likes you as She liked Jain Peredil. However, your predecessor fell from grace. She has not forgotten that, and *you* should not forget that the Remasian leader She truly favors is the Child of Magic. Of whom you are not. Do not tempt your fate."

Jain Peredil, a past me who made bad choices. He let his brothers, the original Four of Rema, the ones who were supposed to end this war hundreds of years ago, die. I won't do that.

I try to smile at Hellene and fail. Evan grins at people he hates all the time, and it scares the hell out of them. I'm no good at scaring people that way. I settle for turning my back to her. "So, you won't summon Order?"

"No." The answer is flat, final.

*Breathe.*

"We will share our decision with the consortia"—the rest of the people in Order's inner circle not present—"in a *jewel*." Theorne grabs his chair, pushing it back to its previous place at the table. I sense his hesitation, but it doesn't stop him from sitting down near me while I'm still standing. It makes me taller than him.

Viveen stays where she is, a few feet away from the table, her chair on its side, as she frowns at me. Maybe she felt me in her head.

I hope she did.

"After we have the majority vote..." Hellene's eyes are on me "...which will be to move forward with the loss of but two Champions, I think the militia should be informed."

"So... we're going to tell everyone Devon and Xijure are dead?" I sit down, studying the fissures the table made in the floor.

"We tell our government, leaders, and fighters that we have suffered a loss," Theorne says. "And we will use the loss as inspiration for our mission."

"And what is that exactly? Tell me again." I sound like the agitator in the back of the classroom who always has something to say.

"To save the world," Theorne says, steepling his hands under his chin again, "by ensuring that when it is reborn, it is reborn with the best of us left behind to populate and nurture it."

And *there's* Order's mess. The prophecy that ruined my life also promises that everything and everyone flying Order's banner is safe if She wins. Only a limited few are privy to the fine print. If She wins, the only other major god on the gameboard—Pandemonium—has to leave, and with Him gone, She intends to wipe the board clean and start over.

She wants a new world. One without the Creations of other gods making things difficult for Her. She didn't Create any of us. Pandemonium didn't Create us.

And so, neither god can control or possess us, not directly. They have to ask for our help in ending the world as we know it, and for a reward? Order will keep some of us—the ones of us in this room and in a few other rooms like this one on other planets, and the people we bargained for.

I asked Her to save my family, my Court, Caea, and her brothers. The Maidens get to keep their entire planet and people. I don't know who the other Circle members asked for, but aside from them, everyone else dies.

I finger the chain of my Stone before taking the warm gem in my palm.

*Breathe.*

Order favors me. She'll make an exception for Devon. I need a private audience with Her. I can't work magic, so I can't do a summons.

*Breathe.*

"Are you alright?"

I look up to find Nialiah beside my chair. Theorne, Viveen, and Hellene are gone. Guess the meeting's over. I lean back. My arms and legs are weak, and a headache brews behind my eyes. But I need to...

*Breathe.*

Nialiah touches my hand, and I gaze at her in full. She's medium height, curvy. The shift dress she wears is the same style as Hellene's, long with gauntlet sleeves to cover her Gift from Order.

Hellene is the one who normally summons Order. But does she do it because she's the only one who can, or is it because she's the one who volunteers? Nialiah's magic should rival Hellene's. No one ever talks about any of The Maidens—Hellene, Nialiah, or Imari—being stronger than one another. I think Lenorans rank them according to age and temperament, not power.

Breathing is suddenly easier, and swallowing is no longer a task.

I turn my hand over, clutching Nialiah's startled fingers. "I think I'll be fine."

Her full lips purse, then even into a pleased smile.

"But I wonder..." I use my thumb to massage the pulse in her wrist. She quirks a brow and takes a seat on the table, crossing one leg over the other, not taking back her hand.

"Yes?"

"Are you able to summon Kahanna?"

Chapter 2

# Lawrence

"YOU'RE QUIET." EVAN'S VOICE comes from behind me.

The entire room is a white space of subtle sound, sickly-sweet vanilla and honey smells, as well as living elements. Nitrogen, phosphorus, potassium, and calcium atoms vibrate around me as looser hydrogen and oxygen atoms flow around them: plants and water. Lenorans use vines, leaves, and grass as wallpaper and carpet. The castle is an indoor jungle.

My power connects to just about everything in the room, reaching out to analyze and spill the tea on what's around me, because I can't see it. I try to remember what the walls looked like a month ago. They were green wood covered in purple foliage. But the mental picture isn't as clear as it was yesterday. I'm forgetting what stuff looks like. Colors and shapes don't seem like real things anymore, just concepts, and it's...

I bite my lip, tasting blood before my power tells me, 'Hey, you've got the chemical components of blood in your mouth. Wanna stop biting scabs, grasshopper?'

"Should I even think this procedure's gonna work?" I lick my bloody lip, liking the sharp sting of pain that comes from doing it. Pain distracts me from being afraid.

I feel Evan's approach before his hands squeeze my shoulders. My brother is fire, a constant burning ball of carbon dioxide, water vapor and... something else. Something warm and—I'll be corny—magical. It's magic fire. Bet Disney would cast him as a princess.

"I'm not about uplifting speeches and *pidge*." Evan's voice is light. "You know the odds of getting your sight back. You listened to the readout."

A forty-three percent chance of success based on my current medical records. The odds could go up once I'm reassessed, or they could go down. I grip the sides of my jeans, thumb pads rubbing the rough fabric. Earth denim doesn't like Lenoran soap.

"But I do think you'll make do with whatever you get, because that's what *we* do." Evan pushes me forward, and I stretch out a hand, sensing a nearby combination of carbon, oxygen, hydrogen, nitrogen: wood. My knuckles strike the hard edge of a chair. I grip it, pat it down, checking the shape to make sure I have the back. Then, I spin and straddle it, resting my chin in a wide groove.

Evan chuckles. "If I didn't know better, I'd think you could see just fine."

The fire moves, the only thing letting me know that he's beside me now. The guy's a ninja. He ruffles my curls, then taps the bridge of the sunglasses I stole from Lyle. My nose twitches, and I push the dark glasses back into place.

"I... um..." Evan stammers. "I wish I could tell you everything will work out how you want it to."

He can't lie, like really can't. Physically incapable. And that's gotta suck when he hangs out with politicians for hours on end. Laughter bubbles in my gut and touches my chest but doesn't escape. I could let it out, but I think it'd turn into something else really fast and maybe then it wouldn't stop. My hands shake and I chew my lip again, tasting salt and copper, concentrating on how much it hurts.

Anxiety, a feeling I characterized as locusts crawling around my insides, is just… anxiety now. Noradrenaline, a hormone I dubbed 'gotta do something', is just… noradrenaline. I squeeze my eyes shut to feel the muscles contract. To push back saltwater. Because I don't want to be this guy.

I'm not this guy.

I try to channel the guy from the party last night. The one who laughs and tells the people around him he's having a great time. That going to Bruhje and letting witch-doctors poke in my eyeballs is where it's at. Nothing gets him down. Nothing touches him. He fries monsters to a crisp with lightning and is learning to use his elemental powers to deconstruct matter and build a Maserati that runs on broccoli, so he doesn't have to eat it.

That guy's me.

"The ship's ready." Evan's voice breaks through my funk. "Your stuff's onboard, and so is your court."

All waiting for that guy.

Evan pulls me up, and I grip his wrists.

"Come with me? Please?" My voice breaks. That bubbling emotion, the one that might start off like laughter, wants to come out again. Gets trapped in my throat. I don't want to be without any of my brothers on a strange new planet. I need at least one of them with me. Evan's so strong. He can be that *for me*, if… if things don't go well.

Evan sighs. "I wish I could go with you, but you know why I can't."

"Yeah." My heart sinks. He can't come because it's crazy enough just sending me out.

If there was a way for the Bruhje doctors to work here, the Allegiances would make it happen to keep me off a ship. Bruhje doctors draw their healing magic directly from their planet's core, which limits them to on-planet procedures.

Evan tugs his wrists free from my hold and drapes an arm over my shoulders. "Come on."

I lean into the support, needing it. Not knowing when I'll get it again.

We step through the door together, and he lets me go. I almost pull him back, but his voice stops me.

"Drill time."

I tilt my head at his shift in tone, from apologetic to playful. His drastic mood swings are kind of incredible. The end of his Rapunzel braid thwacks my elbow, and his fire shifts. Did he just turn and jump ahead? His voice comes from in front of me, but the sound is direct, so he's facing me while still moving. Walking backwards, then. My interest flickers, dulling the growing depression.

"You asked me stuff about Bruhje." His voice is light, but there's a fine undercurrent of nerves. Maybe they're the same nerves making my hands shake and my legs feel like dollar store gummy worms.

"Yeah. You got more?" Devon and Lyle hate taking university-level crash courses in everything alien, but I chug data like Mountain Dew. Evan lived on Bruhje with our uncle Aeric for months at a time as a kid.

Evan's fire surges. Air molecules around me charge. The temperature in the hallway rises, then falls. "This is about Dad."

My stomach flutters. Dad: Devrik Lauduethe.

I put him on a mental shelf this morning. There's too much other shizz to worry about. But he'll be there. Will probably meet me at the landing site on Bruhje. And what should I say, think, or even feel?

"Ev, do you—do you like him? You..."

...never seem happy when you talk about Devrik.

Evan's eyes were always flat when he mentioned Devrik. He doesn't tell stories, just makes blunt statements. The temperature around us stays level, but I feel Evan's internal flame pulse, ready to roar and roast bonfire pigs.

"I love him," he says slowly, his voice neutral, "but I don't like him." A humorless laugh. "Feeling might be mutual. Who knows? I'm not around him much to ask, and he prefers that."

"Ev—"

"Don't count on him to help you, Lawr. He doesn't do things like that. He just... he's a thing that takes up space and eats your leftovers to soak up last night's alcohol." His words are fast, hard. After a short pause, the fire calms, and his voice steadies. "Don't be surprised if Dad's only around once or twice while you're there. Uncle Aeric, though, he'll be what you need."

"Was he what you needed? You lived with him."

"Off and on. I stayed with Uncle Rovn too," Evan says.

Devrik's other half-brother. Uncle Rovn had a hand in the deal Mom made with the Silver Allegiance. I'd love to meet the guy and thank him.

"They helped me with my magic," Evan says. "Figured out how to train me and made sure the councils followed through. Raised me."

"And Devrik?" I ask.

"And Devrik what?"

The words are cold and final. A deep dislike for Devrik creeps in. He's a deadbeat who pawned my brother off on other people. The surges of heat from Evan's inner flame and the unsteady pitch to his voice when he talks about Devrik tell me all I need to know. He thinks Devrik doesn't care about him or us, and Devrik hasn't done anything to prove him wrong.

I don't want to meet him or worry about him anymore, so I put Devrik back on the mental shelf that'll hopefully disappear. I've got better things to freak out about.

Open air: oxygen, nitrogen, argon, neon, methane, swirls out to greet me. The soft squish of grass under my sneakers changes to the crunch of glass pebbles that make up the castle's reconstructed outdoor launchpad. Evan slaps my shoulder and leaves his hand there to guide me towards the sound of multiple voices and the increasingly strong smell of ship fuel.

The conversation dies as we approach. Someone nearby clears their throat. Elements, hydrogen and oxygen, stir and vibrate around them. One of my court members then, Bhela. Her elemental specialty is water. I picture her. Taller than me with straight green hair in a spiky, cheerleader ponytail that looks like it wants a high-five, round yellow eyes, and pale pink skin.

"Hey, Bhela." I keep my hands at my sides. Remasians don't wave or shake hands. Though, nicer people try not to leave me hanging and attempt to grab my hand if I stick it out. Bhela won't.

"Greetings, Leader Four." Her voice is clear and professional, never friendly.

I feel a slight shift in energy, a stronger sense of zinc, iron, copper, and chromium. An earth elemental. "Hi, Tian!"

"Greetings." Tian's voice is deep, and it comes from Bhela's vicinity.

Their energy stays at the same distance. Neither one makes any move to come closer. I don't know if I'm happy they're not fake, or disappointed that they won't pretend to like me. I imagine them standing side by side. Bhela, bright-haired and built like a broom, and Tian with hair like black walnut fuzz and built like a refrigerator. Opposites in everything except not being fond of a half-human brat.

"*Gikak!*" A rush of power, an all-around elemental like me, glomps on my back, not caring that he's probably got twenty pounds on me.

I stagger and laugh, for real. The act of it, the simple flood of joy at somebody who's not family being glad to see me, brightens my day. He's a Hallmark card, a funny one with a mean old lady calling me ugly on the front.

"Chasyn!" My first off-planet friend. The one member of my court of three who likes me. I throw him off but grin as he slings an arm over my shoulder and leans on me.

"Where's Lyle?" Evan moves to my other side. "He knows what time you're leaving."

Evan sounds irritated, which isn't weird. He's a bomb with a busted timer. When I could see, watching him try not to kill somebody for getting on his nerves was Grade A entertainment. Now that I can't, *sensing* how he affects the environment when he's trying not to kill someone might be the better floor show.

"He's got a few minutes before we need to go," Chasyn says. "I mean, you guys probably said all your goodbyes this morning, right?"

A dull pain gnaws on my right coronary artery. "No." I shake my head. "The last time I talked to Lyle was at the party." Where I pretended to be *that guy*.

"Same," Evan says. "And he knows you can't miss your launch window. That *gottlesh—*"

"Leader One!" Bhela sounds so horrified that my gloom cloud fades a bit.

Chasyn chuckles in my ear, and I bite back a laugh. Evan keeps his translator off and speaks fluent English in my presence, so when he tosses out words in other languages, he's cussing. My interplanetary vocabulary increases one roast at a time.

*Gottle*-what?

"Officer Bhela Wenat." My brother sounds cheerful. He might be smiling.

Run, Bhela, run.

"How long have you been in the field?"

"Two *revs*, sir." Bhela's tone is wary. Smart girl.

"That's not long. You're lucky to have passed the trials for my brother's team. Heard you weren't a first choice, or a second. Which means you've got a lot to prove. Nothing better happen to my brother on your watch."

A threat given in the same tone people use to say: *Merry Christmas!* I want to be Evan when I grow up.

"Leader Four will not come to any additional harm now that Bhela and I are allowed to protect him," Tian rumbles.

Chasyn straightens, his weight on me lessening. He coughs and fidgets, his bony elbow hitting my side. Bet the pale redhead's turning red.

I bristle, feeling protective. "Hey, you two being there wouldn't have changed a thing. You read the battle reports." The ones that sound like heroic ballads when told inside Lenore's version of bars: forest clearings with lots of sweet wine I'm not old enough to drink.

"Yes," Tian agrees. "The one where Meklan,"—Chasyn tenses at the mention of his last name—"did not assist you in grounding the lightning that took your sight, and who let you move ahead of him into a hostile situation."

"That was my fault, not his! I—"

Bhela cuts me off, "I may have only been in the field for two *revs*, but that is better than his half *rev*."

"But his talent still places him above you." Evan's voice is cool as I seethe, hands clenched at my sides. "Truth be told, I wouldn't have chosen any of you for my brother's court, but at least Officer Meklan is powerful. You two are just good at following commands. My brother will be better for you than you'll be for him. Treat him as such."

Well shizz. My anger fades as respect for my brother takes its place.

"Sir."

"Yessir."

Bhela and Tian echo each other. Footsteps walk away.

"They're boarding the ship," Chasyn says softly. "*Cratches*."

I nod my agreement.

"I don't like them." Evan cracks his knuckles. "If I'd been there during the trials, they wouldn't be here." Evan had been recovering from surgery after a battle wound reopened while the trials for Devon's, Lyle's, and my courts were being conducted.

"I wouldn't be here either," Chasyn mutters.

Silence from Evan. He can't reassure Chasyn without lying. How does he live with this truth-thing?

"Look." A finger flicks my forehead, Evan's. "I'll meet you there, on Bruhje. I'll find a way. I won't leave you with them. *Gottleshes*." I hear the sneer in his voice. He sighs. "You'll meet way worse than them, though. At least when *they* get to know you, they'll act better. And this guy..."

Chasyn grunts beside me. Did Ev hit him?

"...will look after you until I can get there."

And the tickle that starts in my guts and works its way into my chest is back. My eyes burn.

Shizz.

I rub stupid trails of saltwater off my face.

"Aw, Lawrie, don't." Evan flicks my forehead again.

"What happened? What's wrong?"

And of course Lyle would show up right now. I turn away from the sound of his voice, hoping I didn't just spin around to show another audience of people how pathetic I am.

Evan huffs. "He's getting sent off with a bunch of... what's *your* word? What's that Earth word? Oh. Assholes. To meet another asshole. Where've you been?"

"Doesn't matter. I'm here now." Lyle's tone is sharp. "I wasn't going to..." Hands clamp down on my shoulders, turning me around. A six-foot-two mass of oxygen, carbon, hydrogen, calcium, and phosphorus stands in front of me, and I force my arms to stay at my sides.

I won't be a baby and hug my big brother, not with stupid tears on my face. Not in front of—more masses made of similar elements hover around the launch pad—so many people.

Fugnugget.

"Lawrie, I wasn't going to miss this." Lyle releases my shoulders.

"The launch window closes in a *facet*. He needs to be on board. You should have eaten with us this morning." Evan's fire crackles. It's been doing that a lot around Lyle lately.

But Lyle's been weird. Well, *weirder*.

"I was—"

"Busy," Evan finishes. "Doing what?"

"Guys." They can't fight now.

Cool, compressed hydrogen attached to elements I can't identify flow like liquid in a pond surrounded by aluminum and titanium: metal and ship fuel. A warm blast of fruity exhaust blows curls off my forehead.

The ship's ready to go.

"You need me here?" Chasyn pokes my shoulder.

Chas is scared of my brothers on normal days. It says a lot that he doesn't leave my side in the face of Evan and Lyle probably shooting eyeball sparks at each other right now. He's a braver guy than a lot of people give him credit for, and *he'll* be with me for the trip.

I wipe my face, done crying.

"I'm good. Go ahead and get on the ship." I wave my hand in the direction.

"*Gikak*, if I didn't know better…"

—He'd think I could see. Yeah, yeah.

I wait for the crunching of his feet across the launchpad before I turn my attention to Lyle and Evan. They're quiet, which probably means Lyle's using his telepathy. It's as annoying as parents using code to talk around the kids.

"Hey!" I clap my hands, hard.

Evan hisses. He hates sudden loud noises, but the guy also hears flies burp.

"Sorry." Not sorry. "We're splitting up. Again. Is this how it's gonna be right now?"

"No," Lyle says, but no one has anything else to say.

Bells chime. A boarding call.

"You know I'll call," Lyle says. "And I want you to call when you get there, and right when you find out what they can do, and when they'll do it. And maybe call after you meet... that guy."

Devrik. Lyle hasn't said his name in days. Doesn't act interested, but I think he is. Think he wants to know what 'that guy' is actually like in a way I don't.

"Call me after you call him," Evan orders, but his tone is softer. "And call when you want. But like I said, I'll get there."

"What do you mean you'll get there?" Lyle asks.

"What I said."

Silence. They're probably arguing now. Stupid brothers.

"Guys!" I reach out, feeling for fire and that mass of elements that make up Lyle. My hands close around their respective wrists.

Another bell. My legs are the consistency of Jell-O, and I know my brothers feel the tremors through my hands. I don't want to go alone. I don't want to find out

I'm blind forever alone. I don't want to meet Devrik Lauduethe alone. I don't want to be alone. I don't want to get on the ship alone. I don't want to—

A sharp tug and I fly into a smaller, leaner body. I hug Evan, memorizing his scent: ash, green plants, bitter bark. He rubs my back, then pushes me away. Lyle grabs me next, hugging me just as tight but half as long. He lets go.

His skin and clothes are cold, like he's been in a fridge or underground. The basement floors of the palace are freezing. Is that where he was?

"Call, okay?" Lyle's voice is clipped, urgent. "And I want to see you. Turn the video feed on. I need to see you."

"Ly?" It makes me feel good to know that this brother cares so much, though I need to get over being surprised that he doesn't hate the world and me. But his tone borders on paranoia. "What's—"

Another bell.

"You better go," he says.

I imagine him tucking his hands in his pockets and looking at the ground. He could be freaking out because he hasn't seen or talked to Devon in weeks and doesn't want a repeat from me. Dev not being here has been hard on him. I hug him again and am reluctant to let go.

Evan gently pulls us apart. "Come on."

I follow his fire, feeling the ship getting closer. Lyle walks behind us. The threshold of the craft comes sooner than I want it to. I pat around, feeling the sides of the oval-shaped doorframe. There's no ramp. This ship, the Laglis, sits right on the ground. When it launches, it springs up on something like hydraulics, then shoots into a tube shaped like a capital letter "L".

I saw it once, felt it, and am glad no portal is involved this time. The Laglis is small, made to travel fast. The journey to Bruhje will take the equivalent of two Earth weeks.

Two weeks to work up the nerve to say, *"Hey, Dad."*

I get another hug from Evan, another hug from Lyle.

No words this time.

I know what to do. Call them. Be good. Don't cry again.

A new hand grabs my arm—Chas. "I'll help you strap in."

The door hums as we step on board, and there's a suction noise as it closes and seals itself. Chasyn helps me find a seat and makes sure I'm secure before he sits across from me.

The ship rumbles. I sense its fire but clearly distinguish its make-up from Evan's. His is magic, while the ship's is a chemical compound. The magic is stronger and burning hotter than it had been just a minute ago. As we move away from my brothers, the force of Evan's flame should diminish, but instead it grows.

Wait. Is he wazzed? No, that's more than wazzed. That's wallpaper searing, floor melting fury.

Something just happened.

I want to unstrap myself, to roll up a window screen and look out...

But doing that won't matter.

I can't see.

Fug.

A hand—Chasyn's—on my arm. "It's going to be okay. I'll look after you."

Mmhmm. Yeah. But who's looking after my brothers and whatever the hell's going on down there? "Chas, look out the window. What are my broth—"

My heart leaps into my throat as the ship jolts upward.

A thrill ripples through my system, and I forget brother drama. I almost raise my hands, ready to ride this coaster but also ready to jump out of the line. Up we go, and then out toward a final destination that equals fugged.

Chapter 3

# Evan

*"WE'RE GOING HOME"*—A COMMON statement swapped between my soldiers. But it's true. The Ievisara is home to us. For the last two *revs*, we've been ship-side more than soil-side. Space-bound, always on our way to do something important. Enforce Silver Allegiance policies, incorporate more territories, violate Cold Space laws, commit war crimes. The usual.

I stare at the warship, a massive, black metal mountain of death that I am forbidden to take to go after my little brother. Who's probably not dead at all, but to us, he has to be. Happens all the time. I've dealt with it before.

*Fip.*

I hiss, shaking out my left hand. Blood drips from where my nails bit into my palm. My core burns cold. Grass dies under my heels. Plant life that used to stretch toward me rears back when I pass through. Have I ever been this consecutively angry? A week's gone by since Devon was reported 'lost in action.'

This... Is there a word to describe feeling like a combustion canon with a fried override panel, simmering, ready to fire at any random moment, at any random person?

An iron grip clamps down on my right shoulder, and I whirl around, left leg sweeping out to take down whoever it is. An ice cloud hits me in the face, freezing my eyelids open for a split-*wisp* before I puff out a wall of steam to melt it away.

"You didn't hear me coming." Adonis stands a foot from me, pupilless gray eyes unblinking.

I usually don't hear his feet approaching. He doesn't make noise when he walks unless he wants people to know he's there. But I know what he means. I should have heard him in a different way.

"I'm blocking them out."

"Why are you blocking life songs?" His voice is low and even. To most people, Adonis's tone never changes, and neither do his expressions. He's an umber statue, tall and imposing. But I'm not most people. My first-in-command is no-nonsense... but my best friend/cousin is worried.

I shrug. "I'm not hearing the songs I want?" Can't be a lie or I wouldn't have been able to voice it.

There's an oversaturated sponge in my chest, heavy with mildew and dirty wa-ter. It expands and contracts, sucking up everything—the hurt, the loss, the grief—and grows. It's disgusting, and I want it gone.

New subject.

"Ready to head out?" I nod my head in the direction of the ship.

Plans, strategies, and checklists run through my mind. In three *cycles*, we'll be gone. A mental map of the Cold Space borders in Sector Four flashes behind my eyes. Nazflit troops squat on two moons orbiting an inhabited Allegiance Protected Planet.

They don't know we're coming. I can't wait to get there to burn, shake, seize, and destroy.

Adonis gives me that stare, the one that digs into my soul, saying, 'Please stop.'

But I don't want to. To stop means to lose momentum. My brain is headed towards the future. To battle and glory and things I can tick off a list I need to create. Adonis's iron grip is back on my shoulder. He squeezes until I tilt my head up, meeting his eyes.

"There should be a memorial." His voice is flat.

I shove his hand away. "For what?"

He stares.

*Fip.*

"I'm not having a funeral for a brother who's not dead." It hasn't been confirmed. But if the Allegiances aren't making deals, why would it ever need to be confirmed?

Adonis eyeballs me, reading me like a treatise on subterfuge, and sighs.

I wait for him to say something else, but he doesn't. Instead, he pushes me toward the Ievisara. The doors open, recognizing our body signatures. Cool, recycled ship air brushes across my dry forehead. I breathe in its metallic, manufactured odor, and a light sense of welcome touches me.

Home.

Warmth and belonging coat my skin like another set of clothing. This is my domain. I run this. And I feel better and worse at the same time. Worse, because I shouldn't feel better. Not when I'm falling in line with a decision that leaves my brother for dead.

I was left for dead once. Collateral damage. But my brothers found me.

*Fip.*

Running lights on the floors and ceilings flicker to life as Adonis and I roam the long halls, nodding at supply caches, navigation hubs, and weapons stations that seem to be clean and in good repair. As sterile and surgical as ever, our home doesn't look like it was nearly obliterated months ago in an outer space ambush.

At the end of the main hall, a Tube Port glistens milky white, its doors sliding open at our approach. We enter the small chamber, and I tell it to take us to the seventh floor, our living quarters. The ride up is short and quick. The doors open, and I step out first.

Up here, things are less silver and white. The walls are screens displaying cloudy green Remasian skies and double suns. The gray floors are carpeted, and the lounge is set up for games. A cube floats above a glass table, ready for me to call up the quest I left my avatar in the middle of. A box of black dirt sits on the floor in front of the table.

Oh *pidge.*

I jog to it, dropping to my knees and plunging my hands in the soil. Don't be dead, don't be dead, don't be... I open myself and sigh at the faint wheeze of a flute. One note, two notes. The song is weak, but there.

"You're not dead." I hum the song, repeating it several times, until the seed echoes me. Stronger, louder. I feel the plant inside shivering, ready to root and grow. I feed it a measure of my life energy and grin at its grateful shudder. A sprout of green pushes its way through the soil.

I remove my hands, staring at the black dirt under my fingernails.

The siwi bud's song hums through the soil, as other life songs spring into existence from different places in the room. I sit back on my heels. An approaching woodwind solo tells me Adonis is coming. The air behind me shifts, and I see him kneel in my periphery.

"There should be a memorial." This time, he's firm.

I shut my eyes before they leak and flinch at sharp pain in my palms. My nails again.

Devon's dead to me.

I will rip the world apart and roast every Su and Nazflit I encounter. But before that, I need to bury my brother.

"Let's do it now." I hate dragging *pidge* out. I wipe my hands on the knees of my cargos.

"Not here and not with me. You and Lyle should have one, in private."

I level Adonis with a sour look. "If I thought Lyle gave a *fip*, maybe." That *fipsak*'s acting like his own twin brother isn't being thrown to the *sludge racks*.

"He's being strange." Adonis looks at me sideways, his mouth a straight line.

I frown. Should I be worried? Maybe Lyle's having a secret meltdown that I wouldn't know the first symptoms of because I don't know the first thing about Lyle. Not really. Lawrie should be here. But Lyle let Lawrie go before breaking the news. He didn't want Lawrie here.

I blink, thinking that over. "He *is* being strange." And stupid me for not realizing it. "He spends all his time training or with Nialiah. I haven't seen him with Caea since…" Since Caea lost her little brother too.

Devon *and* Xijure are gone.

"And why was he informed about the situation before you were?" Adonis asks.

"Because he's been kissing Maiden ass lately? I don't know." But I need to find out. The weight of duty and failure sits on my shoulders as I stand up. "I'm really bad at this big brother thing."

"You're better than my big brother." Adonis rises to his feet, face blank.

I side-eye him. "Your big brother's a *dershpin*." But that's not fair. Adonis's entire immediate family is full of *dershpine*. It's not his fault his mom forgot she didn't want any more kids after the first two. A dim spark of righteous fury ignites as it usually does when I think about Adonis's immediate family. They don't deserve him.

"You don't ignore Lyle. You try to know him. You care."

Memories flare. I recall the terror of drowning, the burn from holding my breath too long, then inhaling a lungful of hot water. Everything was green, then black, then gone. Like I went to sleep, but not.And then I was back on an empty battlefield with Lyle in his *underoos* gaping at me like I was in mine. He didn't know who I was then, but he wanted to save me.

A rush of gratitude and a deep feeling—love—almost wind me, because Lyle's my brother. And I want to help him.

I gaze around the living room again. Soft chimes echo from a sound system in the ceiling, an alert that someone else just came aboard. Probably flight crew wanting to double-check equipment.

I sigh and turn to the Tube, not needing to see Adonis's 'I know you better than you do' expression. "I'm going to find Lyle. Run checkpoints with the crew for me."

He doesn't respond, and I don't look for confirmation. Telling Adonis to take over for me is never necessary. He knows. Has known since we were little *mopis* pretending to be older. Before I head to the Tube, he pats my back.

I have four brothers: Devon, Lyle, Lawrie, and Adonis. But my little ones need more attention. The Tube whistles as it takes me to the ground floor, and I step out, new plan formulating: Find Lyle, sit on him, and make sure he's okay.

I KNOCK TWICE, THEN PUSH open the door to Lyle's office. I don't tug on the telepathic link he set up between us to see if he's here, and I don't listen for his song. It feels too invasive right now.

Caea Harliel sits at Lyle's desk with her feet propped on the purple wood. The bottoms of her boots are caked with green dirt. She's been to the marketplace today. Underneath the overpowering sugar and vanilla fragrance of Lenore, I get a whiff of Her Majesty's personal odor: salt, parchment paper, and the randomness of nameless people. No Lyle.

"You haven't been with my brother today," I say.

Caea's semi-full lips quirk into a half-smile. "Hello to you too."

She doesn't change positions as I enter the room, ignoring the vines coating the ceiling and walls as they sing to me. I mute their music, humming a song of apology under my breath. Lenoran décor involves a lot of vines and leaves as wallpaper and ceiling covers. It's bad form to anger living walls.

I sit on the desk, back to Caea and facing forward, noting Lyle's lack of personal effects in this space. No extra clothes are slung over the blue resting bench against the wall, no half-empty cups of kava or balled-up napkins litter the desk or low tables. No broken tools or dirty boots lay in corners. He's so clean.

"Are you wondering why this place looks like no one uses it?" Caea asks.

I snort and tap an index finger on the toe of her boot. "After two weeks, you'd think there would at least be a half a sandwich laying around."

"Not everyone gets as... *comfortable* as you do on foreign soil," Caea says, voice strangely light.

I frown, turning my head to gaze at her. Her wide sienna eyes are downcast and her mahogany skin, usually luminous, is dull.

I tap her toe again. "You calling me messy?"

A soft smile. Caea looks at me, and I swallow at the dark circles under her eyes.

"You said it, not me." She shifts, taking her legs off the desk and sitting up straight. "Are you okay, *mopi*?"

We're around the same age developmentally, but I have a feeling I'll always be 'little' to her. The Remasian Council introduced me as the Remasian leader apparent when I was eight and took me with them to Zare to meet the next generation of Zaran monarch hopefuls. Caea was taller than me and picked me up like a baby and tossed me to Xijure, who was a half-head taller than her.

Sadness coats my words. "No. Are you?"

I don't need her to answer, but I did need to ask. To let her know I understand without saying so. I care about Xijure too.

"Our parents won't accept messages." Her voice is bitter, and her mouth twists as if she's eaten something gross. "Ramesis hasn't said two words to me. I know he's talking to those people he meets on the *intra*. He'd rather talk to strangers than me."

Maybe because it's easier. But I don't say that to her. I also understand dealing with younger brothers avoiding you. "Are you... going to do anything? For Xijure, I mean."

Caea looks at her hands, palms callused from years of working with long blades and daggers. "I'd like to. But I don't want to do it alone. I also don't want to bring it up to Ram." Her shoulders slump. Everything about her is defeated as she looks around, eyes lingering on Lyle's closet door, the place he hides his art supplies.

"When's the last time you spoke to Lyle?" I ask.

"Alone?" Caea's eyes spark with an edge of fury I'm not used to from her. "At the party. Otherwise, he's always with *her*."

Nialiah.

"Same," I say. Pain flashes in my hands. "*Oi vati fip.*" I smell new blood before I feel it. Buying gloves goes on my mental 'to do' list.

"He's probably in The Maidens' Pavilion." Caea studies the ceiling, eyes bright. "I'm not going out there. The last time I went to check, and he was there with her... The look that woman gave me, like I was an interloper. As if I didn't have a right to know where my significant was." Caea pauses, hands clenching into fists. "I had to remove myself."

I shake my head. "I'm worried about him. He's not behaving as he should. He acts like he doesn't care that Devon's... not here, and he's avoiding me." And her.

Shouldn't Lyle want comfort from his girlfriend who's going through the same terrible thing? "Something's not right."

"Grief makes people odd." Caea shrugs and relaxes her hands. "I just really thought he'd open up to me. Before..." she trails off, biting her lip, then starts again, "We were fine. We laughed and explored the marketplaces, and he listened to everything I had to say and looked at me like I was this gift he couldn't believe he'd gotten. I felt... I don't even know how to describe how amazing he made me feel."

I tense as her words start to quiver, slight shock filling me. *Niobe-va*, does Caea love Lyle? Does he love her? Reality spirals away from me as I fathom the possibility of me being the sorriest brother in existence.

How did I miss Lyle and Caea being in love? What else am I missing?

Caea snaps her fingers and I jerk to attention, looking back at her. "Caea, I didn't know—"

She cuts me off with a raised hand. "I won't pretend to be an expert in all things Lyle, but I like to think that I was getting to know him. That he's been more himself with me than anyone else in a long time. Now, he's different, and I'm as worried as you are."

*Fip.* Empathy for her and concern for my brother are solid masses in my chest.

We sit silently for a moment, Caea seeming as lost in thought as I am.

Finally, I slide off the desk, turning to face her completely. "I'm going to find Lyle. I'll do my best to send him to you after I'm done with him." It'd be the least I could do. Maybe they could help each other. I reach across the wood to squeeze her wrist. "If I can't, I'll let you know why."

She nods with a fond smile. "I know you will."

I touch two fingers against my left shoulder, a Common salute, and head for the door.

"*Ayo.*"

I pause.

"If I don't see you again before you take off, be careful on your mission, *mopi*. We're down two. Don't make it three."

I smile at the softness in her voice. "Yes, Majesty."

I venture back out into the hallways. All paths in this place look the same: green, purple, green, purple. Though, each vine, leaf, and blade of grass has its own story. They're ecstatic as I travel through the palace, all wanting my attention, not used to having people like me around. Only Children of Magic commonly referred to as Magic Breeds—faeries—and their distant offspring hear life songs.

No one knows how Magic traits decide which people to wake up in. A handful of my relatives can cast spells, but only a few are any good at it. I'm the only one who hears magic, aside from Adonis. But cousins by marriage aren't the same as blood relatives.

The Maidens' pavilion is an offshoot of the castle. A tree bridge takes me outdoors and leads me into the three-story purple cottage that probably resembles the Maidens' true, respective residences. They all live in houses somewhere out in the deep woods. Apparently, they only come together and stay in the palace when they have guests. Meaning they're never here because Lenore hasn't had known visitors since the Prophetic Cycles hundreds of Common *revs* ago.

The double doors are made of several knitted branches that part for me as I approach. The inside of the cottage suffers from the same purple and green color scheme, but pink, yellow, and white flowers grow in winding patterns along the walls. I pass open doors, not bothering to peek in. I know the Maidens' rooms are in the back.

A woman in a long pink and white dress pops out of an open doorway with a basket of folded laundry. She gasps, nearly dropping the basket, and staggers back, hovering in the frame of the door she'd exited.

I stop walking.

"Y-y-you were not invited in. There was no alert about you being here today."

I narrow my eyes at the way she says 'you', irritation setting in. 'You.' Active Quarters Breeds, beings tainted with faerie blood, aren't welcome in many places. We're 'safety hazards.' But I'm special because I'm important.

I smile and let magic crackle over my skin. Some people flex their muscles; I leak power. "Is my brother here?"

I don't need her to tell me, I hear his melody, but I like that she steps back again. Maybe it's mean to scare her, but I'm sick of the palace staff treating me like I don't belong indoors.

"Yes, Leader One." She bows her head once, then seems to be waiting for me to move on.

"Thanks!" I wiggle my fingers at her and continue down the path. I hear her utter curses under her breath and chuckle, loving that I got under her skin. Didn't know Lenorans knew that kind of language.

The end of the hall opens into a foyer that splits into three new hallways that lead to different suites. One for Hellene, one for Nialiah, and one for...

"Evan?"

Imari.

"What are you doing here?" She stands in an archway, sun from a skylight in the ceiling putting red highlights in her straight black hair. Her inky eyes sparkle as she smiles.

"Looking for somebody." I nod at her. "What's in the basket?"

Her cheeks puff out like a pouty kid's as her eyes narrow. "Answer my question fully and I will tell you. Oh!"

I forget about Lyle and rude Lenoran women as the large, lidded basket in Imari's arms wiggles and a little head covered in golden fur pops out. Two more heads follow it, then three.

"Oh!" The purple basket quivers, and a chorus of excited high-pitched yaps drown out anything else Imari says. She loses her grip, and the basket hits the purple grass floor, releasing a litter of...

"What are they?" I drop to my knees as eight furry pups, a few gold, some red, a couple black and gray, scamper around on four legs. They wiggle short puff-ball tails and pant, sniffing the ground with round black noses and looking around with starry blue eyes. I click my tongue against my teeth at a gold one and it patters up to me, putting its paws on my knee.

"Pafti pups." Imari kneels, long hair brushing my side. Over the cinnamon and sugar in the atmosphere, I smell sour plum.

I pick the golden pup up with both hands, burying my nose in its mostly dry fur, and note a similar scent. I laugh, thoroughly amused. "You've been bathing puppies."

Lady Imari smells like wet dog. And it explains the outfit. Instead of a uselessly long dress that drags the ground, Imari's in brown silk pants and a short tunic. If I didn't know she was a Maiden, I'd think she was some kid who snuck in this place the same way I did.

"Indeed, I have! And they did not like it one bit!" She giggles, snatching up a red pup and kissing its nose. "You love being dirty!"

My chest tightens as a memory flickers behind my eyes: *Imari, small-boned and beautiful, head thrown back as she howls with laughter at something I said. Solid black eyes bright with tears of mirth. Green skin even and soft as I touch her shoulders, bringing her laughing, full mouth in for a...*

I blink, shaking the memory off. Not my memory. She was Corin Peredil's girl-friend hundreds of years ago, in my past life.

"Ah!" I yelp as another pup gets shoved in my face.

"You cannot frown like that in the presence of puppies!" Imari snaps her fingers and fluffy, triangular puppy ears orient toward the sound. She points at me, and they leap.

I'm toppled by a pile of fur and wagging tails. And I can't be mad, heartsick, or itchy for anything else but this. A wave of warmth floods me, pouring from eight little bodies hardly bigger than one of my palms as they lick and nip and sniff. I gather as many as I can in a hug, holding on, reciprocating their energy. They calm, resting chubby bellies on my chest and anywhere else they can find some space and we rest. Tiny hearts beat three times faster than my large one. I hum to them.

"That is a pretty song. Did you compose it?"

Imari's voice sounds over my head. I open my eyes to find her leaning over me. Thick hair waterfalls over one of her shoulders, obscuring part of her face. My hand comes up, smoothing it behind her ear.

My stomach clenches. I pull my hand away, bringing it back to the puppies, stroking their fur.

*Vati fipping pidge.*

Her eyes widen, and she leans back. "Why did you do that?"

Touch her or pull away?

Two of the pups bark once and nip my shirt. My core crackles as my body tenses. More barking. The pups wiggle out of my hold, scampering off to tackle each other and chew things. I sit up, making Imari and I about the same height with her still on her knees.

She runs a hand through the hair I touched. "Evan?"

My heart thuds in my chest as my head reels. Feelings of love and longing blend with memories of Imari dancing in a long blue dress, Imari holding out morsels of food, begging me to taste it, Imari's eyes darker than death, begging me not to go.

I jump to my feet, wanting distance between us, between me, her... and Corin Peredil. My life isn't his, or is it? Reincarnation is a five-headed beast to understand, especially when that beast was in love with somebody who's still alive.

"I'm here for Lyle." I stare at the halls Imari hadn't come out of. "Which hall is Nialiah's?"

I listen to the forced inhales and exhales of a person trying to calm down.

"I think you should respect the distance your brother puts between you."

I turn to her. "Come again?"

Imari still kneels, tilting her chin back to meet my eyes. Her gaze is...

I don't know what that look is.

"Something changed in him when he found his Stone. You cannot fix it."

She knows the past, knows so much about what happened to the Peredils. But The Maidens are secretive. Like there's a curse on their tongues.

I frown. "There are things you can't say. Am I right?"

Imari bows her head.

I sigh, moving back to her and squatting down. My hand reaches for hers and stops. I can't keep touching her. It could send messages, make her forget that I'm not Corin, and that's cruel. I don't hate Imari, but I also don't love her.

"What can I do to help?" I keep my voice low.

Imari doesn't raise her head. "I am the one who needs to help you. And when I know how, you will know too."

More guessing games.

"Why do old people like to talk in riddles?"

Her dark lashes flutter, and her mouth flaps open and closed as she sputters. "Old people? Why you…" She's a girl again, someone not hundreds of years older than me. A tiny fist catches me in the shoulder, and I let myself fall over.

"You… you…" She straddles my abdomen, punching me in the chest with soft knuckles that tickle. I can't help it. I laugh at her, and it brings the puppies back.

Soft fur, wet tongues, and laughter make me let go again. Gods, how long has it been since I did this? Relaxed and simply enjoyed events, let them happen without needing to control the outcomes? My heart hurts, remembering *revs* before the Ievisara was home, back on Rema, or Bruhje or Amphora, with uncles and gardens and animals to care for until they were ready to go back to the woods, forest, wherever.

There was schoolwork, training, potions gone wild, parties that lasted until different dawns under foreign skies. And no interstellar war with world-ending conclusions breathing down my neck, waiting on my decisions. People are dying. Devon's gone.

My body's too heavy now; everything's too heavy.

"Is that a tear?" A soft finger touches the corner of my right eye.

I realize my eyes are closed, and I don't want to open them.

"I am sorry about your brother," Imari whispers. "Devon seemed kind. And I am sorry for Lyle too. And Lawrie. I will help you."

"You keep saying that."

"And you hear no lie in my words," she says. "Which means you can trust me. I have helped you before. So…"

I flinch as little fingers force my eyes open. I squint at her.

"Listen to me now and leave. No good will come from you meeting with—"

"What the hell?"

I sit up, knocking Imari off me and flipping around. Lyle and Nialiah stand in the third archway, Lyle gaping like he just caught me naked and rolling in the grass with—oh. I pluck grass out of my braid as Imari grunts and gathers up puppies to put back in her forgotten basket.

"I've been looking for you." I climb to my feet, ignoring Imari like she's ignoring me. It stings a little, but it's for the best. There's nothing between us, and other people need to know it.

Lyle and Nialiah share a look that sends an odd ripple of unease through my core. Nialiah's hand brushes his arm as she nods to me, then tells Lyle goodbye. She disappears down her hallway, hips swaying.

"What were you doing with her, Lyle?" My voice is smooth, but I'm ready to hit him for Caea.

"I could ask you the same thing." His eyes look over my shoulder, and I follow them to Imari. She scoops the last pup into her basket and moves on to wherever she'd been going before I bothered her.

I smile at him, chuckling at his startled look. "I was playing with dogs. Your turn, now. What were you playing with?" I almost clap at the intensity of his glare. "That's pretty good, little brother. One day, you might scare me."

Lyle looks heavenward, seems to count, then tries again. "So, you're hanging out with Imari, now?"

His voice is oddly strained. I don't think he likes Imari, and that's fair. She's a Maiden, someone who actually spoke with Order back in the Prophetic Cycles. None of them are high on the Trust List, but Lyle's here with Nialiah. Even after traveling and fighting beside Nialiah, I wouldn't close both eyes around her. So, who is he to talk?

"What would it matter if I was?" I look him up and down. He's got bags under his eyes, and his brown skin is ashen. "You look like *pidge*. I came here to talk to you. I don't think you're doing well, and I'm taking my head out of my ass to be your big brother."

He blinks at me. "I don't need you..." He stops when I smile and rolls his eyes.

*"I don't need you"*—the notes in his voice are off-pitch. A lie. And any irritation I have with him fades as his lie blows more warmth into my core. So, he needs me, huh?

I close the distance between us, draping an arm over his shoulder and holding him in place when he squirms. He's a half-head taller and has about twenty pounds on me, but I can take him in a wrestling match. "Walk with me? We'll get food and talk."

"I'm busy."

Not a lie.

"Doing what?" I ask, raising a brow and scoffing. "You're not shipping off with me, or with anyone else. Lenore's a safe-ground. And you're not ready to participate in planning meetings with the councils. You can skip training to spend time with your brother who's leaving soon. You'll be here alone after that. And…"

…you just found out you have to give up on your twin brother.

"I have t-to make plans for Devon." Lyle looks at his hands, and I do too. The skin around his nailbeds are red, swollen, and his knuckles are bruised.

"Are you planning a memorial?" And am I not invited? I struggle to keep hurt out of my voice. Yes, I just reunited with them, no I'm not as close, but I'm still their *fipping* brother. I should be included.

Lyle shrugs. "He's not dead. I'm not having a funeral for him."

His words are guarded. Something I really started noticing after he came back with his Stone. In the months we spent together before he went to find that thing, he wasn't the friendliest, but he talked to me without pausing to consider every word. There's nothing wrong with people thinking before they speak, but this is different.

I start moving, pulling him with me as I head back the way I came. My gut tells me spilling secrets in The Maiden's Pavilion isn't the way to go. Lyle doesn't fight me, but his steps are slow, maybe even lethargic.

"Are you sleeping okay?" I ask.

He shakes his head.

"Eating?"

A sigh.

I fail. And it hurts more than a wet-handed slap in the face. Being a good brother shouldn't be a task I check off another list, but I can't help it. I need to check boxes. And I'm not good at failure.

It doesn't take long to re-enter the palace. I steer us away from main halls, heading for a servant corridor that opens into the east courtyard. There's a tiny kitchen next to the archway that leads outdoors, and I make a quick stop to gather a few snacks and drinks before we head out.

The yellow sun is almost mid-sky, and I wonder where the day's gone. I don't feel like I did enough today for it to be afternoon already.

"Here." I pass Lyle a bag of krosa nuts and a black pear.

The midnight skin of the oblong fruit is bumpy and soft. Clear, sweet and sour juice squirts and dribbles down my chin when I take a bite. I slurp up any excess and wipe my face with my palm. The food hits my stomach, and the empty echo reminds me that I skipped breakfast.

I finish the pear in three big bites and start in on the krosa nuts. "What are your plans for Devon? Do you want to talk about him? Hold a vigil? There are things called memory bracelets. We have them made in honor of people we lose contact with. They..." My stomach roils. Probably shouldn't have eaten that pear after all. "They aren't necessarily meant to honor the dead. Just the gone."

Because it happens. Soldiers disappear. It's likely they're dead, but not uncommon for it never to be confirmed. There is hope they'll come back.

"I have three memory bracelets." And I still hope those soldiers will come back one day, but after too many *revs* passed, I eventually lit candles.

Lyle is silent. I glance over at him. He squeezes the pear so tightly that juice streams over his knuckles. His eyes are dry, lower lip cracked with a healing red scab.

*Niobe-va.* I can't leave in three *cycles.*

"I don't want a bracelet," Lyle says stiffly. "And I'm not having a vigil. And I don't want to talk about him."

Truth. Truth. Lie.

"What made him laugh?" I ask, because I want to know.

Devon hadn't laughed much around me. I watched him train, gave him pointers, but we never had the chance to really relax around each other. There's a hollow space inside me in the shape of an outline of Devon, waiting to be filled in. Lawrie's outline has bones, flesh, and color, and Lyle's has shading that gives his features some depth.

But Devon's? I look to Lyle, hopeful for an answer.

The yellow meat seeps through the top of Lyle's pear. "He laughed at dumb shit. Slap-stick-type dumb shit. People falling down or getting smacked in the face with pies and water balloons. Pictures of cats and dogs in clothes."

"You didn't laugh with him?"

"I don't laugh easy." Lyle scowls at the mess in his hand and lets the pear fall, wiping his hand on his cargos. He licks his palm.

"Sometimes it's easier to laugh when other people are." I can't resist joining in on a laugh unless it's at me. Then, I burn *pidge*.

"And sometimes it's easier to leave when they are, because it's annoying." Lyle stops walking. I stop too, waiting. "Devon isn't dead," Lyle insists, green eyes bright enough to worry me. "He's coming back."

"Okay." Because he's undoubtedly right about the first thing, and he needs to keep talking. To get it out and help me understand what he's feeling, so I can try to do something for him.

I'm not warm and cuddly, but I know 'death' and how it hurts to let go.

"So, I'm not talking funerals and memory chains or vigils, or anything else, because it's a waste of energy. When he comes back, he's going to need time to recuperate, get his bearings, and of course, train. And I want his transition to be smooth. So, there are things that have to be done."

And he's not lying, but there's something else there. A chord under his tone. He's not saying something, and the intent tremors under his words.

I narrow my eyes, suspicion and concern urging me to ask, "Lyle, are you working on something with Nialiah?"

He shrugs.

*Fip.* "Something stupid?"

"No."

No lie. But if he doesn't believe something is stupid, it won't be untrue to him.

*Niobe-va.* My thoughts race through insane possibilities. What could he be plotting with Nialiah, of all people? *Fip.* I should trust her. I've trusted her before, with Lawrie's life, with mine and my friends' lives when she worked a teleportation spell to send us after Lawrie's Stone. She's followed through on everything she's promised on missions, but something about her interactions with Lyle isn't right.

"Little brother, I'm leaving soon. I'm okay with stupid plans, but you need to get me involved. I'll help with whatever it is. Because I'm sure I can do more than Nialiah."

"You can't," Lyle says, voice flat. "And it's fine. Don't worry. I'm just... getting things ready for Devon to come back. Things are going to work out. I'm sure of it."Delusional people speak in trills. Their words are true because, in their fantasy world, what they say is real. When they talk, I hear clear tones with undercurrents of random, sloppy arpeggios, never in the right key. Lyle's voice doesn't trill. He's not losing touch with reality.

He looks up at the sky, eyelids fluttering as if blinking back tears. "We need you to go on your mission, Ev. You have things to do, and so do I. We can really talk when you get back because Devon will be here, and he talks better than I do."

I taste sweet-and-sour pear at the back of my throat. He's scaring me. "Ly. I don't think I can leave you like this."

"Doesn't matter what you think. You have to go. The Allegiances need you, and so does everybody else. We can't lose any more territory. And weren't you going to find a way to see Lawrie too? It'd be good for you to be with him. You two are close now."

And he doesn't sound jealous, only sad.

And right.

Duty first. We can't lose more territory. Too many people will die, might cease to exist, if the Allegiances don't make a move.

*Fip.*

My brother clears his throat, shaking his head and opening the bag of krosa nuts in his clean hand. He pours several into his mouth and crunches on them. "So, let's talk about something else. What's with you and Imari?"

I almost choke on my own breath, caught off-guard. "No—" *Niobe-va*, I can't say 'nothing'. "She had something with Corin Peredil, and I sense it when I'm with her. It's weird."

"You should stay away from her if it's weird." His voice is muffled as he chews. He walks again, and I match his pace. We pass under a copse of trees, thick purple leaves shading us from the warm sun. Shadows make Lyle's face appear older than seventeen.

"You should stay away from Nialiah," I counter. "Caea might be thinking about killing you."

Lyle smirks. "She's got nothing to worry about there."

"Then what are you doing together?" I ask. "She's—"

"Just helping me. She knows things I don't about political stuff. She gets me what I need." He sounds offhand, casual. I unclip a drinking bulb from my belt and pass it to him before unsnapping the second.

"I know what I'm doing." Lye sounds confident. He fumbles with the bulb's cork, and I take it back from him, twisting it off with expertise and holding it out again. He grabs it, but I don't let go. I need him to look at me.

Those fever-bright eyes meet mine.

"When I leave, there won't be anyone else here who is obligated to drag you out of whatever hole you're digging. If you need to tell me something, say it now. What are you up to?"

My brother looks me dead-straight in the eyes and says, "Business."

He leaves it at that.

I take off in three *cycles*, and I pray to any god listening that whatever is about to blow up in his face happens before I leave, so I can clean it up for him. Take care of him, like a big brother should.

I release the bulb and watch him drink.

My lists of things to do spirals behind my eyes, checks flying off their pages, as I miss this mark. But I swear, if anything happens to Lyle, Nialiah dies. Prophecies be damned and worlds be dead, along with her.

I drink from my own bulb, sealing the deal, while letting Lyle walk in front of me.

# Chapter 4

# Devon

THE BEST HAND-TO-HAND combat training I get is in prison. I spring back from a blow meant for my front teeth, then execute a perfect dropkick. My heels connect with my John Cena-sized opponent's chest with a force that feels like concrete against concrete. My knees strain at the impact, but I power through the move, knowing my body can handle it. His bulk yields, hurtling backwards as I flip and land on my feet. I punch the ground like Iron Man before bouncing back up to block punches from a different direction.

Behind me, Mineshka roars as she lays into the jerk who started it all. He'd run his fingers through her hair when she walked by him to grab a stake. She'd driven that stake through his right hand, and then his buddies jumped in. I'd been twelve feet deep into the foundation I was digging for a nearby housing unit when Xijure yelled for my help.

Three against thirty. The odds are always against us.

Turns out inmates don't take kindly to having to share their living space with a king, a leader, and an honor guard from enemy territory. The red midday sun glares down on us, wearing on my stamina but not killing it. Even in this heat, it'll be a while before Xijure, Mineshka, and I give out.

Our prison buddies aren't that lucky but don't ever seem to care.

And why should they? They've got nothing to lose. This nomad-style camp is for lifers. Every few months they're rounded up like cattle and driven on to the next place. They slave away, constructing future towns, pouring concrete for houses and hospitals with mediocre tools they can't truly use to revolt against prison guards with energy rifles.

I imagine spending the rest of my life living in tents that smell like my high school locker room, eight-deep with guys who gut each other over jerky and extra soap. Laboring in unchanging desert conditions, because there are no seasons, and every few months, carrying everything I'm allowed to own on my back across miles of newly terraformed terrain to a new building site. Once it's nice and real people are given the signal to move in, we move out.

*We.* Because this is my unit now.

I nearly eat a kick in the stomach. I grab the guy's caveman foot and swing him around, using his body to take out a few others before letting go. I watch him fly, then raise my hand to catch a mallet aiming for my neck.

A familiar battle cry comes from my left. Xijure disarms Mallet Man and hefts his new weapon like the sword he lost—his Gift from Order. Fifteen men are down. The rest start backing up, bloody and undoubtedly discouraged by the fact that we're not. I take a second to mop sweat off my brow with a long, dirty sleeve. I'm always tempted to rip the long sleeves and pants of the uniforms shorter, but they keep us from frying in the sun.

"You guys had enough?" I'm only mildly winded. If they want to keep fighting, I'm ready. Let's go. Hitting things helps me. It seems to help Mineshka and Xijure too.

Mineshka and Xijure stand on either side of me, shoulder to shoulder. Xijure's light brown eyes glint with fury, and Mineshka's sun-reddened face flushes with a wildness that ignites a desire to keep smashing my hands and feet into anybody who dares look at her wrong.

I owe her protection. I owe her blood. I owe her a brother.

I blink and Loniad's face—bright blue eyes, ever-cheerful, and his wide smile—enters my mind. I hear his barrel-chested laugh and his surprisingly good baritone singing a bar song about mermaids. Then hear the fleshy thwack of a bullet ripping through his throat. See the blood spurt as he falls. Remember Mineshka's gut-wrenching scream of grief and rage.

The leftover inmates right themselves, stepping over their fallen comrades to advance on us. Mineshka's grief and rage are mine as adrenaline fuels my second, third, and fourth winds. I want everyone who lives under the liar Pandemonium's banner to bleed, now.

Xijure and Mineshka tense, and I feel them shifting into lower fighting stances. We're a better team than we were before being dumped here. Shiham, one of Pandemonium's Champions, promised an audience with Pan for my compliance, but Pan shunned him and, in extension, me.

And now we're surplus. Set aside until someone needs us again. Or forgotten and left to die.

Because it's been a month. Maybe longer. No one's coming to get us, not our side, not Shiham. We lost on Disiez when Chief Owelu betrayed us. We lost when Shiham took our Gifts from Order. I lost when all but one of my honor guard—my court—and the crew of my ship were slaughtered while I was right there.

I yell and rush forward. Not waiting for the inmates to strike first. Not warning Mineshka and Xijure I was going to move. I spin-kick the first person I encounter, feeling and hearing bones crack, before—

A tsunami of vertigo slams into me. The world is upside down, sideways, backward. The smell of burnt ozone overwhelms me. Afterimages of my opponents double, triple, before they fall into the sky. I hear retching and cursing. My knees hit the rough, hot dirt. I plant my gloved hands on either side of me, refusing to fall completely.

I won't writhe on the ground. I will not be that helpless. Not for him.

Because I know this power.

Rocks in the dirt ground beneath boots headed my way. A thick boot sole presses between my shoulder blades, pressuring me to go down. But I won't.

A hateful laugh. A hand clenches the awful manbun I've taken to wearing, because I can't cut my hair, and wrenches my head back. The world twists again as a face drifts into view. My focus is slow, but I make out waxy white skin, snake eyes, and a smile burned into my nightmares. The teeth are different. They gleam like black diamonds instead of white pearls. But the monster they belong to is still the same.

"Shiham." I cough after croaking the name. My stomach threatens to rebel. But if I puke in this position, I'll choke on it.

"Devon Lauduethe of Rema." Shiham releases me and removes his foot. "I see that you are making quite the impression here." He motions off to the side. "Take them."

I hear signs of struggling and Xijure and Mineshka cursing creatively. Anger courses through me, but I can't move.

An arm hooks around my neck, the inside of an elbow crushing against my jugular. I'm yanked to my feet. My knees are pudding that can't hold me. The arm across my throat tightens as another wraps around my chest.

Black spots dance in front of my eyes as oxygen becomes a thing of the past. Shit. This... this is how he's going to kill me?

My vision goes completely black, then gray, then black, then...

Air rushes in.

The arm's gone from my throat. But the phantom feeling of it squashing my windpipe remains. Choking in air hurts as my patchy, semi-vision returns to show me the building site's red terrain. My entire being shifts sideways—

"*Fipping* idiot. Lord Pan wishes to see this one," Shiham growls.

The sound of a palm across flesh and a grunted apology.

Dizzying sensations swivel around me. This is like passing out at football practice after too many drills and not enough water. Green and silver sparklers flicker in the corners of my eyes, spreading across my field of vision until they're all I see.

Then Shiham's ugly face plants itself in the middle of the halftime show.

He looks pissed, but maybe not at me. Black teeth gleam, the flare blending in with the sparklers.

"The hell happened to your teeth?" I slur. My head's a rock, and my limbs are barbells.

"A promotion."

The douchebag answered me? White noise roars around my ears. I barely hear what he says next.

"Carry him."

Carry... where? To Pan? But I can't ask because the outside world fades when the sparklers dim. The last thing I see are snake eyes and black teeth.

I RETURN TO REALITY IN a skinny shower stall, ice water hitting me from all sides. A snake-eyed soldier has a hand in the cubicle, holding me up as the water pressure washes the grime, sweat, and stink off me. After a minute, I'm dragged out. Rough fabric rubs me raw, then a shirt and pants that feel like silk are tugged over my body. I want to swing out an arm and smack somebody, but my arms are dead weight.

Blackness overtakes me as white noise roars in my ears.

And then I'm awake again. My eyes snap open. My heart hammers as panic screams through my body. Wherever I am is dark, and whatever I'm lying on is soft. I test my arms and legs. They tingle like they've been asleep and move like I'm treading through hardening cement. But I can move. I roll off the soft thing, hitting the floor on my hands and knees. The pain of connecting with solid rock rings through my palms and kneecaps.

My freed hair falls over my face as my head stays bowed, struggling to catch my breath and slow my heart before it explodes. I swipe hair out of my eyes and sit back on my knees, trying to gain my bearings. Scanning for that bastard Shiham. For Xijure and Mineshka.

My neck groans at all attempts to turn it, so I only look forward. My peripheral vision strains. The room is black rock with a tall gas-lamp in a corner radiating cheap light. A thing sits at the front of the room. It's a table... or altar.

Shit.

A sharp intake of breath sounds from my far right. My neck pops, groans. Still can't turn it. But...

"Xijure?" I croak.

A rough cough, then, "*Fip*. Alive. Mineshka?"

"Here." Rough and craggy, from the other side of the room.

Relief almost makes me face-plant.

I hear bodies scooting across the floor, then two warm shoulders bump mine on either side. Xijure and Mineshka. I can tell by their sizes and the way they breathe.

"Where are we?" Xijure says hoarsely. "There's an altar."

The shaking starts in my hands and makes its way through my entire body. The last time I saw an altar was in a weird dream-walking past life experience with Lyle. Order showed up and cursed our bloodlines with heroic duties.

But this can't be an altar for Order.

Mineshka's breathing gets heavier. "I don't think I can stand."

I know I can't.

And then something says...

**Do not be afraid.**

The words stamp themselves on my brain. I don't hear them, just know them. Like with Order. A dark shape approaches the altar and stands behind it, caressing its top.

**Champions of Kahanna, and guest. It is appropriate that you kneel.**

Only because we can't get up.

My teeth chatter.

**I said there is no need for fear.**

A horrible sound, like billions of nails on a chalkboard, raises to a fever pitch. I cover my ears, watching as the black shape walks through the altar as if the altar doesn't exist. A body forms: legs, torso, arms, head. A porcelain-white face, black hole eyes, shark-teeth, and long hair that sparks like lightning.

Order's Son. Pandemonium.

He peers down at us, jagged teeth in a rictus smile.

**I believe you have been waiting for My offer.**

CHAIRS, A TABLE, FOOD, AND wine. The table is draped in dark blue silk and set with silver plates, goblets, serving dishes, and utensils. Roasted white meat sits sliced in the center of round purple root vegetables on a platter. It smells friggin' delicious. And might be nice... if we weren't sitting across from a seven-foot god.

The low light throws long shadows over His face, making Pandemonium's fathomless eyes gleam. **I apologize for keeping you waiting. I understand that you have been enjoying the hospitality of My people for some time before My arrival.**

I jump as His words invade my mind again. I'm used to Lyle speaking to me with his telepathy. His mental voice never feels like an intrusion; it's a whisper in my ear. What Pan does feels like a stranger puncturing my personal bubble and yelling in my face. Instinctually, I want to punch out, though Pan's nowhere near me.

"We've been here for twenty-three sun rises." Xijure sets his fork down on his plate with a clink. "Your follower acted as if You would meet with Leader Two upon our arrival."

**Shiham often makes promises in My name without My knowing or permission. He is currently being corrected for the accommodations provided to you.**

Did I detect sarcasm on the word 'corrected'? Gods can be sarcastic? Mineshka nudges my thigh, and we share a 'WTF' look before Xijure kicks me, hard. His scowl scrubs any mild amusement from my body. Nerves and fear return. Pan seems... nice. But He's Order's Son—the ultimate enemy, and we're His prisoners.

I push food around on my plate, needing something to do.

Xijure clears his throat and in a steady voice asks, "You said You had an offer for us?"

All the juices in my stomach and the saliva in my mouth dry up. Here it is. The reason this is happening. Back on the ship, a million years ago, I agreed to

Shiham's demand to accept an audience with Pan. Anything to keep Mineshka alive. Shiham said an offer had been extended to Evan, and he'd shot it down. Of course he had. Evan's a badass warrior that breathes fire. He's not scared of anything.

But I am. I grunt as metal bites my hand. I look down to see that I'd bent my fork until it had splintered in the middle.

I let it drop and stare at Pan, waiting to hear what awful sentence I committed us all to because I couldn't be stronger. Because maybe I should have said no and let Shiham kill us all. It might be better than what's to come.

**My offer is simple. Do not fight for My Mother and the war is over for you.**

I blink. That's... "Don't fight? That's it?" My voice croaks. I stare wildly at Xijure and Mineshka before turning back to Pan. "That can't be it." He's lying, trying to trick us. Anxiety makes me want to throw my plate across the room and then turn the table over. I curl my hands into useless fists. I can't fight a god.

**You will have no responsibilities. You no longer have to be warriors. I know that you are both very young in terms of development for your species. You will be relocated to a place that suits your status as god-touched and live in comfort with My protection.**

This is bullshit. My mouth opens, but Xijure's iron grip on my bicep stops me from screaming something stupid. I focus on the king. His facial expression is schooled, calm, distant even. It's the face of a monarch, a leader. A face I can't make.

"And what about our worlds?" Xijure's tone is regal. "Zare, and Rema, and... Earth? The Silver and Gold Allegiances, our people?"

Pan's silence seems to last for hours. My heart pounds in my ears as His unspoken words say it all.

His Champions and their armies will obliterate our homes.

"This is why my brother rejected You." I sound as gravely as a chain smoker. I cough but doubt it fixes anything. "You'll destroy everything if we stand back."

Pan doesn't move, body relaxed in His throne-like dinner chair.

**I am certain that I cannot spare as much as you might desire. When I defeat My Mother, I will restart this universe and build what flatters Me. Peoples and places I did not construct will be erased if I hold no love for them. I hold no love for any place once protected or favored by Mother. She plans to do the same, erasing all things that I have favored if She is victorious, which She will not be, because I have you."**

What? What is He talking about? I glance over at Xijure, who looks just as confused and horrified as I feel. Erased? Pan's going to erase people? Order's going to erase people? Nobody ever brought that up before. No councilor ever mentioned that. Evan never did. Hell, maybe he didn't know. Maybe no one knew.

**However, I *am* reasonable. Present Me with a suitable counter proposition, and I shall consider your terms.**

Xijure's body goes stiff, grip on my arm still solid, his eyes on Pan. My hands unclench, but my stomach decides to take up their mantle and ties itself in two. I'm glad I didn't eat or drink. I'd throw up, and I don't want to go down as the leader who barfed on a god's table. My breath catches. Mineshka touches my shoulder, and Xijure squeezes my bicep until I think it might pop. I don't pull away as we all stare at Pan.

He, in turn, stares only at me.

Because I was the one who said He'd destroy everything. I was the one who made Him explain more and opened the conversation to barter. And my choices are supposed to be the ones that win wars. My stomach folds itself again, and I fight a wince.

But this is good, right? We want to bargain?

But no. There's no way *I* got this far if Evan hadn't.

"Why didn't You ask my brother to make a counteroffer? He'd have been better! He's..." *Smarter.*

**I want to negotiate with you.**

Because I'm the stupid one. Of course an evil god would rather deal with the dummy. But Xijure's here. Xijure can do this.

Xijure eases his grip on my arm, patting it before he lets go. He nods at me, a solemn hint of respect in his eyes. Was that for me? My stomach attempts to unfurl.

Xijure lifts his chin. "Will You tell us what's within reason for You, what we can bargain and hope to receive? We need Your ground rules and expectations, or else we'll just be wasting our time. And Yours."

MVP Xijure Harliel for the win.

Pan sits up straight, a close-mouthed smile gracing His stone face. I don't know if I like that smile. I fight the urge to look away, to see Mineshka's expression or Xijure's.

**Someone will speak with you, inform you of what I might consider as payment in exchange for certain concessions. You will be assigned tasks to ensure you understand what you could lose or gain. You will decide afterwards.**

Crap.

The god's smile vanishes. And so does He.

We're alone in a dungeon, with food, drinks, and the responsibility of writing a proposal that could save or end trillions of lives.

The pitcher of wine in the center of the table, between meats, jellies, bread, and fruit, is tempting. I know plenty of people who drink to forget their problems. To make things easier. They claim words come more smoothly. They could talk to people, loosen up. I need to be loose and smooth since I'm sure this thing with Pan has to be one of my prophecized choices.

"What. Just. Happened?" Mineshka reaches for the pitcher and fills her goblet.

Xijure, who'd been the only one to fill his cup during the meal, finishes his wine in a gulp. "I think we're gambling for our worlds."

I take the pitcher from Mineshka. My hands shake as I fill my golden cup to the brim. The fruity smelling red liquid shimmers. "Are any of you good at coming up with proposals?"

"I'm good at passing them over to my sister." Xijure takes my cup and sips until it's half gone. He gives a tiny smirk. "I somehow sense you don't have much drinking experience. Start with this." He passes the goblet back, then sighs. "I also get the sense that you probably haven't had training in negotiations."

I stare down into my half-empty cup. "What do you think?"

His silence is as telling as Pan's.

"Mineshka?" I chance.

"Negotiations were not in my job description." She pours more wine in my goblet, ignoring Xijure's glare. "Let him drink."

The undertone of 'he needs it' is loud.

We. Are. Screwed.

And moments later, our three empty wine goblets agree with us.

# Chapter 5

## Lyle

*"WHY DID AIMEE CALL YOU?"*

*Fifteen-year-old Devon sounds confused instead of pissed, meaning he's not even suspicious. I should be relieved, but my stomach tangles up like a metal Slinky.*

*"I don't know." If I keep my voice low, maybe it won't give away anything.*

*Devon sits next to me on the porch step. Grandma and Grandpa's old Victorian house is made for hanging out on the wrap-around porch in the summertime. All the windows and doors are open, letting out hot air. All East Coast people don't believe in centralized air conditioning, like smart Southerners do.*

*"It is so friggin' hot. You want to walk to the store? Get some ice cream?" Devon asks.*

*I study him out of the corner of my eye. He's browner than me, and the sun he likes to play under is making him look more like Lawrie. People at the store side-eye* them, thinking racist crap about terrorists, unless we're with our obviously White grandparents.

"You want to run into Aimee." It's not a question. He does.

Images of Aimee in a two-piece swimsuit on the beach skip through his mind. The sun catches her brown-black hair as it falls over her shoulders in long locs. The Slinky in my stomach twists into a figure-eight as I remember Aimee on a swinging bench, half in my lap, her lips on mine while my fingers fumbled over her clothed body.

"Yeah." Dev shrugs and frowns at me. "Unless you wanna call her and ask her to come here. I mean, she does have your number and all."

His eyes narrow, lips thinning. Thoughts revolve in his mind: Does she like him? Does he like her? Is he being weird? Weirder than usual. When did weird become his usual? How do I fix him?

'How do I fix him?' That thought works the knots out of the Slinky. Devon thinks I'm busted. Hates that I can't turn my telempathy off, that it's stronger now. That the headaches are worse, and I don't want to play football because I can't concentrate on any of the plays he makes up. Too much feedback clutters my head, and I can't sort it all and stay 'normal'. At least, not normal enough for him.

"Lyle? Are you okay?" Devon touches my shoulder. "Is it... your head?" He cringes just saying it.

"No." I shrug his hand off.

My head's fine. I think of Aimee, pushing me back on the bench, half lying on top of me to deepen kisses that shoot thrills of excitement through my tongue and into my brain. Pleasure receptors fire as her own feelings of want and need are satisfied and course through me.

*For the first time since I turned twelve, my mind was quiet. No loud outside thoughts, no random emotions from neighbors, no brain being beaten up by strangers and relatives who think a million thoughts per day.*

*Being with Aimee did that. But was it just her, or was it the kissing in general that did it?*

*She wasn't my first kiss, but it was my best kiss... and my first make-out session. And the quiet after lasted all night. If we make-out longer than a few minutes, how long will the quiet last then?*

*"I'm getting you water."*

*I blink. Devon's on his feet, staring down at me. I bite my lip, then gut a Slinky again. He's so worried, even though he thinks I'm weird and a growing danger to the 'cool' rep he's trying to build. This is my brother. Honest, loyal, trustworthy, and too open to lie to.*

*"Dev?"*

*"Yeah?" He kneels, hand on my shoulder again.*

*"I made out with Aimee last night."*

*His face twists from worry to hurt to rage so fast I barely track it all—and then knuckles fly at my face. I topple down the two porch steps and lie on the white paved walk-up. My brother, still on the porch, towers over me, and I blink.*

*The reality of my memory ripples, and fifteen-year-old Devon is replaced by a seventeen-year-old Devon. He glares at me with a coldness patented for me, because he never gives this look to anyone else. And suddenly, I'm seventeen too.*

*This is no longer a memory, but it's not quite a dream. The faint smell of oranges, the only scent I register in dreams, floats under a new odor of burning ozone.*

*"I trusted you," Devon snarls.*

"I..." can't breathe.

"What good are you, anyway? You're not a leader. You're a loser who can't save anyone. Why did you even think you could?"

"I..."

"Give up. You can't save me."

"No." I can't sit up. Can't move... and still can't breathe. It feels like something's sitting on my chest.

"I'm dead, Lyle." Devon backs away, toward the open front door of Grandma's house. Inside, instead of a cuckoo clock and Grandpa's leather armchair, there's a swirling void of blackness.

"Dev, no! Don't go in there! Don't!" Power surges within me, and I spring to my feet. I jump up the two porch stairs, reaching for Devon's arm.

And miss.

He vanishes though the door. Gone. I search for him with my mind and don't feel him. There's a hole where he was. A hole in me. Because maybe he's dead.

I crash to my knees. The porch disappears. So does the house.

And the dreamworld.

THE SMELL OF ORANGES VAPORIZES, and the reek of burning ozone increases. The world is gray and quiet, except for me. I pant, then start as a sound like metal on chalkboards played on a patchy rodeo sound system floods the place.

I clamp my hands over my ears and turn.

Oh.

I bow at the feet of Lady Kahanna.

**This is an unusual summons, Champion.**

I don't know how She thinks any summons that have to do with Her are usual, but She's right. The best way to call Order without anyone else knowing is by requesting Her presence on an *ether* plane. "Nialiah made an astral projection potion for me." I drank it after dinner and drifted away as Nialiah sang me to this place.

An icy blast of wind with a smell of burning wires nearly knocks me over.

I anchor my body and keep my eyes low, waiting for Order to instruct me to look at Her. Out of my periphery, I scan my new surroundings.

I'm on the cold stone floor of the temple She called Her first Champions to. Flashes of a past life, memories of being Jain Peredil, roll behind my eyes too fast for me to grab onto anything meaningful. I get a glimpse of Nialiah half-dressed, a snapshot of an older version of Evan—no, Corin Peredil, narrowing his eyes and calling me a liar. I see Corin's cold, dark blood pooled around slashed wrists. Padain's burial urn.

Jain Peredil failed. He didn't save his brothers. Couldn't save his twin.

I'm not him.

**Stand.**

I wince at the sharp pain inside my skull. Her words are scalpels carving letters on my browbone. My knees tremble as I push myself up. A wave of dizziness makes me wobble before I shake it off.

Her black hole eyes drink me in as Her crackling white-lightning hair swirls, covering Her body like a full-on silk robe. She moves forward, revealing a curvy figure of ivory stone and four large breasts. I straighten my back and grit my teeth as her long, clawed fingers brush my face. Freezing electricity streams from her hand and runs under my skin, wrapping around my bones.

Can't move.

**Speak.**

The muscles around my mouth relax. "Kahine took Devon. The Allegiances won't send anyone out to save him. You said if I helped You, You would keep my family safe. Why aren't You saving him?"

Oh. Crap.

Fear spills from a dark place in the back of my brain down the length of my spine as Her electric current flares in my blood. My lungs seize. My throat closes. There's no air.

**You accuse Me of dishonesty?**

/Inaction. We can't win like this./ Black spots fleck my vision. /We need Devon./

My brain is soup. Can't put together another sentence that makes sense. Blackness fogs my mind.

Weightlessness.

Until air rushes into my lungs.

Pain shoots through my kneecaps and palms as they hit the floor, impact echoing through my body. I gasp and cough. Black spots and chasers like sparklers on the Fourth of July keep my eyes from focusing.

**I do not need all of you to succeed. I only need your choices to align with actions that bring Me closer to having My world. How do you know that Devon has not already made the choices needed for My victory?**

/Our deal.../

A silence colder than the floor chills the temple space. My head throbs and my eyes ache, but my vision clears. Everything flickers like images on a dying LED monitor. Kahanna's body wavers as all ten feet of Her towers over me. Her robe of lightning hair stops before it touches my knees. I sit back on my heels, staring at Her double rows of white shark teeth as She chuckles in my head.

**Are you offering to expand upon Our deal, Lyle Lauduethe?**

/What else can I do?/

Horrible screeching grates my ears and grabs my head in a vice. Her laugh. Her real laugh. **Secure My Child of Magic. I want more influence over him. To do that, he needs to use My gift. He is reluctant. Change that.**

/I can't change my brother's mind./ Not only can I not break into Evan's head and wreak havoc, I won't do it. I draw the line at hurting my family and friends.

**Then you will lose your twin.**

/I can't lose Devon./ There would be no point in being here, making deals, helping Her, if it isn't to save him. He's not more important than Lawrie, or Evan, or Mom... but he is. To me, he is.

/But I won't hurt Evan. You have to tell me a way I can help You that won't hurt him./

Order stops smiling. **What do You perceive as hurt? Do you not want him physically harmed, or is it that you do not want him to harbor hatred towards you?**

/Both./ He can hate me if he wants, but later. After the war. Right now, I need him to care about me. For his own good. /Tell me what to do./

**You only need to plant a seed in My Child of Magic's mind, one that urges him to accept power when it is needed, no matter the source. My Son has gained more of His own followers while destroying more of Mine. The fortune spell warns Me that the time for your final choices is nearing sooner than I would like. Major events will transpire, and your brother will be tempted to draw energy from his Stone.**

**Your seed will ensure that he will not resist further temptation. And then, he will be Mine. And he will live because of this choice. Do you not think it foolish for your brother to reject power when he needs it? Think of the times he would be dead, if not for My gift. You will save both your brothers with this choice, Lyle.**

I shut my eyes, thinking of Evan drowning alone on a foreign planet. His life was suspended by the Stone, and it gave us time to save him. The battle on Nakshera was won because Evan and Lawrie used their Stones. They both would have died there. I tried talking to them about it, how good it is that they have their Stones. All they see is the bad. They're afraid of the power, afraid it's too much and that they won't be able to manage it all. That they'll hurt people they want to protect.

My fear.

And is it right that to conquer my fear, I have to make them lose to theirs? Guilt slithers around me, binding my body like a boa constrictor ready for a big meal.

**In the end, you are saving them all, Lyle.**

They'll all live, and hate me, but they'll live. That was my decision before, and it's still my decision now. My stomach burns, and my gag reflex triggers. But I choose this, and I own it.

Raising my chin, I reopen my eyes, ready for Her instructions.

# Chapter 6

# Lawrence

FAERIES. ARE. WEIRD.

That statement is a complete thesis. If anyone asks for evidence, I'll gesture at the water sprites currently splashing in Uncle Aeric's pool singing "When Doves Cry." Witness Exhibits A, B, C, D, E, and F, who sound pretty good. *Kids Bop* wishes their kids had this kind of range.

"Join us!" a high-pitched voice calls. They all sound like ten-year-old Earth kids, sweet as pie but evil as shizz. I'm told most Magic Breeds have a thing for luring mortals to their deaths or keeping them as pets they forget to feed. Once a person 'joins' them, it's all over.

"The water is sweet!" another sprite chimes.

They don't speak English. Don't really sing it either. But their words translate on a primal level inside my head. My lizard brain screams: 'Run!' while rest of my brain asks: 'How do alien faeries know about Prince?'

I sit cross-legged on a stone porch that juts into Uncle Aeric's yard, or rather the woods behind his house. He calls it a yard. Air molecules bounce in frenzied patterns while water molecules rotate in smooth circles. Combined elements vibrate, identifying themselves as plant life, rocks, dirt, and magic.

Magic is like matter on Bruhje. It clings to my skin like a cheap shower curtain, checking me out, poking at my power and deeming it interesting. Magic plays with the wind and earth, triggering my senses on the hour: *I'm not touching you. I'm not touching you.*

I hate Bruhje.

*Splash. Splash.* I shudder at a chorus of wild laughter, a sound very similar to Evan's cackling—the Lauduethe line has ember sprite in its DNA, angry little pyromaniacs that probably howl metalcore.

The buckets of joy in the pool switch songs. They have an entire catalog of 80s Earth pop music at the ready whenever I come outside. They beg me to sing with them if I won't swim, not deterred by me putting in my earbuds. I don't really understand why they insist I come to them when they can easily get out of the water and rush the porch.

Uncle Aeric says it has to do with the Old Magic that Order forged them from. Fae don't enter mortal homes and don't come into areas already occupied by mortals. If I beat the sprites into the pool one day, they won't dive in. Wonder what happens if they try?

A shrill note from a pitchpipe, nicknamed *Fae-Away*, cuts through the air. I grimace as the sprites shriek like kindergarteners and my stomach bottoms out as tiny rips in the fabric of reality teleport the little jerks away. The water stills, and the air calms. The sticky cloak of magic draped over my body lightens, like wet clothes drying in the sun. Still gross, but not as annoying.

The smell of nickel and copper nears me. Uncle Aeric has a metallic scent, like he's got bionic parts, but it's his earth magic. He can encourage plants to grow and cause the ground to shift, as well as cast spells and infuse potions with magical power.

It's amazing how differently magic users can smell from one another depending on the type of craft they work. I had no idea.

"Why do you like sitting out here with them?" Uncle Aeric's voice is medium-deep and smooth, like a DJ's before they warn the world that they're about to play slow jams for an hour. "You know they'll drown you in heartbeat, right?"

"Because I'm not getting in that pool." The water smells like bread and honey. Sprite pee.

Uncle Aeric laughs, and I respect that it's loud and real. There's been too much nervous chuckling, fake cheer, and awkward silence in Uncle Aeric's house.

My court and I landed a week ago. Enough time for Devrik Lauduethe, my fugging father, to say more than, *"Wow, you got big!"* to me at our initial meeting, but he hasn't even looked at me since then.

I expected indifference from him based on everything Evan shared with me, but it still comes as a sucker punch to experience it in person. I wish I could see how he looks at me, *if* he looks at me, because there must be something there. I'm his son. But I get nothing from him, and it makes me feel cold. Everyone walks on eggshells when he and I are in the same room for more than a few minutes, and it sucks.

A warm hand touches my back, and a rush of elements signals an incoming body as my uncle sits beside me. I hate that I can't see him. Evan said Uncle Aeric doesn't look much like any of us, but something about him keeps people from questioning his relation to the Lauduethe line.

"Whatever prognosis you get today will be good," Uncle Aeric says. "We'll know what to do from there on out. It's better to know, right?"

Is it? "I don't know." The healers could tell me, *'Yes, we can fix you'* or *'No, you're blind for good. Live with it.'* My heart stutters like a raggedy old car.

I spent an hour lying on a cot days ago as a healer poked my brain with magic, inspecting the damage to my retinas and checking my occipital lobes. Soft music played and the gender-fluid healer hummed, all to calm my pounding heart. The results took a while to process. Uncle Aeric and Chasyn waited for me in the healer's lobby. We left the clinic after being told when to return.

The healer was casual and friendly. They offered me candy and recommended a place to eat nearby. Chasyn ate my food, and we came back to Uncle Aeric's house to pretend my last chance at getting my sight back didn't depend on a healer who carried around salt-flavored lollipops.

"There are so many options for you," Uncle Aeric says, voice tentative but positive. "So many jobs and opportunities if things don't turn out how you want. You have a rather influential support system. You can stay here with me and... that guy who looks a lot like you."

I grimace. Mentioning Devrik while trying to cheer me up isn't the way to go. "He doesn't want me to stay."

"This isn't his house." Uncle Aeric doesn't miss a beat. "But also, he does." He sighs. "My baby brother is... someone you have to get to know. He means well, but he's complicated. Your Uncle Rovn and I are to blame. Our dear old dad too, may he rot in peace." He pauses, words turning bitter as lemon rinds.

I wondered a lot about Grandpa Kavka Lauduethe and why no one talked about him much before I got here. Turns out nobody talks much about him because none of his kids could stand him. Only Uncle Rovn attended his funeral, and that was more out of ceremony than caring.

Uncle Aeric continues, "Dad ignored Devrik, same as he did Rovn and me, so Rov and I spoiled him. Devrik never had to fend for himself. I just… I felt bad for him. Dad always had better things to do when it came to me, but my mother didn't. Rov's mom didn't have anything more important than him either. So, we each had at least one parent looking out for us. We were raised to excel. Riki's mom might as well have given him away. She didn't even know where he was half the time."

I lean in, curiosity beating out trepidation about the healer now that Devrik's mother, Hyacinth, a former Amphoran princess of a small country who ran off with a younger person, is in the story.

"One time, I was supposed to get Devrik for a holiday break and bring him here. I took a commercial shuttle to Rema, and he wasn't even on-planet. That bubble-brain Hyacinth let him fly off with a group of older kids to follow a music group. Who cares that he had prior plans or that those other kids sniffed crater dust? I wasn't arriving soon enough, and she needed her house child-free. He didn't come back addicted to anything, but still."

A crinkle of paper and the brief scent of watermelon. Uncle Aeric eats candy in place of aspirin. Whenever there's stress in his voice, he rummages around in his bottomless pockets. A paper-wrapped candy works its way into my palm.

"Evan told me not to count on Devrik." I explore the edges of the wrapper with my fingers, freeing the hard candy. Hoping it'll work a calming miracle on me too. "He let on that you'd be the one to take care of me here." And Evan was right.

A snort. "That *gak mopi*."

"What was he like, you know, when he was here with you?"

"Ev?" Uncle Aeric blows a raspberry. "He nearly burned the place down twice. Got lost in the woods I don't know how many times partying with wood sprites. He wanted me to critique every magical thing he did. Everything was 'how can I do this better?'" He chuckles lightly. "Great student. Made my kids jealous enough to try harder."

Uncle Aeric's kids are adults and live off-planet.

"Was he hyper?" I ask, trying to picture a pint-sized Evan tearing up the place. I want him to have been like me, a ball of directionless energy always kicked outside until it stopped bouncing.

Devon and Lyle are a pair, even when they hate each other. I daydreamed about Evan being the forever missing left sock in my laundry basket. And sometimes, I think he could be. And damn, I wish he was the one sitting next to me. My eyes burn and I rub them, refusing to let tears escape. Instead, I lean further into Uncle Aeric, waiting to hear more about my brother.

Uncle Aeric laughs. "He's mellowed out some, but he's always been a very direct, competitive little beast with a lot of energy." His shoulder bumps mine. "You're asking like you've never met him before. Did you guys not get along? I can beat him up if he was a *cratch*."

I shift, planting my hands behind me on the warm stone porch and leaning back, wishing I could see the sky. "He wasn't. I like Ev a lot, but he can be… distant. Like, I know he's different with his court than with me. I wanted us to have more time together." I half-grin, imagining us both staying here with Uncle Aeric, running wild. The dream makes my chest hurt. "Maybe he can take me out partying with the wood sprites after all this shizz is over." If we're not dead, that is.

Uncle Aeric slings a slim arm over my shoulders, and I scoot closer to him. "He won't. Those things won't eat him, but they'll eat you. At least, we think they might. We never find anyone they take, just their clothes. Sometimes, their shoes."

"Shizz! How often does that happen?"

I feel him shrug. "Tourists are warned. They still go camping anyway, wanting to get *digis* and *reels* of the Magic Breeds. We had a couple of ambassadors from Earth a few years back who thought it was 'wild' that we had faeries. Never found anything of those guys."

Fugnugget. My brain clicks, and the black cloud riding high over my head, fat from fear of impending doom and sadness over a missed childhood with Evan, makes way for a scientific discovery. The 80s crap. Bet one of those human tourists had an iPlay. "The sprites in the pool sing old Earth songs."

"Huh. Really?" Uncle Aeric sounds intrigued. "You know they sing what they think you want to hear. Anything that might make you get close."

"That's freaky. And you say they look like..."

"Your faerie brother," Uncle Aeric says. "You know, pretty, but shorter and younger, with pointier ears and longer nails. Don't run off to study them or anything. Not even with Ev. It's not safe."

"You don't think Evan would protect me?" That doesn't seem right. Evan seems to like playing hero.

Uncle Aeric is quiet for a minute too long. Not able to kill the reflex, I turn to 'look' at him.

"He might not be cognizant enough to realize he needs to protect you." Knuckles crack, a family habit. "How much do you know about what it means to have active Breed blood?"

"People can be afraid of you if they know about it," I say.

I flashback to the portal spell Nialiah and Imari worked to get us from Lenore to Nakshera. Something about the magic used triggered a change in Evan and

Adonis. For a few minutes, they'd gone from the guys in charge to… guys who might eat us. Oh.

"Depending on how much is active in you, you get affected by shifts in magical pressure. And those things bring pressure. It's hard to concentrate sometimes."

Uncle Aeric has active Breed blood. It's a drop compared to Evan's ocean, according to him, but I assume that's why Ev likes him so much. There are plenty of other reasons too.

Uncle Aeric squeezes my shoulder. "All right, nephew. You seem better. Not so gray anymore. We need to flag a railer and head to the clinic. Your healer commed right before I came out here to get you."

I frown. "We're using it again?" The zipline cart through the South Bruhjen Brush and into the Third Capitol is fun, but the raillery is public transport. I'd rather travel in Uncle Aeric's rover today.

I hear him stand, and he grabs one of my hands to pull me up. Once I'm on my feet and grunting at the pins and needles in my legs, he says, "This railer is just for us. A little extra coin gets you privacy."

I bow my head, awed and humbled by how much this guy understands without me having to say anything. "Thanks."

"I don't need thanks. Just, when you meet your uncle Rovn, be prepared to say *I'm* your favorite uncle."

He laughs again, and I hear it this time. A touch of the wild, like the sprites, like Evan. I wouldn't be lying if I told Uncle Rovn that this guy is my favorite uncle. Fear and anxiety want to eat me from the inside out. But Uncle Aeric will be there to feed me watermelon candy and make sure no strangers see me break down on the way to the clinic and back.

HEALER WESGRIFF SERVES UNCLE AERIC, Chasyn, and I salty-sweet cookies. Their footsteps shuffle away. Leather creaks like fresh kneepads—a chair being sat in. I lick my cookie. Tastes like kettle corn. Much better than the salt-pop from yesterday, but I'm starting to think this person has a fetish.

"Let us not take any more time than necessary to get to the prognosis." The healer's voice is young and bouncy, like a chibi from an anime. "Lawrence, the photoreceptors in both of your eyes are significantly damaged. Your healers on Nakshera and Lenore were very good. They stopped any further deterioration, but the cellular destruction caused by the overexposure of photons was already enough to result in your immediate blindness."

I nibble the edge of the cookie and lick crumbs off my lips. Doctors always start with junk you know. Get to the goods.

Or the bads.

A cookie crunch sounds from my left. Sounds like Chasyn just bit his in half.

"Your occipital lobes are healthy and ready to receive information from your retinas," Wesgriff says. "I can replace some of your rods with a technique known as inseiving and revive your cones if it takes."

Giddy, fizzy energy shoots through my system. I drop my cookie and jump to my feet. "Sweet! When can you do it?"

"Lawrie." Uncle Aeric's voice. He tugs on my sweatshirt, but I can't sit down again.

I'm getting my eyes back.

"We can perform the procedure as soon as tomorrow morning," Wesgriff replies. "I can have my assistant clear my schedule."

"I knew something good was going to happen today, *gikak*!" Chasyn claps my shoulder. Guess he's on his feet too. It's a party. Let's go find those Prince-loving sprites. I can look up the words to '1999.'

"Boys, please sit down." Uncle Aeric's tone is fatherly, the one that tells you the teacher just called home about that frog you launched across the room in science class.

My stomach lurches, anxiety creeping back in. Uncle Aeric is fun, and this is good news. Fun people not celebrating good news is an omen, a crop circle... Shizz. I feel around for the arm of the leather chair. No one helps me find it, and I'm grateful. Once I catch hold of the cushioned appendage, I sit.

"What are the complications to the procedure, Healer?" Uncle Aeric asks.

Complications.

"Another cookie?" Wesgriff's voice is kind.

Which means whatever they say next will be brutal.

My body shakes. Uncle Aeric rubs my back. "No, thank you," he says. "Please proceed."

"The process of inseiving involves inserting charmed nanocirm organisms into the occipital lobes. They will be programmed to travel through the optic nerves and into the retinas."

Little creatures hiking through my brain. Okay.

"In your brain, the occipital lobes have two major pathways through which they send the information they receive and process. One pathway is to your temporal lobe, the other is to your parietal lobe. These control..."

"Auditory and sensory perception," I murmur.

"Nanocirm must be implanted in large quantities, to ensure that at least ninety percent of the colony will follow the proper pathways to the injured regions they must repair and encourage to regenerate. The other ten percent may migrate through other pathways, venturing into those other portions of your brain."

Okay.

"Nanocirm must be extracted. Rogue organisms may not return to their insertion points. They may, instead, burrow and hatch additional nanocirm. With no further programming, they may die, which is desired, or they may build new structures inside your temporal and parietal lobes. This could cause—"

"Damage and blockages in those parts of my brain." I might get my eyes back, but lose the ability to hear, taste, feel, and smell. I might not even be able to recognize what I see.

"They could also migrate further, spreading to other regions of the brain."

Shizz.

"How likely is this to happen?" Uncle Aeric asks. "Do you have statistics?"

"This particular procedure has only been done thirty-seven times. It has a complete success rate of sixty percent."

"And what's the rate of people leaving here worse than they came in?" My voice is rough. Uncle Aeric's hand remains on my back.

"Ten percent achieve partial success. Color vision restored with some night blindness. Impaired vision with need of future corrective lens surgery."

They're stalling.

"Thirty percent achieve a status of restored optic nerves and retinas... but without the usage of their occipital, temporal and parietal lobes to process the information, it is useless. These patients..."

"Lose all their senses." My words are flat.

"Oh kid," Uncle Aeric sighs.

"I understand if you will need some time to consider treatment," Wesgriff says. "Though, I must inform you, the longer you wait, the lower the rate of a complete success will be. Taking a few *cycles* to ponder this is recommended, but you must reach a decision within one week, or your chances decrease by five percent."

Shizz.

"We'll have an answer for you soon," Uncle Aeric says. "Will you still have flexible availability?"

"For one of Order's Champions, I will make availability."

"And there are no other treatment options that could possibly give him partial sight or something similar?"

"Not with which I am familiar," Wesgriff sighs.

My uncle is thorough. Asking more questions that will probably make sense when my brain is ready to think about them. Blind forever, senseless forever, partially blind. The percentage is higher that I'll be able to see, but it's sixty percent. Thirty percent is high too. I can't lose everything. But if I don't try...

"We'll be in contact." Uncle Aeric helps me up.

## Chapter 7

# Lyle

NO ONE STOPS ME AT the door of the Maidens' Pavilion anymore. The Maidens' disciples are used to my visits, though they side-eye me when they think I'm not paying attention. Their thoughts stay neatly veiled, and I'm not tempted enough to dip inside. Who cares if they think I'm messing around with Nialiah? I only care if their gossip gets to Caea.

Damn. Images of her, dark-skinned, sharp-witted, and gorgeous, fill my head. And I grimace because I didn't make time to see her yesterday. I was busy creating plans, scheduling a training session with Evan this afternoon before he goes tomorrow. Had to get it perfect, or else he'd think something was wrong.

The base of my stomach burns in the same place it has since talking to Order. I don't know what it means, but I hope it's an ulcer, or something equally terrible. Karma needs to bite me somewhere.

I pass through the garden that leads to the Maidens' respective corridors and jump back as a barking fluff ball throws itself at my leg. I don't like dogs. I move on as it nips at the hem of my pant-leg and hear a whistle.

The puppy-thing yips and bounds toward the back of the garden, where Imari probably is. I speed into Nialiah's hallway to miss Imari's greeting. I hate pretending to like Imari. It's a waste of energy. When I reach Nialiah's door, I knock once and wait.

"Enter."

She sounds like a lady pharaoh from an old movie, eternally bored. Probably with me. I don't react to her the way she wants me to. The oval door opens, and I step into Nialiah's world where everything is Ferrari red and Porsche black. A protest to all the green, purple, and brown in the palace. Bed-sized pillows in varying shades of crimson are flung all over the floor, prepared for the woman to flop down and lounge at any given time.

Nialiah lies on her back, staring at a ceiling enchanted to look like a night sky full of dark, shifting clouds.

I don't wait for her to acknowledge me. "Did you finish it?"

She sits up so slowly that I feel my life pass me by.

I count to ten. "Nialiah, did you—"

"Yes." She rises and glides to a door near the back of the room. Her long dress flows behind her. She doesn't like anyone going into her workroom, so I wait for her, palms beginning to sweat.

*Shhhh...* the Stone whispers. Cool energy trickles from its facets, soothing me.

"You are certain you can go through with this?" Nialiah's purring voice floats from the workroom. She follows a second later, carrying a corked yellow gourd. She stops in front of me, and I try to ignore her cherry Jolly Rancher scent. Once she learned I liked it, she started wearing it daily. "I mixed the halif with faro berry juice. The drink will be sweeter than normal, but that can be easily explained by the berries being a bit overripe before I squeezed them this morning. This information will not register to Leader One as a lie since it is true."

She holds the gourd out to me but doesn't release it when I try to take it.

"I believe my dosage is correct but err on the side of caution and do not let him finish the container. Halif can be poisonous if ingested by beings with active Breed blood. Do you truly wish to risk it?"

No. Of course not, but... "It's the only way to get in his mind without him knowing."

Nialiah's black eyes feel omniscient as she studies me, then releases the gourd. "You must monitor his vitals carefully after he loses consciousness. You will know within the first few *wisps* if there is an adverse reaction." She produces an injection tool from a long sleeve. "This is an antiserum. It will loosen his muscles and reopen his airways if anaphylaxis occurs. You may also have to use it if he doesn't wake after a *jewel*."

I stumble to one of her pillows before my legs give out. I sit, clutching the juice gourd, tempted to pour it out. I'm going to poison my brother. My ears ring as my body shakes.

*Shhh...* cool energy seeps into my bloodstream and the tremors ease. *The Maiden is competent. Her measurements are correct.*

Cherry Jolly Rancher invades my nostrils. Soft hands cover mine. Nialiah is beautiful, ageless, and somewhat decent at times. "You do not have to do this, Lyle. Kahanna says She will do what She can to help Leader Two, that She will intervene if She feels his life is in danger. It is no promise to bring him to you. Should you risk damaging your relationship with Leader One beyond repair for something not guaranteed?"

Order didn't say how She would intervene, but Her word on doing something is better than knowing the Allegiances are doing nothing. Devon would save me. He might not do it this way, but he'd try. And his dumbass would fail because he's too Devon to push limits or morals.

*He will not know. Neither of them will. Only you will know what you risked and what you accomplished. You make your decisions out of love. Love is never wrong.*

"Do you love your sisters, Nialiah?"

She releases my hands, feathery lashes fluttering. "Hellene and Imari are not my blood, Lyle. My true sisters were lost during the First Sector war, and I moved on."

Which means she doesn't understand, *can't* understand my reasons, because she could 'move on.'

"However," she adds, her words light, "if my true sisters were alive, I would protect them at all costs."

I stare at her as she looks away from me. She never talks about herself, aside from

reminding me that she knows what color underwear Jain Peredil preferred. She usually smirks when I squirm. Sometimes, it seems as if she delights more in making me uncomfortable than when she does something I actually respond to. Even though my only responses have been to push her away.

But right now, in this light, with her speaking in that tone as I'm about to do something terrible, maybe I'll give her something she wants—"How did they die?" I ask—attention.

Her smile is softer than her next words. "Rissen, Gisa, and Maris were formally educated in healing and opposed the way Lenore had always been removed from joining the Sector War efforts yet asked for continued protection. They left here to serve as combat medics. I did not stop them. I envied their ability to just... leave.

They were not tied. They were beautiful and free. They wrote me long letters about all of the new worlds they saw and all of the people they helped."

Her smile fades, and I brace myself for what comes next. "Then after a few Common Years, the letters stopped." And she's quiet. I wait for her to finish, but nothing else comes.

Shit. I sit up, trying to think of something to say. Words of condolence.

"They should not have died." She grabs my hands again. "I would have made deals for

them too, but I would not deceive them."

I cringe as her gaze burns me. She wouldn't lie to her sisters. But… "You know my brothers wouldn't listen to me if I tried to tell them what's going on."

Nialiah lets go of me and is silent for another long moment, so long that I stand up, because I don't know what else to say or do. Do I go now? Am I dismissed?

"My sisters would not have listened either," she says. From her seated position, she passes me the syringe full of an antidote to the poison I'm going to feed my brother. A fragile new understanding hovers between us.

A timepiece from another room chimes. I meet Evan in an hour.

"Thanks." I say it because I should. This is a favor, even if Order reached into Nialiah's head and told her to help me out.

She doesn't answer, and when I look back at her, she's lying down again, looking at her ceiling. Not for the first time, I wonder if she's searching for something in those enchanted clouds. The timepiece chimes again as I leave the room, venturing back down the hall and into the garden.

The same, red-furred puppy that attacked me earlier sits in the hallway's portal. It barks, scampering into the garden. Good riddance. The garden is pretty, purple grass, pebbled-lined ponds, small trees... and a short, barefoot Maiden in what looks like brown overalls with her hands on her hips, scowling at me.

"What?"

"I could ask you the same." Imari's eyes drift to the gourd in my hands. "Did Nialiah mix something for you?"

"I don't sleep well." It's not a lie.

She comes forward, feet noiseless through the grass. I take a few steps back, looking down the exit hallway. I don't really know what her powers are, but she's not part of Order's VIP really. She knows the deal, and she, along with the rest of Lenore, will be saved for Order's New World, but something she did keeps her out of the special club I'm in. I don't care what it was, but I don't want it affecting me or my brothers.

Her hand wraps around my wrist, and I have to stop or drag Imari along with me. "What do you and Nialiah talk about?" she demands.

I shrug, and her grip tightens. Her eyes drop to my chest, as if she sees through the fabric of my shirt. The Stone's energy thrums, warming the skin over my heart. Her mental voice floats through my mind like a leaf on gentle water.

*Trust no god.*

The same words Corin Peredil said to me all those months ago. The ones I replayed over and over but erased after I accepted my Stone. In the end, Corin Peredil lost for not playing the game right. I can't take a loser's advice. And Imari might have been part of the reason why Corin hadn't played his cards right.

I push a thump of telekinesis against her fingers and watch them release my wrist as they splay. "I'm meeting my brother in a bit. Is there anything you want me to tell him for you?"

Her large black eyes don't waver. "Ask him to stop by to play with the puppies before he takes off. They would love to see him again."

I bet you would too. I smile at her, a quick curve of my lips, and force friendliness into my tone. "Sure thing. Later."

And then I walk away. I'm not telling Evan anything. The best part about Evan leaving is the fact that Imari is staying here. One less thing to worry about.

Juice and poison slosh against the tough skin of the gourd, mimicking the acid in my stomach as it rocks. I make a pitstop into my room to change into sweats for training with Evan, and to throw up.

* * *

"YOU'RE NOT AS BAD AS you led me to believe," Evan says as he lights candles by blowing on their wicks. He plants them in glass holders, making a miniature circle between us.

I sit across from him, panting, sweaty, and light-headed. He spent an hour teaching me basic hand-to-hand combat moves and making me run through them with him. It was weird. I'm not the athletic Ladreth—Lauduethe. Don't get what Devon enjoys about working out until it hurts, but it was fun seeing Evan in his element.

"You're a good teacher," I say, and he grins.

"I like training people." His tone is wistful. "I'll admit I prefer training them in magic over fighting. But you lack the necessary components for the former."

"Are you power-shaming me?"

I'm rewarded with his laughter. Makes me feel good. I don't often make people laugh.

I use a small towel to mop sweat off my brow as Evan completes his meditation set-up. He pours a flask of herb-dirtied water into a shallow bowl and places it in the center of the ring of candles. The water boils as if it's on a burner, steam rising and making the place smell like honey cough drops and mint. The clear smoke burns and cleans my airways at the same time, like vapor rub.

I lean back on my hands and let my eyes wander. Evan's workroom is a forest trapped inside a fifteen-by-eighteen-foot space. The wall vines are insane, sprawling across the floor and hiding the ceiling. White flower petals settle over everything like dust.

"Was there ever furniture in here?" I ask.

"A table, some stools, maybe a couch," Evan says. "Tossed them all out. I needed more room to do physical magic."

"Can't you do that in the training rooms?"

Evan levels me with a dark look. "Not with my Stone."

A flare of hope catches me off-guard. "You're working with your Stone?" Buds of relief want to sprout inside me. If he is, then his opinion on the Stones must have changed. I won't have to do anything. I can just appreciate whatever weird yoga-meditation session he wants to run now.

"I'm trying to strengthen the wards around it," Evan says. "I don't need it telling me things while I'm trying to concentrate. If I use it, I want to choose the spell, how much power I take, and when that power stops flooding out of me."

My heart palpitates. If he's using his Stone, even warded, can Order do what She needs? Can I back out?

*You know better*, the Stone says. *Ensure Her claim. Save him, Lyle.*

"You okay?" Evan sits on his knees, green eyes murky with concern. "You look shaky. Was the workout too much?"

I shake my head. "The workout was okay. I haven't eaten today."

Evan sighs. "Is your stomach still bothering you?"

"Yeah."

"You need to get checked out. Maybe that's what we should be doing right now." He starts to get up. "I'm awful at meditation junk anyway. Let's—"

/I want to spend time with you. What if you go out there and never come back?/

His expressions crumples, grief and guilt making him look younger than he already does. And guilt has me swallowing back another dry heave. It's true that I worry he won't come back, but I didn't have to throw it at him like that.

*Yes, you did*, the Stone hisses.

Evan settles across from me again, staring at me over the circle of candles. "You know I can't promise you anything about being safe or staying safe, but please know that I want to return to you." His smile is weak but genuine. It reflects in his eyes.

That's family love. I see it in the gestures of my close relatives, sense it echoing through their thoughts and feelings. And they deserve a new world.

"I know you don't hate me," I say. "So, uh, show me this terrible meditation technique of yours. It might give me some blackmail material to use against you."

Evan quirks a brow. "Blackmail?"

It takes a minute for me to realize he's unfamiliar with the term. I really need to get a translator, but I'm terrified of the idea of someone sticking a needle in my brain stem to insert one. "Blackmail, something embarrassing or incriminating I can hold over you."

Evan chuckles. "Hah! I'd call that extortion."

"Why do you know that word and not 'blackmail'?" I ask.

"I don't know." He shrugs. "Okay, so breathe deeply. In and out, clear your mind of petty *pidge* like blackmail. And we're going to start this off with movement. Follow me. Doesn't matter if you get it perfect, just do the best you can and remember to breathe slowly but deeply."

We end up doing one of those cool down sessions fitness instructors lead after workouts, but the cough drop smoke takes me to a higher place. By the end of it all, my body feels lighter.

We sit in our original spots, the candles still glimmering.

"Well?" Evan says after a while, and I look at him.

"I can't blackmail you for this. I feel better, more focused." My stomach is less fiery.

"This is the place you should be when you practice using your powers," Evan says. "Psychics always have to find an inner peace. I know it sounds *blikky*, but it's true. If you want complete control, you have to be steady, grounded, and clear."

This is a state of mind I only achieve with my Stone, but I got here on my own today. Cold energy stings my chest, and I wince as the Stone radiates displeasure. It's like ice creeping through my bloodstream.

"Do you want to try something? Some telekinesis maybe?" Evan asks. "Or do you want to work on your mental shields? That's something you can do alone if you want to trance. I'll guard you."

Trance. Sensuen taught me how to fall into one, but I've never tried it without her.

"I can trance and work on my shields. I remember how," I say. My hands quiver, body tensing.

Evan frowns. "Do you need to stop?"

"N-no, I don't need to stop."

His brow furrows.

"It might take a while for me to go under and figure things out. You really want to stay here?"

Evan looks unamused. "Even with wards, I wouldn't leave a tranced psychic I don't hate,"—he grins, drawing out the word 'hate'—"alone. It's fine. I brought mission reports to read, and... you brought snacks." He reaches for the bag of krosa nuts and the gourd of juice I half-emptied before leaving my room. He shakes it and gives me a look. "Really? You brought something you already started in on as a snack for us both?"

"It's really sweet. You might not like it," I say. It's a chance for him to put it down, say he'll pass. It's not my fault if he chooses not to drink the poison.

My heart pounds in my throat as Evan tastes the juice. He smacks his lips. "It's good to me. If you don't like it, I'll drink the rest." He takes another swig and nods at me. "Do your thing. I'm not watching."

I take a deep breath, closing my eyes, and panic. Nialiah said don't let him finish the gourd, but that's vague and I can't control how much he slurps down. What if I didn't dump out enough? What if I dumped out too much? What if I have to use the antiserum? The injector tool feels like a rock tucked in the pocket of my boot.

I struggle to breathe calmly. I need to seem like I'm trancing, doing what I said I would… until I hear it. A soft thump. A sound that can only be made by a limp body hitting the ground.

Damn.

I open my eyes, then wrap my arms around my stomach as intense pain tears through it. His legs are still crossed but his upper body is sprawled to one side, the gourd in the grass a few inches from his fingers. I get up, pausing to wait out the dizzy spell and the need to puke, and kneel beside him. I straighten his legs and turn him completely on his side. I've watched enough hospital and paramedic shows to know to roll unconscious people over. I check his pulse and almost sob at finding it steady. I fumble to get the injector out of my boot and set it on the grass near my thigh.

*Touch his mind. See if he stirs.*

I don't want to. I want to shake him awake, but it won't work. Nialiah said to use the antiserum if he doesn't wake in an hour, meaning he's out for the count. And I can't waste it.

Closing my eyes, I knock on the door to Evan's mind, waiting, just in case he's awake in there. I have permission to touch his surface thoughts, a link that keeps me, Devon, Lawrie, and Evan connected, so we can talk to each other. But that's as deep as it goes. His inner door remains closed to me. Non-humans are mostly aware of psychics and are taught to shield their minds early on. Some are better at it than others.

Evan's mental walls gleam like titanium, strong and cold. I might be able to break them, but I'd leave my power signature behind. My attention shifts to the door. I knock on the thick metal again, then push, stomach on fire, heart in my mouth, as the door swings open.

The smell of strawberry milkshakes and opened ketchup packets welcomes me as I step into the cogs and wheels of my brother's mind. Sunlight filters in from a skylight, illuminating a mall with an infinite number of floors. If there's a ceiling, it's well beyond my range of vision. This place reminds me of an indoor outlet center.

Is this the old Katy Mills Mall?

I gape, my own memories flittering around me. A Christmas tree and Santa's workshop are in the middle of an empty food court. A kiddie train cruises by with no one aboard.

When we were little, Mom brought us here. I peed on that Santa Claus, Devon bit him, and Lawrie stole his hat. I don't remember Evan here with us... or maybe I do. I squeeze my eyes shut, hearing a little voice sagely letting me and Devon know that Santa Claus is a hoax and that he saw our presents in Mom and Dad's closet two weeks ago.

My eyes open, scanning for the five-year-old who spoke to me, but the mall is still empty. I wander around, peering in glass store windows that swirl with emotions and memories. I touch the glass and flinch as one of Evan's memories sparks in my mind, about to display. I snatch my hand back.

No. It's bad enough that I'm inside his walls. I won't tamper with anything unnecessary.

Where do I need to go?

*To the center.*

To Santa Claus?

If I was anywhere else doing anything else, I might laugh. An absurd thought strikes me and now, I need to know. Am I going to have to sit in Santa's lap to get this over with? Evan has a weird sense of humor.

My footsteps reverberate, bouncing off walls. Too loud for the quiet. If Evan was conscious, this place would probably bustle with energy and motion. Music might play, NPC characters might rove by stores or order food that I'd smell cooking. Santa's seat would be occupied by a pot-bellied grandpa in a trash wig and beard.

I approach Santa's workshop. A waist-high, white picket fence borders a living room-sized synthetic snow rug. Carboard gingerbread people with candy eyes and cloth scarves peep through the windows of a plastic log playhouse. Wrapped gift boxes of various sizes are scattered under the tree. I pass through the fence, walking across the fake snow that leads me toward Santa's red throne.

*Not there. Keep going.*

I pat the arm of the chair as I move on to the massive, white-frosted Christmas tree. The presents are on a red velvet blanket bunched around the base of the false spruce. I pick up a present, surprised that it's heavy. Something rattles when I shake it, and the little kid in me wants to rip the green and red paper off. I set it down.

*The tree.*

I look to it, inhaling the sharp, piney odor of Christmas, and...

It hums.

What is this? I tilt my head back, staring up, and up. The tree stretches toward the mythical ceiling of the mall. It's boundless.

And not a fake Christmas tree.

It's a manifestation, like this mall. I stretch out a hand to touch its rough trunk.

*The roots.*

I sit on my knees, moving presents and peeling back the blanket to reveal a hodgepodge network of gnarled roots that vary in size. They glitter like ocean glass caught in sunlight. Their energies sing respective notes. Evan hears life songs, says every living thing has one.

Is this his?

I release the soft blanket and lean forward, panting and dizzy, as fear screams between my ears. I could ruin my brother with the wrong touch. Destroy him from the inside out. Kill him if I—

*Set me on a root.*

The Stone is cold, calm. So rational. I latch onto the feeling. Needing the panic to stop. I slip my hand under my shirt collar, palming the Stone, letting soothing vibrations run through me before pulling the necklace over my head. My sapphire glows a rich, royal blue in my hand, and I hate letting it go. Carefully, I place the Stone on the thickest root. Its colors brown, green, and blue. It shines brighter than the others and sings its note loudest.

My sapphire sparks, and I shield my eyes in the crook of my elbow as the Stone pulses. Planting Order's seed. Smoothing away reservations and assuring my brother that it is wise to take power when he doesn't have enough. That it will save more than it hurts. I hear the words the Stone whispers to my brother.

*Accept your gift. And yourself.*

The root's colors flicker, light, dark, light, dark—a struggle. He's fighting it. I count heartbeats. One. Two. Three. Four. Fi....

The light stabilizes, the colors still vibrant, their gloss the same. But something's off.

I retrieve my Stone, draping it over my neck. Not realizing how naked I felt without it.

It's done?

*Kahanna will reward you.*

I nod. Okay. Yeah. She'll do Her part now. And planting the seed wasn't so bad. I walk away from the tree, admiring its infinite reach toward a ceiling that might not exist, and shake my head at it being disguised as a Christmas tree. Only my brother.

My brother who will be fine. It's done, over.

But as I head for the door that will take me outside of Evan's walls, I hear it.

The silence of the mall is thunderous, the loudness of the white noise smothered Evan's life song before. But now that I know the song is there, know its sound, it's obvious.

And wrong.

One of the notes in Evan's song is wrong, changing the harmony. The mistake is small, but it's there. Will he hear it? Will he know?

Can he fix it?

*There is nothing left to be done here.*

I cross the threshold, closing Evan's inner door and throwing my awareness back to its point of origin. Inside my own head, I open my eyes. See my brother curled on his side, dead to the world after trusting me. And cry.

Chapter 8

# Evan

SEVEN *JEWELS* AFTER TAKE-OFF, and I still can't stop thinking about the parting look Lyle gave me. He hugged me like I was going off on a suicide mission and stood back afterwards, hands in his pockets. I've never seen Lyle cry, and I am under the impression that even under pressure, tears don't come easily to him. He beats himself up, makes himself sick, but his eyes remain dry.

Regret about leaving him behind had me re-checking third and fourth diagnostic reports from the navigation and armory stations. Soldiers gave me knowing looks and sent me what I asked for the first two *jewels*, and after the third *jewel* they told me to take a break.

An avatar of myself stands in a virtual arena of cheering, stomping people, ready to play Ringer, a virtual contact sport. The 3D construct of a tournament projects from my gaming cube. The cube throws a myriad of revolving colors down on the clear glass table it hovers above. I flex my fingers in the sensory gloves. They tap into my biorhythms, syncing me with my undefeated avatar.

A new player appears several *kiuts* away. She's broad and yellow-skinned with two curved antennae situated on her forehead above round black eyes with orange sclerae. A Karch. There aren't many Ringer players from that part of Sector Nine.

She bows and I return it, then wave my hand so that my avatar produces the first energy ring.

I ready myself to pitch and freeze at the sound of the Tube opening. Four people file out, Desiri grumbling. Something barks. I call up a timeout screen and send an invitation for a rematch, time 'to be announced.' Disconnecting, I peel off the gloves and whip around to face my court.

And Imari. I gape at her. What the—

"Look what I found squatting on Deck Three with a basket of rats," Desiri sneers, amber eyes glinting with suspicion. Her long, copper-brown hair is twisted in a knot atop her head and her bicep and thigh holsters are loaded with black-bladed knives. She must have been fire-blading. She likes working certain mage-crafts in the cargo overflow areas.

"Why?" I step toward Imari, still in shock.

She's in a sleeveless, green pantsuit a shade lighter than her skin, clutching the purple thatched basket she uses as a carrier for her Pafti pups. She looks at me like a savior. Makes me wonder what all Desiri said to her on the way up.

"What are you doing here?" I ask.

"You have a horrible memory." Her voice is firm. She tilts her chin, a proud stance. Her long black hair is wound and tied at the base of her neck, but the extra movement shakes it free.

I stare at it a *wisp* too long before blinking. "I didn't forget an invitation."

Adonis and Jalee fan out around Imari. Jalee seeming peeved, Adonis inconvenienced. He heads for the galley in the open common area, probably for kava. Jalee folds her slender arms over her chest, high cheekbones and narrowed brown eyes making her look judgmental. I don't miss how Imari stiffens as she glances at my second and third-in-commands.

She locks eyes with me. "I told you that I needed to help you, and when I learned how I could, you would know. Well…"

I wait. She stares.

"Well, what?" Desiri snaps. "You snuck on our ship like an assassin and say you have information, and now you can't share it?"

"I said he would know." Imari rounds on Desiri, not intimidated by her anymore. "It is not quite time for him to know yet, but that time is approaching. And I must be near."

Desiri cocks her head.

"Or maybe you're just running away." Jalee's voice is a cool wind. She wears standard gear, tan cargos and steel-toed battle boots, but no ammo jacket. The sleeveless tank most soldiers keep under their gear fits her upper body like a second skin. Black on medium brown.

"Are you? Running away?" I focus on Imari. She's not lying about thinking she needs to help me or knowing how, but that doesn't mean there isn't an ulterior motive.

Imari scowls. "Perhaps I am doing both. My destiny lies in traveling with you, but I also do not object to… getting away. I can count how many times I have been off Lenore."

Her tone is melancholy. And I catch a shadowy glimpse of sad black eyes from a previous life where a younger version of this Maiden told me she wasn't allowed to travel anymore.

"Your first trip off-planet since the Prophecy Cycles was to Nakshera with us, wasn't it?" I ask.

"Yes." She presses her painted pink lips together. "I need to see more of this world, and I did not think you would mind so much. You like me. And I come with friends." She sets the basket on the gray carpet and opens the lid.

Four puppies, gold, red, gray, and black, sit on their tiny rumps, wide eyes staring up at us. They yip and bounce to their feet, thwacking each other with their puff-ball tails.

"I figured that I should bring one for each of you. And forgive me, I chose for you. You favor this one, Evan." She reaches in and lifts out the golden puppy I'd made first contact with *cycles* ago in her garden.

The puppy pants, tail wagging furiously. I take the giddy mound of fluff from her, bringing the pup to my chest for a welcome hug and letting him sniff at the pockets of my uniform. He squeaks and snuffles, nipping and tugging as I rub his back. I'm ready to forgive Imari for somehow bypassing my security and invading my ship. She gave me a puppy.

She takes the red and gray ones by the scruffs of their necks, holding them toward Jalee and Desiri. Jalee wavers, then melts. She takes the gray puppy and makes clicking noises as she snuggles it.

Desiri hums at the red puppy. Everything about her posture is calculating. "How big do these things get?"

Imari seems taken aback. "Oh, they can get quite large. Standing on their hind legs, they might be taller than me, after they mature."

Desiri takes the pup in one hand, gazing into its eyes. A small smile graces her full lips. "It's about time I had a familiar on the field with me. How's training them?"

"They can be very obedient," Imari says slowly, her hands still out like she's holding the puppy Desiri took. "Uh…you wish to train it for battle?"

"What else would a mage do with a dog?" Desiri settles the red pup over her right shoulder. "Don't worry, Maiden. Kiaku and I are going to be partners. And you,"—she flashes a toothy grin at Imari—"are now safe from retribution. Enjoy the rest of your time onboard. I can find comfortable quarters for you on the eighth deck."

The final puppy chirps in the basket. I shudder as the artificial air in the unit turns crisp. Our breath makes clouds in front of us. Imari picks up the puppy and goes to where Adonis stands in the food prep area holding a cup of kava in both hands and glowering at every puppy in the room.

Ai.

"Those things will not remain on this ship," he says.

I open my mouth. Adonis hates animals indoors. Detests when they're messy. And abhors when they're mine. My laughter is nervous.

"Oh, get over it," Desiri drawls, crossing into the galley. "He's leader, not you, and he loves furballs. Now move so I can get some water for my familiar." She bumps Adonis away from the cold box with her hip as she speaks to her dog. "We start your training today, Kiaku. No grace period."

*Fip.* The temperature drops another degree before Adonis releases the vapor in the air and walks to his room. The atmosphere warms.

"Oh." Imari hugs the black dog. "Forgive me. I did not—"

"He'll adapt," I say, entering the galley as well and patting her shoulder. A strange feeling of familiarity seeps through my hand as it contacts with her bare skin. I pull back, flexing my fingers. "Adonis and I share a flat on Rema. He ignores my pets there too. I'll take this pup as well." Wanting to touch something else, to rub out my tactile memory of her soft skin, I reach for the last puppy.

The black pup is timid and shy, nothing like the bold gold pup in the crook of my left arm. Adonis would like this quiet one, if he gave her a chance. Most people I know in tune with nature magic love animals. Adonis is the exception. He's not even a fan of gardening. He may be the worst active Quarter Breed I know. The only stereotypical thing he does is sleep around.

I nod toward the couch. "Do you want to sit down and tell us how you got aboard or what you think is going to happen that requires you to be 'near' me?" A vague sense of foreboding tiptoes up and down my spine, and I doubt that she's going to tell me anything pleasant.

Imari looks at her booted feet and nods. She shuffles out of the galley and heads for the couch, and I share a look with Jalee. She joins me, her pup yipping at the gold and black pups resting on my forearms. The black pup shivers, heart racing. Poor baby's nervous.

"Do you think Hellene and Nialiah know she's with us?" Jalee asks in a low voice.

"I don't know. She doesn't seem close to either of them. But she could be on a mission." I never know what to think when it comes to the Maidens, but Imari is different than Hellene and Nialiah. Not so grouchy or beyond reproach. She seems more comfortable away from her sisters.

Jalee scratches her pup behind its ears. "I don't trust her, Evan. She looks at you like you're someone else. It's worse than Nialiah with Lyle. Nialiah's toying with him. Imari..." Jalee shakes her head. "She wants something from you that you shouldn't give her."

"What do you think I want to give her?"

A corner of Jalee's mouth twitches, a tick when she's irritated. "You look at her like she's someone else too. Don't let her hurt you."

Jalee leaves the galley and walks through the common room, passing the couch. Jalee's earthy scent lingers where she stood beside me, and I bite the inside of my lower lip. Jalee, my voice of reason since we were primary school-aged, has never steered me wrong.

Metal scrapes the stone floor behind me. Desiri's pup laps water from a clay bowl near the mage's steel-toed boots. Desiri kneels to set down a plate of raw, pink fish, grated into chunks. My golden puppy whines, and Desiri huffs at me.

"Set them down and talk to the green girl. I'll stay here and monitor. You might need a witness."

"Just what do you think I'm going to do to her?"

She grins and the poison-blue barrettes pinning back her bangs glitter. I roll my eyes and kick at her as she chuckles. Desiri should be an assassin-mage, running dark market cartels as part of her family's business. She became a warrior-mage in training when she joined my court at nine Common *revs* old, but she never downplays the sneakier skillsets she grew up with.

I set my puppies on the floor, pushing the black one closer to the others as she shies away. "Go on. Good girl." I don't leave until my puppies start eating.

"I know a great recipe for an elixir that gets blood stains out of fabric." Desiri's tone is conversational.

I reach out, tapping into the canned song of artificial air and shift the notes so that it gives her a shove. I march away to the rough sound of her laughter and the yips of startled pups.

Imari has her knees to her chest, black eyes roving around the room. I drop down beside her, and she bounces slightly from my added weight on the couch cushion.

She doesn't acknowledge me right away, still studying the common space as if trying to get a read on us.

"This is cozy," she finally says. "I like it very much. It feels inhabited. Is this your usual residence?"

"Most of the time." I pick at a loose thread on my cargos. "There are a few things I left behind that would make this place my real home." Bigger musical instruments, pets, plants. "I rescue animals and cultivate endangered plant species on Rema. The smaller plants I could bring. The animals and larger plant species I had to find temporary homes for."

"I am sorry your nymph does not like the pups. Is it the reason you have no animals aboard?"

"Partly. But really, I never know how much time I'll have to take care of anything. *Fip*, a few of these plants almost died while we were on Lenore."

She looks crestfallen. "I should not have brought you the pups. I saw how much you loved them. I wanted you to have a nice gift. Something from me."

My eyes widen as she looks up at me. Her face... a flash of memory shows her beaming as she holds heaping handfuls of green sea glass in both palms. I hear my own laughter and her voice saying, *"From me. My feelings for you are as transparent. Do not ask me if I love you anymore. You know the answer."*

*Fip.*

"Imari, what do you want? And don't say to 'help me.' I get that. You did or didn't do something for Corin Peredil and you're guilty. Now, you're flying off to battle with us. Because that's where we're going. We're entering hostile space and landing in the middle of a border skirmish. This isn't a vacation cruise for you to see more of the world. What do you know? Are we heading into a trap?"

Imari frowns. "If you think about it, this whole war is a trap."

I can't fight a growl, but I stop when she laughs.

"Impatience is your Achilles tendon. You charge forward, overconfident in your abilities to conquer hardship and win favor."

"You're not talking about me."

"I am and you know it."

"I'm not overconfident. I train, hard." My words are clipped. How dare she? "I trust my skill because I hone it. My opponents have to be very good, or damn lucky." Her glare is so venomous I want to scoot away, but I refuse to give ground, so I change tactics. "Corin Peredil was the cocky one. He thought he was better than he was. He challenged Order and—"

"Shut up."

"...and She saw to it that he died."

"That was a mistake! She never meant for him to die!" She clamps both hands over her mouth.

Score one for me. My pulse throbs in my throat in anticipation.

"She wanted him for me... as a mate."

Like an animal? *Vati fip*. Order is sick, and Imari? The jury's out.

I keep myself in place as she continues, "He was safe, but he could not leave things alone. He wanted too much. Thought he could have it all his way. That She loved him for more than his genetic make-up that She could not copy on Her own. She can influence breeding..." Imari looks away from me, ducking her head. I know I look intense.

"Influence breeding?" I press.

"The Leaders of Rema, all of the Marked ones before you, and people of the Lauduethe line. The last Peredil was a woman. She married a Lauduethe, and Kahanna saw to it that Lauduethe men and women bred with fae. Her magic forced couplings. She lost Her Corin and needed another, but he was too unique to come by easily or quickly. She worked and waited for hundreds of Common *revolutions* for you, Child of Magic. And you... are better than Corin. His magic was nothing compared to yours. And partnered with Her gift? She wants you badly."

"And, according to that, *you*," I say, my inner fire crackling. The smell of burning cloth hits the air and I jump off the couch. *Fip.* There are scorch marks where my hands were. My clothes are cool, treated to be flameproof.

Imari hugs her knees. "But Kahanna will not get what She desires." She speaks to a ghost I can't see as she stares straight ahead. "I loved Corin. You bring memories. He is a part of you, but you are not him. When you gaze at me, sometimes I see specs of him in your eyes. But those specs of Corin Peredil are dwarfed by the presence of Evan Lauduethe. So young, and so very confused. You are the same soul but washed to be a blank slate. Your individual experiences shape who you are now. It is not fair of me to wish you to be someone you are not. I let Corin go before I boarded this ship."

Her song is true.

"This thing I must do for you is something I could not do for him. I did not know how," Imari says. "It will be a parting gift, so I can let you go as well."

"But you won't say what it is."

I don't know what to make of her. I want to think she's disgusting. She shows no shame or remorse at being a willing part of Order's breeding project.

A breeding project that I'm a product of, but... a phantom of longing from deep inside me wants to hold her, kiss the top of her head, and tell her she doesn't have to give me anything in parting because… because it doesn't want to be parted from her. It loves her, and when she said she loved Corin, there was no lie. She would have been willingly bred to someone she wanted to be with. But obviously, he didn't know that. How could he?

"What do you know of fortune spells?" Her sudden random question hits me in the face, dragging me out of my thought spiral.

"Tricky as *fip* to cast, and the outcomes are almost never worth the cost." My body cools as my core temp drops to semi-normal. I'm safe to touch the furniture, but I'm going to catch Hades for singeing the couch again. "Why? Are you planning on casting one?" *Pidge*. "Did you already cast one?" She shakes her head. "I do not dabble in that type of magic."

"The only people I know who play with it do parlor tricks. Stuff to fool non-magical tourists. I caught a guy ripping a family off on Jipor." He screamed so loud when roots pierced through the ground and grabbed his ankles, binding him to the floor. I made him give the currency he stole back and left with his lunch. Jipori cheese and egg sandwiches are delicious.

Imari's shoulders sag, and I latch onto the motion. Guilt-ridden shoulders love to droop.

"You didn't cast a fortune spell, but someone you know did." I breathe carefully, regulating heat.

Squeaky barks and puppy feet bound my way. The gold pup puts its front paws on my shin. Crazy little thing isn't wary of my leaking magic. I lift it with one hand as I focus on Imari. I'm told that my full attention on a living creature feels like dozens of razors boring through flesh. It's a Breed thing that I avoid unless necessary.

Imari flinches and glares at me, chin on her knees. "Fortune spells and Kahanna's Prophecy of the Four, Evan. Think about it."

Desiri enters from the galley, her gait slow. A hunter's stalk. She's been eavesdropping. She comes to stand shoulder-to-shoulder with me as we take identical stances in front of Imari. We're warriors sizing up an enemy. The tone of everything darkens as small clues about the prophecy and the past fall into place. I set the pup down and nudge it to move along, not wanting it to be in the line of fire while betrayal, shock, and holy fear play a raging game of Ringer in my gut.

"The *fipping* prophecy is a fortune spell," I murmur.

Imari probably knew this from the beginning. *Niobe-va.* I flashback to the cell under the castle in Lenore, and the Ruj general who told me The Maidens had secrets. The Remasian Council too.

"What are the parameters of the spell?" I ask.

There's a sound in the hallway. Adonis appears, glancing from me to Desiri and joining our united front before Imari.

Imari bristles. "Stand down and I will share."

"It doesn't work that way, Maiden." Desiri's voice is silky. "You're on our ship. The only people who give commands here are us."

Imari sighs, looks pointedly at me, and folds her arms over her chest.

"Answer the question," I say.

"I am not afraid of you. If I were, I would not have come aboard. So, until you behave—"

"We can toss you in a holding room," Desiri says, studying her nails. "Since you gave me a puppy, I'll make sure it's a nicer one. There's a princess suite for dignitaries in custody."

"Oh, for goddess's sake!" Imari shouts. "Kahanna's fortune spell was cast in Her favor. However, a proper fortune spell must always have a finite element of chance. She can win, but there must be a wild factor. And so, she gave that component to the Four. You have a select number of unknown choices to make, and what you select can literally change the winds of war. She must guide your choices to maximize Her likelihood of winning."

Hm. Now that's interesting. My anger cools as intrigue takes the wheel. Desiri grins at me and backs up a step to sit on the edge of the glass table in front of the couch. Adonis relaxes his stance, and I perch on the couch arm beside Imari.

"So, the Four—my brothers and I—have a set number of choices to make. Any idea how many?"

Imari shakes her head. "But I am sure She knows."

Well, *fip.* I glance at Desiri and Adonis, then back at Imari. "Do you know why She picked the Four as the wild factor? They were the youngest and least influential people at that table. Why not the Zaran monarchs?"

Imari's smile is sad. "She did not choose the Zaran monarchs to give the so-called 'burden' to because there was no magic in their blood at the time. She did not choose The Maidens because the blood magic from Lenore's patron goddess keeps Lenorans from being susceptible to Her influence. The Peredils, leaders from a lesser Silver Allegiance power, were tainted. Not only did they have magic in their bloodline, but their magic was Hers. It came from Breed blood, and over the Common Years She made sure there was a lot more of it."

My magic is Hers. I suppress a shudder.

"So, it's easier for Her to manipulate my decisions." I'm speaking, but there's a disconnect to what I'm saying. Like I'm talking about someone else, because I can't possibly have something inside me that makes me vulnerable to Her influence. "If I got rid of the Stone right now, would I still hear a voice in my head?"

"A voice and a longing to retrieve it, yes," Imari says. "Once you accepted Her gift, She gained purchase within you. But you know that."

I do. Deep inside, ever since I drowned in shallow water, I've felt the Stone urging me to embrace it. It never stops.

I'm going to burn something else. Cool water mists my forehead and bare forearms. Adonis. My body temperature lowers and hovers around normal, and my inner flame calms. I shoot Adonis the grateful look I invented for him when we were kids.

Imari rubs her arms. "Being under a fortune spell means we must operate in a careful manner that will not alert the caster that we are deviating from Her Will until the right moment."

"You want to turn away from Order?" I ask. "Because of what She did to Corin? You loved him enough to risk Her wrath?"

We stare at each other. She swallows with difficulty, and her black lashes lower.

"Imari, being on Order's side is what is going to save us from extinction, right?" I say it softly, not wanting to scare her into shutting down. I don't trust Order's game, but I saw planets implode, vanish, after losing ground to the enemy and not swearing fealty to Pandemonium.

But something's not right about Order's promise. It's an unspoken thing Champions of Pan have taunted me about.

"I apologize, but I cannot disclose more at this time. This will have to be enough to satisfy you." The chords in her voice have a strange resonance. Not lying but holding back, as always.

Desiri groans and climbs to her feet. She waits for a cue from me. Am I *meffed*? Am I happy? Desiri tries to ally herself with my moods. It's a mage trait: mirror the boss. Good for intimidation.

I slick damp curls off my forehead and stand. After two deep breaths and more cooling energy from Adonis, I roll my shoulders. "Let me offer you a room. We have an extra one on this floor." I have no idea what state it's in, but letting her stay on the seventh floor with us is a token of trust. People give more information to those who believe in them.

Desiri grunts in disappointment and snatches my whining gold pup off the floor. "I'll be on Deck Three."

Adonis stares at the puppy, at me, waiting.

I nod. "I've got this."

He glares at the puppy one more time before taking his leave. If Imari's going to say anymore, we've got to dispel the hostile crowd. Former love without his threatening friends around is less intimidating.

Imari's lips part, and she looks uncertain. I don't blame her. My smile at her doesn't seem to help much. "Follow me."

She hesitates, and I'm still. I won't reach for her or grab her arm. I want her to follow me on her own, and if she doesn't, then Desiri can show her to the princess suite. After a minute, Imari gets up, brushing imaginary wrinkles out of her clothing.

I head to the empty room beside Jalee's. Bright dance music soaks through the walls, and I snort, picturing Jalee in there bouncing around instead of spying like everyone else. She won't do that in the common room where a soldier might come up and see her acting 'undignified.' I think we're the only ones who know she can dance me under a table.

Imari's footfalls are quiet behind me, and I don't feel the need to make additional conversation with her. She can't say more, and all I have are questions. My insides ripple with nervous energy. Fortune spells need blood, even the small ones. The spell Order worked had to have taken rivers of it. Who had She sacrificed?

I push open the door to the extra room, and stale air rolls out. Dust particles tickle my nose. I wipe at it with the heel of my palm. "Let me activate cleanse control." One of my favorite things about living ship-side is having cleaning spheres that suck up dust and dirt and spritz out sanitizing fluids.

"No." Her hand ghosts over my elbow as she breezes past me into the room.

A medium- sized oval bed made of beige metal slumps against a far wall. A pale brown wardrobe rests across from the bed, and beside it, a tiny yellow desk with a matching backless chair. The bed's tan sleeping foam is bare.

Imari stops walking mid-room and spins to face me with a pale smile. "I would like to clean this place myself. And unpack a few of my things."

Things? I look her up and down and blink as she extracts a flat red pouch from a deep side pocket camouflaged by the folds of her baggy jumpsuit. She shakes the pouch out like a wet towel, and it expands into a full-blown satchel. She chucks it onto the bed and raises her arms over her head in a long stretch.

Yawning, she says, "Corin did not enjoy cleaning. I do not suppose that you do."

I don't reply, and she smirks.

"Did not think so." The smirk fades, along with the humor in her eyes. "You do not have to stand guard over me. I am not here to hurt you or anyone you care about. You are unsettled and angry. I keep giving you vague messages, but I promise that all will be made clear when it needs to be. Let me have your trust."

"Only if you tell me one thing." I can't keep myself from saying it because my mind circles around the question.

"I told you—"

"How much blood did it take for Her to work the spell?" I know my face is flat.

Her expression freezes, worry making her eyes glitter. I don't think she's ever seen my true business face. The one that says, 'I'll do what I have to.'

My muscles are tight, my flame controlled. I reach for my song, needing it to ground me. I hum the memorized melody and pause. My second movement has five measures of straight sixteenth notes that jump octaves like arpeggios.

But one of the bars doesn't—

"One thousand souls."

My body goes cold.

I stare at Imari. Her deceptively young face and large eyes are laden with sorrow and regret. "An entire generation of worshippers offered their lives in exchange for Her undying love."

*Vati pidge.* My heart weighs more than rest of my body and is hard as concrete against my ribs. Temple sacrifices usually involve daggers and troughs of blood. "And did She?"

"What?"

"Love them?" After what they gave, the pain they endured.

Imari's smile is humorless. She reaches for her satchel, untying its sash and pulling out a purple blanket. She lays it on the bed, smoothing it with her hand. "What do you think?"

*Fip.* "This war isn't going to end well for any of us, is it?"

She continues stroking her blanket. "Before I was born, my mother wove this for me." Her voice lilts, a pretty song. "Strands of her own hair blended with fibers from the manes and tails of blessed single-horned beasts were knotted into symbols of protection and embroidered onto this fabric. It was to protect me from harm because she knew she would not be able to do so. She did not survive my birth. And so, I was an offering to the temple of Lenore."

Imari's not answering my question, but I'm not upset. The sound of her voice captivates me. I sit on the dusty bed, examining Imari's blanket. It's old, the edges frayed, color faded, but still beautiful. Purple fabric with ivory and onyx strands of hair weave in looping designs across its face. The patterns sing their own medleys, subtle magic. Not enough to hurt anyone, but it could make a person with unsavory intent nauseous. My fingers trace the soft fabric, and its magic pulsates under my skin.

"I lived in the main house of worship until I was old enough to devote my life to Niobe and Dane, but as it turned out, dedication was something I could not do."

Her story sounds like Jalee's. I see a quick image of my second-in-command, small and skinny, nine Common Years old, holding back tears but ready to take my hand. She would have been a temple priestess on her planet if she hadn't been chosen for my court, a complete pacifist whose magic would be used for healing arts. I know she regrets it.

"Why couldn't you do it?" I ask. "Did Order call you then?"

Imari sits on the bed with me. "Kahanna graced Lenore. We hadn't seen Dane or Niobe in centuries. They abandoned us, as They did everyone else, and Kahanna came and suggested our current form of government. Instated The Maidens as oligarchs. Then, She chose who would forever wear the mantles. Hellene was the noble who argued to build a democracy. Nialiah was the powerful witch of the Northern Forests. I was a temple girl who swept up after services."

"Why did Order pick you?"

Imari says she's the weakest Maiden. The one who can't cast on people. The most expendable.

"Why me, indeed."

Her warm hand rests on mine, and her liquid black eyes slowly turn me into someone else. My mouth opens, ready to remind her I'm not Corin, but love for her swells beneath my surface thoughts.

Not my love for her.

I push and shove, but it won't recede. It rises like lake water on a rainy day, threatening to flood the shore. My shore. And I can't fight it.

Do I want to fight it?

Yes. We're talking about death and blood and gods and I'm furious. Fire should crackle

beneath my skin. The bed should heat and smoke where I touch it.

Her face is close.

Death and blood. One-thousand souls.

Her breath smells like sugar berries.

Gods and lies. Too many sacrifices.

Her skin is soft. My hands don't burn it.

Too many lies. Too many...

A hand in my hair.

....

Warm pink lips crash into mine.

# Chapter 9

# Devon

"NO, LEADER, DON'T SHAKE IT."

It's too late. A mini-mountain of bright pink seasoning bobs in the white soup before sinking to the depths of the large pot. I clutch the bottle it came from and offer the Zigti matron what I hope is a charming grin, because I'm pretty sure I ruined dinner for fifty.

Paka's light blue skin blushes a deeper blue as she laughs and pats my hand before snatching the empty bottle of spice. "I should have warned you that the lid was loose."

"I'm sorry. Is it really spicy or salty? Can we... add water?"

I liked to cook at home, but I'm used to being in a fully stocked kitchen and not feeling guilty about throwing out batches of food I mess up and starting over.

Easy access to grocery stores loaded with food and having money I never thought about being short of made me... a jerk. Like a celebrity only famous for being rich and carrying around rat-dogs in their purses.

Their kind of stupid isn't supposed to be mine, but it is as I sit in a mobile kitchen, helping Paka stretch a meal I could eat by myself to feed thirty kids and their parents.

Paka smiles at me, her thin face warm, motherly. A sharp pang in my chest almost makes me flinch. It's been months since I've gotten that look. Used to roll my eyes at it and tell Mom I was too old—but I always liked it. One of Paka's cool, six-fingered hands touches my face.

"I have two sons," she says, voice mild. "They're both with war parties, off-planet. I've haven't seen them in *revs*, but every now and then, a message gets through from one of them. Full of pictures and epic tales of cooking nightmares."

I snort at the laughter in her eyes. "I usually do a better job than this in the kitchen."

"I can tell by the questions you ask." Paka pats my cheek. "Yours aren't simply 'where do I put this?' or 'the yellow one?' You inquired about tastes, levels of spiciness, and consistencies. But I do doubt you've ever had to sacrifice quality for quantity when it comes to food." Her pinkish gaze sizes me up with a nod that doesn't make me proud. I like when women look at me, but she's not appreciating me in the way I'm used to. Instead, "You've never had to go without."

Not even in a prison camp. It's hard to wrap my head around the fact that less than a week ago, I was an inmate. Barely a day passed after our meeting with Pan before we were packed up and shipped out on our first Pan-Mission: relocating locals.

I look away from Paka, staring into the soup I messed up. We can't throw it out and start over or we won't have enough food for the rest of the migration. Planet

Inrarch had three habitable continents, two connected by a land bridge, and one across a black ocean. The Golden Allegiance blew up the one across the ocean and did a good job herding the people left on the other continents into pockets so they could mine the planet's magic core deposits.

No one would dare do that to planets like Bruhje or Amphora. Those planets have rich people and fancy governments and big cities and tourist traps. Inrarch has villages, tribes, and chiefs. Bigger planetary factions land and offer money to people to go fight for them, and the young adults leave. The population is old and very young. Grandparents watching over their grandkids because their sons and daughters left to join different armies for a chance to get away from here. I think some of them come back for their kids once they make enough money to set up on a 'civilized' planet, but I think a lot more don't.

I start as the pot beneath me sizzles. Paka stands on the other side of it, pouring in a bucket of water. "I..." I step back, watching the soup bubble.

"Adding water is fine," Paka says. "The soup will be tangier than usual, but it's not ruined, *krewie*."

*Krewie.* My translator prods my brain stem, throwing out words like *sweetie, honey... hon*. She called me 'hon.' I grin at her, and she nudges me aside with her thin hip.

"I'll salvage the stew and bring a few servings to you and your friends." Paka stirs the pot with a large metal spoon. "I know you have more important work to do, Devon."

I shake my head. "No, this is just as important as,"—staring at the blank document Mineshka and Xijure and I keep deleting—"anything else I'm doing. Those little kids need to eat and, well..." I crack my knuckles, an odd feeling rumbling in my stomach. The Gold Allegiance wrecked this place, hurt these people, used them. The Silver and Gold Allegiance are allies, making me a part of it.

I didn't do this. Wouldn't do this, but... Crap. I rub my face, flashing back to Ilea flooding Disiez right before someone shot a hole in her middle. A double-gut punch. Ilea's dead. Murdered. But not before *she* murdered.

How do I feel? Who do I feel for?

"*Krewie.*" Paka's cool hand is on my face again. It smells like salt and potatoes and the weird cedary spice I spilled. "You had no part in what happened here aside from helping us pack our lives into this caravan and escorting us to better soil. You do what older people tell you to."

I open my mouth. "I'm a Champ—"

"You're a child," Paka corrects. "You were recruited just like my sons. Didn't really have a choice, did you? You go where people put you and do what they say."

My head swims a bit as her words sink in. I'm a leader whose destiny is to make choices, but the most important ones that have to do with me, I don't make. Order chose, the Allegiances chose, then Shiham chose, then Pan.

"At least here, you're doing what you think is good." Paka ruffles my hair. "I watch you with the younger children. When you help put things together or carry water barrels for us. You're a good boy."

I don't know why my eyes burn at that or why it feels so good to have a lady who seems old enough to be my grandma messing with my hair. I'm not a little kid like those babies in the trailers waiting for soup. But...

I lean in and let Paka hug me. She's a head shorter and skinny from too much going without so her grandkids can have more, but her presence folds around me. Warm and gentle.

"Thank you for helping us, Devon. We appreciate you."

She pulls back and smiles at me before shooing me out of the kitchen-trailer and into the arid Inrarch night. A few tiny, blue-skinned kids huddle around a circle sketched in the yellow dirt. A black rock sits in the center of the circle. A kid swats it with a stick, and kids shriek and laugh as they run in the opposite direction the rock rolls.

I raise a brow at one of the brats who looks at me. He grins with crooked teeth and gestures for me to come over and play. I played a version of tag with some other kids earlier. Guess I'm the fun guy now. I wave at him, and he hesitates before mimicking me. It gets the attention of the other kids who look confused, then copy the first kid.

I forget that waving is an Earth thing. It's cute how they want to do what I do. Caught some kids doing my 'Devon walk'. Or what Mineshka refers to as my 'Devon walk' when she saw them and cracked up.

Haven't heard her laugh that way since Loniad.

My heart slams into my ribs, and I blink back wetness.

I walk faster to the oblong, brown trailer given to me, Mineshka, and Xijure near the back of the circling of similar trailers. It's like circling wagons from that old school video game about heading West, only there's no typhoid fever or deer to hunt. No animals or edible plants, really. The land is yellow and dead. Trees sag, grass wilts, and the sun stays hot overhead, leaving plenty of desert heat behind for the evenings.

The place we're going is supposed to be green, more like an Earth prairie, but we'll see when we get there. Could be that the Gold Allegiance will come back and roast that too or at least try. A Su army is enroute to be permanently stationed between new settlements. Hopefully, one or both of Paka's sons might be with them, so she'll have someone to help her.

I reach my trailer and knock before pushing open the creaky metal door. Dim light greets me as I step onto a padded floor. I untie my boots and kick them off beside the door before shutting it.

"You're back earlier than I expected." Mineshka sits at what I'd call a card table with the compal we've been sharing laying in front of her. The place is musty with BO from three people not afraid to get nasty and sweaty with the folks in camp.

"Yeah, well, I'm a kitchen nightmare, so I got kicked out early." I come to the table and plop down in a flimsy chair. I let my head loll backwards to glance at the bunks. Two stacked beds built into the back wall with another nestled beside them tucked under a round window. Xijure's big frame curls on the single bed.

Worry flickers through me. "He still feeling weird?"

Mineshka nods. "He said to wake him up when you got here. But if the sound of that door didn't do it, I'm not going to."

A week of loading a village onto a trailer caravan, rough riding through a wasteland, and a canteen of questionable water took Xijure down. He fights it, but I'd rather him sleep than burn himself out on what I can do more of. I don't mind extra chores, like pushing trailers out of mud pits. These muscles have to be used for something, huh?

"That's fine. You, uh, work anymore on..." I shrug at the compal. I see a few words on there. About a sentence.

Mineshka shoots me a tired look. "Dear Great Pan."

"Didn't we decide that start was too corny yesterday?"

She swats me. "But we didn't come up with better, so it's back." She sighs and runs a hand through her sweat-matted red hair. She made a ponytail out of four huge braids to keep it off her shoulders and out of her eyes. "This shouldn't be so hard. 'Don't kill our worlds.' It'd be selfish to just list ours, but too many planets and people could be too much, so how do we pick?"

Which is why we keep starting and deleting this list. Places like Earth, Zare, Amphora, Bruhje, Lenore are obvious. People we love are on those planets. Pan didn't tell us what places of His own He's saving. Maybe all. Didn't tell us what all Order would save but hinted not many. That His deal would be better.

"List our planets again, and then let's think about…" I start.

"Resources. It's cold, but what Allegiance-owned planets are the most useful."

"No, which planets have the most people. Or the most space. Maybe we can migrate people, like we're doing now." It's a good idea.

"Migration isn't that easy," Mineshka sighs.

"When it's life or death—"

"It isn't that easy! Not everyone is as good-hearted as you." Mineshka rubs her eyes. "A lot of people are like the ones who kill this place to steal the magic under its dirt. Those people don't want to share ground with refugees."

"If they don't have a choice, they'll have to!"

"So, you'd force it, like a dictator, and ignite planetary skirmishes that you'd have to ignore or get lost in mediating forever."

"No! I…" And we're back where we always end.

Mineshka's grin is sad. "We have to *nicth* people, Devon. It's the only way."

*Nicth—damn, screw, throw to the dogs.*

"How…" I stop, shaking my head. People do this to others all the time. All the effing time. How can they, though? How do they choose and not get eaten alive by the faces of all the people they laid in front of a bus?

"It's better some die than all, right?" Mineshka says, tapping the table. "But the ones who live won't be thankful, because they might not enjoy how their lives change."

"Wish we could root out all the ungrateful assholes and put them in one place and circle it for Pan to get rid of. That's our sacrifice."

"Choosing individual assholes to delete is much easier than picking groups to save as a whole." Mineshka nods. "We could sponsor a contest that only the greedy would enter. Gather them up in luxury ships and blast them off to Pan."

She chuckles, but there's nothing behind it. It's not funny. I laugh anyway.

We sound empty and old.

I reach for her hands, wanting to cry at the tremor in them. "If I really had a choice, I would go back in time and listen to Ilea and Xijure when they wanted to leave Disiez right away. We would all be on Lenore drinking weird fruit juice and watching this shit play out with people who can decide stuff like this and sleep like babies."

Mineshka purses her lips. "And we'd be stupid, thinking they were choosing correctly because we wouldn't know what was at stake. We wouldn't know about *these people* being killed off by our own Allegiances. Next time, Pan will send us to another place just like this. With people we've wronged."

But we didn't. Paka said...

I close my eyes. "He's doing this to make it harder on us. I bet He thinks we'll see something that will make us turn on our side."

Our side.

I'm supposed to feel some patriotic obligation to that side. But I don't. I just know where my family is. I don't do politics just people. Can...

"Mineshka... Pan just said write a proposal. We're assuming planets and Allegiances. Why can't we just pick people? Why can't our plan really just be to burn the assholes? Can we try that instead?"

"Devon, we don't have *revs* to do this. That would take so much research. We'd have to interview and visit, and..." She shakes her head at me, heart in her eyes. "*Babila*, no. We can't."

Frustration makes me want to break something, but I won't. A busted chair is one that can't be used, and these people need everything they have. And that thought makes me want to break something else. Because assholes have everything they need, while nice people eat watered-down soup and have to boil and bleach their water or end up with gut worms.

"Min, this—"

Goosebumps pepper my arms as a chill runs up my spine and my ears ring.

What the hell? The musty air turns sweet and flowery, and something makes the atmosphere strange, different. It's like... like magic being worked, only I can feel it. It tingles and—

"Devon, don't move."

Mineshka sounds terrified. My first instinct is to move, to throw myself in front of her. But the wide-eyed fear on her olive-toned face freezes me in place. She's staring at something behind me. Something that has to be standing close to Xijure, who's too sick to even wake up when he'd normally be on his feet scavenging for a weapon at the feel of whatever the hell's in this room.

I shake myself out of the terror-trance Mineshka casts, fighting through the hair-raising electric field of power in the air. I jump to my feet, turning, ready to fight, and my arms fall slack at my side.

At the sight of her.

A woman with dark mocha skin and large silver eyes. Black hair coils around her heart-shaped face. Full red lips part as she inhales. Holy hell. Holy... Where did she—how did she—why is she... Intoxicating bliss smothers me.

Will she kiss me?

Love me?

Have me?

I feel myself moving. To where she sits on my bottom bunk, ignoring Xijure as she watches me, unblinking gaze beautiful. I've never seen anyone so beautiful.

"Devon, stop!"

A hand grabs my arm and yanks me backward. I plant my feet and don't budge. Feel a smaller body slam into my back. Mineshka.

"Devon, please. Focus. You have to fight the pull."

Why? If she's pulling me, I want her to. The woman crosses her legs, lashes lowering but not quite blinking, and then her gaze shifts.

It moves past me.

I stagger to one side as her power, that perfumed mushroom cloud of desire, dissipates. I'm dizzy. The room's too hot.

I look at her again. Still gorgeous. Still alien. But I don't have to have her anymore. Why did I want to have her? I don't understand. My head hurts. "What are you? How did you—"

Mineshka's hand grabs my bicep. "It's a nymph, Devon. A Magic Breed. They spirit people away. Don't look into her eyes."

*Now* she tells me that. "What's a nymph doing in here? Don't they..." I don't know what they usually do. But isn't it weird that one popped into a trailer?

"This planet does have a magic core," Mineshka says. "But it's not... Just, just stay still. Act uninterested. It might leave if we're boring."

"Like an animal?" I lower my voice and keep my eyes averted from the woman, instead looking at Xijure. The king's still a lump on his bed. Please don't let that thing turn on him. I don't think I can get to him fast enough to help, to shield him.

"Kind of," Mineshka says hesitantly. "No sudden movements."

We stand still, me barely breathing as I run through a mental catalog on what I know about nymphs. Not much. Adonis has nymph blood. He doesn't blink, and neither does she. He also doesn't talk much, and she hasn't said a word. "Do they—do they eat people?"

"No one knows what happens to the ones who don't come back," Mineshka says. "But no one here's complained about Magic Breed herds."

"Herds?"

"Sometimes they—"

The nymph uncrosses her legs and stands. She's a few inches shorter than me. I watch her long, silky black dress swish between her legs. Bare feet peek under the skirts. She stops a foot in front of me and I feel it. The power pouring off her, only it doesn't draw me in like it did before.

Goosebumps fleck my arms. Every instinct in my body screams at me to run. There's danger. This is a predator. She'll eat me. She'll... I steal a glance at her perfect face and notice her eyes looking beyond me.

Behind me.

At... Mineshka's hand tightens on my arm.

"Mineshka? Is she watching you?"

"Y-yes."

"I like your song."

The world stops when the nymph talks. Her rich alto wraps my brain in silk. I want her to speak again. To me, not Mineshka. I want to reach out, to touch her face.

Mineshka's hand on my arm grounds me. Keeps me in my spot. Breaks the spell again.

The nymph doesn't come closer. "Your song is drenched in grief, but the notes are strong. The phrases long, the beats plenty. May I taste it?"

I puff out my chest, shifting to put Mineshka completely behind me. I'll get eaten by the nymph while she runs. That's how this is going to go. I'm ready to announce it. 'Eat me instead.'

But instead, the nymph hums and steps back.

Can I tell her to get out of here? She's not tasting anything today. But my arms are heavy. I couldn't swing on that thing if I tried. Her eyes are on me again, and my ears buzz. My skin's on fire. I want her. I need her.

"Kahanna sent me."

My body goes cold.

Kahanna—Order.

"I only needed to find you this time," the nymph says.

"Wh-what does that mean? Does it mean we're being rescued? Someone's coming? Do you know about my brothers? Are they okay? Are they coming?" Words spill out of my mouth, tumbling over each other. So many questions. I need so many answers. Giddiness trumps fear. Order is going to save us after all. Order sent someone to find us. Order…

...isn't a good guy. She might not be bad, but She isn't good.

We'd leave here and go back to another god who wants me to make choices for Them. Will Order tell me who She's saving, offer to let me save more? Would She listen and spare the people here and others, like the good god She's not?

And should I care if it means I'll go back to my brothers, to Lyle? To people who can make smarter decisions than me? I could go back to them and let them meet Pan and write a proposal.

The nymph stares at me. "I know nothing more."

"But—"

"I will find you again. Do not die before then."

And she vanishes. *Poof.* She was there and now she's not. The smell of flowers and the sting of magical energy disappear with her. My bunk appears untouched. As if a magical woman hadn't just sat there and drifted across the floor, flirting with—with Mineshka.

I turn slowly, realizing Mineshka's grip on my arm is still tight. "Min?"

One hand covers her mouth as she trembles. "I'm okay." Her voice is high.

"Sure, you are." I frown at her. She's not who she was when I first met her. Of course she's not. Her twin brother bled out under her hands as she tried to put pressure on his neck wound. If Lyle—I almost double over at the horrible idea of it. She's not okay, and that nymph said... "That thing said your 'song' is 'drenched in grief'."

Mineshka shrugs and releases my arm.

"What does that mean?"

"What do you think, Devon?" Her voice lowers, tone despondent as her arms hang limply at her sides. "My brother is dead. Body lost under an ocean. My parents, if they even know anything, were told by strangers that Loni is dead. Magic Breeds hear life songs, the music of your soul if you will. Did Leader One never explain this to you?"

Evan? "Not like that, no."

And if he had, I'd lost interest by then. I know he hears music I can't and can make nature do things by humming or whistling. It's weird, but so is he.

"Can that thing hurt you with your... your soul music?" Did that sound as stupid as I think it did?

Mineshka's eyes are clouded. "No. It just... It can make them more tempting. Breeds can change songs, you know. Make you love them. Make you happy."

The pull I'd felt. When all I wanted was to get that woman. "That's..."

How my ancestors got laid by faerie people, I bet. I mean, if they all look like what we just saw, it might not have taken all that much singing, but... damn. "She's coming back."

"Which is good, since Order sent her." Mineshka nods.

"But..." I flex my fingers, not knowing what to say next. That nymph was too interested in Mineshka. Might want to do something to her. Order might want to save us, which is what I wanted weeks ago, but being rescued by Order might not be what we need.

"Min, is it really good that Order might get us out of here?"

She shrugs again, like nothing matters anymore. "We'll go back to our families."

I cut her a sharp look. "But what happens after that? Would it be better for our families if we—"

"I trust no god, Devon." Mineshka's interruption is blunt. "Gods let people die. The only thing we must do is live and fight. Whatever choice keeps us alive for another day is what I choose. If Pan returns to us before Order sends that thing back, then our choice is Pan, because to not choose Him means we die sooner."

Simple. Not right. Not wrong. Just practical. I hate practical because I think it might border on wrong.

Mineshka turns away from me, heading back to the table, to the compal and our blank document. I inch my way over to Xijure. The king sleeps on his side, one knee pulled to his chest, face creased in pain. Sweat dots his brow.

I touch his shoulder to see if he'll stir. He inhales sharply, but his eyes don't open. He'd slept through the nymph and her magic. He's sleeping through being touched. Worry and fear make me shake him. What if he's unconscious? What if—

A fist shoots out, nearly catching me in the eye. I jump, stumbling backward as Xijure jolts upright. He glares at me through bleary eyes, but I don't see any recognition there. "Xijure? You good?"

He groans and mutters something my translator doesn't catch before flopping back down. He clutches his stomach, and I come back to stand over him.

"Xijure?"

"Do we need to fight?" Xijure's voice is husky, breathless as he grits his teeth. His pain-glazed eyes are on the ceiling.

"Ah... we don't need to fight." But something happened.

His eyes slide closed, seeming relieved at my words. He's tired and sick, and I feel like a real jerk for waking him up.

"Everything okay?" he presses after a minute.

"Uh…" I could tell him about the nymph, and Order, but…

He winces.

I won't.

"Go back to sleep, man."

That his breathing changes almost immediately, face going slack with sleep, is freaky, but it makes me feel more confident about having decent judgement. I don't always trust it because smarter people always use theirs first. The wiser people here are sick, or grieving twins.

I glance back at Mineshka, who stares at the compal. Ready to work with or without me.

I reclaim my seat at the table and reach for the compal, nervous about testing out this new confidence, but I have to. "I think what we need to do is create a list of pros and cons for Pan and Order. Once we figure out what might make Order a more ideal choice for us, we can write out what Pan could offer that would make joining Him better."

Mineshka blinks, dark blue eyes brightening. A light smile lifts her lips as she punches me in the shoulder. "*Babila* is thinking like a leader." She rests her chin in the hand she used to punch me with. "And it's about time."

Her smile finally reaches her eyes, and I wonder if the nymph would hear a little hope in Mineshka's song now.

I tap the screen, staring at the strange symbols that mean nothing to me. "Uh…"

Mineshka laughs. "How about I write while you talk?"

I love her laugh. The sound helps me block out any lingering anxiety and focus on the task at hand. Operation 'Who's the Better God and How It Works for Us'.

"Let's make it a chart."

Squares and rectangles dance across the screen as Mineshka creates a format and I puzzle out how to word my first pro and con for both gods.

# Chapter 10

# Lawrence

THE SLIDING BACK DOOR GRINDS over its rack and feet approach. The man smells like sweat and malt liquor. Not quite beer, but just as nasty. Cloth falls around my shoulders, a blanket. And he sits beside me.

The sprites in the pool cheer and start singing a Remasian jig. I pick out a few words I've heard soldiers on the Ievisara mumble around me.

"I hate that damn song."

Devrik speaks to me in English, the words heavily accented. His voice is lower than Uncle Aeric's, the sound of it striking a chord deep within me. Buried beneath bundles of random memories and facts, I know that voice. Feel my face pressed against a warm chest as it rumbles through tone-deaf lullabies.

My mind's eye shows me fuzzy images of a man with dark shoulder-length curls, green eyes, and skin as coconut-brown as mine. He smiles with his full face as I look up at him, maybe from a crib or bed.

My absentee father. A complication I don't want or need right now.

My head is full, maximum thought and feeling capacity met hours ago when I left Healer Wesgriff's office. Pros and cons of going through with the procedure war inside me.

On the one hand, it shouldn't be that big of a deal. I don't need to see to live. I've proved that. I've been fine. Better than fine, in fact. I've got a power that helps me connect to the world without eyes. I can still hear, taste, and feel. I can keep all that. Or I could gamble for my eyes and lose it all, or some. The winning ratio is weak. I should just opt not to do treatment. It's too risky, but I want to see again. I really, really want to see again.

The shakes from Wesgriff's office return, and I clutch the blanket around my shoulders.

Devrik clears his throat, reminding me that he's still there. Taking up space, breathing my air, wanting to finally have a conversation about—I don't know, being my dad—that I couldn't care less about right now. If I ignore Devrik, he'll leave. He can't actually want to be out here anyway. He sleeps all day and parties all night. He should be getting ready to go out and meet whoever it is that's more important than knowing me.

"You're taller than I was when I was around your developmental age," Devrik says. "Perhaps you'll outgrow me."

I'm silent. Leave, Devrik.

He coughs. "Aeric told me about your appointment this afternoon. He, um, said it was up to you. And..." Knuckles crack. "I know how hard it is making life-altering decisions."

The tremors through my body increase as I fight back a growl and the urge to punch this guy. "What decisions have you made? According to everyone I talk to, you don't do shizz."

An audible exhale. More knuckles crack. "I didn't have to leave Earth, you know. I could have stayed, with you and the twins, and your mother."

Incredulity fills me. "And let Evan be shipped off into outer space by himself? You actually considered that?" What the hell?

The earth beneath the porch quivers. Atoms of carbon, nitrogen, and potassium making up the soil shudder, ready to fracture. I clamp down on my power, not wanting to create a sink hole. Uncle Aeric's porch doesn't deserve a burial. Only Devrik does.

"He would have gone directly to your uncle, Rovn, and eventually here to Aeric. They raised him when he wasn't training anyway. He didn't need me. I just… fell back into the person I was before. But if I stayed on Earth…" I hear him swallow. "On Earth, I was starting to become somebody else. Joey, your mom, she expected things of me. Held me to a standard. Trusted me to help her take care of you. I think… I think I was better there."

I turn toward the sound of his breathing and narrow my eyes. I have no idea if my sightless stare is imposing, but I hope to fug it is. I want to melt him with my glare. "So, you generously sacrificed yourself for the sake of your son, when you think you shouldn't have?"

The porch grunts and dips. I reach out, forcing molecules back together.

"No!" His voice jumps an octave. Reminds me of Devon. "I-I needed to come with Evan. I did. But I knew that if I didn't—"

"Someone else would handle your business. So, it wouldn't have been that big a deal in the end. Nice."

"That's what people around here would have assumed," he says. "Had I stayed on Earth."

I let my eyes close, take calming breaths that don't work.

"And, before you assume it, I didn't come out here with Evan because I wanted people to think better of me." His voice stays in that higher register.

He is definitely Devon's sperm donor.

"So, why did you come out here then?"

A louder knuckle crack and a hiss of pain. Good, hope he broke something.

"I didn't want him to be alone." His tone deepens again and softens. "He would have had Aeric and Rovn, but they would have been strangers at first. Rema was foreign. And he would have been afraid. At least I could stand by him, hold his hand, and introduce him to the strangers and show him around the foreign places. Make him ready to take someone else's hand and make sure my brothers were a part of everything."

I frown at the urgency in his tone, like he's telling me confidential information he would be thrown in an oubliette for.

"Your Uncle Aeric is an entertaining guy, right? And you haven't met Rovn, but you know he helped you on Earth. Both of them have strong political influence, and no Silver Allegiance official is trying to *meff* them off. They protect Evan in ways that someone like me can't."

"Shouldn't you have political influence?" I ask, eyes still narrow. "Weren't you an ambassador?"

"Yes, but that wasn't a fair appointment. Rovn had a heavy hand in it," Devrik says, frustration bleeding into his words. "When I wanted to stay on Earth, Rovn worked to make it so. And when I left Earth and brought Evan with me, Rovn and Aeric made sure Evan got suitable magic training, because there are no craft academies on Rema. I've never done anything weighty on my own."

"And you want me to feel sorry for you?" The porch creaks again as I lose my grip on the potassium atoms beneath us. "Is it an apology for ignoring me up until now? You know what I'm dealing with. You know I might just have to say fug treatment and be blind forever. Yet here you are, telling me *your* sob story. I'm crying for you, man. You're rich and can party all the time and don't have to do shizz in this war but hideout. You..." Oh, it's on now.

"The Allegiances sent Mom away and banned us from talking to her, but they didn't say *you* couldn't have anything to do with us. We've been out here for, what, three months? Evan almost died again. I am fugging blind. Did you check up on us? Even worry?"

"Of course I worried."

"What'd you do about it, though?"

"I watched the *reels*. I talked to Rovn. He kept me informed. Lawrie—"

"Lawrence."

He pauses. "Lawrence. I am a joke. When I show up, so do rumors and nasty people you don't want around you. You want me to stay away as much as possible. You're my son. By the gods, you look just like me. People will want to make you less than just for that. They'll assume you're unintelligent. The public associates Evan with Aeric and Rovn's prestige. No one ever thought less of him because of me."

I growl and get up, stomping off the porch and into the yard.

The sprites burst into a spirited rendition of 'Girls Just Wanna Have Fun.' Warm droplets of water from the pool hit my skin. I sense the nearness of joined hydrogen and oxygen atoms and dense clouds of magic in the shapes of elementary school students.

"*Ayo*! Come away from there!"

I open my mouth. That's all the time it takes. I can't finish the start of a sound before it grabs me. A hand, its fingers hot like desert sand, locks onto my bicep. I fly backward, into the flowing mass of $H_2O$. Wind hisses around my ears. I scramble to tug at elements, hydrogen, oxygen, anything to slow me down, but the magic clenching my body is too heavy to fight. More burning hands latch onto my limbs. I hit tepid, honey-sweet water. Before I can take a breath, my body goes under. I'm drowning in water and terror.

Hydrogen and oxygen are immovable. Magic owns those elements. I feel the molecules swim around me, but when I grab hold, I can't manipulate them. Can't stop them from dragging me down. Chasyn said to never fight an elemental magic user with their element of choice. It's too much of a struggle to seize control of the element. Use something they don't have.

I reach for the earth. Sense its strength. Feel it rise and touch my feet. A sprite tugs me to its chest, small and childlike. More bodies swarm me. I keep my mouth clamped shut. Can't inhale water.

Earth pushes us all upward. My head breaks through the water's surface. I suck in hungry breaths before losing my hold on earth. Magic weighs me down, snatches me under the water. I call for earth again, pulling at the ground, filling the pool with dirt. A high-pitched whistle pierces the air.

The *Fae-Away*. The sprites hiss, hands releasing me. But they don't scream. Don't teleport. The whistle. It doesn't sound like the times Uncle Aeric blew it.

"Lawrence!" Devrik yells. He's close.

Air cyclones around me. I feel its formation. It becomes a wall, a barrier. Its outer edges ignite—Chasyn, Tian, and Bhela using their power together. The sprites whisper, and magic shoves against the flame. Water surges and quells.

I can help, but...

I can't see them. I sense the particles making up the bodies of my court, but when they use their power, I can't discern who's who. Similar elements ripple around them and the sprites, distorting my perception. If I push, I take the chance of pummeling allies. I could kill somebody.

My heart thumps so hard it hurts, and my stomach quivers as magic rips at the wind vortex and beats out the protective flames. Shizz. Am I going to die here, now? The sprites are stronger than me and my court. They're Magic Breeds, Order's creations. The ones everyone claims She can't use. Crazy powerful, but with mush for brains. We can't win, not like this.

My Stone's in my room. But even if I had it, I can't help without more accuracy.

A whistle pierces the air again, high and sharp. The correct sound. Uncle Aeric's here. The sprites shriek, and the world falls away as time and space tears. The sweltering magic in the air vanishes. I flop back in the dirt as the last of the wind dies around me.

People yell my name. Cool hands shake my limbs. Someone picks me up.

I hear the sliding door to the house open, and cool artificial air brushes my skin. Whoever's carrying me sits me down on a couch or chair. I slump, fingers gripping the soft cloth beneath me. Holy shizz. Holy fugging shizz.

"Get him something to drink," Uncle Aeric orders.

"Lawrence?" Devrik's voice comes from in front of me. He sounds freaked. "Are you all right? You have to talk to me. Aeric, did they *nazzle* him?"

"No, I don't sense any residual magic. I'll still do a cleansing." There's a depression beside me. I must be on the couch.

My body quivers from the inside out, heart going so fast it vibrates. Those things tried to kill me. My death theme would have been sung by Cyndi Lauper impersonators. I couldn't fight back, and I couldn't help anyone. Like on Earth, someone else had to save me while others got hurt around me. I'm regressing.

Weeks ago, I brought lightning down on a shadow beast, banished it to Hell, saved Evan, Adonis, Jalee, and Desiri. I want to be someone who helps others, who saves the day. And I was on my way to becoming a hero. But now I'm back to Phase One, a scared Earth-kid feeling helpless and dangerous. I could have hurt my court just now.

I can ask for harder training. There has to be a way to get back to where I was and keep building. Daredevil did it, but not in the limited time I probably have. Because there's a war on that I can't forget about. And Daredevil isn't real. This is.

A cold glass of liquid is pressed to my lips. I sip bitter juice gritty with minerals. People move around the room: Chasyn, Tian, and Bhela. I decipher their individual elemental affinities now that the chaos is over. Uncle Aeric rubs my neck. And maybe he's the one holding the juice.

I bring shaky hands up to take the glass, fingers brushing the large hand supporting the cup. Not Uncle Aeric's hand. Devrik's.

"Can you speak?" Devrik presses.

I clear my throat, lowering the juice to my lap. "Y-yeah."

"*Niobe-va...*" Uncle Aeric groans. "What in glory hells were you doing? I told you to keep your distance! They were one *wisp* from spiriting you away! That would have been it. No one knows where they go. We'd never find you."

He shakes me and Devrik moves. Uncle Aeric's hands are gone, and Devrik touches my arm. "Leave him alone, Aeric. It was my *fipping* fault. Are you okay?"

I hold my breath for a few seconds, wanting my voice to be level when I speak. I cough, making sure my throat is free of juice. I need to sound clear and strong. "I want the procedure. Can someone com the healer and schedule it ASAP? I need to see."

"Lawrie," Uncle Aerie says, "I think we need to take all of the allotted time to consider all of your options. There are therapies to get you acclimated to—"

"How long will they take? Can therapy get me back on the battlefield in a few weeks, a month?"

"There doesn't have to be a battlefield. You don't have to fight anymore. You shouldn't be fighting. We'll see to it."

"Right." Devrik's still next to me. He touches me. "We can—"

"Weren't you just telling me what all you *can't* do?" I sneer at Devrik and turn my attention in Uncle Aeric's direction. "I only want to hear from you. If I don't fight, what do you think our chances are at winning the war? I don't know if you know, but I bet you saw. Did you see those planets disappear when the Silver Allegiance lost ground?'

I shudder, recalling the black holes devouring worlds while I watched on a viewing cube. So many people just *gone*, for no other reason than being born or just being on a planet that belonged to the 'wrong' side, a losing side.

Uncle Aeric breathes faster. "I've seen it before."

I hate his tone. The helplessness in it. Uncle Aeric hasn't never sounded like that. "Do you know what it means? What's actually going on when that happens?"

The hum of the cooling system keeping the house a comfortable temperature is loud when no one speaks.

"The Maidens told us that if we don't win for Order, everything under the Allegiance umbrellas, and even the Cold Zones that won't join anyone, will get sucked up, just like what you saw."

The cooling system's whir sounds like a lawnmower now.

"When Evan found his Stone, and we all got brought out here, it…" I trail off, needing more juice.

"It reignited the war, set off some type of celestial clock," Uncle Aeric finishes for me. He sounds so tired. "I know, but that won't stop me from wanting all of you out of it. This is a valid way out, Lawrie. You acknowledged it. You don't have the time to train your body and powers to adapt to your current condition well enough to be a piece in this game. Leave it."

"And lose?"

"You don't know that—"

"I don't know what my prophetic choices are, or that I've made all the ones that need to happen or where I need to be to make them. But I can guarantee where I need to be isn't in this living room." I shake my head and sip more juice as I make a decision.

I need back in the game. I can't tap out and leave everything on my brothers and the other Champions. I brought down lightning. People on Lenore sing songs about it. I'm a hero with a lot more to do. Adrenaline and a little of my former crazy warm my pool-chilled blood.

I want to help. Back on Earth, I wanted to help. On Nakshera, I was awesome. I want to be that hero again. To stop people I care about from blinking out of existence.

Fug. My hands won't quit shaking because this can go epically wrong. I can lose everything, but hell, if I don't, I just might lose it anyway.

"I want the procedure."

Devrik touches my arm. "You're... sure?"

My throat burns despite the juice. Guess I did inhale a little pool water. I nod, and he grunts.

"I'll make the arrangements." Uncle Aeric's surface tone is sedate, but I hear anger and fear warring beneath it.

Weight on the couch shifts again. Devrik sits where Uncle Aeric had been.

"Do you want me to go with you for the procedure?" he asks.

I ponder it, not long, not hard.

"Not really." His efforts are too little too late, and I don't want him with me for something so... I swallow hard, fighting pinpricks of fear stabbing out from the darkness behind my eyes. I don't want Devrik. Wish I could trade him for a brother, or mother, or Dad. My real dad, a guy on Earth who looks nothing like me but who was with me when I broke my first bone and taught me to ride a dirt bike.

Devrik doesn't touch me again, and nothing else is said between us. I do give him minor props for not leaving the room until Uncle Aeric returns to say Healer Wesgriff will perform the procedure tomorrow. I head upstairs alone, knowing the others will talk about me when I'm gone, but I don't care.

I just made a choice, and now I've got to sleep on it.

UNCLE AERIC TAKES US TO the clinic in his rover this time. He drives like me, too fast, sprawling all over the wide, stone-paved roadways, and ignoring the people who shout at him. The windows are down, and I lean my head out, enjoying the cool breeze on my face and the dull smell of burning chocolate and charcoal pencils from whatever fuel source Bruhjen vehicles run on.

We park and I run my hands along the smooth leather of my rover seat and get out to touch the slick metal edges of the vehicle's side panels. I take my time marching up the steps to the clinic, savoring the sound and feel of my heavy footsteps. The thick glass of the clinic's doors is cold, and the recycled air that greets me is colder. The tips of my ears burn.

No cookies or candy are offered in a lobby so quiet I hear Uncle Aeric and Chasyn's nervous swallows. We barely said good morning to each other before we got into the rover, and no one speaks now. Chasyn squeezes my shoulder and pushes me forward, probably in the direction of a chair. Uncle Aeric cracks his knuckles behind me, truly a family habit.

Another door opens, and Wesgriff's high voice greets us. Then slender fingers, not Chasyn's or my uncle's, touch my arm. "If you are ready, we should go."

Ice water trickles through my veins. *"If you are ready..."*

Arms hug me. Hands mess up my hair and pat my back.

Words fall past my ears. Chasyn and Uncle Aeric might be telling me their most embarrassing secrets, but I'll never know what they are. Fear talks louder than them as Wesgriff leads me out of the lobby and into a different room, one that smells like tangy fruits and leafy vegetables.

"You may remove everything but your undergarments and leave them on the floor," Wesgriff instructs before a cottony bundle of cloth is pressed into my hands. "This is a modesty cloak. It pulls over your head. There are no strings or buttons. Three steps to your left is the procedure table. Lie flat on your back.

There is an open orifice for the rear of your skull. Do not be alarmed when you feel it. When you are situated, say the word 'Ready'."

Footsteps that I'm sure are louder than necessary move away from me. A door opens and closes. My arms shake so bad I almost drop the stupid cloak. Shizz.

I move, feeling around for the procedure table. My hand smacks into a structure made of metal and cloth. I toss the modesty cloak at it, then strip. T-shirt, jeans, sneakers. Don't know what logo anything has on it, don't know the colors, but no one laughed at me this morning. It'd be douchey to laugh at the blind guy.

The blind guy who might be better off as he is.

No. Not thinking that. Not turning back.

My clothes and shoes are a pile at my feet. I tug on the modesty cloak, a big t-shirt really, and rub the fabric across my chest and abdomen. It's as soft as the fluffiest blanket fresh from the dryer, the smell clean and pure as warm bathwater before soap and shampoo. I flex my fingers and toes, memorizing the feel of the joints working, lick my dry lips, tasting salt, and relishing the burn.

I clap my hands, sing the alphabet backward twice, and wish the people in the waiting room were my mom and dad and brothers and sister.

A deep breath, in and out, as I drag rough hands over my face and through my hair.

Here we go.

I climb onto the table, my feet enjoying the reprieve from the cold floor. I mentally file every sensation of situating myself on the cushioned table. My head finds where it needs to go, the back exposed to open air, but my neck supported.

This is my choice. I'm doing this. Can't turn back.

But yes, I can.

I can still say 'I changed my mind'. I can get up, put my clothes back on, and eat salt cookies until I puke, because I know the healer has cookies somewhere. And then, I can leave.

But I'm not going to.

"Ready." My voice shakes.

A few seconds pass before the door reopens and closes. Footsteps near me. Cool fingers touch my forehead. "I will use magic to make you sleep. You will feel warm, and then you will feel nothing. Do you have any concerns before we proceed?"

My empty stomach gurgles. It sucks that I wasn't allowed to eat before the procedure. I want to taste those fruit pastries Uncle Aeric makes from scratch one more time. Drink more sugary milk that tastes like vanilla ice cream.

"No."

Warmth sows through my forehead, branching downward, sprouting through my torso and limbs. I feel free, comfortable, bodiless. Smell, sound, touch, and the taste of a dry mouth quickly fade. Until all my senses are as black as my vision.

Chapter 11

# Evan

EVERYTHING UNDER THE MED TENTS smells like various types of smoked meat. The different skins of soldiers burn in unique ways. Scaly yellow skins turn white, oily black flesh goes gray, and smooth pink bodies char bright red. Puss oozes, blood flows, and soldiers cry as medics inject them with anesthetic to dull nerves before treating deep wounds.

It took us more than two weeks to get here and, in that time, two more attacks occurred. I make rounds at the camp with Adonis, Desiri, and Jalee, stopping at bedsides to greet and give praise. There are twenty-seven wounded in this tent, thirty more in the one before, and twenty in the one before that. The morgue tents hold double the numbers, rapidly increasing as the medic tents' numbers drop.

I touch my fingers to an unmarred yellow forehead of a woman with feverish blue eyes. Her neck and shoulders are smooth and chalk-white where scales have fallen off. Her breath wheezes in her chest.

"Thank you for your service," I whisper. Her slack lips tremble, like she means to talk. I shake my head, sorrow filling me. "Tell me later."

There won't be a later for her.

I move on as Jalee takes my place. She murmurs prayers over the woman, as she does over most of the people I know won't make it. There's a look, a smell, that tells me when it's over. They usually die within *jewels*. Half the soldiers in these tents will die within *jewels*.

I've lost count of how many tents like these I've visited on the field and how many dying soldiers Jalee has blessed. The words I offer the dying and the prayers Jalee gives have become automatic. This part of the job *should* get easier over time; I should be immune to the grief that comes with death, but I'm not.

"Leader Laudue—Leader One!" a baritone voice calls.

Adonis and Desiri fall in, flanking me on either side. We turn as a unit.

Captain Unferla, Rank R7, Gold Allegiance, jogs and comes to a stop in front of us. "Nazflit scrimmers are on the horizon."

I nod and tap two fingers to my left shoulder. Acknowledged. "Jalee?"

I don't need to look over my shoulder. I feel her at my back a split-*wisp* later. We exit the tent to meet my outer court, fifteen soldiers standing at attention armed with shoulder cannons, side lasics, and utility belts loaded with sharps and leather pouches full of materials needed for their own individual magic user quirks.

My outer court was selected for me when I was twelve, all of them older magic users with years of military service before auditioning for my team. They treat me like a little brother off the field, but on it?

They salute.

We march to join a combination of Silver and Gold Allegiance warriors—three hundred strong. The enemy's numbers should be even. The allied company before us kicked ass, and the price they paid is matched by the body count of dead enemies.

The air smells like iron and sulfur. A dusky orange haze rusts a normally pinkish-blue sky, war pollution that will take a week of rain to cleanse. The rocky soil gives our military march a crunchy beat as we move. The soldiers ahead of us part so that my court and I can bring our troops to the front line and meet First Captain Bilowe.

The woman doesn't turn to look at any of us; her gaze is fixed on the horizon where the silhouette of Nazflit scrimmers becomes clearer by the *wisp*.

"Leader One." She's a head taller than me. Her tone is the bone-tired rasp of a leader who's lost too many people in a short period of time. Her gray-blue eyes flick over to me, gaze both appraising and disapproving. "I wish you weren't so young."

Truth rings in Bilowe's words, but it's a sad truth.

I square my shoulders. "Be glad we're here. What's left of Nazflit over there doesn't stand a chance." I don't smile, because when I'm not doing it to scare people, smiling makes me look like a kid, and she already thinks I'm too young.

She lifts her chin, eyes forward again. "The troops are briefed. They know to give you and your full court space." She eyes the people with me, probably noting the slight differences in the standard uniform between my inner and outer courts and my regular soldiers. Only magic users wear utility belts with multiple pouches.

"The shield spells will be set first, to protect our side from magic fallout," I say.

"And you're going to cast something huge, and we should all jump for cover," a perky voice chirps. A head pops between Bilowe and me.

Major Finara Borks, four Common Years older than me and one of my favorite leaders to work with from the Gold Allegiance. "Fire spell?" she asks, smoothing flyaway pink curls off her face. The rest of her hair is trapped in a tight bun at the nape of her neck.

"A flame-tapestry, yeah." I smile at her. She doesn't need reassuring that I'm old enough to fight with her. "Then, a water-web behind it." I look over my shoulder at Adonis, who gives a slight nod.

Followed by Desiri's wind furies and various magic volleys from the outer court, while Jalee holds our shields. The army will flood in after we wipe out half the enemy. It's what we do.

"Enemy has passed the border triggers." The hard voice resounds through the secondary compal interface cuffed inside my right ear. A soft vibration thrums through my wrist, my primary compal, a device Devon calls an alien Smartwatch. I roll up my sleeve and acknowledge the written message.

"Jalee, ward up." I turn my eyes to the sky.

I feel the start of her shield spell crackling as she invokes the name of several elements and unnecessary goddesses. Her spellcasting is archaic in the eyes of most, but she prefers to honor her lineage and cast like the Danecian witches she came from.

As soon as the heavy magnetic force of a gargantuan earthbound ward needles my senses, I hold up a hand. The signal that I'm going to cast. And ten beats later, Adonis will cast.

I draw from my core flame, exhaling it into the atmosphere, and mentally grab hold. I shape fire and air with invisible fingers, braiding layer after layer and watching a massive quilt of bright orange and red flames shoot upwards. The plaited inferno spreads—and sputters, trembling, patterns loosening.

My core huffs and spews more energy into the spell. The fire tapestry wavers.

*Fip.* What the *fip*…

I give it more power. The fire shifts from orange to yellow, cooling.

No. I reach out, stroking the air, listening for its song, humming it back. *Feed the fire*, I croon. *I know your song. I can sing it too. I am with you today.*

But the song I sing doesn't match the wind's score.

"Evan?" Adonis's voice rings through my compal.

I analyze the score and what I sang. Did I miss a note? I hum again. And again. I'm flat. I try to correct, and… I'm flat. The fire wobbles, the blanket topples in the direction of the ward and the team. *Vati fipping pidge.*

"Evan?" Adonis and Desiri say together.

"Fall back!" I shout, then push, throwing out pure energy to knock the unraveling fire tapestry forward.

Nazflit scrimmers scream overhead and explosives drop. The fire covers the first onslaught, roasting their front line. Not what I had in mind, and not what we need. My spell was supposed to destroy forty percent of the enemy's forces.

I tap the cuff on my ear. "Adonis, now." I threw our timing off. The plan is *pidge*, but the Nazflit troops aren't waiting for me to get it right.

Hot vehicle exhaust from the second wave of Nazflit troops fans my face as they roll over their fallen comrades. Their energy weapons open fire, slamming into Jalee's shield spell behind me. I throw up my own personal shield spell and deflect a hit that should have punched a hole in my chest. My shield sparks like a short fuse, the magic flickering.

The *fip*? I send more power into the shield spell as I dodge another blast, hurling myself into a forward roll and coming up in a kneel. Explosions shriek around my ears.

An icy fog unfurls over the field, freezing Nazflit in their tracks—Adonis. That's ten percent down. I'll take out another five. I gather power in my fingertips, focusing and charging it with fire and wind—the notes... the notes... I can't grasp the notes.

Natural melodies and life chords slide through my fingers, hitting the ground, turning the grass beneath my boots black. Dead.

*Pidge.*

Another blast. The enemy fires laser cannons, destroying their own frozen soldiers in their charge.

Why is my magic not working?

I can't run a diagnostic, not here. A wave of electric-blue water geysers up and waterfalls onto the oncoming soldiers. Adonis again. He's doing too much. He's trying to take down the people I was supposed to. Desiri's wind furies screech around the water, cycloning past me, slashing through Nazflit troops.

"Evan, fall back." Adonis in my ear.

Right.

A blazing sword swings toward me and I jump back, kicking out. At hand-to-hand, I'm still stronger than a lot of people. I break the soldier's sword arm, then his knee, then his neck. More find me. I was a loud beacon of broken magic earlier. The enemy has to know who I am after all that. They rush me.

The Gold and Silver Allegiance armies behind me roar battle cries, passing through Jalee's shield. Feet stomp, weapons fire. Heavy gray smoke clouds the field, along with the chilling fog from the water attacks Adonis launches from... I don't even know where he is. I can't see through the gray soup in the air.

I drop low, ducking a slash from a weapon, flipping to the side to avoid an energy shot. My swinging fists connect with flesh and crack bones, every hit and kick I deliver designed to kill.

I can't spare mercy. A weak combat move could mean a broken spine—or worse, a capture.

I blur, charging my movements with core fire. Faster. If they can't see me, they can't counter my physical blows. I lose track of the bodies falling in my wake. Panting, heartbeat in my ears.

I can't keep this up.

I draw my lasic, substituting energy blasts from the gun for punches. But the blasts are slower than my hands. Not as effective. I could try another a spell, but that would take too long. I reach for the dirt, listening hard for the sound of anything beneath it. The songs of roots, grass, trees... They're all jumbled. A symphony of errors my brain can't sort. I can't use any of it to help me win.

What the *fip* is wrong with—pain explodes through my ribcage.

I keep my balance, but I can't breathe. Something grabs me by the throat, dragging me. I reach up, gripping a foreign wrist and forearm and pulling down, snapping the bone. The soldier howls. Air rushes in, but I can't get a deep breath.

Think the *spuccum* broke one of my *fipping* ribs.

Half my vision tinges red as fire heats my face. My limbs tremble as I fight rage. Anger is a bad thing. Control is better. But... but... the cacophony from the ground irritates me. My magic is broken.

More people come at me, and I fling myself into more hand-to-hand combat, firing up my steps. At least my body works like it's supposed to, but breathing fast enough to maintain the oxygen level I need to keep up this speed is more difficult with an injured rib. Sweat stings my eyes, and my vision doubles. I take a hit, barely dodging a sharp projectile. An explosion rocks the ground, and I lose my footing. Take a hard blow from behind.

I can't make out individual sounds anymore. Don't know who's winning. Just know this is all wrong. This was not the plan, and the plan should have worked.

*I* didn't work.

My compal crackles to life in my ear. I hear someone saying retreat. Hear someone else say they're being cut off from the rest of our forces. Hear someone crying about an entire battalion lost.

No. No. No.

It won't go this way. Can't go this way.

*Devour.*

I flinch at the cold whisper that chews through the back of my skull.

*Devour.*

The word claws its way centerstage, echoing through my core, reigniting the flame by singing my life song. But there's a weird note in it, clashing with the others. Its sharpness makes everything else flat. I can't harmonize or resonate with other songs when my signature key is incorrect.

*Devour.*

The voice of the Stone is beautiful. Its song is perfect. Not sharp. Not flat. My inner flame heats in response to the voice. Power surges through me, my life song twining around its flawless rhythm.

*Devour*—the composition for that spell is simple. Five notes, an almost elementary arrangement. I can manage it. But I don't like using the Stone in battle. Things always get out of hand. Too much is destroyed. I can't... Said I wouldn't ever...

*Devour*—the only song I hear clearly. Straightforward and pretty with long, mournful notes that can summon eaters from a lower *ether* plane. Microorganisms that dissolve flesh and bone. That spell is...

*Devour.*

...perfect.

My fingers unsnap the damper bag I keep the Stone in. The emerald glows as the warding around it parts. Energy swirls around me, fortifying my magic and patching the broken chord in my song. I hum the opening notes of Devour, willing the air to take it and spread its chorus.

Gray battle smoke bleeds red as the screams start. The coppery stink of blood taints the atmosphere. I complete the song, not needing to repeat it. The energy from the Stone fuels the encores. I rock on my heels in time with the beat of the continuing melody, caught up in the swells of its passion. As the tune crescendos, billions of sharp-toothed microorganisms billow over the Nazflit soldiers attempting to flee.

They won't make it.

Curls plaster against my forehead, sticky with the blood the creatures leave behind.

I won this.

My ears ring—not with music, voices. Yelling at me to stop.

Stop? But I still see enemy troops on the other side. See vehicles, armored shells disintegrating, the soldiers operating them firing weapons at what they can't see without magic.

*Victory is yours.*

It is. The power swaddles me. I block out the desperate pitches in the voices wanting me to end the spell. We haven't won yet. Just a little mo—

"Evan!"

My stomach clenches at the horror in Jalee's voice.

"Our team!"

Our team. Our... The massive cloud of blood envelopes me on all sides. Devour is ravenous, and there are only so many Nazflit.

I whip around, needing to see. Is it...? Did it...? I grip the wind, whistling to it. It obeys. Blood-thickened air thins, allowing me to see the bright blue water wall encapsuling what's left of the Gold and Silver Allegiance soldiers. I can't see Jalee, or Desiri... but I see Adonis, standing with his arms raised. Trembling.

He can't hold that. And if he lets go, the teeth come in.

Stop the song.

*Just a little longer.*

Adonis sways. Someone touches his shoulder, but they can't offer him any magic. Nothing to give him strength. The water wall turns purple, the light brilliant—and too much. I hear it. Over the screams of the enemies being eaten alive, over Jalee in my ear, over the beautiful song of Devour. Adonis's clear life song pours into the water's composition. A sacrifice. Terror grips me.

Stop the song!

The banishing spell. I need the words. But my brain can't find them. My fingers fumble for the pouch. If I cut the power... the monsters remain. They were called here. They have to be sent away.

Reluctantly, I feel the Stone's power leach through me, teaching another tune to weave into the air. The notes of Devour transition into those of Homecoming. A faster song with sharps and trills. The invisible monsters hopefully vanish. The air stays wet and red. Screams fade. I can't tell if anything's changed, but...

I break into a run, body heavy like I'm wading through sand. Exhaustion from burning too much energy in hand-to-hand and unleashing Devour and Homecoming wants me to pass out. Black spots dot my vision, but I can't stop.

I hit Adonis's barrier at full speed, freezing water chilling my limbs. The fact that I pass through to the other side completely dry speaks to the remaining strength of the barrier. It pulls water off my skin to feed itself. The water wall surges upward, arcing high and crashing to the ground behind me, becoming a raging river flooding toward what's left of the Nazflit. Cleansing the air and ground.

I stand a step away from Adonis, panting, watching his body shake. Catching him as his eyes roll back in his head and he falls forward. Too many people talk at once. Shouts of victory, nervous roll calls, the nonsensical chatter of chaos.

"Did you see that?"

"The air turned to blood!"

"Goddess-touched."

"Praise the Leader."

I sink to the ground with Adonis, pulse pounding in my throat as I check his vitals. His lungs wheeze, his heart vibrates at an alarming speed. He's going to... His body stills, then seizes. I roll him onto this side, letting the seizure finish. Watching. The blood on my hands stains his skin and uniform.

My stomach lurches. I'm going to throw up, but I won't do it here. I have to...
I check Adonis's pulse again as he stills. Weak, barely there. His chest shudders.
*Niobe-va.* I reach for his song, to pour strength into it, but... the notes of mine
clunk around searching for a key.

The Stone hums in its pouch

It fixed my song before.

The wrongness of my life score hurts my ears. Scratches my mind. I reach for
the Stone, and it rights my melody. Together, we help Adonis, strengthening his
chords, feeding our life force into his. He coughs, but his eyes don't open.

"Evan." Jalee uses a voice best suited for soothing cornered animals.

Hot tears spill onto my face.

She squats beside me, body covered in dirt. Her hands reach out. I stiffen, not
wanting comfort. She grabs the pouch, fingers drawing it closed. Sealing the ward.

But I still hear it.

"Get it away from me." My voice is hoarse.

The chaotic chatter in the air is still about me. Awe, fear, and reverence tremor in
strained voices. In my periphery, people move. Inspecting the field beyond us as
Adonis's river recedes. I think all the Nazflit are dead.

I lean over Adonis, ear over his lips. His breathing rasps. His heart sounds weak.

"Get it away from me," I repeat. My words tremble.

I feel it being unhooked from my belt, leaving my person. Faint outrage flickers
through me. I curb the desire to strike Jalee and take back what's mine. My Stone.
*Fip.* I hear it in my head. Sense it stirring in my magic. It's worse than ever.

I turn my full attention on Adonis. His body's too cold. Skin too dry. "Medic?" I choke out.

"Almost here," Jalee says. She echoes my movements, checking Adonis's vitals, brown eyes stealing worried glances at me. "Ev, what happened?"

My jaw locks, and my throat dries out. My mouth barely opens, voice croaking as I say, "I—"

"What the *fipping* hells did you do?" Desiri runs to us, dropping to her knees in front of Adonis's head, checking his pulse at his neck and touching his cheek. She stares at me, and I flinch, waiting for it.

Desiri should stab me. Jalee should hex me.

Both are silent as a medic in green and white reaches us. The man gapes at me, hands shaking.

"Do your job," I hiss at him. "He needs fluid and nourishment. He used too much life energy." And I can't give him more of mine without the Stone. But with it... I clamp a hand over my mouth and jump to my feet.

Exhaustion hasn't forgotten about me. My head reels as I stagger to a nearby bush. I continue to heave long after I'm empty, feeling my intestines touch the base of my throat. A hand touches my back and I jump, almost toppling face first into my own sick.

"What's wrong with you?" Jalee's voice is grounding.

I spit a few times and dry heave twice before I can talk. "I don't know." *Niobe-va.* "Did I...? Is anyone on our side dead?"

"You mean, did anyone die because of that *pidge* you unleashed?"

Jalee swore. She only does that when she's terrified. Oh gods. I spit again, leaning over the bush, not wanting to see her, not caring that the reek of vomit mixed with the overpowering twang of too much blood wants me to throw up again.

"No." Jalee squeezes my shoulder. "Our side retreated as soon as they saw the red tide. There are some injuries but no fatalities from…" Her fingers hurt. "Did you summon eaters?"

I nod. Because I did. And didn't think about anything else other than needing to win. Not letting the troops down because I couldn't perform. I had to prove that I couldn't lose.

"I didn't tell you to adapt the shield spell or to retreat," I murmur. "You couldn't have worked up anything to counter the eaters fast enough, even if I had. You could have…" *been devoured.* The only person who'd been safe on the field was me.

Breathing is a chore. Oxygen rushes in, but I can't exhale quickly enough. Pin-pricks of light fleck my vision. Because…

I didn't think.

Couldn't think.

I sense the Stone on Jalee's body, and I want it back. I start to reach for her but stop. A gut-wrenching feeling of dread fills me.

"Something's wrong with me." I close my eyes, trying to catch my breath, clear my head. I concentrate on my life song and personal rhythms, but I can't find them.

Jalee's hand shifts from my shoulder to my back. "You have to breathe out, Ev. I'll count and you blow out in three counts. Come on."

I let her sweet voice teach me how to breathe again. The vertigo in my head slows. She rubs my back and stops counting after a minute.

"Your magic failed," she says. "I saw you try to correct and conjure. It didn't seem to work."

"Nothing worked. I'm off-key." My voice goes completely hoarse on the word 'worked'.

"Leader One!"

"Leader Lauduethe!"

I straighten, wiping my mouth with the back of my hand. Jalee hugs my shoulders, and we turn in tandem, her putting herself slightly in front of me. Captains and lieutenants approach, their faces—is that admiration? Are they ready to celebrate what I just did?

I could have... I look beyond the approaching commanders, needing to see Adonis. Desiri's still kneeling, the medic is still crouching. They block my view of Adonis's upper body, but his legs don't move. The medic waves a hand, a signal for an evac. A white stretcher whizzes toward them. It stops and the medic and two other people, assistants who appear as suddenly as the stretcher had, lift Adonis onto the floating hammock.

My breath catches in my burning throat as fear chokes me. I count. Inhale: one, two, three. Exhale: one, two, three.

"Jalee." I don't sound like myself. "Take over."

Her callused hands grip my elbow before she nods and nudges me on. I stride past the commanders who start, like they're going to follow me.

"All debriefing will happen in the war tent." Jalee puts bass in her voice when she's in charge.

I feel the attention shift from me to her and my shoulders slump in relief as I reach the stretcher. Adonis's dark skin is ashen, and his chest struggles to rise. I grab his cold hand—my head jerks back. Desiri's got hold of my bedraggled braid.

I shudder, turning to her, eyes on the drying blood in the crevasses of my knuckles.

"What happened?" Her voice is low, meant for only me.

I shake my head slightly and gulp before looking her in the eyes. There's no judgement, only concern. She holds the end of my braid in one hand, scratching flecks of crimson from its strands.

"Jalee's in command. Be her second?"

Desiri frowns at me for a long *wisp*. "You sure you don't need me to be *your* second right now?"

I don't answer. She doesn't make me. Instead, she sighs and thumps me on the back, hard. "Take care of him." And then she marches away.

The stretcher moves, hovering between the med team. I jog beside it, not losing my grip on Adonis's freezing hand.

*"Take care of him."*

Because I've already done a wonderful job of that.

I shouldn't touch him. Shouldn't be near him.

We pass soldiers, filthy from the aftermath of my spell and maybe the fighting before, their uniforms grimy with blood and soil. Some are polite enough to pretend not to stare or cringe away. Some point and whisper. I hear it all.

They think I'm an otherworldly presence. Something to bow to, then run from. I'm not one of them. I'm one of Order's Champions. Some of it's true, the rest is *pidge*. Don't bow to me. I'm not an otherworldly presence. And I'm not goddess-touched. I'm goddess-cursed.

The overpowering stench of death and dying in the first med tent hits me harder than it did earlier. Half the beds are empty. The dead soldiers must have been moved after I went on to visit the second and third med tents. Two medics rotate between the remining troops populating beds at the rear of the tent, and the others must be out on the field.

Adonis is transferred to a clean bed, and the medics get to work. One runs diagnostics by holding a short silver rod over Adonis's body. A 3D image rotates above Adonis's middle, displaying vital statistics in symbols I don't understand.

"Leader One, we need you to step back," a medic says.

My hand doesn't want to let go. I force my fingers to release and shudder at the loss of contact. Though his skin is cool, hand limp, I detected life. Sensed blood flowing through still digits. I'm a *kiut* away, but it's too far.

I shut out the chorus of disjointed life songs. When had it gotten this bad? I had perfect pitch on the Ievisara, in the tent. It wasn't until I tried for a greater spell that I noticed—

My brain clamps on the thought, choking it silent. I can't even lie in my own head. I did notice it before. On the Ievisara. Something was wrong inside, but it hadn't been enough to stop me from being with Imari. My body knew hers in a way that scared me but didn't stop me from touching her. She knew where to touch me too. We fit together like two halves of a whole born hundreds of years apart.

Corin was with Imari that night, but so was I.

It made me forget something was wrong. I went to my own bed after, but I slept easy and woke ready with nothing but the mission on my mind. Living with her in our space as we traveled was pleasant. She kept out of everyone's way, and when we finally touched dirtside, she was all business. Imari wanted a vocation. She was happy learning how to use the machines to mend uniforms and boots, and sterilizing equipment with chemicals instead of brews.

I left her, smiling, as I whistled and joined my inner court to talk strategy with other leaders before visiting the wounded.

I *fipping* forgot. And Adonis sacrificed himself to save people who trusted me... from me.

I sit down, hard. The grass floor of the tent is dry and prickly. The thick fabric of my uniform pants protects my backside and legs, but fine blades slice the pads of my index and middle fingers as I grind my hands into the soil.

Ragged notes moan to me, and I shut them out. That song is wrong. Or rather, *it's* not wrong. I am. I'm not hearing what I should.

I could be sick. Maybe it's a virus attacking my core, spreading into my other senses and *fipping* up my interactions. It happens. Being sick and working deep magic is dangerous. Viveen *raxed* me for it on Rema. I'd been sixteen and didn't want to pull my team out of a battle at the last minute. I had promised to fight; I was needed. And I'd cost the planet a wealth of currency in damage because my fried, fevered brain couldn't focus my fire.

I press the back of a bloody hand to my forehead. No fever.

But I knew that already.

"Leader One?" A soft voice, a rusty smell. Someone else with a lot of blood on their clothing approaches me.

My eyes are closed as my head rolls forward. "How is he?"

"Honorable Maeve severely depleted his lifeforce, but he will recover."

My lungs take in more air, and my head stops being heavy. I nod at whoever's talking, hoping they think I'm all here. That I'm not having a mental breakdown over something I should be used to.

It's not the first time one of us has been hurt in battle. Desiri was almost disemboweled in our last fight. I was punched through the chest by an *ether* beast. And several skirmishes before that one, I died. For a few minutes, maybe a *jewel*, a *cycle* at most, I was dead. I don't freak out over injuries.

Unless I cause them.

"Leader One."

"Yes?"

"You need to wash."

I open my eyes. A slender medic with small braids piled on top of his head peers at me from a squatted position. His green and white tunic is spattered with blood.

"Working hard?" I study the dried blood on his front.

"Was transferred from Med Tent Two." He sighs, breath sounding heavy with exhaustion. His light purple eyes gleam. "But I hear I'm going to get to take a break soon, after what you just pulled out there."

My stomach churns at his awe.

"Forty-nine wounded on our side, and only thirteen fatalities," he says. "I came in here right before you all marched out to meet the Nazflit. Was expecting another rush of soldiers I couldn't save to flood in. Instead..." He smiles. "Instead, I get to come over and ask after you. I can walk you to your ship if you prefer to bathe there."

"I'm not leaving this tent." Adonis wouldn't leave me. I steal a look over at his bed. A portable white curtain hides him now.

The man nods. "I figured that. The soldiers' cleansing chambers are... well, they're disgusting right now. I can let you into the medic chambers. The pods are at the rear of each tent." I start to shake my head, but the medic grimaces at me. "Leader

One, you're drenched in blood and what I'm sure is vomit. You reek. I don't think that Honorable Maeve will appreciate rousing to that aroma."

A laugh escapes. I clamp a blood-crusted hand over my mouth to catch it. But the image of Adonis's offended face—a raised brow and a single nose twitch—makes me laugh so hard it hurts, running both hands through my matted hair and letting them rest above my ears.

The medic chuckles with me. "I think you might live."

"Huh?" I would wipe tears of mirth from my eyes, but I don't want to get blood in them. My skin crawls from the sensation of tears and drying blood creeping down my cheeks.

"You looked ready to expire a *wisp* ago." The medic rises to his feet, knees cracking. He offers a hand down to me.

I don't take it, but I stand too.

"My name is Heka." He bows his head to me. "I only received my stripes to practice on the field a Common month ago. My sister..." He swallows. "My sister received her stars to be a soldier at the same time. This is our first battle. She went out onto the field for the first time just now and didn't have to fight. I don't have to treat her for injuries or worry about someone else doing it, because..." He bows his head lower this time. "Thank you."

It could have gone so wrong.

It *did* go so wrong.

I wave off his 'thanks.' "The cleansing chambers are in back?"

"I'll let you in."

Heka's pace is brisk as I follow him through the tent, ignoring the wide-eyed stares of medics and patients. Murmurs swell. All the gossip is about me commanding an invisible tide of flesh-eating monsters. No one talks about the air being soupy with blood afterward. They mention Adonis's water wall but don't say why it was needed.

We arrive at the rear of the tent. Three white pods the size of hydra eggs, large enough to be full-service bathrooms, hum. Heka taps the round door of one, and the image of a keypad appears. He enters a code, and the door hisses and rolls upward, revealing a clean, alabaster room with a square glass stall for cleansing, a basin for quick washing, and a head for waste. It smells like fresh ice and mint.

"Take your time," Heka says. "There are uniforms in the basket by the cleansing chamber. Feel free to use one."

I step inside and the door seals behind me, shutting out the murmurs and leaving me with the mechanical hum of the pod. I cringe at the blood I track on the white tile floor, and the red I leave on the white basin of the sink where my fingers touch it.

I don't know if a person maintains this area, or if they have a cleaning program or machine. No living person should have to pick up after me. I shed my uniform, turning the place into a murder scene that I'll scrub myself. Then, I climb into the chamber to drown in cleansing fluid.

Chapter 12

# Lyle

SHAKING OFF THE LETHARGY FROM returning to my body isn't easier after the sixth time. Nialiah says my soul travels to the *ether* to meet Kahanna, which leaves my body temporarily dead. It breathes shallowly, and my heart beats a few times a minute, but if someone ran an EEG, there'd be no detectable brain activity. It's only right that I come back to a corpse after dealing with Her.

My heart pumps harder, my pulse returning to normal, blood flowing into limp limbs. I notice the soft, consistent sound of snipping scissors. It pauses. The scent of passion fruit nears me, and I roll my head to one side, seeing the swishing fabric of Nialiah's belted night robe as she approaches me. She holds a pair of sheers and a headless flower. They disappear to her left with a muffled clunk.

"Well?" The bed depresses as she sits. "Did Kahanna find Devon?"

I flinch at his name, at the flash of pain behind my eyes, at the burst of anger I can't act on because my arms and legs are still useless sandbags. Damn Kahanna and every creature She made. I let extra saliva collect in my mouth and swallow, trying to wet my throat, but my voice still rasps like a terminally ill patient.

"She says She sent something after him but wouldn't say what or how long it'd take to bring him back."

Nialiah tuts and helps me sit up. My head lolls onto one of her shoulders as my back rests against her torso. I wonder what Lawrie would do if he saw me in bed with Nialiah. He'd be disappointed to find out that she doesn't want me like that. She enjoyed teasing me. Claimed it helped pass the time, and because she knew I'd never accept her advances, she had nothing to worry about. Though I'm nice to look at, she'd put Jain Peredil behind her centuries ago. She told me so after my second meeting with Kahanna.

More stories came after the third and fourth check-ins. Stories about her and Hellene's first meeting, about her parents. Snippets from her distant past that encouraged me to share a few memories of my own, about my life on Earth and what it was like being smothered by my powers and brother. She's a good listener.

And isn't who I thought she was. I'm sure she's not who anyone thinks she is.

The rim of a wooden cup presses against my mouth and I sip from it, gazing at her. Nialiah gives me the little smile moms give their kids when they clean up after themselves. She's fond of me in that way now. Like I'm something to raise and mold. I told her I'm not a kid she'd want to have, and she chuckled and went back to one of her little projects. She's always brewing or mixing or smithing cursed jewelry with precious metals and gems.

It'd been a shock to find out Nialiah isn't lazy. She lounges around for show. Under the table, she peddles wares and makes a small fortune she donates to that little planet Lawrie's Stone was on. It's weird that aside from the woman who transports the goods Nialiah sells, I'm the only person who knows. She shared it with me, because—well, hell, we're both in deep crap if anyone finds out what we're up to. It makes us friends.

My heart beats easier at the thought. I need a friend who can know everything and not hate me for it, because she chose it too. A friend who has answers to hard questions and sound theories for when she doesn't.

I sip more water. "Would Kahanna lie to me about helping Devon, Nia? You know Her better."

Nialiah tuts. "She *would* lie, but not about that. I believe that She did uphold Her word and sent 'something'. Will that 'something' work is the question. However, it is not wise to question Her or visit that plane too often, Lyle. You simply must wait."

I'm tired of waiting. My muscles scream as I force them to sit up straight. To take the cup from Nialiah and finish the water. A plate of berries and cheese appears next, and the cup is taken away so I can eat. My stomach's been a black hole I can't fill lately. Nialiah says it's from traveling between planes.

"If She can't find him... if he's in trouble and She's too slow, we need another plan. Maybe we could contract a rescue team. People do that sort of work, right? We could pay them to go out, and they'd do it so no one else would know—"

"You mean *I* would pay them. You do not know how to access your coin without alerting someone that you are doing so." Nialiah smirks. "You would be borrowing money from a dangerous woman."

"Dangerous to who?" I shoot back.

I'm not afraid of Nialiah, and she knows it. I'm also serious. I set the empty plate by my thigh and turn so I'm fully facing her. Her long hair's plaited and wound on top of her head in a huge bun.

"Nia, would you help me pay a team to find Devon?"

"I wish you had asked for that before you asked me to summon Her." She sighs. "Though, I might have refused you, because..." She tilts her head, black eyes softening.

And without touching her mind I know—because before Nialiah didn't like me enough to risk her own connections on something treasonous.

Her lips curve in a toothless smile. "I will think on hiring a team but know that it is a difficult task, and the likelihood of success may be lower than the goddess rescuing your brother. All of our communications can be compromised, and if She were to find out you doubted Her word?"

I shudder, recalling Kahanna's fathomless eyes and sharp sneer as she pushed me out of the *ether* this time. I'm supposed to be her favorite Champion, but I don't think it'll last much longer if I keep pissing Her off.

She's pissing *me* off, though.

I drop my head in my heads, Kahanna's ugly eyes replaced with Evan's, his concern clear when he'd asked me if I'd be okay before he boarded his ship. Black guilt pounds inside my skull, threatening to become a massive migraine. I didn't deserve his worry, didn't warrant the hug. Not after I poisoned him. The radio silence between us as he travels is a blessing in disguise. I don't know if I can talk to him without breaking down.

She can't renege on what She promised, or I'll lose two brothers. If Evan finds out about me, and there's no Devon to show for it all, then that's it. And Lawrie? He probably wouldn't talk to me either.

Dammit all. Lawrie. I haven't heard from him since he arrived on Bruhje. Don't know what his healer says. What's going on, aside from Devrik Lauduethe 'ghosting' him and Uncle Aeric being 'really chill'. I should leave this room and send a message to Bruhje, find out what's happening there. It's not overly safe to send multiple messages to one location, but I have to know.

There's a knock at Nialiah's main door.

I'm no longer surprised that Nialiah cusses. She hates being bothered in her rooms. The bed bounces as she gets up and glides to the door. I lean back on the pillows, stretching my arms and legs and straining my ears to listen to the muffled conversation between Nialiah and one of the Pavilion attendants.

None of The Maidens' attendants react to me in Nialiah's bed anymore, and no one talks about it. When Caea glares at me, it's because I'm distant, not because rumor says I'm sleeping with Nialiah.

Dammit it all again. Caea. Just. Just... I roll onto my side, tuning out Nialiah and the other voice. I want nothingness. A pit where there are no thoughts or memories or feelings.

*Shhh...* The tickle of the Stone's touch runs over my skin, creating a blanket of silence that starts in the center of my spine. It stretches, reaching down to my feet and slowly spreading toward my neck, ready to cover my head.

Yes, please.

"Lyle?" Nialiah's voice rings.

The quiet blanket pauses at my chin. Almost. I could ignore her. Slip away. I don't want to talk anymore.

"Lyle, get up." Her hand on my shoulder. "We are needed. The Silver and Gold Allegiance Councils have called a meeting with the Champions."

The Stone rips the blanket off me, and the real world comes crashing back. Meetings with Champions mean war business, god business. I consider pulling one of Nialiah's real blankets over my head—

Pain stabs my temples like knitting needles burrowing through the skin and bone. I jerk upright with a gasp. Nialiah jumps back, staring at me.

"Are you—"

I get to my feet, sighing at the release of pressure in my head. I rub my temples, trying to erase echoes of phantom pain. When I accepted the Stone, my constant headaches all but vanished. Getting them again now dredges up nightmarish memories, mistakes, things I can't undo. Flashes of a heart-shaped silver face with silver eyes filled with hate, glaring at me. Shoving me. I cover my eyes.

"Lyle, if you are ill..."

"I'm not." I just... "I don't know what I am, Nia. Let's just go."

Everything's up in the air. I can't control what happens next. Don't know if I'll win or lose. Or if my family wins or loses. I'm just moving now. That's what I am. Moving. Doing. Whatever She wants.

*Whatever She wants is wise.*

Yeah. Sure.

I head for Nialiah's door. It's closed again. I open it and stand in the threshold. A dark fog fills the space between my ears with a dull hum that cancels out anything that cares right now.

Nialiah joins me, squeezing my wrist. "Do you want me to leave first, and you follow, so we will not arrive together?"

I hear her, even register it. Thoughtful. Though the Lenorans don't gossip about us, Caea sees us together more often than not. I shake my head, bracing for pain that doesn't come. The hum between my ears is steady, flattening spikes of worry. The Stone is warm against my chest. I focus on that comfort, on the hum, find a space that floats in the center of the grayness in my brain and drift forward.

"Meet you there." I'm toneless, letting myself fall into not quite a trance, but a neutral state that's good for psychics learning to control their powers, or on the verge of a meltdown. A place I needed years ago, but no one on Earth could teach me how to get here. Evan got me here with his training before he left, but he's not here to coach me anymore.

*Stay in this place.*

Yes.

I leave the Maiden's Pavilion, not missing the presence of Imari and her dog-things. She packed up and went back to her manor in the woods, and neither Nialiah nor Hellene miss her.

On autopilot, I head to the decision hall. As I near it, more people in uniforms buzz by me, some in the gray and tan jumpsuits of the Remasian army, some in Zaran black, others in plain clothes. Their minds are like glass beads on thin stings being pushed and pulled in all directions. The glass is transparent. Through it are flecks of color and other imperfections I can see but don't have to touch, hear, or feel.

It's nice.

"Lyle?" Caea's voice from nearby. "Are you okay?"

I feel her closeness. Let it stir something in me as I bob out of my neutral zone to take her in. Her pretty face swirls into true focus, dark eyes appraising me. I don't smile at her because I don't think I can pull off a real one. Instead, I reach for her arm, looping mine through hers, and tense as she pulls free.

"You don't get to do that right now," Caea chides. "I haven't seen you in two *cycles*. And the last time I did, you wouldn't touch me. Wouldn't talk to me."

"I talked—"

"No. You didn't." She narrows her eyes at me, arms at her sides.

I think back. We'd been outside her room. I'd gone to tell her goodnight before I went to see Nialiah again. Caea hadn't wanted a 'goodnight'. She wanted to talk about Xijure and Devon and memorials. And I'd wanted her out of my face and head. I don't remember what I told her. But it couldn't have been bad, or she'd have punched my head off. Had I just left?

"You look like *pidge*," she says.

"And you look beautiful." Because she does, even when she doesn't. The fog starts to clear, and my stomach aches with more guilt. I bow my head. "I'm sorry I haven't been the best... person... to be around."

"Or not be around," Caea shoots back. "You keep disappearing. Avoiding me." Some of the anger in her posture wanes, and her shoulders slump. "Look, I know... I know what..." She bites her lower lip. "I lost a brother too."

A tear wets her cheek. I watch it slide over her lips before she wipes it away. I don't have to tap into her emotions to know her devastation, because it would be mine if I lost a brother. But I didn't, and maybe she didn't either.

I didn't ask Kahanna for Xijure.

I should have asked Her for Xijure.

But that might have been too much, and Devon means more. I included Caea's loved ones in my first deal. That's enough. If they can't get themselves to the end of the war alive, then it's not on me if they don't collect their ticket to Kahanna's new world. My choice was to give them a chance.

But Devon's non-negotiable.

To be around Caea would mean to talk. To share and feel the hurt from my deciding someone she loves so much is someone I have to let go. I have to. Pain spreads throughout my stomach. She wouldn't understand that. Shouldn't understand that because her brother would be non-negotiable for her. She'd hate me, and I don't want hate. Don't need it. Not now.

"Lyle?"

There's my name again. All of her anger is gone as she frowns at me, touching my brow with the back of her hand. "Your skin's clammy, and I'm not just being mean when I say you look like *pidge*. You can skip this meeting if you want..." She trails off, gaze going beyond me.

"It is not your call to dismiss Champions from war councils, Majesty."

Theorne. His oily voice drips on my nerves.

He plants himself in our conversation. "If Leader Three is not well, he can seek medical services after he receives his new mission."

New mission?

"I thought this was a meeting, not a mission briefing." Caea's words are sharp. She's not afraid of Theorne. He can't do anything to her, because Kahanna didn't see it fit to brand the Harliels with curse Marks. Not that I'd let him do anything to her if he could.

"What are we walking into, Councilor Theorne?" My voice is smooth. His smile is pasted on, superficial with a dash of malice. What he said tells me that the real 'meeting' probably happened hours ago with only the Gold and Silver Allegiance Councils in attendance, no Champions. Unless the Champion was Hellene.

A growl builds in my chest. Members of Kahanna's inner circle aren't supposed to withhold information like this from each other. I'm supposed to get a heads up, never be blindsided. But...

Doubt wraps around the growl.

What if...

*You are the favored.*

I push my power outward, pricking Theorne's brain with a telepathic needle. I force my face to remain a careful blank as he fails to conceal a flinch. "Headache, Councilor? You're welcome to join me on my visit to healers after the... briefing."

The fake smile on his face widens, and the malice deepens. "You were indisposed, Leader Three, or else Councilor Viveen and I might have informed you of certain matters. However, we do understand that you and Maiden Nialiah have additional duties to attend to."

My heart bucks. I look at Caea and wince as she storms into the meeting hall. I'm going to save that woman just to have her never speak to me again *before* the end of the world.

And hell. I want to speak to her. About anything but war. Want to be with her.

I shove Theorne with my mind, loving to see him stagger backward. "That was uncalled for, Theorne."

His bright blue eyes glitter. I never know if it's with hate, fear, or a heathy blend of both. I could rip into his brain and find out, but that means opening myself to whatever slimy things are on his mind. I think it's childish to brand anyone good or evil, but Theorne, Viveen, and Hellene willingly signed agreements to damn billions while lying to their faces.

I at least did it to save people. Theorne and Viveen aren't saving anyone but themselves, Kahanna told me. And Hellene? She has an ulterior motive for pushing to save Lenore. Nialiah's hinted as much.

"Careful, child." Theorne lowers his voice. "You are playing a game you do not fully understand, and you will not be the reason we lose everything now. The mission given to you today will be simple, and you will accept it without objection."

I glare at him. "Depends on what it is."

"Depends on what you still want." Theorne steps closer to me. "To be one of Kahanna's pieces means She moves you however, whenever, and wherever She pleases. Your gift is needed."

We stare at each other.

My gift is needed? I don't gape and don't want to lose any edge I have by asking a question that might seem dumb or naïve. I weigh what I say next.

"What's the mission? Tell me before I go in, so I can be cool about it."

Theorne frowns again, seeming to mull over my words. Maybe not understanding my slang. I don't care. He's a smart guy. He'll figure it out.

"You are going to bring a president and her people over to our persuasion."

"A diplomatic mission?" Incredulity fills me. I'm no politician. I'm not charming or even knowledgeable.

"A hostile takeover," Theorne says slowly, as if speaking to an unruly toddler. "Or, as you may put it, a meeting of the minds. I hear you have talent for influencing others to desire what you want."

Tires screech in my head. Silver eyes.

"I—"

*You must fulfil your initial bargain.*

I curse under my breath and nearly choke on my question. "Anything else?"

Theorne tilts his head, studying me. "You will receive further information inside and more once you reach Siodde." He watches me a moment longer before heading into the meeting hall.

I shiver, unnerved. That man makes the ambulance-chasing lawyers Mom complains about seem genuine.

Mom,

I miss...

The Stone is hot against my chest. Grayness fills the space between my ears, and a dull hum guides me back to neutral. That place where I can't feel hurt or lonely. This place is okay with waiting.

Waiting for orders.

Waiting for Devon.

Waiting to know who'll hate me before everything ends.

I drift into the meeting. The room is already filled with projections of world leaders, councilors, and soldiers. Their transparent constructs sit on risers fashioned into throne-like chairs. A real table sits in the center of it all with Caea, Ramesis, Hellene, Nialiah, Theorne, and Viveen around it. No Devon, no Xijure, no Evan. No Lawrie. No Imari.

My court's lost in that sea of projected officials. I scan for them for a few seconds, then don't care if I find them. It's okay. I already know our mission. The meeting is called to begin. I take a place beside Ramesis instead of Caea, avoiding her eyes. Ignoring Ramesis's glare. And wait for my mission to be further explained.

*"DON'T YOU EVER FEEL LIKE it's cheating?"*

*I jump at the sound of Padain's voice. Hadn't felt him enter. His mind resonates with mine when we're close. More poetic people might compare us to a harmony and melody. Which is one way to describe twins, even ones that come from separate eggs. Padain's nothing like me, though his mental wavelengths even out my choppy ripples.*

*But not lately.*

*Haven't needed his presence. The Stone's enough now. I don't turn, don't get up from the divan I'm sprawled across. My rooms in our old battleship are the same as always, with lots of overstuffed furniture good for napping, muted gray and blue colors that are easy on the eyes, and bland smells. It's designed for someone with frequent migraines. I don't need this anymore. But Padain never changed it, so I'd still have my safe space.*

*Padain sits on the divan, rear end by my head. Not a good position, which is why he sat like that. I push myself up and sigh. "You said something to me?"*

*"Yeah." Padain's gaze bores into the side of my face because I'm not looking at him.*

*I don't want to. I didn't register his earlier words, but I can probably guess what they were about and be right. So, I wait for him to repeat himself.*

*"I said, 'Don't you ever feel like it's cheating?' Using your powers in that way. Making people who don't agree with us think what you want them to."*

*"Better than fighting them." No one died today, because it never occurred to the enemy that they should draw any weapons or execute any attacks. Instead, they loaded their ore and mined minerals onto our convoys and severed all trade with the Nazflit. It'd only taken a careful infiltration mission and a jewel alone with parliament. Seeds of suggestion get easier to implant with practice. I hadn't broken a sweat or gotten a headache.*

*"It changes them, though." I feel Padain's heavy gaze shift away from my face. "The people you manipulate. They behave strangely after. They twitch like they know something's wrong, but they can't figure it out. It... It seems like it hurts them."*

*"Better them than us," I murmur.*

*"What?" The word is soaked in disbelief and righteous anger.*

*Annoyance builds inside me at Padain's tone. "Nothing. You can't tell me you'd rather kill people than leave them behind with little ticks."*

*"They're not little ticks, Jain! Those people look disturbed. They probably think they're going crazy. And maybe they'd rather me kill them than to not be in control of their own mind. To wander around like... like..." He stops, and I feel his eyes on me again.*

*Oh.*

*Oh.*

*I fold my hands in my lap, bowing my head. Letting the sickness and guilt rise from my gut into my throat. Because...*

*"Like Corin," Padain finishes.*

*Does Corin wish he were dead? Would he if he was conscious enough to be aware of himself as he is now? I don't know how much he truly understands or remembers of his time for the few moments that he's lucid.*

*Swallowing is harder to do around the growing lump in my throat. I told Padain I'd done something terrible. Something I regret. But I couldn't say what. Not then. Not ever. I can't bear the thought of him hating me. Not when I did this all for him, and Aman, and Corin.*

*If only Corin hadn't been so cocky and reckless. Only that's like asking outer space not to be black. Corin was what he was. And now he's not, and I can't fix him.*

*She won't fix him.*

*"Jain, I want you to tell me something. Right now. And I promise I won't get angry."*

*His voice is low, sincere. I can sound like that when I imitate him. Only, no one believes me when I use that voice, because I'm not Padain. I'm neither honest nor selfless.*

*"You've spent time with Maiden Nialiah. Spend more time with the council, with Viveen." Padain nudges my shoulder. "Look at me, Jain. Tell me. They're all closer to the goddess than us. They know things that they tell you. I know they must. Aman thinks... he thinks that you..." Padain shakes his head.*

*My stomach twists in knots. Aman thinks that I what?*

*He's designated himself Corin's protector these last few months. As if I wasn't the one who'd been doing the bathing, feeding, and just general care. As if I was the one who... I rub my face. Feeling the warning aura of a migraine I'm not supposed to have anymore.* Fip. Fip. Fip.

*"Jain, did Order hurt Corin?"*

*The question is blunt, rushed, loud. Too loud. Pain and panic roar in my ears, and I don't answer.*

*"Jain?" Padain sounds desperate.*

*I feel it. Padain reaching out, sense his wavelength. His aura seeking mine, ready to calm it, to organize it into corresponding patterns. To help me, like I wanted him to weeks before, when I'd gone to him. But...*

*Cool energy washes over me. Pushing Padain and his connection away, as it heals and quiets the storm of pain overloading the receptors in my brain.*

Shhh...

Yes.

Tell him nothing. Protect him. Save him.

*Save him.*

*At all costs.*

*At all costs.* "Order didn't hurt Corin, Padain."

*My brother's shoulders slump, and his sigh is relieved. He smiles at me, his large hand on my back. "Good. You don't know how much better I feel. Aman was so serious when he told me what he suspected. I said it was crazy. If you knew anything like that, you'd tell us."*

*I smile back. Selfless and sincere. Selfless, because for once in my life, maybe I am like him. I'm doing this for others, for him, for Corin and Aman. They'll live to see Order's new world. And I'm sincere because I didn't lie. Order didn't hurt Corin.*

*I did.*

❧❧❧

THE NEXT DAY, I BOARD a spaceship. One smaller than the ones that'd taken my brothers away. This one is made for quick, short travel with small delegations, just me, my court, and surprisingly, Caea—who doesn't want me out of her sight, and unsurprisingly Ramesis—who doesn't want another sibling out of his sight. The flight takes a few hours, and I manage not to say a word to anyone.

I pretend to sleep or trance. No one bothers me when they think I'm resting or getting my head together. They know I have work to do when we land. My court will help me, but the brunt of changing the minds of President Isiphe Akitsa and her cabinet is on me.

Last night, Kahanna spoke to me without me needing to go to Her. Told me Akitsa's alliance with Kahine needed to end. Told me Devon's skin is darker, hair longer, muscles stronger. She knows where he is. So, I'll use my power to tear down whatever She wants, to bring my brother home. To save him.

*At all costs.*

It's nonnegotiable.

A prickle of pain presses against one side of my head as something tries to burrow in. Guilt?

Am I doing the wrong thing? Is it too much, too far? What would Devon think? What would—

*Shhh.*

Cool relief and numbing gray billows between my ears. No pain. No excess thoughts. No emotion.

An arm brushes mine. Caea's as she secures her strap for take-off. She breaks the silent treatment I'd gotten since the mission briefing. "Are you all right, Lyle?"

I think I should be glad, excited that she's talking to me again.

Gray fog clouds my eyes, slows my smile.

*Shhh...*

And when I respond, it isn't to her. "Yes."

# Chapter 13

# Evan



"THAT CAN'T BE COMFORTABLE."

I crack open an eye to find Adonis staring back at me from his supine position on the bed. I sit up, attempting to stretch and flinching at a punching pain in my ribcage. Oh yeah, that's a fracture. *Fip.* The chair I'd dragged over to Adonis's bedside isn't the best choice of sleeping arrangements for broken ribs. Which is why I picked it. I wasn't supposed to sleep.

Adonis's skin lost its ashy hue after a few hours of nutrients, but his eyes are still shadowed. I lean forward, placing my hands on the soft bed pad. "How do you feel?"

"Drained." He frowns at me. "What's wrong with you?"

"Busted note."

"I don't hear it."

I shrug, replacing my hands with my face on the bed pad, the top of my head brushing one of Adonis's elbows. "How do you think it got by me? You have to dig. It's in there deep, and I don't know how."

"Do you think your life song is evolving?"

My breath is shallow. Life songs sometimes alter themselves, gaining new time signatures, key changes, and extra measures as people mature, but… "It shouldn't *fip* with my magic."

We listen to the sounds of other soldiers snoring, the quiet hiss of medical machinery, the gentle footsteps of night-shift medics making rounds through the tent.

"How did the battle end?" Adonis asks.

"All of the Nazflit that came here are dead. Jalee's sitting vigil with our soldiers that passed on. We lost thirteen today."

He sighs.

"If not for you—" I begin.

"Why did you do that?" His voice is neutral.

Wish I was neutral. "We needed to win."

"We could have won without that."

I don't raise my head.

"Was it the Stone?"

"I used it to power the spell."

"Did it tell you to choose that one?"

He shifts with an audible grunt, and I move to help him sit up. I press a button under the head of the bed to make it rise and support his back. His dark gaze dissects our surroundings.

His 'room' is a tiny square cordoned off from the rest of the tent's population by a white hover curtain. A slender cylindrical machine sits on a small table on the other side of a bed that's just large enough to cater to Adonis's long legs. Clear fluid flows from the cylinder, trickling into a tube that leads to Adonis's wrist.

He rubs the injection site before plucking out the needle. He watches blood pool, then holds out his other hand to me, palm up. I blink, then smirk. Next to my chair is a small hamper loaded with white linen. Just in case I got cold while pretending not to sleep. Courtesy of Heka.

I yank out a sheet, fold it over and over into a small square, and put it in Adonis's open hand. He presses the cloth against his bloody wrist and sighs, his attention coming back to me.

"Do you ever wonder why all the spells The Stone selects are abominations to natural magic?"

I shake my head. "Hadn't thought more beyond '*Oi vati fipping pidge.*' I could have killed you and everyone else behind me."

"Time to think beyond it, then." Adonis grimaces, applying more pressure to his wrist. His opaque eyes gleam.

I hold my breath.

He removes the sheet. No new blood seeps from the wound. "Why did you use the Stone?"

"I already told you…" And suddenly, I can't say anymore. My throat closes off like it does when I attempt to lie. Something behind my eyes pulses, the start of a headache. *Niobe-va.* I did it because we needed to win is no longer the truth for me. "I…" My heart pounds against my broken rib because the answer is… "There wasn't another choice. I tried to think, and that spell was my only choice."

"It wasn't," Adonis says.

"I know that now, but out there…" I run a hand through my tangled hair. I washed the blood out of it but didn't comb it, just bunched it up and tied it back.

I'd cut it all off if I didn't think Jalee would kill me. She likes the braid. Thick plaits are things priestesses on her home planet Faran wear. She gave up the look after her first kill in battle but declared me worthy enough to wear it for her.

Maybe she won't mind me shaving my head after what happened today.

I swallow. "It spoke to me, through the ward."

"How? You and Jalee strengthened that ward."

My ribs throb in time with my heartbeat. *Fip.* "I… I don't know." I can always feel it, but the new ward shuts the voice out. Had shut it out, until now. My thoughts jumble. Word salad shuffles though my brain as I flounder.

"Did it change on the ship? Could Imari have tampered with the ward?" Adonis's grip is steel on my forearm.

"I don't…" Imari's big black eyes shine in my memory. Her honesty sings to my recycled soul. "No. No. It's not her." Imari would never willingly hurt Corin, or me.

"The council then. Viveen. Did you feel the *rax* activate at any time?"

I shake my head. The leadership Mark down my spine, the one that tells the worlds I'm one of the Four, didn't burn or twinge. "She doesn't have the reach to activate the curse from this far away." The farthest I've ever been from Viveen before a punishment was a few rooms over. And…

"Viveen hasn't used the *rax* in a while. Not since we came back from Nakshera." Not that I've given her reason to. We've been on the same page lately. Defeat the enemy. She doesn't need to use the shock-rod curse on my back to make me behave.

"You need a diagnostic. Let me—" Adonis pushes back the blanket over his legs and tries to get out of bed. I hit the button that reclines the back of his bed and watch him wobble without support, then push him down.

He lies flat without a fight. His eyes close; the hollows beneath them make me sick.

"I'll ask Jalee in the morning," I say.

"If that thing is talking to you—"

"It hasn't since the battle. Jalee took it away. I think she bound it a few more times and put it on the ship. It feels distant." But...

"You still sense it." Adonis opens his eyes, staring at me. His eyes reflect worry, and maybe failure.

*Niobe-va*. "Adonis, it isn't your—"

"Uncle Rovn trusts me to protect you."

I blink.

"When we were little, and you didn't speak anything but your weird Earth-talk, and you ran around me in circles, and pulled me up trees and made me build stick castles in mud, I thought you were crazy."

"You were so boring." I don't know where he's going with this, but I like thinking about six-year-old me and a little Adonis who was around the same developmental age. It's a welcome distraction from the now. But not if it hurts him. His eyes glimmer, like he might... "AD, it's—"

He holds up a hand to shut me up. "I thought you were crazy, but I really just didn't know how to deal with you. You were... I didn't do things like that. Not before that season. I read and watched my mom do minor magic and practiced it until she was angry that I was better than her at it. I didn't want to do dumb things with other kids, and I thought it was fine. But then you showed me that it wasn't fine and that I did want to play. And one day..." He puts his hand on top of my head. "One day, I decided you were my brother."

I smile at him, stomach calming. Ribs not aching so much. "Was it before or after the double-headed snake incident?" Two heads, one belly, but both tried to eat us at the same time. I chuckle, thinking about Aunt Dahlia and Uncle Rovn's faces when we came home covered in snake vomit.

A long-suffering sigh from Adonis. "Luckily for you, it was before." One side of his mouth quirks. "*Gak mopi.*" The wetness in his eyes doesn't fade. "Before we left Amphora to go back to Rema, Uncle Rovn took me aside. He told me that he wanted me to stay near you. That you would need me more than you'd need anyone else. Because it hasn't been easy, has it?"

And now my eyes want to mirror his. But I already *fipping* cried today.

"I don't want the Stone to break you," Adonis says. "I don't want you to be a Champion of Order or be somebody who chooses how a war ends." He laughs, briefly, without humor. "Why couldn't you just be a normal leader of Rema? One of the ones who serve forty *revs* and retire to live out whatever fetish-fantasy they hide from the masses? You just... you can't be normal, can you?"

I snort. "Who wants to be that?"

He ruffles my hair.

"I'm sorry I'm a freak of nature," I mumble. "I'll try harder to be boring."

"I think that is the only thing in your life you'll ever honestly try and end up being horrible at."

"I *squelk* at sitar-playing," I say.

He blinks. Adonis only does that once a *jewel*. Point for me.

I rest my face on the bed again, and he keeps his hand on top of my head.

"Ev?"

"Yeah?"

"You're not allowed to die on my watch."

"You either. And you almost did." And it was almost my fault.

"You *will* let Jalee cast a diagnostic on you in the morning. And you won't touch that Stone again until she says you're alright."

I nod into the mattress.

"And after I'm recovered, we're going to analyze your song and repair it."

I hum.

"And you need to let a medic scan your ribcage. I saw you flinch."

Of course he did. Because that's what he does. Ever since we were little, and I pulled him up trees, and made him fight snakes beside me. I won't be the reason he dies. Ever. I listen to him breathe, content to stay here for the rest of the night, basking in the knowledge that he's going to be okay.

The hand still on my head yanks on a tangle.

"Ow!"

"Get your ribs scanned."

I glare. He stares.

"*Cratch.*" I get to my feet, fighting to keep a grimace off my face at the flash of pain in my chest. I look heavenward instead of back at him. "Fine. I'm going. Don't expect me back here before sunrise."

"Good. Maybe you'll sleep in a bed."

I grab the edge of his blanket and pull it over his chest. "Sleep well. I'm... uh..."

He swats my hand away and turns on his side, putting his back to me. "We won the battle. We only lost thirteen. I'm alive. Nothing to be sorry for. Now, get out."

"Love you too, brother."

Silence. I grin and drift to the rear of the tent to consult with a medic.

RIBS TREATED, PAINKILLER SWALLOWED, I hunt for Desiri. She might be sleeping in the Ievisara for the night. With Jalee sitting vigil, Desiri knows to rest in case I can't resume my commanding role and she needs to step in for a sleep deprived Jalee.

Desiri could also be napping in a dorm-tent because she's like me. I never feel right about snoozing in my nice, cushy ship when our ally soldiers spend their nights in tents on the battle ground. Not every planet has fancy live-in ships for their leaders and soldiers. These armies from the Silver and Gold Allegiance are from poorer nations. Their ships for warfare hold the bare minimum, made for carrying weapons and fundamental supplies. Soldiers get bunks and communal showers, a room to eat, a room to train. The tents might be more comfortable.

The Ievisara is a flying palace to them. I don't want to sit in a palace with soldiers out here ready to kiss my boots and hand-peel my fruit. The ones I pass on sentry duty bow deep at the waist and stare at me with stars in their eyes. Most don't even wait for me to round a corner before they whisper things like, "He's short for a god."

Growling under my breath, I continue walking through the village of white, green, and tan army tents. Nightbirds cluck, and soldiers on night-watch talk and laugh. The smell of fresh laundry and pressed leather wafts from the partially open flap of a tent with no sentry. There's a machine that washes and folds uniforms and linens and mends shoes. It's massive and earns a tent to itself.

I tilt my head as the sound of a woman singing drifts from the tent. Her voice puts toads to shame, and I'd know it anywhere. At least, I think I would. A wave of nostalgia washes over me, along with that awful sound.

I let myself into the tent and stand in the threshold, watching Imari sing to the shirt she dances with. She goes up on her bare toes and twirls, shirt sleeves fluttering as she hits a high, sour note—that turns into a shriek when she notices me.

Imari lobs her fabric dance partner at my head. I catch it in one hand as she waves her arms and rants. "You—you—you—!"

I shake out her partner and rest it over my shoulder for a slow dance. She puffs her cheeks and balls her hands into fists as I swivel closer to her, stroking the shirt like it's hair on the head of a real dance partner.

"You are such a child." She snatches the shirt off my shoulder and tosses it over hers. Her irritation evaporates as she gazes at me. "Your eyes are bright. You have been medicated."

"Stretfaur." Burns like *pidge* going down, but it raises tolerance thresholds, so nerves don't fire off pain signals.

She frowns at me, wiping sweat off her brow. Her green skin glistens with sweat, and her black hair is pulled up into a sloppy bun that looks heavier than her slender neck can hold. She wears a soldier's uniform: cargos and a flak jacket sizes too big. The sleeves are cuffed and rolled up to her elbows.

My mouth opens. She's…

"Stop thinking about how cute I am." Imari pushes my shoulder. "I know that look."

"You don't know it from me."

"I know it from someone close enough to be you." She turns serious and brings a hand to my face, knuckles pausing before brushing my skin. Her expression asks for my permission, and I lean in, cheek touching her hand.

"What are you being shy for? You can touch me, Mari."

She bites her lip and rubs my cheek, then lets her fingers travel upward into my hair. "You liked what we did?"

"It was good." I look her in the eyes, seeing the hope in them. We haven't really discussed what happened between us. There'd been flirty teasing, but not much more, as we existed around each other on the ship. "A little weird, but…" I shrug. "I liked it."

I like you. But I don't want to tell her, because 'like' isn't love. And love is what she wants, what she said she'd given up on. It isn't a lie. She's taking what she can get from me.

"I should g—"

"No." She won't let me pull away. "Sit and talk with me."

The laundry tent—suds and crud—is greenhouse warm. Its clean scent tempts me to stay as much as she does. Tables are laden with dark green, black, and gray uniform parts and boots in varying stages of falling apart. A pile of folded bed sheets sits on a large mat in the middle of the grassy floor. Imari takes my wrists and walks backward, leading me to the mound. She flops down, tugging me to her, and I let myself topple with her.

I control the landing, straddling her waist and keeping my full weight off her. Knees sinking into small mountains of fabric, I smirk as she sparkles up at me.

"Thought you wanted to talk." My voice is husky, heart speeding up. Instinct demands I kiss her. I've done enough talking today. I lean in.

"We should talk." Her warm lips graze my forehead, then she pushes my chest.

I flinch out of reflex. My ribs don't actually hurt.

Her face falls. Suddenly, we're sitting up with her probing my ribcage. "You *are* hurt. No one told me you were hurt."

"I didn't tell anyone until about a *jewel* ago." I let her touch me, enjoying the soft look on her face and the cautious taps of her fingers.

"You used the Stone," she breathes. "You said you would refrain from it. The battle site must have been bleak."

I shake my head. "The only thing that was bleak was me. The Stone controlled me. Made me think I didn't have any other choice but to use it. And..." And Adonis thought that Imari had something to do with that.

The sorrow in her demeanor tells me I was right, though. This Maiden would never hurt me. However...

"Imari, maybe it's time to tell me what you're hiding." I need to know if it has anything to do with what's wrong with me now. If she can fix it.

She wraps her arms around my waist and rests her forehead against my collarbone. "Not just yet."

Frustration brims under my skin, and my core flares. The blanket beneath us steams. Heat doesn't bother me, but it must be uncomfortable for Imari. She doesn't move. Instead, she squeezes me tighter.

"What must be done has to be performed between sunsets on a planet with dual suns, on ground that has recently tasted blood."

I try to pull away, wanting to see her face, but her hold is strong. "You're casting a spell?"

"A summons."

The word strikes me in the injury I can't feel. Pins and needles prickle across my skin. "On a planet with dual suns? You... did you get us stationed here?" The exact timing is too perfect to be coincidental.

The longer she hesitates, the more I want to shake her. Adonis was right about her after all. I try to pull away again, but the woman's arms are an iron vise around my waist.

"This battle was happening with or without you," Imari says. "But having you come here, with me, put us where we need to be. So, yes, I told Hellene that you should be sent here. You were going stir crazy on Lenore, and Hellene was eager to be rid of you for a while."

"Imari..." The snarl rumbles in my chest. What the *fip* did this woman get us into? What did she *fipping* let me lead my people into? If I had hurt anyone on our side today, it would have been her fault. She—

"My love."

I stop breathing at those words, the note in her voice.

*'My love.'* She said it as a name, my name. And her shivering timbre was beautiful in its truth. But she can't—

"Nothing about this war between gods is as you believe it to be. The fortune spell and the truth of your bloodline curse are trivial facts in the face of what the true outcome of this war will mean," she whispers. "I know what will happen, my sisters know. Corin was never to know. My only duty was to keep him ignorant, and I failed. And when She…"

Her voice breaks as she trembles. "When She broke Her promise to me by placing the curse that led to his death, I cast a 'vow' on myself. Is it strange that I can spell myself, but not others?"

I don't move. Not wanting to disturb her. Not wanting her to stop talking, from finally revealing what the *fip* this whole war is about.

"She will not be the death of you again."

The warmth of her head on my chest leaves. She tilts her chin, gazing at me. Tears rim her black eyes and roll down her face. Her nose runs, and sweat mats dark tendrils against her temples. Crying is never pretty, but it's real and raw and a deep urge begs me to smooth the hair off her face and kiss her silent. Do it now.

I want to, but I don't. Because she needs to finish. She thinks I'm going to die fighting for Order. She wants to save me from that. But the war won't stop because she found a way to hide me, and I won't run from it. I have the power to help worlds of people if I win in Order's name.

Only, I watched planets loyal to Her die. All of Her divine interventions cause a loss of sanity and mass destruction without a care. I do Her work to save the worlds within the Allegiances, to save family and friends and people who trust me enough to put their lives in my hands. But my hands are bound to a goddess who doesn't give a *fip*. Whose Gift doesn't listen when I say stop. Who doesn't rescue planets full of Her own people. Who sacrificed one-thousand faithful followers as an opening gambit.

Rough cloth brushes over my face, dragging me back to reality. Imari stands, making herself taller than me. She strokes my hair and leans forward to kiss my forehead again. A kiss for something being left behind. She'd called whatever it is she's about to do for me a parting gift so she could let go.

She smiles through tears and snot, then straightens her shoulders. "Order must die, and I know how to kill Her."

"What?" Of all the things I thought I'd hear today, that was not it. "You think know how to kill a god? Are you cra—"

Imari presses two fingers to my lips. A universal hush, but not for me. I nip her fingertips, and she squeaks. I climb to my feet so that I'm taller than her. "Your secret is that you want to kill Order?"

She glowers at me. "My secret is that we *need* to kill Order. If you want your worlds and all that you love to survive, both Order and Pandemonium must die."

She takes a step back from me so that an arm's length separates us, but it feels like a chasm. My feet are at its edge; one push and I'm dead. My body wavers, the fear and exhilaration that happens when I free-fall makes me dizzy. Do I ask more, do I just leave because she's crazy? Or do I listen for more? Because Imari might be insane, but she believes she's telling me the truth. There's no madness in her eyes. No glint of a zealot. She's nervous, wringing her hands, expression imploring.

I swallow and step off the invisible ledge between us. The sensation of falling sweeps through me, but she catches my hand and I'm steady. Waiting.

"Whichever god wins this war means to start this universe over," Imari says. "If Order wins, She means to wipe the board clean. Only Lenore and my people, and a few political leaders who were able to offer Her something She finds invaluable are to be saved. Your planets will die, like the ones you saw that day. The people will not feel anything. They will simply cease to exist. Everything She Creates later will be loyal to Her without needing to be enchanted or swayed by gifts."

I rip my hand out of Imari's and jump back as smoke rises from the mound of blankets and several tables. My core roars with heat, and the air shimmers. My pores release steam, because, "Pan's Champions were right." The Maidens and the councils and Order have been screwing us over. Tables burst into flames.

Imari gasps and rushes to the laundry machines, pulling manual override levers. Slots open and cleansing fluid sloshes onto the ground. She detaches a body-sized tube that pumps suds from a portable reservoir inside the laundry machine and sprays the tables and linens.

"Get yourself under control!" Her command is shrill. "*This* is why I did not tell you on the ship or in my garden!"

Under control? My entire mission is a godsdamn lie. Which makes my life a lie because it was given to the cause. This *pidge* on my back? The *rax*? All so I could die not saving anything but the bitch Goddess who—

"Evan!"

...who'll kill us all. Everyone is going to die. If Pandemonium wins, His Champions tried to tell me that He'd save them. That maybe He'd save me and my brothers if we didn't fight Him. If Order wins, She'll save none of us. None, but...

"Why Lenore?" My throat is dry. Too much fire. I hum to calm myself, but it doesn't work. *Niobe-va*. I'll save Order the trouble and kill us all right here.

Imari aims the spewing tube of cleansing fluid my way. Ice-cold froth hits me full blast, knocking me off my feet. The ground is spongy from cleanser and sooty from smothered fire and smoke. I lie back in the muddy mess, letting the cold liquid seep into my borrowed uniform, lowering my core temperature. When shivers set in and my teeth chatter, I dare to exhale. No steam, no smoke.

The fires around the tent are out, the flame-resistant beige canvas slightly darkened but not burned. The boots, uniforms, tables, and linens are another story. Fabric and leather are charred beyond repair, metal tables bow in the middle from exposure to extreme heat. If the fires lasted a few moments longer, the smoke and flames would have escaped the tent, threatening the rest of the camp and warning everyone that Leader One's lost his mind.

"You cannot stay like this." Imari kneels in the mud beside me. "Your body will shut down."

I'm not good with cold. My main elements are fire, air, and earth because they generate heat. My best spells involve ignitions. I run hot. On Earth, teachers and nurses always thought I had a fever and would send me home if they touched me. If they only knew I was full of fire. Fire that dies in extreme weather.

I stare up at Imari's worried face. "Tell me your story while I can't torch anything. Why will Order save Lenore? Why is She saving you?" I shut my eyes. Because there's another half-told secret. Imari must mean something to Order. "Why did She want to save Corin, so she could pair him with you? And does She want you and me to do the same?" I concentrate on how cold my body is, on my sputtering inner power source. "Order didn't Create you either. I know why I'm special. Why are you?"

Imari pulls at me, tugging me up from the marshy ground and struggling to strip off my soggy shirt. "Some of that I cannot answer until the first sunset." She flings my shirt to one side and chafes my arms. "Presently, I can tell you that Lenore is a center for magic. Order must have a focal point, a base if you will, from which to destroy and build. She cannot stand on, nor Create from, nothingness. She is not that powerful. She will draw from Lenore's magical core and the magic of my people and Create Her new world around us."

I sound dead. "All the worlds around you would die, and you were okay with that."

"I would have had him." Her voice breaks. "Lenorans only love once, Evan. We cannot give our hearts and take them back like mortals can." She hugs herself and looks down. "She promised me that he would walk with me forever. Then She killed him."

"This is revenge." I set my jaw, focusing my full attention on her, waiting for her to squirm.

She doesn't. "This is revenge."

"What happens if both gods die? Won't everything disappear?"

Imari shakes her head. "Kahanna and Kahine did not Create worlds, only beings. And those beings will not be missed."

I mull the information over. "So, we'd be godless after?"

Imari shrugs. "Who knows? Maybe new lesser gods will come to fight for this place. Maybe older gods will return to clean up what they once Created. It will not matter to me, because Kahanna and Kahine will be gone. In this moment, this lifetime, they are the biggest threats to survival. We can fret about what happens when 'the after' comes."

She says 'the after' as if murdering gods is a task to check off a list. History tells horror stories about those who trespass and anger the divine. It's why people worship and curse in the name of gods. Gods can create and erase life, give power, and take it away.

How do you kill something like that?

"What are the ingredients for a god-killing spell?" Because my gut says whatever needs to be melted down won't be goods we can purchase in a market.

One side of Imari's mouth smiles. "It is not a god-killing spell, but it will bring forth the weapon needed to kill Kahanna and Kahine. Do not worry about ingredients. I have them all. And no, the sacrifice of a thousand souls is not on the agenda."

I hear what she doesn't say. Not a thousand souls, but she doesn't eliminate the factor of mortal sacrifice. I frown at her. "What do you need?"

"I need..." The rest of her mouth smiles, and she goes to a bowed metal table. Digging through burned clothes, she locates an untouched shirt and a pair of pants and throws them at me. I catch them, cocking my head at her, as she winks. "I need for you to get dressed and take me out of here."

I gape. "What?"

"I want to ride in one of the rovers, across the plains. I want to dip my toes in the pink river one of the medics told me about. I want to go into the village beside the river and taste its famous fish porridge and have native red tea."

I think I need to lie in the mud again. I might start another fire.

"We have hours before the second dawn. No one will look for either of us until then. Well, they might look, but no search parties will be sent out until after the second sunrise." Her black eyes dance, the deep dimples in her cheeks enhancing her white smile.

She really wants to go out and do these things. The strange desperation in the tightness of her body and tone of her voice settles the kindling heat under my skin. But we were just talking about god-killing weapons and summoning spells. How did she switch from that to needing a night on the town? She truly has lost her mind.

"Imari..."

"The soldiers here say Lacak Village never sleeps. The shops will be open but not crowded because of the recent fighting. We will be free to roam and buy and taste. I... have never done such things."

She finds an uncharred towel and comes to me, rubbing the soft square over my chest and arms as I continue to stare.

"Before I was a Maiden, I had no money, only devotion. After I was a Maiden, I never had to pay or shop; things were brought to me. I never got to be anything other than a vocation."

Her melancholy eats at my soul, rousing the parts of it that are more Corin than me. He hates her despondency. The gnawing ache in my stomach not dulled by the painkiller assures me that I hate it too.

"So, you want to play before we summon a god-killing weapon?" I raise a brow.

She mirrors my look and drops the towel. "Play with me." She snatches the shirt from my hand and gets it over my head, pulling it over my shoulders. When my head pops free, all I see is her joy. She knows what I'm about to do.

I work my arms through the sleeves of the shirt. It's loose and sticks to patches of skin that are still damp. I groan and unbuckle my pants. "Turn around."

She laughs and goes up on her toes, kissing my nose and twirling around as she had earlier when she danced with the shirt. Her voice is flute-like. "I have already seen it, so there is no point in turning."

"Thought you wanted to go out?" I replace my pants and tap her shoulder. She's radiant as she links her arm with mine.

"I do. Now, let us steal one of those rovers and once we are far enough away, you will teach me to steer."

"Steal? We can just ask—"

"No." She jerks me after her, breaking into a jog and forcing me to keep up.

We push through the tent door and into the warm open air. The breeze smells like a mix of bonfire and clean laundry. The mess we made will be gossip for *cycles*. The newbie soldiers assigned to checking the suds and crud tent might *pidge* their pants in the morning.

"It is more fun to be naughty!" Imari leads me to where rows of dirty black and brown rovers wait for a morning wash beside a lopsided tent with no light inside. "This one!"

She picks the filthiest one of them all. A six-wheeled vehicle with grooved, hard rubber wheels a head taller than she is. The body of the rover is made of thick black metal, the windows of sturdy, dark-tinted plastic. I open a door for her and boost her inside, snorting as she scrambles onto the wide leather seat, then make my way to the driver's side.

She won't tell me what ingredients go into making or summoning a god-killing weapon. She's also very sure this weapon will succeed at its task and that the gods must die for the worlds to live. Imari knows what I'll do to protect others. My court. My family. People who trust me. And now, she wants to go out, like tonight's our last. Maybe she thinks I'd agree to die. And if that's what it takes, she might be right.

If the spell works.

I climb into the rover and key a generic override code into its front panel. A triangular navigation pad hums as it unfolds, and I grip its padded rims. My heart thuds, but I keep my voice neutral.

"You know where this pink river is, right?"

She laughs. "Get us out of here."

I trigger the engine, and the rover starts. Sentries round corners, staring at us in confusion. Imari waves, and I pull up on the navigation pad. We rocket over the clearing at the edge of camp and out into what could be my last night.

Chapter 14

# Devon

THE LAST FOOD TRUCK DRIVES away, full of fruit and vegetables from a harvest that would have rotted in the sun if left in the field another day. Planet Ehro is green, covered in fertile pastures that produce more food than there are people to eat it. A Silver Allegiance army from a trio of united planets brought disease and no medicine. Didn't care that this world lost a third of its population due to a plague. They took harvests in exchange for guarantees of protection from other Allegiance armies that didn't like that Ehro chose to remain impartial with all its resources.

Ehro fed Su and Nazflit worlds too, and recently decided to only export to Nazflit and Su, who never bullied them. Now, there aren't enough workers to farm the lands and fill the trucks. Nobody to get into the thick of it and be a foreman to analyze tasks and figure out how things can be done faster by whom.

"What time should I be back in the mornin', Leader Two?"

I glance over at the man who'd spoken and laugh. "You look like you jumped in a lake." His dark orange skin is slick with sweat, his coveralls damp. "Take a break and join the second shift tomorrow."

"But—"

"No buts. You earned it, my guy." I clap him on the shoulder, not caring that my fingers get all gummy from his sweat. It's working sweat. I'm drenched in it too.

Olg grins at me, and I feel a boost of comradery. He's a young guy, maybe a few years older than me, big, likes working with his hands over crunching numbers and reading documents. He really gets a kick out of the fact that me—Leader Two, the enemy's Champion, likes grunt work. I don't mind riding in hot, uncovered buggies from field to field. Jumping out and lending a hand when things get rough. Getting under trucks when stuff gets stuck.

"You sure you hafta' leave in the mornin', Leader?" Olg asks. "We never had a head foreman like you out here. I can't count up all the crops we saved and all the coin we're gonna pull in on account of it. You're gonna make us rich."

My face burns at the praise. "I mean..." I mop greasy hair that escaped my stupid man-bun off my face. "I just..." I saw a problem. Saw what nobody was doing and got out there. Then started showing everyone what I was doing until they did it too. And rinsed and repeated. And got so good at it, I got carted around to different places to do the same thing.

Mineshka had waved me off, staying behind at our last site with Xijure who's still a little shaky on his feet. She'd smiled at me in a way that made me feel proud and off I'd gone to get dirty and stinky and... solve problems.

"You're good at getting people to work with you. Building them up." Olg clasps my forearms. "Hope you can find a way to stick around."

I watch him trek through the empty field ready to be replanted. The green land reminds me of Disney cartoons from back in the day with smiling suns and singing cows. It's surreal, but almost wasn't. So much had been left to go to hell. And I helped slow its descent. Maybe somebody will pick up my written logs, my practices, and continue what I started in this region. I was… well, the people here call me a hero. Don't think I deserve that title, but…

I didn't know I could actually solve problems. Under all the grit and heavy-lifting, I had to do some multiplication and division. Had to come up with strategies and workplans. Had to be fair and considerate. I even anticipated problems and instituted fail-safes.

I'm a boss. No, this work isn't rocket science. It's about labor and people, and… I really care about that kind of stuff. I like watching people become confident about what they're doing. Laughing and sharing water, helping each other with tasks that take two pairs of arms, not one. It feels right, natural.

And when someone calls out the word 'Leader', I don't look around for anyone else. Not another brother, not Xijure. I know who they're talking to. I trot to the truck I'd been gifted after days of site-hopping—a circular, black vehicle that rumbles around on six thick, spikey wheels. It roars and grinds like a monster truck, and I'm in love. I call her Roach, because that's what she reminds me of.

I throw open the rounded door and climb into the driver's seat. The controls are like driving a stick. Which I can do. Grandpa showed me when I was fifteen and let me practice in parking lots and back roads that summer. I'd needed time apart from Lyle. I punched him. Hard. And didn't want to stop after the first swing. So, I knew I needed to get away from him.

The way he'd looked at me then… It was like something died between us. Something neither of us could fix with sweat and hard work. Or pretty words and offers to stop seeing a certain girl who will forever go unnamed for me.

My chest hurts, thinking about that day, and Lyle. Always Lyle.

There's a hollow space in my head where he should be, a constant presence even when he doesn't say or do anything. Xijure said a while ago that our separation was harder because of Lyle's power, because we're twins. His gift wrapped around me, and when it got dragged away, it pulled a bit of me with it. It hurts.

I need to see my brother. Want to see him. Want him to see me, and all of this. Look, Lyle, I'm not so stupid. I can captain these people like I did the football team. It's not really that hard, I just had to think I could.

I chuckle as I start the truck. Roach's engine purrs beneath me. The gas she runs on smells like fossil fuel, and the nostalgia of that stench almost breaks me in half harder than missing Lyle. Damn.

I want to go home.

I push Roach into drive mode and cruise down the roads, surveying plowed and harvested fields. Workers in wide-brim hats and coveralls clean up, ready to go back to their homes for the night. A few people wave and holler 'goodnight!' I wave back and roll down the window to let in the sweet smell of ripe fruit, fresh air, and wannabe diesel.

How much longer until I can go home?

My emotions are at war. I love being 'the man', but would I give it all up for a Coke, a bag of Cheetos, and a show to binge? For a few hours of Barbie Goes to Prom with my baby sister? For a weekend spent cleaning out the garage with my dad? For a regular old day of Lyle and I ignoring each other and going on about our lives, him off on some date, me heading out to run for a few miles in the sweltering Texas heat?

Yeah.

And soon, maybe I will. Mineshka and I finished our list for Pan last night.

And it's good. Though, I'm sure not everything's spelled quite right. There might be some typos, some missing things. But it's... it works. It maps out what we need from Him, and what we're willing to give. Not much. But it's something, and if He could meet us halfway, maybe we can talk more.

Who knows? We don't know how to deal with gods. All I know is that what He has us doing now, after Shiham and all that darkness, hasn't been bad. In fact, it's been better than anything I did while with the Allegiances. I know what I'm doing, feel in control. Like it. People need me to help them, because others haven't been kind, have been wrong.

And all that wrong was done by the Allegiances.

I can't ignore it. Know it's what Pan wants me to see. I'm sure Order could send me to a bunch of places that were wronged by the Nazflit or Su. It's a game, but at least Pan told me I was playing one. Order didn't. That's where the problem lays—now that I'm seeing problems, plain as day, and figuring out ways to solve them.

Problem: Order withheld information that might have made the Peredils, Harliels, and Maidens choose other sides.

Problem: Pan didn't. His followers claim to know the game. Were given all of the information before they chose.

One god laid it all out, the other manipulated. Pan isn't good, but neither is His mother. Do we trust the god with the deal, or the goddess with a prophecy that suits Her needs? Either way, worlds die.

Wish I had music to blast. Some rock, or hip hop. Hell, I'd even take some bubble gum pop. Senseless beats, stupid words to make my mind empty. I frown, wondering if the empty I want now is what Lyle needed when he took those mind-drugs.

I'd been an ass about those and need to apologize. Need to see my brother.

It takes an hour or so to get back to the camp I'd left Mineshka in Xijure in. It's all-white tents and boxy RV-looking setups. The RVs buzz with cold air, the cooling units rumbling like massive power generators, but it feels so good inside I don't care about the noise. My Roach is louder anyway.

I roar into the space behind the RV that's mine, Xijure's, and Mineshka's. The people offered to give Mineshka her own space, and we'd both balked. Then, I thought about it.

Mineshka is a woman. She should have privacy from us. However, she'd shook her head and insisted on sticking with the two smelly guys that take up too much space and brag about the size of the craps we take after lunch. Though, we hadn't done much of that lately. Xijure hasn't been up to it.

I push open the door to the RV, and cold air gives me a hug and kiss. Sorry, Roach. I think I'm cheating on you with this place now. I think the tractor that pulls it has a stick-shift-like driving pad too. The strong scent of meaty stew hits me right off, and my gaze goes to the kitchenette area. Xijure—he's up—sits at the small kitchen table, watching a pot on the countertop burner plate.

"Hey." I shut the door and make my way over.

It only takes a few steps. The RV's small inside. Bigger than other places we've had, but there's still only enough room for the three of us. When we're all inside, we constantly trip over feet or have to squeeze by each other to get through doors to the small rooms. There's a bedroom with bunks, a bathroom, and then the rest is a studio.

Xijure gazes at me, tired eyes with dark hollows beneath them glimmering. "You stink."

I stretch my arms over my head, wrists smacking the low ceiling. I bring my arms down, catching a strong whiff of my man musk. "Yep."

"Mineshka's in the shower. You're going in as soon as she gets out."

I laugh. "What's with all the hate? I smell like a hard day's work."

Xijure rolls his eyes. "You smell like a dead *sanrat* after it roasted a few days in that sun out there."

My translator taps on my brain stem. *Sanrat, a Kantar regional slang term for Saniritas, rodent species (large). Similar to Earth opossums with skunk glands.*

Gross. "Okay, I'll shower. Whatcha cooking?"

"Somebody brought it over. I'm just heating it up some more. To kill bacteria." He looks at his hands on the table, jaw set, like he's embarrassed. It pisses me off that he's mad at himself.

"Dude, it's fine." To overcook food and boil all of our drinks so they're always too hot to want to drink after work. Parasites in bad water took him down hard. He'd be an idiot not to be paranoid and extra careful now, and I'm glad of it. "I don't want bugs in my belly either. So, thanks."

Xijure grunts, and I sit down across from him. He pretends to be offended by my stink, but I don't think he minds. He eyeballs me for a minute. "You're doing good things for these people."And I don't think he just means the people on Ehro when he says that.

I shrug. "They should have people do good things for them."

He nods. "Everything we're being sent to clean up after are Allegiance messes. Pan's trying to turn us against our side."

"It's not hard to do," I say. "But I bet Order could take us to places just as bad, and it'd be Nazflit or Su's fault."

Xijure blinks at me, a flash of something in his eyes. Appreciation? Respect? I've been on the receiving end of a lot of these flashes since he's been sick.

Xijure flicks my forehead, something he does when he says I'm staring at him like a weirdo. "I'm starting to think neither god is better than the other, but—"

"At least Pan is transparent?" Mineshka steps into the room, long hair wrapped in a towel. "Whew. *Babila*, you smell like…" She breaks off, laughing at me, full on. She beams at me when she's done, and my heart warms at the fondness on her face. She reaches over to ruffle my greasy hair. "I won't be able to call you *babila* for much longer, will I?"

I shrug, liking her attention and not. She'd come into all of this thinking of me as a baby brother, someone to look after. I should mind it, but I don't. Not from her, and especially not now, when she's acting like she cares about life again. There are still very dark times where she's quiet and snaps at everyone, even me, but it's gotten better.

Mineshka winks and moves to the burner, raising a brow at the bubbling stew. "Tedew brought this for us?"

Xijure seems impressed. "How can you tell?"

"She likes the black spice." Mineshka turns the fire off under the burner. "It turns the vegetables purple." She grabs a metal spoon, stained with brown stew, from the counter beside the burner. "I think this is safe to eat, *dibu*."

*Dibu… dear one.*

Xijure earned his pet name recently, while Mineshka watched him pick at food and hesitate at drinking from water bottles. It's strange that I'm outgrowing *babila*, darling, as Xijure becomes *dibu*. Xijure's the man, but now, I am too.

"I'll serve it then," Xijure says.

Mineshka passes the spoon to him and takes a seat beside me at the table. Weeks ago, she might have argued that she was already up, so she'd serve food. Days ago, I might have said, 'Save your energy, man.' But Xijure needs to do something.

I completely understand how it feels to watch other people working their asses off and feeling guilty that you can't help. He's just not up to it yet.

"Harlew likes our proposal," Mineshka says.

Harlew, mother of Tedew and a Champion of Pan who likes to juggle and tell ghost stories to little kids after dark. Fun lady with a gentle laugh and eyes that crinkle when she smiles.

Nothing like Shiham or anything I imagined a Champion of Pan to be. She giggled at the thought of Silver and Gold Allegiance folks telling scary stories about the people in the Su and Nazflit Alliances and was disturbed to find out Allegiance folks had never heard of Pan having any Champions. Pan's people have always known about us: The Maidens, the Monarchs of Zare, and the prophecized Four. They waited, prepared.

It doesn't sit right. There's no way Order didn't know Pan had people on His side, but why would She keep that a secret from Her own Champions? It would have been better for us to know and prepare. We could have been ready for Shiham, but no. I scratch my neck and thank Xijure for the bowl of soup he sets down in front of me.

"Harlew is kind," Xijure says, "but she had suggestions too. She says we need a little more structure, and there were some things she bit her lip on."

"What's important, though, is that she didn't laugh." Mineshka takes her bowl from Xijure and blows on the broth. "She read and seemed to consider it. After she made her remarks, she smiled again and said it was good. That she would mention it to others."

"Other Champions of Pan?" I ask.

"I'm not sure." Mineshka sips her soup. "But if there are more Champions like her and less like..." Her face darkens, and she returns to her food.

"Y-yeah." I blow steam away from my bowl and watch the purple veggies bob in the brown broth. "I... How do you all feel about leaving for home? Like, if that nymph-thing comes back and just takes us away? Do you think about what we'd say to the others? I mean, I know what I'll say to Lyle and Lawrie, but Ev? Not so sure how he feels about some things. And Xijure, what about your sibs?"

"Caea and Ramesis hate fighting." Xijure sits with his own food. "If they could pass their weapons on to someone else, they would. But Dev, this bargain with Pan won't stop a war. It might make some want to engage in peace talks with outlying communities occupied by Su and Nazflit, but not every place is like the ones we've been to. And not everyone within the Allegiances is like our siblings, or us. This war is old, and there are people who just want to win. Seize land."

"Even if it means so many other people die, cease to exist? They won't be slaughtered as wartime causalities or killed as war prisoners or starve to death because the time after big wars really sucks for the people who lose or are just poor." My voice breaks. "Guys, these people will just disappear, without a choice. If our people know that—"

"But in knowing that, they'll also know that if the 'other side' doesn't choose to bargain, they'll be the ones who disappear without a choice," Xijure says. "Our people have been at odds with Nazflit and Su for so long that establishing any trust between us might be a fantasy." He frowns at his food, and my own stomach turns at his obvious discomfort.

"What do we do if we leave here? Seems like any good we could do might only be from this end." I eat heartily, wanting Xijure to see that the soup is good. Nothing tastes off. "We'd be shadow Champions."

Xijure blinks at me and snorts a laugh. "Shadow Champions? Because that sounds trustworthy." He takes a tiny sip of his soup before he looks at me again. "To do that would mean we'd tell any help coming for us to return home empty-handed, and we'd be stranded here. Relying on Pan to honor His words of protection. *Some* of His people have been nice, and He seems fair, but we can't accept any of this at face value."

I wasn't hungry when I sat down, but as soon as the food hits my stomach, I'm a bottomless pit. Could be stress-eating because... Am I thinking about not wanting to go home now? That's what my mouth said, but my brothers are 'home.' Lyle is 'home.'

We eat in silence, everyone seemingly lost in thought. We keep coming back to the same issues. We can't trust Pan. But can we trust Order? We want to go home. But if we trust Pan, then home is better protected from where we are. I think no matter what we pick we'll be wrong. I just wonder which version of wrong will cost the most lives, because that's what we're gambling with. Lives.

Xijure pushes his food away half-eaten. I don't get on him to try more. He ate more than he did yesterday. Instead, I take his soup and finish it off. I hate seeing food wasted after having to stretch rations between way too many people on our last mission. My stomach finds room for more stew.

Mineshka sets her empty bowl on the table and looks ready to say something. I lean in—she's interrupted by a knock on the door. Three hard knocks. None of the people here would knock on our door like that. They'd find it disrespectful. I wave Mineshka and Xijure down and get up to see what whoever it is wants.

The knocks come again, sharper.

"What the hell?" I stalk to the door and swing it open. And gape as a multitude of emotions flip through me, horror, rage, shock... rage. "You."

Standing in the portal of our door is snake-eyed Shiham with several hulking bodyguards behind him. His bloodred eyes look me up and down as I shake, struggling to keep my fists at my sides, before he says, "Greetings from our Lord Pan. My crew and I will be joining you for takeoff in the morning."

The kitchen table makes a loud noise as it undoubtedly gets knocked over in Xijure and Mineshka's mad rush to flank me. We glare at the snake men together, my teeth grinding together at Shiham's laugh.

I want to kill him. But would that screw up what we have with Pan? Will everything be null and void if we're able to rip that band off Shiham's wrist along with his head?

"Don't be like that, Champions of Order." Shiham has the nerve to look taken aback. "I've only just arrived, and I didn't want my presence to be a surprise when you came aboard tomorrow. There is bad blood between us, yes? I was hoping to, uh… how you say in your language, something about tools and burying them?"

I seethe and practically feel anger radiating off Mineshka and Xijure on either side of me.

Shiham chuckles softly, eyes glinting with dark humor. "Ah. Well, I look forward to serving our Lord Pan with you. Have a pleasant evening." His words drip with condescension as he holds my glare too long. Slowly breaking eye-contact, he signals for his bodyguards to move back so he can step off of our wooden stairway. They leave, heading for an RV a few cars down from us.

I punch the air where he'd been, imagining my fist smashing through his mocking smile, then whirl to face Mineshka and Xijure, speechless and furious. Mineshka's white with rage. She storms back to the kitchen table, kicking it before righting it. Xijure watches her before reaching past me to close the door. He's angry, I see it in his tight posture, but I also see the regal restraint.

"We've dealt with decent people so far." His voice is cool with a slight undercurrent of tension. "Now, it's time to see what working with Pan is truly like."

My fury slowly blends with incoming anxiety. I lock our door with a shaky hand, then turn to watch Mineshka cleaning the kitchen like she's scrubbing down a murder scene.

"Did it have to be Shiham?" It's not a question, and I can't stop grinding my teeth. "This has to be some kind of test." A cruel one.

"Shower, Devon." Xijure walks past me, heading to the bunk area. Probably to lie down.

After throwing a few more air punches at imaginary demons wearing Shiham's face, I do go shower. And I scrub hard with bar soap and a rag, to get rid of stink, dirt, and dark thoughts of Shiham and what the morning will bring for us all.

"WE CAN'T WORK WITH HIM." Mineshka crosses her arms, eyes burning embers.

"We're not. We're working with Amagorle," Xijure says. "Shiham is just traveling with us to the next spaceport and then he's gone. It'll only be a few more *jewels*."

"Why'd he pick Ehro of all places to hitch a ride?" I grumble, but I already know the answer. Shiham's new fleet is parked in the same spaceport as Amagorle's much larger one. Amagorle is yet another Champion of Pan. Pan seems to have no shortage of Champions, and none of them will give us an exact number of how many more of them are out there waiting to work with us.

Amagorle split with her larger army to hand off special supplies to Harlew on Ehro, as well as to pick us up. Once we reach the spaceport, we're to join Amagorle's army on a mission to nullify and clean up a massive oil spill on a populated moon. We met Amagorle a few hours after Shiham darkened our doorstep. Apparently, the landing sites on Ehro were designed for emissaries to pop on and off planet without a lot of noise and fanfare. It's said to be an easy rendezvous point, which sucks for the people when enemies come to town.

Amagorle is bubbly and curious about Champions of Order. She can't get over the fact that Xijure and I don't just look young but actually are. The youngest of Pan's Champions, Shiham—asshat—is over sixty Common Years old, which makes him damn near eighty in his own years. That's a lot of time to learn to be the perfect monster.

"They should have made him stay behind and leave with Harlew's crew on another ship," Mineshka growls.

I shake my head, thinking over what was said by Harlew this morning before we boarded. "Shiham's on Pan's shitlist right now. He doesn't have a choice in how to get around or where to go. The new fleet he's picking up is supposed to be much smaller than his last one. He's been stripped. Did you see his teeth?" I only noticed after breakfast.

"They're white," Xijure says. "The onyx was removed. Must have been painful."

"Not painful enough." Mineshka's voice is liquid fury. "Let's add more to our proposal. I get to be the one to extract the monster's white teeth and feed them to him while he chokes on his own blood."

I shudder, the visual making me sick—but then I see Loniad prone and convulsing on the ground, Mineshka trying to hold his neck closed as he bled out. "I'll hold him down."

We share a dark laugh that makes Xijure frown.

"We can't attack Shiham."

I punch the ship wall, not hard enough to break through the material, but a spiderweb of cracks fans across the light blue surface. Amagorle's ship is light and airy, done in pale blues and yellows with bunks for soldiers and a galley for games. It doesn't deserve the abuse, but it's either this or hunting down Shiham and doing something we'll regret later.

Though, I do wonder how much Pan would mind, since Shiham's obviously out of favor.

"We'll be civil," I say, "But if Shiham starts shit, then—"

"Then we get that gift off him and show him how well we fight when there's no cheating," Xijure says. His eyes glitter, and he finally joins in on the darkness between Mineshka and me. "I hope he does starts *pidge*."

I nod my agreement and watch Mineshka pace. I worry that she'll jump Shiham alone and start a fight she can't finish on her own. I'll have to be her shadow. Because what happened to Loniad and Ilea will not happen to her. I bargained for her life, and I'm going to keep her alive.

"Let's talk about the next mission," Xijure says. "The oil spill... on a satellite planet I've never heard of. The Su and Nazflit territories are vastly uncharted, but their maps of our territories are disturbingly accurate."

"It always seems like bad guys are the most informed." Just like on TV and comic books. Heroes win as a result of plot armor or luck, not skill and knowledge. In the real world, there is no plot armor.

Xijure grunts in agreement. "But we're becoming better informed. Let's go to the galley. We can sit at the round table and—"

The lights go out.

The room's draped in blackness so dark I reach out to grip Mineshka and Xijure's arms to make sure they're still here. "What the hell?"

"A blackout," Mineshka whispers. "But there are no running lights on the floors for safety."

"No, there are running lights." Xijure's voice comes from the floor. Did he kneel?

"Then why aren't they on?" Mineshka asks.

Xijure has no answer.

"Maybe they're no lights because there's no power?" I offer, but I'm honestly confused. Why would any lights work if the ship's power was out? Oh, holy hell. "If the power's out, will the ship…" Fall out of space? But no, no space doesn't work that way. Does it?

"The ship will drift in orbit without thrusters," Xijure supplies. "And running lights run on reserved power. They *should* be on."

"Unless someone doesn't want them on."

"Mineshka, no conspiracy theories, please," Xijure says lightly.

"This is not a conspiracy theory." Mineshka's voice is firm. "Think, King Leader. Without running lights, traveling on a spaceship is highly dangerous. Which means additional help not already there would be much slower to get to the main control rooms, or the navigation bay, which are all places where the power can be tampered with and that are advantageous for mutinous members to seize."

"It sounds like conspiracy to me," Xijure says slowly. "I say we sit down and wait for the lights to be restored. We can talk through our new ideas."

"Or we could check out the navigation and control rooms, just to be sure nothing's wrong. Maybe lend a hand." The need to mediate is strong in my chest. I don't want Mineshka and Xijure to fight.

"It's danger—"

"We jumped into an ocean to retrieve a rock that could have been imaginary," I counter. "Dangerous isn't a good argument."

A grunt from Xijure. Did he agree or did Mineshka hit him?

"Fine."

Fine? He gave up that easy? I know he's still feeling a bit off, but... "Are you okay?"

A breathy laugh comes next. "Are any of us okay?"

Touché.

"Hug the walls," I say after a moment of silence. "I'll take lead since it was my idea. But Mineshka, you've got the best spatial sense out of all of us. Let me know when I'm going the wrong way."

"Lead." Mineshka pats my arm.

"We're behind you." Xijure's voice is level with my head again. Guess he stood back up.

Running my hands along the wall, I guide my friends out of the room and into the hall.

BLOOD. NO MATTER THE RACE or the body, it all has a nasty coppery tang when it pools and sits. I cover my mouth and nose with one hand, swallowing hard as my world flashes back to the bodies of my crew. Of Loniad lying on the ground. At the explosion of blood from Ilea's middle as her guts were blown away by an energy blast.

Oh god. My boots squelch across the metal floor, slippery with a stinky liquid that can't be…

has to be…

is.

Blood.

Choked gasps echo from behind me. The others know too.

Blood is everywhere. And if the lights come back on, we'd eventually see them. Bodies… of Amagorle's people. Because it would be her people, not Shiham's. Because it would Shiham who did this.

Dammit, Shiham.

Hate and rage are black emotions that wrap around me like pythons, squeezing until I'm ready to pop. Only, I don't pop. I move faster, now stumbling over soft, yielding masses. People. The bodies. Oh no. Do I… should we… I step on someone else and stop. Xijure and Mineshka do, as well.

"What do we do with them?" I ask, shaking. We can't just leave them out to be trampled on, can we? It's disgusting. I can't keep myself from thinking about my crew's bodies, Loniad's bodies, all left lying there on Disiez. Ilea's body had been on Shiham's first ship, but I don't know what they did with it.

"We don't have time to honor them now, *babila*. We will come back. Now is time to fight. Listen…" Mineshka squeezes my hand, and I hold my loud breath to hear what she needs me to.

Without my own harsh panting in my ears, I hear it. Voices talking. People laughing. And the accent, the laugh—it's Shiham.

Mineshka hisses our location at me. Just outside the navigation room. We approach slowly, listening to the party of excited voices behind the door. A party to celebrate killing more people. Fury brings my leg up to kick in the door. I don't care about stealth or the element of surprise or battle strategies. I only care about making Shiham bleed.

Light from runners on the floor illuminate the faces of Shiham and his eight-person crew. Of course the runner lights work in here. Of course they do. I glare at Shiham and his group of murderers. That's all they know how to do, kill. And this time...

"You killed your own allies." I'm cold. My words are icy. "Where is Amagorle?"

Shiham beams at me, white teeth gleaming. "I believe you *stepped* in her on your way here, Leader."

I see red as I charge forward and get caught in a wave of stomach churning, head-screwing nausea. I barely feel my body crash to the ground.

Shiham and his power.

Behind me, I hear retching—probably Mineshka and Xijure.

If this guy would fight fair, take us on without any godly gifts, I'd rip his head off. And I'd hold onto that decapitated head like a bowling ball, fingers through its eyes, and hurl it against a wall. I don't care that it'd be gross and awful. Or that I'd be killing something. Because he deserves to die. Over and over. Because he's a piece of shit that's killed so many others and doesn't care. Laughs about it. Makes jokes. Amagorle was his ally.

He's evil. He's what people of the Allegiances think Pan is. And if more of Pan's Champions are like Shiham, then... then maybe there can't be a deal. Pan obviously can't control Shiham. Can't even keep him from killing His own. And Pan hasn't told us how many Champions He has. Evan had a number, a tally of shadows he counted in a fever dream, but that's not concrete. Order has ten Champions. Pan could have dozens.

Heavy footsteps, rubber squeaking across a blood-soaked floor. The sound stops near my head. My pulse pounds in my ears. The steel toes of boots flecked with blood fill my vision. One rears back, readying itself for a kick.

Two good kicks in the head might crack my skull.

I squeeze my eyes shut. Will my arms to move, to cover my head. Try to command my body to roll over, get up. If I don't, it's over. Over for real.

I don't want to die.

Move.

Move.

I don't want to die.

If there's anything listening right now, Order, Pan...

I don't want—

Screams unlike anything I've ever heard erupt around me. My senses flood back.

My limbs come to life, and my arms fly up to cover my head, my ears. I roll onto my side, stomach heaving. I gag and hurl two meals before struggling to my feet. My eyes open last.

And holy shit.

Shiham and his monsters are on the bloody ground, eyes wide and sightless. The running lights flicker, casting long shadows on them and the bodies of the allies they'd killed. And on her.

The nymph from before. The one who'd told us that Order sent her.

Her bare feet plod through the blood and over the bodies, heading right for me.

I stumble backward into a body in motion. Arms catch and steady me. Xijure?

"Devon… what is that? What is that thing?" Xijure croaks. His breath near my face is awful, but I don't step away because it'd bring me closer to the nymph.

My mouth opens, but I can't talk as she stops directly in front of me.

She watches, eyes full black, unblinking.

Xijure's fingers dig into my arms on either side. I feel myself being pulled, shifted, backward. He's trying to pull me behind him. But no. No, he doesn't need to protect me. I can…

Her gaze is unnerving. My body shakes. I feel Xijure's tremors as well. He stops pulling. He pants. "We need to run. We need to run."

"You can't run from Magic Breeds." Mineshka's voice is rough. "You can't. They'll hunt you. She'll hunt us. Through this ship."

"But… but…" Xijure gasps, and I hiss as his fingernails break my skin. But I can't make myself tell him to let go because she's still staring.

Then she finally speaks. "This place is empty of anyone who would harm you. You may do with it what you like. My task is complete."

"Wh—" I start.

A smaller hand grips my bicep above Xijure's iron grasp. "Devon, all of Pan's people on board are dead," Mineshka says quietly.

So? But I don't say it. Know I'm missing something.

"The ship is ours."

Ship is ours.

It's…

"You can pilot." I remember. When we were going to escape Disiez with just me, Loniad, Mineshka, Ilea, and Xijure, Mineshka said she could fly.

"I can take us back to Lenore, or anywhere. We can turn off the tracking systems and go dark. Plot a path outside of radar. I can also work navigation."

Mineshka. I want to turn and hug her, but Xijure's still gripping me too tight. And the nymph is still there. Does she want something? She said her task was done. We can go back to Order, to our families.

She walks around me and stops. I shake Xijure off, hating the strangled sound he makes, but don't look to see if he fell down or whether I hurt him. I turn to see the nymph, the bigger monster that'd killed Shiham and his group and doesn't look strained or stressed, standing beside Mineshka.

Her hand stretches out, touching Mineshka's cheek. Mineshka remains still, eyes wide as the nymph's slender fingers trace her cheekbone.

"You are beautiful." The nymph sounds half asleep, her words a lazy drawl.

Mineshka says nothing. Should I? Do I?

But Xijure catches my arm again. Lips at my ear. "What's it doing?"

"Won't you come with me?" The thing's voice draws me in. My head swims, and reality feels light, airy. Wonderful. But only here, where she is and wherever she'd take me.

I want to say I'll go. Only, she isn't talking to me.

Mineshka stammers. Licks her lips. Her eyes still large, and sad.

The nymph waits. I have a feeling it could stay there, watching, waiting, for days, weeks. What's time to a Magic Breed? Aren't they supposed to be immortal? I can't grasp that a creature similar to this is part of my family tree. Some of that weirdness is floating around in my DNA, unused.

I think about Evan, the one magic is alive inside. Oh, he's weird, but not like this.

"Mineshka," I whisper. "Mineshka, tell it 'no'."

Why would she say 'no', though? A subtle surge of desire makes me want to say, 'yes' when no one's asking me anything.

Mineshka should say 'yes' and take me too.

She should say....

No. No. She should say 'no'. We have to go home. We can go home, and... and warn people. Warn everyone about the gods, about both Pan and Order and that everything isn't what they say. Pan's deal doesn't have to be the only way if enough people know what's going on. Smarter people can help us figure it out.

"Mineshka!" I snap. "Mineshka, tell her—"

"No." Mineshka's voice is so soft I barely hear it.

The creature tilts her head. "I hear your longing."

The sway, that pull comes back. Stronger. But Mineshka said 'no'. I want to lend her strength, but I'm drowning in the weight of thinking that maybe, maybe, maybe Mineshka is wrong. I'm wrong. She should go. Go.

"No," Mineshka repeats.

"No," the nymph echoes.

Then disappears. It's gone.

The spell breaks.

"What just happened?" Xijure sounds lost.

"Order saved us," I murmur. I crack my knuckles, trying to work the tremors out of my fingers. We could have died here. The nymph could have stolen Mineshka or worse. But instead, here we are.

I think we all breathe a collective sigh of released terror.

I smell the heavy coppery scent of blood and the sour tang of puke. See the bodies littering the floor. Feel my torn skin healing from Xijure's sharp nails. My knees are weak, my stomach aches.

It's disgusting. Sickening. Shiham's people, they probably needed to die, but not Amagorle's. Not Amagorle. And Pan could think we did this. Killed two of His Champions when we didn't kill any. Because who else was here to do it that might have wanted to?

Hell, maybe Shiham was going to set me, Xijure, and Mineshka up to take the fall for Amagorle had he lived. Who knows what he had planned, because the bastard's dead, and I'm glad of it. I kick his corpse, once. Twice. Think of Loniad and Ilea and keep kicking until his flesh yields and Xijure pulls me away. Holds me back from doing more damage. Because I want to stomp his brains into the floor.

He killed so many people who were good. Who shouldn't have died. Who were people I knew. People I cared about. People who cared about me.

Shit.

I cover my face, not caring that there's blood on my hands from lying on the ground earlier. I smear it upward, into my hair as I run my fingers through it. Then, I turn and look at my team. My remaining friends. Xijure and Mineshka. Mineshka, with tears streaming down her blood-stained cheeks. Xijure, who looks gray and ready to pass out, as sick as he had been only days ago.

And I know I'm in charge right now.

I take a deep, disgusting breath, full of death and sickness and everything wrong with this picture, and say, "Mineshka, kill the tracking and plot a course for Lenore. Xijure, draft a list of people you think we can trust. We're going to tell as many of them as we can what they need to know about these gods. And we'll stop Them. Someone has to know a way to stop Them without picking sides and leaving half to die."

Mineshka scrubs tears off her face. Xijure stares at me, gaze calculating.

Uncertainty flips in my chest. Did I push too far? Say something crazy? What should I have said...?

But then Mineshka salutes and Xijure inclines his head—a motion of acceptance.

"Yes, Leader Two," they say in almost unison and move to do as I commanded.

I'm in charge, and we're going home. Where I hope everything is okay, because it won't be when we land and break the news.

Chapter 15

# Evan

IMARI DRIVES US BACK TO camp. She's a fast learner and only nearly puts me through the dashboard once on the way back, as opposed to the seven times she'd done it on the way to the village the Pink River runs beside. She's good enough to drive with one hand, while the other plays finger games with one of mine.

She steals glances at me, blushing each time she finds me staring back at her. I turn completely in my seat to memorize her as she concentrates so hard at staying on the dirt roads and making every turn.

I think about the past several weeks of living with her. She marveled over little things, like making the perfect smoothie and having several flavors out each morning for me to try. She knitted and asked shy questions about the virtual games I played. Here, she dove headfirst into learning to iron and fold clothes.

In the village, she'd never eaten off a used spoon or swam naked in a river, lake, pond, or ocean.

How can she be hundreds of Common Years old and have only lived for a few weeks of them? She makes love like someone who hasn't done it often. In all that time, Corin Peredil was her first and only lover, until me.

She smiles and tickles my hand. "You are making me nervous with all this staring. Look forward."

"Looking forward's boring." She's more interesting. She sticks her tongue out at me and massages my fingers.

"I will be boring too, soon. You will know every inch of me."

"I think I already do." I turn and lean back in my chair, laughing when she smacks my arm.

This is nice, and if it all ends in a few *jewels*, I'm glad it was this way. I take her little hand and kiss it. "Thanks."

She glances at me, gaze shuttered, and doesn't reply.

It makes my stomach flutter. There it is again. The confirmation that what's to come is going to be final for me, and "It's okay, you know."

I'm ready to sacrifice myself to save her and everyone else. It's a small thing in the face of something so great. I don't want to die, but the drive to preserve this place is stronger than that want. It's just how it has to be. Probably how it's always had to be.

The almost calm resignation taking over my body is unnerving. I should have died a month ago, when the shadow beast punched through my chest. I'd given myself up for my court—my friends. I'd been ready to die in exchange for their safety. *Hades and Ether*, I also should have drowned in the shallow pool I found my

Stone in. My lifespan was up a long time ago. I'm living on borrowed time. So, what does it really matter if I go now?

I suppress a shudder and sit up straighter. I can do this. I need to.

She frowns and grips the wheel with her steering hand as she rubs my palm. We're silent until we pull onto the campgrounds. A small crowd receives us and peppers us with questions about where we've been. I tell them out fooling around in the Pink River. The soldiers laugh, Imari hides her face in shame, and I grin, delight in her embarrassment brightening my mood, until we run into Jalee, Adonis, and Desiri who don't think we're funny at all.

I ask for privacy, and we go to Ievisara where Imari fills them in on Order's true intent and the spell Imari wants to work. There's stunned silence from Adonis and Jalee and shouting from Desiri.

I watch them cycle through the same emotions I'd experienced last night when Imari enlightened me in the laundry tent: righteous wrath, betrayal, fear... resignation. *Hades and Ether*, the resignation. It's the same as mine. We're so used to *pidge*-work we all just take it. Nothing's ever easy or without cost here.

*Niobe-va*, I feel so heavy.

Desiri and Adonis insist on going with Imari to gather the supplies she brought with her for the spell. They want to see what comprises a spell to call forth a god-killing weapon. As Adonis and Desiri start to follow Imari, Adonis shares a meaningful look with Jalee, who in turn glares and grabs me by the braid.

She drags me to her room. It's bright and decorated with pastels and tapestries of her family. Her mother and sister in their white and gray Danecian Priestess robes with braids in their long hair. Her sister is going to be coronated high priestess next season, and Jalee's already made plans to attend the ceremony. She invited me, Adonis, and Desiri and hopes Desiri won't come. And Desiri, knowing this, accepted the invitation and openly shops for embarrassing gifts to bring Jalee's family.

The passive aggressive barbs and looks crack me up. It'd be a good time, if we all could go. I've only visited Jalee's home planet, Faran, twice. She's only been home once in the past three *revs*, but she comms her mom, sister, aunts, uncles, and cousins whenever she can spend more than a few *jewels* on the line.

I'm glad she has that. It's hard to be jealous of someone else's relationship with their parents when you care about that someone very much. It keeps her level-headed and kind, something the rest of us need, and she knows it. I love her 'mommy' vibes as much as I hate them.

Jalee pushes me down on her bed and instructs the room to burn basic, cleansing herbs.

"Are you falling in love with her?"

"What?" I struggle to find my balance. Her bed is too soft. I wobble and have to plant a hand behind myself to stay sitting.

Jalee stands in front of me, squinting into my eyes. Suspicion twitches across her face.

I fiddle with the end of my braid. Some people might call it a nervous tick. I don't think I like talking about actual relationships where I want to do more than play. Imari is definitely a 'more than play' person for me. My heart beats faster.

*Am* I falling in love with Imari?

I lick my lips. "I don't know."

Jalee grunts at me, looking frustrated. "Evan, we talked about this. You know she's thinking of you as Corin Peredil."

"She's not."

"And that Corin Peredil is affecting your perception of her."

"Not anymore, Lee." I reach out, taking her hands. "He's there, but there's a difference in our feelings. I can tell."

"Can you?" Her eyes bore into mine.

And I look at my lap. "I don't know."

"That's what I thought, and I don't like it. I think you shouldn't explore it either. There are other people out there where things aren't so messy. You don't need to get tangled up with her. Why are we agreeing to this spell? Imari has dropped bomb after bomb. I know you and Adonis sense she isn't lying, but is her judgement of what needs to be done really the best? That's what I don't trust."

"But I do."

"Why?" Jalee demands. "Because you think you could fall in love her now?"

I shrug, because I'm sure I could fall in love with Imari. Just as Corin had, but differently, because we're different people. But that's not why I trust her.

Jalee's rough palm is on my forehead. "You always think you know what you're doing."

I don't, but I have to make people think I do.

"And we always catch you when you don't."

I smile as she finger-combs my fly-aways.

"We'll catch you this time too." She pokes my cheek. "Let me see what's wrong with you."

"You don't have to do this." What's wrong with me and my magic won't matter for much longer, and diagnostic spells are *crachaes* for everyone involved. "Don't waste your energy—"

"Lie down." The words aren't forceful, but her stern expression leaves no room for argument.

I lie back on the bed, legs dangling over the edge, and inhale the smoky herbs. This is going to *plore*. I count backward, shifting into trance mode, feeling myself drifting, half aware, half not, and sense Jalee's magic at the edge of mine.

"Relax your walls." Her voice is melodic, soothing.

I ease my mental barriers. Jalee's magic entering my body is a smooth sensation of satin and silk thread caressing my nerves. A distraction to keep me from tensing when she—I gasp—

"Relax."

—reaches in. Diagnostics are like hands in my ribcage, peeling my heart and lungs back like annoying skin flaps to reach my true center. I choke as Jalee digs.

"Your core isn't in sync with your life rhythms, but I can't sense why. Your energy is fine. Your magic is..." I feel her wince. "...volcanic."

A fist clenches my windpipe. I cough hoarsely, air struggling to find a way in.

"*Niobe-va.*" The pressure is gone, but the hands are still in my chest. "Don't fight me. I need to go a bit deeper."

I try to suck in more air and gag instead. "Just do it. Push." I sound like a drowning man.

Pain drills a hole through my spine. My arms and legs are numb. I forget to breathe... and then it's over. The hands withdraw. My organs fall into place, but phantom fingers haunt me. I open eyes I didn't know were closed and stare at my friend. There's a worried crease between brows.

"I can't see what's wrong with you. You need a specialist."

"It's fine." I sound awful. I roll onto my side and dry heave, moaning in misery. *Fip*, I hate diagnostics.

"It's not fine. Are you sure you want to proceed with Imari's plan? I vote we don't and that we call one of your uncles. How about Aeric, and you can check in on Lawrie?" She sounds pleased, like she's making a case I'll listen to. I kind of want to. I like her hopeful tone, but that's not what has to happen.

"You can call him after the spell." I can say that, because she can call him. She just won't need to. Gritty, sour guilt floods my mouth in the form of saliva. My stomach palpitates and I jerk away, dry heaving again. Oh, this *plores*.

"I wish you'd change your mind." She sits beside me on the bed. I hear her ask the delivery system for water and chimin leaves. She's going to make tea for my nausea. I grin at her and hug her waist from my prone position.

"I love you," I mutter.

She snorts. "Be quiet."

I close my eyes to the sound of the supplies arriving in a service chute built into a wall. Jalee's weight leaves the bed, and I sigh at the lack of warmth in the area she'd been in and rest, knowing she'll be back.

Times goes by too fast. I choke down Jalee's awful tea, let her re-braid my hair, then rise with her when Desiri comes in and says Imari's ready for us outside.

We march through the Ievisara with purpose, keeping conversations with the soldiers on board at a minimum, and soon we're out on the terrain. Desiri guides us to a private clearing that reeks of blood. A tent is set up, the door flap left open to reveal Imari and Adonis inside. I ignore the question in Imari's eyes and the wariness in Adonis's.

We take our places around the ring of candles planted in the ground. Nervous sweat beads my brow as I avoid stares in my direction as I wipe it away.

"Are you—" Desiri asks.

"Good." I nod at her, at everyone, then look directly at Imari. "Let's begin."

Imari offers me the soft smile she'd shown me in the river boat. Fluff and lace cushion my fear, and I smile back, because I really want to love her. Might be close to it, or falling, as I said earlier, and nothing about Corin Peredil is making me feel anything.

I take one of her hands, savoring the touch for a *wisp*, before taking Adonis's as well, and listen for instructions.

THE CHANT IS SIMPLE, ONLY two phrases with words no longer than two syllables. The candles crackle with green and blue flames. I only notice now that there are five candles, one for each of us. I stare into the spark that represents my soul and sing hastily memorized words.

Imari's voice increases in volume. She's the soloist while the rest us of are the chorus. Warmth spreads, entering my hands on either side, crawling toward my core, which lashes out. I stifle a gasp, struggling to fall back into the chant as the energy from the spell and my core magic wrestle each other. *Fip.*

My body cools, and the candles flicker. Imari squeezes my hand, and new energy floods the space around my core, sealing it so that it can't interfere. The magic of the chant, the power of residual life energy lingering after so much death in one place, circulates through my body.

I try to look at Imari. Did she just temporarily fix me by feeding me more power? But I can't look away from my flame as it deepens from aqua blue to navy. The sensations of reality fade, and the only thing that exists in this new empty space is me. I'm the fire as it burns upward, stretching, reaching into the sky, slicing through glistening silvery layers of atmosphere.

I breach a surface that parts like water and pull myself onto a translucent shore made of thick, clear glass that glows in the darkness. My footsteps clink across its surface. I look down and get hit with vertigo. Through the floor, *ka* below, I see myself, sprawled on my back, eyes open but glazed with a milky hue. Like I'm dead.

*Fip.* Is this it? I'm dead?

I squint. All my friends are on their backs, eyes wide and sightless. Except for Imari. She sits in front of her flame, lips still moving. In the center of the ring of white candles, there's a large silver bowl with a sprinkle of blessed water, a sprig of lasal root, a short, braided chain of hair plucked from all our heads, drops of blood from our fingertips.

"Did that *mikrit* just sacrifice us all?"

Desiri's voice thunders in the silence. I whirl to see her, Jalee, and Adonis moving toward me, crowding around to peer at our bodies.

"It was a travel spell, like last time," Jalee says.

"Except we didn't come out of the travel space," I murmur. "We're between *ethers.*"

"We can't stay here." Adonis's words are slow. "We'll die."

And maybe that's the cost. My body's heavy. It wasn't just me. It was all of us. And I didn't warn them. I thought... "*Vati pidge*, Imari!" My voice is cold, calculating. Good. I sound in control.

"She's got our blood," Desiri says through clenched teeth. "Evan—"

"I thought it would just be me!" The words tumble out. "I was the sacrifice. A Champion for... for a weapon to kill Order."

"You trusted her," Adonis says. Almost loved her.

And look where that got us. I fight the urge to be sick at her betrayal. She'd toyed with me. The want to claw my way down to the living plane and throttle Imari burns like lava. How had she been able to lie to me?

"But this means we win, right?" Jalee's tone is soft, wondering. "We saved everyone by doing this. The cost was just us and Imari can get what's needed?"

I stare at her.

"You aren't the only one who would have sacrificed themself for a greater purpose." Jalee glares. "But it would have been nice to know beforehand."

"I didn't—"

"You had us participate in this spell thinking it'd kill you!" Desiri growls and shoves me. Adonis steps back, expression so blank even I can't read it.

"It meant we won, and I knew you wouldn't do it if you knew I'd die! I thought it had to be me! I asked Imari and..." She didn't actually answer me. "*Niobe-va.*"

"I can't look at you right now," Desiri grumbles. She stamps the ground, as if it'll break and send us crashing down to the plane below.

The barrier between us and the lower plane is thick. Only spirits pass and continue.

Desiri stomps again.

"De—" I cut myself off.

Imari looks up. And *Hades and Ether*, she sees us.

"Imari?" I kneel, placing my palms on the cold glass.

She smiles, and my anger dulls, because she's so beautiful.

"Good. You made it!" Her voice has a chiming quality to it, like she's speaking through a glass tunnel.

"What did you do, witch?" Desiri drops beside me, pounding on the floor with a fist.

"Sent you on your way to get what you need." Imari looks smug. "You are between the spirit and godly *ethers*. You are as high as mortals can travel."

"Between the what?" Jalee squats on the other side of me. "What do you mean between the spirit and godly places? We can't be here! It's a violation!"

"Only if you do not have a rite of passage." Imari reaches for something beside her.

"We don't have that!" Desiri says. "Your stupid chanty spell isn't enough to get us through a godly gate! You better be able to get us..." She stops.

Imari holds up a large, white-handled, silver-bladed dagger and positions it over her navel.

Dread hits me with metal knuckles. "No!"

"You were right that a spell like this demands blood, Evan." She strokes the length of the blade. "But you were wrong about the type of blood. The blood of a god's Chosen Champion is not potent enough. Therefore, not a suitable catalyst to open the doorway you need."

"Imari..."

"This spell has a final destination. Just like the one that took us to Nakshera that time." She looks up again. "Traveling into an *ether* and then back down to a living plane simply requires power. Ascension necessitates the blood of gods."

"Imari, you're not a god!" I hit the glass. She's gone crazy.

"I am not a god."

"Then, why—"

"But my grandmother is. My father was half. My blood dries silver."

She's not lying.

"Why was *I* Chosen to be a Maiden? The poorest excuse for a temple girl. The worst Maiden. Why would Kahanna want me, Evan? Why put me in a protected position? Why desire me to be with Corin... or you? What did I tell you She wanted and why would it have anything to do with me?"

*"My grandmother is."*

Cold truth sets my teeth on edge. "Your grandmother is Order. You-you're a quarter god."

"And godly enough to be your rite of passage." Imari's tone is light.

"How?" Jalee leans forward. The brightness of the glass makes her teeth and eyes glow. "How are you Her granddaughter?"

Imari half-smiles. "Kahanna covets lineage. She wanted Children to help Her Create. Kahine is Her first son, spawned from solely Her, and He is barren. Kahsal was Her second son, one She conceived after lying with a mortal, and She favored him because he was able to give Her what She wanted. Fruit. So, Kahine killed him and my mother, before Kahanna could save them. Eighteen *revolutions* later, She and Kahine began the war."

A war that isn't over space, or planets, or life, or power after all. "Are you saying the war really started because—"

"Kahanna loved one son more than the other," Imari says. "And She wants Kahine and everything He has Created and loved to be gone. She will start over in a world untouched by Him or any other god. She could start Her family again with me... and you. You would bring Her Children of Magic with the intellect She cannot Create, and they would be of Her true line and able to help Her Create more life."

Full Magic Breeds with the balanced mental facilities of mortals.

*Fip.*

"Why didn't Order just find Herself another mortal boyfriend and make more demi-god babies?" Desiri asks.

Imari quirks a brow. "What makes you think She has not tried? It seems Her womb is limited."

I slam my mind shut on the nightmare that is Order, a quadruple breasted, shark-toothed, lightning-haired monster goddess sleeping around with random mortals. "How do you know there aren't more? Nobody knew about you." Or rather, we didn't know.

Imari traces her belly with the knife. "We sense each other. I felt my father die. I am aware of Kahanna and Kahine. Their auras hover in the furthest recess of my mind. They will know when I die, so you will not have much time." The knife stills over her navel again.

"I-Imari, I... I..." I should say it. I want to say it. She's dying for me and everyone else and deserves the words.

"Evan." Imari's smile is radiant, worthy of a goddess. "Tell Corin I loved him... and that the spell worked."

My heart shudders, then pulses like it might burst at any moment.

"I..." I can't lie. I feel her hands stroking my hair as we sit in a boat, drifting down the river under full moonlight. Smell her hair as she rests her head against my chest.

Her eyes sparkle and, if possible, she smiles brighter. That wonderful laugh floats upward, and I reach out a hand as if I can catch it, hold it.

"I know you care, and I love you, Evan."

She plunges the knife into her stomach. I can't stop watching as she jerks the blade upward, body falling forward to bleed into the silver bowl in her lap.

"*Fip,*" Desiri whispers.

Hands grip my shoulders, pull me back to sit on my heels, and cover my eyes.

"Don't watch that anymore," Adonis says.

Tremors wrack my body. "I was falling in love with her."

"Yes." Adonis removes his hands but stays close.

I've seen so many people die, some of them I was connected to, but none of them made me feel like this. Hollow, but dry. I don't cry because there are no tears inside me. It feels like there's a hole in my soul. Small, but I miss what was there. Had it been her? Had she and Corin been soulmates, making her mine as well?

What do I do? How do I fix this gash in my essence? Air whistles through it. I hear it, sense the emptiness, and want to plug it before it fills with something rotten.

"Guys." Desiri sounds awestruck.

I don't care.

"Guys!"

Adonis grips my shoulders again. I grunt as I'm turned. Pale light from the crack of an opening portal hurts my eyes.

A doorway yawns open into a garden of rainbows. Its flowers and foliage glitter like prisms made of sugar crystals. The sky is as black as space, filled with white-hot stars that flicker like digital panels winking out military codes. An invitation.

A rite of passage.

Imari gave us this.

I would have died for this. Jalee says she would have too, and Desiri and Adonis might have, as well. Imari beat us to it. She really was a Champion. Not the poorest, or the worst. And I won't waste what she gave, hole in my soul or not.

I rise to my feet, and Adonis, Desiri, and Jalee close in around me. I look at my friends, memorizing the lines and angles of their faces, the resolution in their eyes. The flowers on the other side of the door glitter, the white stars shine.

"Ready?" I don't need an answer.

Jalee takes my hand on the right, Adonis grips my wrist on the left, and Desiri grabs my shoulders. If crossing the threshold of this doorway spits us through a wormhole to nowhere, at least we'll be together.

Without a countdown or battle cry, we pass though the godly gate.

Chapter 16

# Evan

THE GARDEN OF RAINBOWS TURNS out to be a large, enclosed space with gold-veined, black marble floors and massive window walls that look out into a night sky. Triangular flower beds of multicolored, crystal-petaled flowers jut from the walls, lined by tall bushes with rainbow prisms for leaves.

There's no smell, no sound, other than what we brought with us. The flowers don't have an odor. Bright blue water silently churns in a black fountain in the center of the hexagonal room.

"Is it me or...?" I whisper, but it's still loud.

"It's not you," Desiri says. "What's wrong with this place?"

We move in a cluster with me in the middle. I stop at the fountain, studying the faceless statue in the center spouting water. Along with no physical sound, the water has no song. Nothing does. And without a song, nothing in here is alive. At least, those are the rules downstairs.

"Are we trapped?" Jalee asks. "I don't see any more doors."

"It does seem like a box," I say. "Maybe there's something else we need to do."

Only, Imari didn't share that with us.

"This is great. A trip to a godly dead end." Desiri steps up onto the fountain, pacing around its circular ledge.

I dip a finger into the water. Nothing. It's not hot, cold, wet. I'm only aware that I'm touching it because I see my hand interacting with the liquid. I bring my finger to my mouth, sucking the moisture off. I taste the salt of my own skin. My tongue only recognizes the texture of my finger pad. The water doesn't exist. I touch the stone edge.

The marble's not rough or smooth. I detect its shape with my hands, identify it with my eyes. The fact that it doesn't yield to my touch means its solid, but what the *fip*. "What is this?"

"An unfinished corner."

I spin around. Desiri leaps off the fountain and puts herself in front of me. Adonis and Jalee flank my sides. A tall woman materializes through a wall. Her deep brown skin glistens like a polished stone, her large, unblinking gold eyes seem to drink in every fiber of my being. Pressure prickles at my temples, hisses in my ears, squeezes my joints, before letting go all at once when She looks beyond me.

Her body is draped in the same prisms on the leaves and flowers, covering her from chest to ankle. The colors shift as she drifts toward us. Her hair is made of the same material, refracting light as it floats around her face, spilling over one shoulder. The multicolored hues of her clothing and hair bleed and blend the nearer she gets, until they're solid black.

She stops, standing a head taller than all of us. "Do you appreciate this form?"

I stare. She's beautiful and strange and probably not mortal. We're on a godly plane, yet she looks, feels, and sounds like a woman. "Are you an avatar?"

Her head tilts. "No."

Jalee gasps, and I turn to look at her. Her hands are over her mouth. She drops to her knees in a dramatic bow. The woman watches. We all watch, until Jalee speaks again, forehead pressed to the marble floor.

"Glory and praise to the bountiful Goddess Niobe."

*Niobe-va.*

"*Fip*—I mean... *Pid*—I..." I drop to my knees, mimicking Jalee's pose. I hear Desiri and Adonis follow suit.

"You may gaze upon Me," Niobe says, Her voice without intonation.

I sit back on my heels, looking up at the greater goddess Niobe. The mother of so many planets within so many sectors. The creator of Rema, Lenore, Amphora, Faran, Bruhje, and probably Earth.

She makes no expression as She observes us. "I have never entertained mortals in this Place, but your rite spoke My name. A rite that reeked of Kahanna." The gold in Her eyes smolders as they focus on me. "*You* reek of Kahanna."

I shudder.

"I desired to see the mortal so bold as to come here in My name with Her taint singed into his flesh, core, and mind."

She's directly in front of me.

Adonis, Desiri, and Jalee make choked noises as their bodies skid across the marble tile—away from me. Their mouths open like they want to scream, their eyes fixed on Her.

Their lips form words, 'Don't...'

Hot fingers burn my chin as it's yanked upward. My teeth clack together, and my neck strains. I'm forced to gaze into Her burning eyes. Tears blur my vision. She's too bright, but She won't let me close my eyes. I try to but can't.

"Why are you here?" Niobe's voice is so simple, one layer, an easy tone. Nothing about it sends terror down my spine. Even the bright eyes aren't menacing. She isn't angry, doesn't seem bloodthirsty. Just fascinated. Like I'm a specimen that's done something unexpected.

I struggle to clear my throat. It's hard to talk in this position. "I'm here because I want to kill Kahanna."

I don't know if that is the right or wrong thing to say. Her face gives me nothing to go on. My heart pounds, and I take deep breaths through my nose, hoping it's enough air not to pass out. This goddess could smite me right now. I can't get away. She's holding me too tight.

She hums, not loosening Her grip. My jaw is about to detach. I hear the bone and muscles creaking. What does She want me to say? What does She need to hear? My ears ring. She becomes a golden blur in my watery vision. I have to blink, but...

Relief.

I sag, falling forward on my hands, gulping air, and feeling endorphins and adrenaline course through my system, unsure of what to fix first. I keep my eyes on the ground, arms shaking. What do I do... what do I do...?

"You know that Kahanna would erase your existence." Niobe doesn't sound surprised. "Look at Me."

I sniffle, nose running and wipe my face with the backs on my hands before complying. I sit back on my heels again.

Niobe's taking me in. "Why Kahanna and Her Son have chosen not to combine Their efforts is a mystery. They would have succeeded long ago."

"It's not..." My voice is clogged with snot. I bow my head to cough but don't think it'd be a good idea to spit. I swallow hard and try again, "Kahanna had two sons. Kahine killed the other."

"Oh." Said like I told Her it was sunny out. She doesn't care.

"I want to kill Her." I force steel into my voice, hating that I'm hoarse.

"You cannot," She says.

I swear I hear Jalee in my ear, feel her hand on my arm, telling me to calm down, to wait. 'Patience,' she'd whisper.

"She can only be slain by the Hand of a Divine."

Patience. I close my eyes.

"Why did you believe *I* would raise My Hand?"

Okay. Nerves and hope tickle their way up my throat. Adrenaline and endorphins figure out their path. I'm pain-free and ready to spring to my feet if needed.

"You Created the worlds She wants to destroy. People there still worship You. Don't You..." ...feel anything? Do Gods even feel things the way we do? I don't think so. Imari told Corin she didn't feel things the way he did. She blamed it on being Lenoran. It was probably more than that.

"I left those worlds to their own means. My Sister was the One who Nurtured them. In case you are not aware, My Sister was slain in that world."

*Fip.* But She's still talking to me. She's either bored or She wants something.

"Who, if you don't mind me asking, was responsible for... Dane's death?" Dane—Jalee's patron goddess. Her family is made up of Danecian Priestesses.

The silence stretches. I chance a look behind me at Jalee, Adonis, and Desiri on their knees, staring back at me, fear making them all look younger than we are. I see the kids who played with me between training sessions. I taught them Hide and Seek, Freeze Tag—learned Desiri and Jalee had to be picked for different teams because they fought too much when left alone. We were such babies. And maybe we're not that much older now. Not to a lot of people—military, government officials, gods.

We have eighteen and nineteen Earth years between us, less than that in Remasian and Common Years, and here's where it ends. No one will know what really happened to us. The war will be fought and lost and, because Order will erase everything, we won't even be recorded as missing in action.

Niobe sighs, and I turn my attention back to Her.

"Try as I might, I cannot forget that a trivial god is the reason My Sister is dead."

I shiver. Her voice, previously emotionless, is now permafrost.

"However, that is not enough to persuade Me to raise My Hand."

She moves to the fountain, dipping a hand in the water... and notes rise from the formerly silent pool. Did She just give it life? I track Her movements as She ignores my friends in favor of Her flower beds. More music joins the chorus. We're watching a goddess complete Creation. I should be amazed, honored, but I can't be. She needs to finish what She was saying.

"What is your name, Tainted One?" She's behind me.

I stiffen. Should I turn around? But if She wanted me to be facing Her, She wouldn't have come up behind me. I remain in the same position, willing my voice to be steady as I answer, "Evan Lauduethe."

"And what would you give Me, Evan Lauduethe, as payment for raising My Hand?"

There it is. An exchange.

Gods like blood. I can't offer Her a thousand souls, or even four. They're not all mine to give, and She could be like Order. Given a thousand souls, yet She still found a loophole to abuse the *fip* out of. I can give…

"Me. I can only offer myself."

We're dead. It's over.

Her hand is like magma contained in thin plastic as it clamps onto the back of my neck. Fire scorches down the length of my spine. The Mark—the curse, bites down, magical teeth clenching my backbone, threatening to snap it. My muscles convulse as my consciousness seems to detach itself from what's going on. I know I'm seizing. I know it hurts, but I know that from the outside as I rise to a higher plane.

"I do not need a Champion."

Niobe's voice is different here. Bolder, painful, but still not as invasive or imposing as Order's.

I'm above the garden. Another plane jump where I can see the dimension below, but the ground floor is empty. I should see my body, my friends, maybe even Niobe, but there's nothing in that marble room but the garden.

Here is blank. All white, except for me.

Niobe appears, now in a long dress that matches the space around me. New sounds emerge. Breathing, and the rustling of clothes. Adonis, Jalee, and Desiri are behind me, still on their knees, like I am. Good. I don't want to be alone. I want someone to know what I offered, even if it's only for a minute and then we're roasted by heavenly fire.

"I am a Creation Goddess," Niobe says. "I engineer worlds and inspire life. I am a Mother of many things that need Tending."

Patience.

"I harbor no desire to produce celestial offspring to do this Tending, as that would dilute My power. However, I cannot oversee all that I love and Create. This leaves doorways open for lesser gods to enter and take root."

Up here, I don't feel dizzy from hyperventilation or light-headed from my heart pumping too fast. There's no nausea. So, I can be calm. "What would You have me do?"

"Serve Me."

I already serve a goddess, and it's not working out, but... Patience.

"You will Curate. Watch My loved creations and draw power from Me to remove stains."

"Like with Order's gifts?" I ask.

Niobe stares at me. I talk too much.

"Kahanna did not Create you. She needed Gifts. I need nothing to use you. But I like for My servants to be willing, indebted, grateful. You... and you..." She looks beyond me. "...shall be these things."

Wait. "Just me," I say, feeling déjà vu. I've said this before. I remember the battle on Nakshera, that shadow beast would have killed all of us, but it only wanted me. I know they'd sacrifice themselves. I know they want what I want, but... "Just me."

"No." Adonis's voice is strong.

I face them. They're all glaring at me.

"Absolutely not," Jalee says. "We came through that gate together."

"Damn straight," Desiri says. "It's all or nothing, *gak mopi.*"

"You don't know what She wants. If you'll have to change or—"

"Evan." Adonis's tone is flat. "Shut up."

If I could feel sick here, I'd probably throw up. I can't make deals that I pay for with my friends' lives.

"What are Your terms, Mother?" Jalee bows her head.

*Fip.*

Niobe smiles. Her teeth are white diamonds, and Her face softens. She becomes what Jalee called Her, a mother, in that look, but it can't be real.

"I *did* love the ones you come from, girl," Niobe says. "They worshiped Me because they knew they should. Here is your opportunity to worship properly again."

I wait for another curse to trace Order's. Something else to hurt me if I don't obey that will now be extended to my friends.

"You will be My regents across the Greater Creation Board, and you will be Altered. There will be no limit to your days, for you will no longer age. You will know pain and loss, for those you love will pass on as you continue. You will not know legacy, for you will be infertile. These powers will not be passed through a bloodline, for I will always have you."

Immortality, as a servant.

"You will come when called. Duty will not allow you to rest or delay its fulfill-ment. This means you will abandon your needs and the needs of those you feel obligated to, to serve Me first."

"Will it take us away from killing Order and Pandemonium?"

Niobe's smile graces me as well. "Your payment will not be demanded until after My Favor to you has been enacted. If you should survive, then you shall be fully Altered to serve."

"Wait, I thought You were going to Alter us now, so that we can fight—" I start.

"I will imbue you with what you need for Kahanna and the Other one." Her full lips curve into a sneer. "Use that power wisely, for it will be more than you have known. After I fulfill My bargain, yours shall begin when I command, and you shall not be able to renege. I will take you then."

"Take us?" Desiri asks.

"You cannot complete the Alteration on a lower plane."

"And then we can go back?" I ask.

Her mask of indifference returns. "You shall be able to go wherever you wish. However, time passes strangely in other realms. Those who would remember you may have ascended to the spiritly planes before your return. The ones around you now are who you should hold dear. For one day, they will be all you have left of the life you knew."

I lick dry lips. "You're not guaranteeing that what You give us now will kill Order and Pan. But if it *does* work, then we're yours, forever."

Her eyes glitter, and She gestures below. The garden beneath us vanishes. The black marble room is bare. "That is the start of a new world. One you will protect and help Nurture. I Read you, child. You would not be opposed to such tasks."

Growing gardens, helping things live? If this was a regular job offer, I'd snatch it off the table. It's the forever thing that ties my tongue in knots. But to save the world and the people in it, my needs can't matter much. Never could.

"Just to be clear, if we kill Order and Pan, nothing about our world will die because there are no gods anymore, right?" I ask. Nothing can be left ambiguous.

"Do you know how many worlds would be dead if they all needed the presence of a god?" Niobe's eyes widen slightly. "Even Kahanna's foolish creatures would live."

Another lie exposed and dispelled.

"Would our world, the place we left to come here, be one of the ones You'd enlist us to protect?" I'm sure world means universe in this conversation.

She seems to contemplate it. "You may protect that world as you see fit, but if you are called to serve elsewhere, you will abandon it. You are saving that place from Kahanna and Kahine. That is the bargain."

And it has to be enough because I have a feeling She won't offer more. After this war, if we win, the world we were born to will be someone else's problem. It'll have heroes and leaders who aren't us.

"All right." I look Her directly in the eyes. "I'll serve."

I hear my friends echo me, then feel the red heat of Niobe's hand clamped on the back of my neck all over again. Awareness of my body returns to me in a volcanic eruption. A sensation of falling tosses my boiling blood through a warp hole. Magma sears through my veins. Every cell twitches and spasms. My arms flail, trying to slow my plunge into a bottomless hole of space.

I hit the ground hard. The impact snuffs my body's process of internal combustion. My

face stings where it smacked the floor, and my head throbs.

Please don't be a concussion. I push up slowly as my limbs come back to life.

The floor is cold, and the air smells familiar. My eyes flutter open, and nostalgia and homesickness make my body temperature do a disorienting dance between hot and cold. I'm surrounded by colorful stores for toys, clothes, and shoes. To my left is a circular lobby with smaller shops and stalls inside of it, selling food and sweets and frothy drinks that froze my brain when I drank them too fast.

I clamber to wobbly legs and stomp feeling back into my feet. A kid-sized red, green, and blue train buzzes by me, heading towards a large Christmas tree in the center of the building—a mall. I'm on Earth. I laugh.

I'm home.

But it's also not real. I spin around, searching for Jalee, Adonis, Desiri, or Niobe. The only people here are like ghosts. They move around but don't see me. They talk, but their words are nonsensical. Snippets of conversations I must have overheard a long time ago.

Music plays. 'Jingle Bells.' I hated that song, because I'd sung it too many times in kiddie choir concerts where I was always stuck with the solos. I *fipping* remember the itchy elf costumes with the pointy ears and shoes. I watch a lady with long blonde hair move by me balancing a squirmy brown-haired toddler in her arms while holding... my hand.

"Mom?"

She keeps walking.

I follow. Gods, she's so pretty. She's pale-skinned, and her light hair doesn't have darker roots or an undertone of brown. So different from me and my brothers. But there are things about my face that resemble hers. The contours of our noses and eyes, our brows. People would think I was her son in a way they don't think I'm Dad's if they glimpsed us together.

Little me skips next to Mom, pointing at the looming Christmas tree, babbling about Santa Claus, who he—we—know is a fake. I was born able to hear the truth. But Devon and Lyle thought Santa was real, and that was fun, because my mean little ass teased them about not getting presents. I grin and want to keep following but can't. My legs won't go past the tree.

My family—because now I see Dad trailing behind Mom holding the hands of two little brown-haired boys, Devon and Lyle—passes the tree, heading for a toy store.

I strain to keep them in sight as they disappear into the store. Once they pass through, they're gone. I wonder if there's anything even in there. I tuck my hands in my uniform pockets. I'm wearing the borrowed clothes from last night. My chest aches, and I rub it.

Okay. This is more than a memory. If Niobe sent me here, there must be something for me to find or know. I look to the Christmas tree, and my legs regain the ability to move. I walk toward it. As I near, I notice Santa's chair is empty. The elf stations are abandoned. Lunch break? I walk around the tree, cursing 'Jingle Bells' and pause.

'Jingle Bells' isn't the only music playing.

I lean forward; the scent of pine, strong and sharp, burns my nostrils and my ears perk. The Christmas tree hums an up-tempo song full of trills and sixteenth notes with a time signature of… I stop breathing. That's my song.

This isn't a Christmas tree.

This is where my core and life song meet. The heart and soul of my magic. What does She want me to do here? I reach out and the song crescendos toward me. I hum along, rocking to its beat and stumble when it falters. The harmony clashes and the rest of the song trembles, some notes accelerate while others slow. The melody becomes a muddy mess. My ears beg me to turn it down. It's awful.

It's me.

What in *Nth Hell* happened?

"This place is interesting."

I jump-turn and nearly fall back into the tree. Niobe, dressed in green, sits in Santa's chair. "Explain this." Niobe gestures in the direction of stores, the food court, and Santa's workshop.

"It's a shopping center on Earth, during the Christmas holiday season. People come here and buy gifts for their friends and family and..." I nod at the chair She sits in. "That's Santa Claus's seat. Little kids sit in his lap and tell him what they want for Christmas."

"And what happens then?" She leans on the arm rest, placing her chin in one hand. Such a casual gesture for a major goddess.

"Ah... well, then the elves take a picture and parents print out ugly Christmas cards to send to grandparents."

Niobe's golden gaze wanders over to Santa's Workshop, a fake log cabin with signs made of green foam and white and red candy canes. Curly letters spell out 'North Pole'. I think about the story of Santa Claus and smirk. Kids believe anything if there are enough toys and candy involved.

"I am assuming this Santa Claus does not bring gifts to children?"

I shake my head. "Not even a real guy. Just a symbol of the season."

I follow Her gaze to the blinking, frosted tree that spirals upward into the unknown. A symbol of life, mine.

"I was able to remove Kahanna's claim on your body, but I could not clear the taint from your mind without delving deeper. I do not touch souls without permission. So, we are here."

"I don't know what happened." My life song slogs through second and third movements that sound like out-of-tune, amateur musicians sight-reading a symphony of errors. "My magic is going crazy because of this. The only thing that fixed it was Order's Stone." I exhale and grit my teeth, anger flaring. "She did this."

"I will allow you to locate the imperfection," Niobe says.

She reclines in Santa's chair, lifting something off the small table beside it. A box of sample chocolates? She opens it, poking at randomly shaped cocoa candies.

I stare at her for a moment longer before focusing on the tree. Closing my eyes, I concentrate on the mess of notes tumbling over each other, sorting through each. I can't stroke any into their rightful places. Something's keeping the notes from correcting themselves.

Deeper.

I move to the base of the tree, pine needles scratching at my cheeks, and kneel. The song is louder, stronger, the closer I get to the roots. A large root pulses, a discolored tumor bulging from its center, pounding at a slightly quicker pace than everything else. An infection. I reach for it, placing my hand on the hot, grainy wood. Lightning shoots up my arm as a C-sharp trills in my ears. My key signature is natural, no sharps, no flats. The C-sharp is wrong. I snatch my hand back.

The monster goddess planted this *pidge* in my body, in my core and essence. She invaded and poisoned me. Hate is a dark emotion I avoid when possible. Currently, it's not possible. I hate Order.

I rub my arm and reach for the tumor again. The same white-hot pain strikes, but it doesn't stop me from willing my hand through the flesh of the wood. My arm burrows into the root, elbow deep until I feel something solid and warm. Smooth, like a stone. I rip it out and pain tears through my abdomen. I cry out and look down, expecting to see blood burbling out of a hole in my intestines. Imari disemboweled herself, and so did I.

But my shirt is clean, intact. My middle aches like it's recovering from severe trauma, but the intense pain fades. I hold the black, palm-sized stone in the palm of my hand. It's like my Stone, except an onyx instead of an emerald. Same smooth faucets and edges. I run a finger along its curves, detect its heat. The note it sings is beautiful, but it doesn't suit my melody. One wrong note ruins everything.

I listen to my song. It's still a jumble, but one righting itself. Woodwinds scramble to find their places. The tempo adjusts. The torn root begins to heal.

"All of this trouble, because of you." I squeeze the stone and stand, venturing over to Niobe, who is eating chocolates.

"Found it." I present the stone to Her.

Niobe spares it a glance. "Did you discover how it was fused to your core?"

"I..."—don't want to sound stupid, but—"...how do I do that?"

"Do you know a memory chain melody?" Niobe selects a dome-shaped chocolate, squishing its center between Her index and thumb. Red goo oozes out. She brings it to Her mouth, nibbling at the red paste.

"Any memory melody?"

"One that resonates."

Because we have all day. I know fifteen of those songs. I hum through six of them before one makes the stone hum back. Its voice is a haunted echo, a recollection. I sit down on a blanket of fake snow, swaying as the stone sings. Note after note collects into one song—a familiar life song. A misty, melancholy downtempo composition that belongs to—

My family bustles out of the toy store. Mom still carrying Lawrie, little me still holding her hand. Dad walking, hand, hand, and hand, with Devon and...

Dammit, Lyle.

I drop the stone on the blanket and lower my head into my hands.

My little brother would not do this. Not the little brother who dream-walked and spent time in my head while I was dying. Not the kid who threw his life in the garbage to make sure the Silver Allegiance Council sent somebody to rescue me. That guy stuck to my grouchy ass like a boil, to make sure I behaved during rehabilitation after a severe battle injury. That guy doesn't eat or sleep and operates on autonomic when he grieves.

Why would he help Order? Because how else could he even get in here, if not for Her assistance?

*Fip.*

I snatch up the stone and hurl it across the mall, hear it break something.

Lyle wears Her *fipping* Stone all the time. Says it helps him deal with his power, stops the head pain, and quiets the noise of hundreds of outside thoughts. Bet it whispers to him too.

Order wouldn't have had to offer him much more than peace of mind to make him wear Her influence. To get him to betray me, though, She must have told him something, made a real bargain.

Dammit, Lyle.

Hurt envelopes me. He helped Her burrow inside my soul. Looked to Her for something he should have come to me about. What could She give to him that I couldn't?

Nausea turns my saliva sour.

Devon.

A wave of grief and an ocean of guilt flood my system.

I didn't protect Dev. Didn't fight to go after him. Consoled Lyle as if Devon was 'dead.' In my mind's eye, I see Lyle falling apart all over again, looking ready to die himself.

I told him about memory bracelets for people who went missing without bodies being produced. Pretty much said give up and was terrified that he would give up more than hope that Devon was alive. Thought he'd do something dumb. And then I left him alone. It wouldn't have been hard to turn him with an offer to save his twin.

I let that monster get my brother.

I leap to my feet, a red blaze roaring in my ears and clouding my aura. If She told Lyle She could bring Devon back, Lyle would sell his soul. He sold me—or maybe he didn't. Did he really know what would happen? He doesn't see a problem with using the Stones. He thinks they protect us, and what he helped Order do made me need the Stone to use my power properly.

*Fip*, Lyle!

If he was in front of me, I'd punch him in the teeth. But I'd help him find them all after, would even help him put them back in. Stupid little brother. I should have brought him with me, screwed the Allegiances, and gone after Devon. People would have joined me. But I didn't because governments who don't give a *pidge* about me rule my world.

Steam unfurls from my nostrils.

"You are angry." Niobe's voice is calm. She's eaten all the chocolate.

"This isn't anger." Anger is something normal people feel. The snowy blanket at my feet bursts into flames. "This is rage."

My life song is clean and clear, strong and powerful. Ready to annihilate the goddess who dared touch my family and destroy any councils stupid enough to get in my way.

Niobe's smile is something I'm truly beginning to like. She holds out a hand for me to take. I close my eyes as disorientation whirls around me. Instead of falling, I hurtle upward and am thrown onto the sensationless floor of Her Marble Room.

That's what I'll call it now.

"Evan!" Jalee rushes to me, helping me stand up then shoving me away. "You're hot!"

Adonis approaches and dusts me off, frowning. Desiri stands a distance away from us, staring out into black space. Adonis presses a hand to my temple, eyes unfocused. "You're in-tune."

I nod and feel his cool magic settle over my skin, struggling to bring down my body temp, but I won't let it.

"Niobe healed you?" Jalee asks.

"I healed me." Ice flecks my skin, and I hiss at Adonis.

"You're going to set your clothes on fire," he says. "I don't want to see you naked."

I sneer at him, breathe a wreath of flame, then smoke and count. Centering. Control. I'm taking it.

"Order's got Lyle."

"What?" Jalee asks.

"She—"

"*Ayo...*" Desiri, who'd been quiet when she's never quiet, unless she's stalking something, sounds nervous. "Does that look normal to you?"

I look out the window wall. Stars circle, converging into one, increasing in size as they gobble space. Moving closer to…

"*Niobe-va!*"

**My next unfinished projects,** Niobe's voice is a broad stroke in my mind**, are you four.**

"What does that mean?" I shout. Niobe is nowhere to be seen.

"Get down!" Adonis grabs Desiri and slings her to the floor, then pushes me and Jalee down, before throwing his body over us.

As if that would do anything to protect us from stars going nova.

White is all I see, hear, and know.

I hate gods.

All of them.

I hate

hate.

✦

WAKING UP IS LIKE RISING from the dead. I would know. My mouth tastes like ash, and my eyes burn like I've been scratching them for *jewels*. I sit up, bones cracking, body damp, clothes wet with sweat. I scrub my hands over my face and force my eyes open.

There's rough coughing on one side of me, retching on the other, and a string of curses from across the way. A tangy smell of copper and silver hangs heavy in the air.

The world around me slowly comes into full focus. The thick canvas of the tent. The circle of candles. Desiri teaching me creative ways to curse someone's relatives to several hells and back to be quartered over hot coals. Jalee showing me what she had for breakfast. Adonis wiping his mouth.

There's something else. I won't look that way. The smell comes from that way.

Imari's that way.

I hear Adonis moving in that direction. Hear cloth tearing.

"E-Ev? Wh-wh…" Jalee sounds like she's swallowed glass. "D-do you…D-did we—"

"Meet your patron goddess?" Desiri spits off to the side, getting to her feet and kicking over several candles. "Yeah, Priestess. We sure did. We…" She stops, floundering in a very un-Desiri way. She weaves like a drunk.

"What's wrong with you?" I ask.

"Shhh…" Her amber eyes are wide as stares into thin air. "I can…" She reaches out, hand closing around air, but I clench my teeth as a wind whistle screeches at her touch.

"Ow! What the *fip*?"

"I did that," Desiri says, still gazing around in wonder. "That was… I just touched magic, didn't I? I think I can see the air moving. It looks like—"

"Blue threads?" Adonis asks.

Desiri can see Magic Threads? Only people with Breed blood can see Threads.

"Is this what you see, Adonis? Am I seeing Threads, like you?" Desiri reaches into the air again, this time more gently. A soft flute plays a long-tone.

"Desiri, only nymphs see Threads."

"Do they look like tapestries all together?" Jalee's voice is still shattered, her eyes watery and red-rimmed.

Adonis nods. "They can."

"*Niobe-va,*" she murmurs, running a hand through her disheveled hair.

"She changed you." I rub Jalee's arm. "You can see magic, probably weave it."

"And you, are you different?" She wraps a hand around my arm.

I shake my head. I don't feel different. "Adonis, do you?"

He shakes his head. "I'm not sure."

Okay. I rise to my feet, helping Jalee up as well. I don't look at the ground near Adonis. I can't. "We should... should clean up. And then, we need to rally the troops. Tell them."

"Tell them what?" Desiri asks, still playing the air, strumming random notes. She can't hear the song she plays, doesn't know how horrible she sounds. I flinch, and Adonis looks pained.

"Tell them about our mutiny and see who wants to join." Because we're killing a goddess and saving my brothers. I'm also staying in control and not setting fires.

And not looking at the body on the floor.

"Hey, Ev?" Jalee tugs at the back of my shirt. "There's a burn on your neck. Looks fresh."

I bring my hand up to touch the skin and hiss at the tenderness. It doesn't hurt unless I touch it. Niobe held me there. *Vati fip.*

My fingers work clumsily at tunic buttons. When I can't get the last few undone, I rip through them, shrugging out of the shirt. My skin breathes, glad to be free of damp fabric. "What do you see?" I catch my braid and swing it over my shoulder.

"*Niobe and Dane-va.*" I shift to look at Jalee's stunned face, then turn so Desiri and Adonis can see as well.

"Tell me?" I run my hands along my spine, as if I'll feel it. As if I have ever been able to feel it. "Do you see it?" The Mark. The birthmark that stole me from Earth, that signed me up for a war, that curses me.

My friends look gray, shaken. Jalee traces the length of my spine with her fingers, then says, "It's gone."

I extend my magic, searching for the Stone's presence, listening for its song, and sense nothing.

It's *fipping* gone.

No more choke collar. No more having to do what Viveen and Theorne say. No more prophetic duty. I exhale, feeling freer than I have since I was twelve and had to understand what was expected of me as a future leader of Rema.

But how long before Order notices? Imari said Order would feel her death. She wouldn't know why or how Imari died. She might come if She actually cares and find us here, before we're ready.

"We have to go," I say.

"Yes. To clean up, and then figure out what we're going to tell people," Jalee says.

I shake my head. "No time for writing out speeches. We need to rally the troops as soon as possible. Take whoever wants to believe with us. We have to get as far away from…" I do it. I look at the ground where she should be. A tan blanket soaks through with silvery, red blood. "Order might come for her, and we can't be here if She does."

"*Pidge*." Desiri pushes open the tent flap. "I'll gather the soldiers on the west side of camp."

"East," Jalee rasps.

"South," Adonis says.

"North. Meet at the Ievisara in an hour. Whoever's not with you is on their own." This revolt can't die before it begins.

Desiri, Jalee, and Adonis rush out. Sunlight filters in through the skylight and the closing tent flap. It's still daytime. I pull my compal out of my pocket to check the time. A *facet* and a half since Imari worked the spell. Twenty Earth minutes that felt like twenty *jewels*.

Niobe's words haunt me. *"Time passes strangely in other realms."*

My hands shake as I part the tent flap, needing to go. But I can't.

I take a step back and kneel beside the blanket. Gently, I pull it back and see her. Gorgeous, glossy black hair fans around her body. Carefully, I take her shoulders and lift her, tilting her head to rest against my chest. I smooth hair off her cold face and close her staring eyes. Using the pad of my thumb, I wipe blood from lips I kissed not so long ago.

"I'm sorry." The tears that hadn't been there in the *ether* fall. I caress her round cheek, wishing the stink of blood isn't everywhere, so that I can enjoy the scent of her body one last time. "Gods, Imari. I'm sorry."

I hug her, shivering, squeezing out the last of the tears, because I can't talk to soldiers with wet eyes. Soldiers have to see strength. They need to see a leader.

I'm unMarked, but I can still boss people around with the best of them. I'm not Leader One, Champion of Order anymore, but I'm still Leader Lauduethe.

I lie Imari down on her back and cover her with the blanket again. "I threw away Order's Gift, not yours."

I push open the tent flap and step out onto a new battlefield.

## Chapter 17

# Lyle

I HATE MYSELF.

I can't stop seeing the look in Isiphe Akitsa's eyes when she realized what I was doing to her. The shift from absolute terror to dead complacency in the span of a few seconds. It was too easy to do. To reach in and crush the president of a moon's morality and plant the suggestion to give everything, the natural resources, the military, the wealth, to the Silver Allegiance without question.

The authorization took a day, and the mining of the large moon started the day after. So many people were packed onto ships and spread out, placed in resettlement camps already crowded with displaced people still waiting for new homes after years of being shoved aside.

Caea stood beside me, overseeing everything with a severe face and icy eyes. She spoke to me like she spoke to her soldiers: brisk, without nonsense or smiles.

She didn't find me afterward. Didn't knock on my door while we were on the ship journeying back to see if I was okay, as she would have before. She left the ship, trusting that someone else would get her stuff and bring it back to her quarters in the palace.

We've been here for a day, and she hasn't come to me. I know I should go to her, or I'm going to lose her. I don't want that. Not at all. Especially not now. Because I think...

I shiver, rubbing my arms as I walk down the corridor, through a familiar hallway.

I think I can't do this. I can't be Order's Champion. I can't go on another mission like that one. Can't do those things. It was too easy. So easy I didn't bleed or ache or feel tired. I just touched the woman's face and the Stone fed me what I needed to make her docile, to slip into her mind, under her defenses, and cut every chord that made Isiphe Akitsa who she was. All for Kahanna. All so She'll do what She promised.

But I don't know if it's worth it anymore. If people will want to live in a world where so much awfulness had to happen to achieve it. I don't think I want to live there. Think I'll push my brothers and family and Caea through and ask to disappear with what isn't chosen. It can't be that bad to not exist. To not feel or think or scream because this isn't what I planned for. Not what I wanted.

And Devon's still not here. Not here... And if he's not here, maybe She couldn't find him. Maybe he really is dead and She's stalling. And I'm screwed and screwed people and it's just... over. Can I let it be over?

I stumble over the threshold of the Maiden's Pavilion, feet knowing the path to Nialiah's rooms. I come here, because I don't need to impress Nialiah. I don't have to guard my words or think about how I phrase things. Nialiah understands without judgement and is honest in her responses. I think that she may even be good. A long time ago, she wanted to help a lot of people, strangers even. I can't say that.

I don't knock. Her bedroom door knows me. It opens as soon as I reach it, and I step through.

"In the parlor, Lyle." Her voice drifts from a side room. Her parlor, another room of large red and purple harem-style pillows, wall-candelabras, and a high glass ceiling spelled to show a different sky from another planet. She still won't say where.

I enter, immediately assaulted by the heavy smell of fruity perfume. My sinuses clog, and I rub my temples as I scan for her. She sits on one pillow with another propped behind her back as she reads from cream-colored parchment. A wooden box sits beside her folded legs full of folded parchment. Letters?

I haven't seen much paper in outer space. Most writing comes on a screen of some sort. The only exceptions are the heavy books in the palace library, but they might be older than the Maidens and can't be touched.

"Join me." Nialiah's eyes never leave her letters.

I trudge to her pillow and lie down. It's big enough for all of me to fit without pulling in my legs. I roll onto my back, looking up at the funny sky. "What are you reading?"

My voice sounds nasally, like I have a cold.

Nialiah waves a hand and the strong smell of perfume fades, leaving behind a light scent of apples. She glances at me. "Better?"

I sniffle. "Yeah."

She folds her letter in half and sets it on her lap. "I knew a man who wrote so beautifully that I fell in love with him."

Nialiah fell in love? "With your ex-husband?"

She reaches for another letter in the box and carefully unfolds it. "He is not truly an 'ex' as you would put it, as our ceremony was never sanctioned. We did refer to ourselves as being in union, but it was never real. So, it was easy to part ways when he could not accept my vows, easy for him to find another place and a new way." Her voice is strange.

"Do you miss him?" I ask.

A half-smile. "I think of him more."

"Ever since you saw him, right?" His planet was the one Nialiah, Evan, and Lawrie had gone to, to find Lawrie's Stone.

"Before that as well," Nialiah sighs. "I… remember simpler times, but all of it was so long ago that sometimes it seems as if none of it was ever real."

Long ago for her is centuries. It's hard to imagine and even harder to believe that she can remember back that far, or that shit was ever simple. Not when gods were always a commonplace in her life.

"Nia, I think…."

Her hand smooths my hair in a rhythmic motion that lulls me. I let my head loll to one side to look up at her. Her eyes are on her letter, but she still asks "Hmm?"

"What do you think Kahanna would do if I… if I can't do what She wants anymore. Would She kick all of my brothers and family out of the deal and only save Lenore and those other government assholes? Or do you think She might look at what I've already done and honor that as *some* payment. Maybe let my brothers and my sister and mom and dad in. Do you think I did enough for that?"

The parchment flutters into Nialiah's lap as her full attention turns to me, her black eyes wide. "Lyle, She will destroy you. You know too much. You have been in Her inner circle."

"And that's okay." I don't have the energy to sit up or make big eyes or even change my voice or facial expression. I'm tired. And done.

It's over.

"She can kill me. Or I can do it. I know I can."

"You know you can what?" Nialiah's hand freezes in my hair. Her eyes shimmer.

"Nia? Are you...?"

Wetness rims her eyes. She sighs, the breath shaky, and lies down beside me. I don't flinch as she turns, props her head on an elbow and rests her other arm across my chest.

"Sweet child, no. I will never let you do that to yourself." She rubs my chest over my heart, seeming to need to feel it beat. After it does, twice, she asks, "What happened on your mission? Tell me what you are feeling now?"

My words flow, even and smooth. They always do around her. I'm a snake. I manipulate people, kill their souls, make them do what I want. So many people lost their homes, and a good woman is a puppet for Kahanna now. And as a reward, Kahanna will erase her and all of her people. They're cannon fodder, unnecessary, because they won't be a part of Her new world.

I helped Her mark other people as unnecessary. I hate that I can do that. Hate it. Hate me. And Devon would hate me, and it'd be okay. Because I think...

"My brother's dead, Nia."

She strokes my cheek.

"I did two very awful things, for nothing." My eyes burn. But I don't want to cry. It'll make things worse. "I killed that woman. She can't ever go back to how she was. Not after what I did. And Evan... What if I changed him? I haven't talked to him since he left. What if that seed I planted made him like Isiphe?"

"Who is Isiphe?"

"The woman I ruined."

Nialiah shifts so that her body is higher than mine on the pillow and guides my head to her shoulder. I don't fight it. It feels good, warm, and she smells like apples and spice.

"You cannot let Her know how you feel," Nialiah says. Her voice is gentle. "She can do much worse than killing you."

I close my eyes. "Like what happened to Corin Peredil?"

Nialiah strokes my hair. "Corin was eaten from the inside out by madness. Such a brilliant young man. His life should not have ended that way. None of their lives should have." She's quiet for a moment. "They never should have accepted Her gifts. Not the Peredils, not the monarchs. They were all too young and naïve. They knew nothing of dealing with gods, as you still do not."

"What do I do then, Nia? Tell me why I should keep caring. I don't have to wait for Her to do anything to me, you know?"

Her fingers pause. "You will not be allowed to leave this room, if you truly are thinking of harming yourself."

"Harming myself." My own mind collapsing on itself almost killed me months ago several times. It didn't because I found ways to get rid of the pain. If I don't do that anymore, how long would it be before my brain popped for good?

"You are staying here tonight." Her words sound final.

And that's fine. I don't have anywhere else to go. My quarters are in an empty hallway. Devon's room is next to mine, Lawrie's and Evan's across from ours. A cold tingle nips at the back of my neck, and unease spreads through me like cracks across thin ice.

A premonition, then. I'm not a precog, but I get hints of things to come. Sensations that tell me to turn left instead of right. Leave now, instead of later.

Now it tells me those rooms might always be empty.

No one's coming back to them.

The burning in my eyes becomes wetness. I really didn't want to cry.

Soft lips press against my temple. "Lyle."

"Hm?"

"I want to tell you something. Something that I would have kept from you, because you seemed so determined to work with Her."

"What is it?" I ask as she brushes a tear from beneath my eye.

Nialiah hums lightly and looks up at her foreign ceiling. "I plan to leave, Lyle."

"Leave the palace? To go back to your house in the woods, like Imari did?" No, it can't be that simple. She wouldn't sound so grave. Unless she's been worried about leaving me here. I really needed our talks. "Nia, if you're ready to go home, go."

And then there'll be another room in this place empty of someone I care about. Another room no one will come back to. The ice continues to crack.

"Not my house in the woods, Lyle."

I frown. "Then where?"

She points at the sky. "To the man who wrote so beautifully about me and my shack in a swamp deep in the Northern Woods. I used to roam barefoot in skirts and pants always stained with mud, with grass in my hair and ragged nails. I loved being out in the thick of it all, being the woman others came to for fertility tonics and revenge potions."

What? Her tone is husky with sincerity and a hint of wistfulness. But I can't picture perfectly polished and refined Nialiah like that. Dirty, sloppy, living in a swampy place with muddy feet.

"I was a common witch," Nialiah chuckles lightly. "Well, maybe not so common. My magic is... formidable."

Understatement.

"But I was not a person someone would invite into town and show off, as you might say. People secreted to me. I was respected in a way, but not accepted. Then, one *cycle* a young man appeared, looking for a love potion, but left with nothing but a promise to come back the next *cycle*, and the next. Every morning after he left, I would find a letter waiting for me at my bedside. After sixty-six letters, I woke to a promise necklace and a life partner who was wonderful and kind and who wanted to live in my swamp instead of his big house. Who was willing to give up a career in foreign affairs and never look to leave Lenore, because I had no desire to abandon my devotion to the people who needed me, but who also would never acknowledge me in public."

"Why?" Why would anyone want to do anything for people who didn't appreciate them? I'm so confused. "Nialiah, you—"

"Loved Lenore and its peoples and its magic, and I would have done anything to protect and preserve and help it prosper. Anything."

"And so?"

"And so, when Kahanna became our patron goddess and changed our government and selected me to become one of Her Maidens, I accepted. Lenore had fallen into dark times, with disputes between leaders. It was a divided place of factions, until it was united under one government, an oligarchy of three. The high born, the common witch, and..." She trails off.

"Imari. The weak link, right?"

Nialiah blows a raspberry. One of the most unladylike things I've seen her do.

"Imari is anything but a weak link. Unfocused, undriven, does not know how to use what she has, but never weak."

"So, Kahanna picked her because she does have strong magic."

Nialiah laughs. "It had to do with more than that."

"What else was there?"

"Blood, Lyle." Nialiah sits up, letting my head slip off her shoulder. "There is blood. Kahanna had another child, and that child had a child with a Lenoran. And then that child fell in love with a leader and Kahanna saw Her chance to finally correct Her formula for the perfect, powerful yet ungodly beings."

I sit up with her, horror mounting as an epiphany ruptures my brain "What?" The child had a child with a Lenoran who fell in love with a leader. "Imari? Imari and... and..." Oh shit. "Corin Peredil. Shit! Imari and Evan. Nmedilah!"

She smiles at me. "They do seem very fond of each other."

"But it's not real. It's Kahanna and Imari trying to—"

"No, it is not Imari. Imari truly loved Corin, and she cares for your brother."

"The seed. The seed I planted. Do you—what if it wasn't just to make him listen to Her and use the Stone. What if—what if it makes him go after Imari when he really doesn't want to?" I... How do I feel? I was so close to not caring about anything, because I ruin everything. But... "I wanted him to stay away from her. I knew she was bad news. I knew it."

I'm worse than shit. I'm....

"Lyle, breathe please."

"No, no, no..." I try to get up, but she pulls me down. "I have to..." I don't know.

The Stone pulses. It's the first time it's woken up since I came back to Lenore. It wants to speak to me, to soothe me, but I push it out of my mind. Not now. Not now.

"I need to contact Evan and tell him never to come back here. To just go away. But what good will that do, huh? If I blow the deal, turn on Her, he's doomed anyway. You don't think She'd help my brothers at all. But well, maybe She'd help Evan because She wants his..." I groan. "What am I doing? What am I doing?"

It's unraveling. My mind feels like the cracked ice that signaled bad things to come. The Stone tries to send out healing energy, but I don't want it. Didn't know I could force it back. Not accept it. Ignore it, like Evan tries to and could before I....

Nialiah rubs my back. "I will get you something to drink and then I want you to lie down."

"No, no, no, I can't lie down." I shake her off and rush out of her rooms, faster than she can scramble up. Faster than she can run.

Every swear I know runs through my head, faster than my legs can pump. I'm out of the Pavilion. I head for one of the gardens, the one Evan took me into before he left. When he was worried about me. He shouldn't have been. He shouldn't have cared. That whole time he was thinking of ways to help me, and I was planning on hurting him. Helping Her do perverted things.

I ruined my brother, like I ruined Isiphe. And, and Devon's dead, and everything is wrong, and I want... I stumble through the garden. It's not fenced in. Lenorans don't believe in fences. The garden spills out into the woods. I can get lost out here and just not come back. I don't have supplies, won't stop for any. I'll wander until I can't.

Or until I trip.

I'm airborne for a full second before my shins hits the grass first.

"You clumsy *cratch*!"

I get to my knees, staring wildly at Caea, who scowls at me over a ring of lit candles with a friggin' hand-painted portrait of Xijure in the center. A memorial? My heart, already pounding from the run, quakes, ready to burst.

Go ahead. Burst. I don't want to be here anymore.

"Lyle?"

I get to my feet, but my ankle gives way as soon as weight hits it.

Caea grabs my wrist. "Are you okay? What's wrong?"

"Everything I can think of!" I scream at her. I try to get up again, hopping on one foot. I'll limp out of here.

"Whoa, whoa... tell me what's going on."

"I'm a piece of shit that hurts people." I nod. That was right. And hey, I'm talking to Caea like I felt I couldn't for so long. She deserves to know. "You kissed a piece of shit."

"Lyle—"

"A piece of shit that hurts people and... and..." I look at the painting of Xijure, of him in fancy clothes, smiling and happy... "And my brother's dead."

Devon's dead.

And I can't anymore.

I drop down in the grass, on my knees, shaking, trapped, and just can't.

Arms fold around me. "My brother's dead too."

"I'm sorry." I think I mean it. I'd want someone else to mean it if they said it. "I'm sorry."

She squeezes, but I don't move my arms to hold her back. I can't.

My head falls on her shoulder, soaking her sleeve with tears and undoubtedly snot. Don't care, because I can't. When the tears stop, Caea doesn't push me away. She continues to hold me, and I realize that her head's on my shoulder and my sleeve's wet too.

Because her brother is also dead.

I find the strength to bring my arms up and hold her. More tears flow. They won't stop for me or her. I don't know where all the water comes from. My cheeks and chin burn from the salty rivers my eyes bleed over them. Breathing is difficult through the fabric of Caea's sleeve. We both pant through sobs. Her body shakes against mine, as if it could break from sadness.

Maybe it can, and mine can too. We could both die here, but I'm sure she's not ready to expire yet. I should do something, but every time I try to help people it goes to hell. I'm probably killing her now, just by being near. I need to leave, to get away from her and other good people. I start to push away, but she clutches me tighter.

"Stay with me," she whispers. "I miss you."

"You shouldn't," I rasp but comply, remaining in place and resting my head on her shoulder again. Awareness blurs. I fade as I lose track of time.

Shouts come from somewhere inside the garden. Several voices, calling for Leader Two. I think Nialiah's sent people after me, but then they shout for Majesty Harliel as well.

Caea pulls away from me, staring into my eyes. Hers are simmering pools of sorrow and something else, something for me. It stirs an emotion, a vague longing I don't have the energy or desire to muster a reaction for. Caea helps me up, letting me lean on her, and starts walking us toward the palace. The place I'd run from. I don't want to go there.

"Caea, no."

Footsteps and light from spheres temporarily blind me. I blink, and my court comes into focus: Sensuen, Orion, Falun, with Ramesis and several other Zaran soldiers. Ramesis's face is wet, and Sensuen beams like a proud mother. Orion and Falun smile.

"What? What is it, Ram? Why do you look like that? Why do you all look deranged?" Caea has words where I don't.

Because I sense it. The happiness they're openly projecting. They're bristling with something they want to tell us. Something they all know we want to hear. They're sure of it.

"What is it?" Caea asks.

"He's coming home," Ramesis says.

"Who—" Caea starts.

"Xijure, Caea! Xijure… and… and Devon. They sent a message. They're on their way here. They're coming home."

My brain stops. My heart stops. I see spots. Hear words. I think I react. I feel people touching me. I even think I laugh.

Because I can.

I can.

She did it. Kahanna did it. I did what She asked, and She followed through. I'm awful and shitty, but it was worth something.

I think I kiss Caea. Think I spin her around and then we all run back inside for an emergency meeting with the councils. A meeting where we're going to talk about Devon and how he's alive and on his way.

The Stone pulses beneath my shirt, warm and welcome.

She saved my brother.

And for that, I push everything—about Imari, about Corin, and even Evan aside, to think about later. When Devon is here.

Because Kahanna didn't lie to me. She saved my brother.

# Chapter 18

# Lawrence

*"YOU'LL NEVER GUESS WHAT MINKUE was able to smuggle in for you!"
I shake a wooden box. The fruit inside it rattles like rocks. Dice fruit only blossoms
once a year for a week, each dice tree only yielding one feathery petaled fruit the size
of a fist. The pulp is syrupy and disgusting, but Corin loves it, and I'd love to see him
eat.*

*His room is dark. Thick drapes shroud the windows. The only light comes from two
candles near the foot of the bed. I make out the outline of his body, sitting on the
floor in front of them, back hunched, with something over his shoulders—a blanket,
a coat. The fabric drags across the floor. I enter the room, hoping I don't step on
anything important. Or living. Corin's rivercats are a menace. None of the mangy
felines are bigger than my foot, but all of them hiss and snarl like they're bears ready
to rip me apart. A pair of them chewed up my boots while my feet were still in them.*

"Corin?" I stop in front of him and shake the box again. "I'll give you a hint. They're sticky. And disgusting. And you scoop out the middles and add them to your porridge and crunch on the rinds to get on Theorne's nerves."

I smirk, imagining Theorne's scowl at a younger Corin showing up to a war room meeting with a box full of dice fruit. There was nothing like seeing that cratch flinch with each crispy snap of fruit shell and the corresponding dribble of orange syrup down Corin's chin. He didn't have to eat it so messily. He did it for effect, and Theorne never failed to give us something to laugh about.

I miss having Corin in meetings.

I kneel in front of my brother, setting the box of fruit on the floor so that the candlelight catches its angles, and frown at him. The bones under the ashy brown skin of his face are prominent, his eyes sunken. Dark gold hair hangs lanky and greasy over his narrow shoulders. "Cor, it's dice fruit. Fresh, just harvested yesterday. Minkue was able to get you six of them. Can you believe that?"

I put on my storytelling voice, the one the kids like so much when I do obligatory school visits. Who knew so much of being a leader involved going around making the public think you're their best friend, favorite son, and beloved uncle? I don't mind visiting the kids. Corin didn't used to either.

"Brother?" I touch his shoulder. "Six fat dice fruit. And I've got spoons in my pocket. Or we could go to the kitchen and blend them into a drink, or..."

"Aman? When did you come?" Corin's husky voice lacks any hints of its former musicality. My stomach clenches. Everything about my brother is fading away.

I force a smile. "Just now. I have treats. Let me open the curtains, so you can see how big these nasty kruks are! I don't know how you eat them!" I start to my feet, but a bony hand grabs my wrist.

Corin's gaze is intense. My chest tightens at the fever-bright gleam in his eyes. My free hand goes to his forehead, checking for a high temperature. The skin's oily and cool. He releases my wrist, his hand falling back to his side, eyes focusing on the candles.

"Spirits don't like light, Aman."

"There aren't any spirits in here."

That's it. I'm opening the windows. I move to get up again, and he doesn't stop me.

"You haven't been able to work magic in weeks, so I know you haven't summoned any ghosts." I reach the first curtain and feel along the wall beside it for the adjustment knob. Sunlight pours into the room, a thick square of it spilling over the bed onto the floor.

Corin pulls the blanket over his face. How long has it been since he's seen daylight?

I unlock the window and push it open. Cool, salt-tinged air flows in, the new elements tickling my face as they rush by. Soon, all four windows on the sea-facing wall are open and I'm reminded that Corin's favorite colors are gold and green.

I gaze around the space, taking it all in. "Niobe the Great, behold Corin's dungeon! I forgot the walls are green and that bedspread is gold. And look, there are plants... wilting... in every corner. And is something alive on that dinner plate? When's the last time anyone's cleaned in here?"

Probably the last time I was home, which was a month ago.

It takes three long strides to reach the foot of the bed and only one rough yank to get him up. "You're coming to my room. I'll send someone in here to... to do something, but you're with me."

He doesn't fight me. People have to care to fight, and I don't think he does.

I gasp as he leans against my shoulder, resting his light weight on me. As if standing straight is just too hard. "First, we'll get you bathed and changed into something clean, and... I'll have someone prepare your fruit. Porridge is good, right?"

*I talk to myself as I shuffle him out of the room. I don't think I expect him to respond to me, and it hurts, because I'm used to this silence. It's not the quiet of someone ignoring me or even pondering my words to know what to say next. It's an absence of presence. My brother isn't here, and I'd give anything to know where he goes.*

*The house is empty today. Padain went riding, and Jain... I don't know. He might spend as much time alone as Corin does these days. We're falling apart. The war is killing us on and off the battlefield. We don't share meals together anymore. I don't know the twins' schedules. I only see them at meetings. We're sent to different planets and territories, spending months on ships flying here and there without direct word. And now that Corin's unfit for duty, he's left here alone. Aides come by to make sure there's food and water, but they obviously don't do much more than that.*

*When we invested in this house, we thought it would help. But it's rare that we're all on-planet at the same time, and when we are, we're not here long enough to pass more than greetings. Corin gets neglected.*

*The walk to my room from his is short. My door is open, and I usher him inside, pushing him onto my unmade bed so I can run bath water. I'll wash his hair too. He doesn't like my cleansers, but that's too bad. If he'd keep himself clean, then he wouldn't have to suffer my inorganic products.*

*"If you can, go ahead and get undressed!" I call through the bathroom door. I'm not optimistic enough to think I'll come out and find him disrobing. I'll have to do that for him.*

*I sit on the edge of my round, silver bathtub, watching the bottom fill with blue water. Once the tub is full, I shake in cleansing crystals from a cannister and urge the water to stir itself, pushing hydrogen and oxygen molecules around. "Okay, Corin. Here I come."*

*I leave the silver bathroom space and head into my adjoined bedroom.*

"Fipping pidge!" My heart jumps out of my throat at the sight of Jain sitting on the bed tugging Corin's tunic over his head.

"Good morning to you, Aman." Jain always sounds bored. It's his default tone, before he thinks to adjust it for his audience. Psychics are cold pieces of work. I've never met one who honestly likes to interact with people. My brother is no exception to that, though he tries with us.

It helps that he has Padain to speak for him. Or rather he had Padain. I don't ask, because I know neither will tell me about it, but something happened between them. Between all of us.

And it's Her fault.

"I thought you were gone for the day," I say.

Jain attends private council meetings. He seems to get on well with Theorne and Viveen nowadays. They consort with him, and he often knows about missions and decisions before us.

"No." Jain tosses Corin's dirty tunic on the floor and leans in, brushing Corin's long, tangled hair off his neck and back to stare at the divine Mark on his spine. His fingers hover. "It's still there."

"Did you think it would go away?" I ask. "Nothing I've learned or read ever mentions gods retracting curses."

"Why do you keep calling it a curse?" Jain studies me, green eyes like probe-knives. "Order has only made Her Choice visible. He is Her only Champion that displays Her personal touch on his body."

"He doesn't seem to like it much." I narrow my eyes. Jain looks tired, strained. "And he didn't start..." I wave a hand at Corin as he stares straight forward, shivering without his shirt. "This didn't start until after that Mark appeared. He said he was cursed. She's punishing him. And this war, it's out of control.

"We can't win without Corin's strategies. We can't win without him being able to use the Stone. Fipfak, Jain. Majesty Yarhine was practically beheaded. She's not going to make it. And her brothers are leading the Zaran forces like idiots. We've lost Sector Six. We're losing Sector Eleven. Order's not talking to anyone but The Maidens, who I think are only telling us what they want us to know. And you know what, I think there's something more. The Gold and Silver Councils, there are people on it who—"

"Shut up, Aman." Jain's voice is deadly. He brushes Corin's hair to hide the Mark again and stands, shifting Corin to work off his pants. "You don't understand what you're talking about."

"I don't understand?" I'm the genius of the Four. If I don't understand, who does? "Jain, you don't trust anyone besides maybe us, yet you're defending The Maidens and the councils... and Viveen and Theorne?" I thought he'd just been playing them close to his chest but maybe... "Jain, what do you talk about with Theorne and Viveen? Why are you so supportive of Order all of a sudden?"

Not all of a sudden. His support started a few weeks before Corin made his first battle mistake—a misjudgment of the placement of certain troops that shouldn't have happened. The situation had been too basic for someone as brilliant as Corin to overlook such a trap. From there, he spiraled.

And Jain had been quiet, not chiming into family discussions Padain and I had about forcing Corin to see a physician, until it was clear our older brother was broken. And when Jain did enter the conversation, he never associated Corin's illness with anything divine. He blamed the stress of war, the guilt of losing soldiers, the failed relationship between Corin and Maiden Imari. Perhaps ill-fated love broke h im.

Jain stands Corin up, catching him as he sways. "I'll bathe him. I've done it before." He looks away. "I came back here after my meeting to do it."

*And because Corin is rumpled and oily but not wild child-level dirty, Jain's probably been doing it for a while. I almost palm my forehead. With all that hair Corin has, if it's not washed or combed often, it mats and locks. The servants don't touch him. I haven't been here, and I think Padain might eat his own foot before he washes someone else's.*

*"Jain..."*

*"You and Padain are the better fighters," Jain says simply, guiding Corin to the bathroom. "I'm better here with our council and with him." Guilt darkens his eyes—at least I think it's guilt.*

*But why is he guilty?*

*"You didn't answer my question, Jain. What do you, Theorne, and Viveen talk about in the Third Hall? I know you three meet there alone. And when did you become such a staunch supporter of Order?"*

*He doesn't answer. Irritation festers under my skin. I march to the bathroom door, lingering in the archway as Jain helps Corin sink into the bath. The tub is deep, and I'd filled it with water enough to touch his ears if he wants to lounge. Maybe that wasn't such a good idea. I urge the water molecules to poke at the tub's side drains and smile when the water level recedes to just below Corin's breastbone.*

*Jain nods at me, then turns his attention to Corin.*

*My middle brother is so very good at deflecting conversations from himself. He doesn't like talking. It's a defense mechanism, but he doesn't need to defend himself from his brothers. Unless he's hiding something.*

*"Jain—"*

*"What makes you think I didn't support Order before? I accepted Her Gift, same as you."*

*"You didn't like it. You complained. You didn't want to be a leader. You wanted to stay back and take an advisory role."*

*"But none of that ever mattered. This is the vocation I was given by a god. There's nothing I can do. Should I resist it forever? That's meaningless and tiring. So, here we are."* He relies on his default tone, but his jerky movements as he twists Corin's hair into a knot atop his head betray his emotions. I meffed *him off*. Good.

*"What do you, Theorne, and Viveen talk—"*

*"The war! We talk about the war and how to win it."* Jain glares at me. *"What else would we talk about, Aman? Are you accusing me of something?"*

*I step back. His expression is foreign, dark and...* Pidge. *The air feels heavy, like he's pressing it with his telekinesis.*

*"You and Padain."* Jain picks up the sponge and squirts orange cleansing gel onto it. *"You find fault with me at every turn. I'm not invested in the war. I don't care enough about our people or our troops. I don't seem like I wish for victory. I don't want to be here. I'd run if I could. Is that all of it?"*

*"I..."*

*Before. Before we encountered Order. Before Rema met the requirements and was allowed to join the Silver Allegiance of Planets. Back when we were fresh from our specialist academies.*

*Jain didn't want any part of what Corin, Padain, and I had planned for our future. We bullied him into our dream. The Peredil brothers, the last of the former royal bloodline of Rema, becoming leaders. We were ready to make Rema a universal power. No more backwater planet status for us. We deserved the greatness that came with being part of a planetary allegiance: the protection, the shared technological and magical advances, the acknowledgement. "I do everything you want in the end, don't I?" Jain washes Corin's back and shoulders. "I used my powers to fight. I accepted a destiny that only the insane would open themselves to. I sit on war councils and listen to thoughts and feel the emotions of world leaders who hate each other and couldn't give a pidge about the people they're sworn to protect. It hurts, Aman. But I do it because you want me to."*

*"Jain, I..."*

*"And now, this." He swallows and drops the sponge into the bath. "It's not going well. The war. We're losing. And we need a way out." Jain takes down Corin's hair and parts it into multiple sections with his fingers. The motions are deft and done with a familiarity that makes my heart ache.*

*My legs feel weak. I stagger over to my brothers and sit on the floor in front of the tub, entranced by the frothy sound of Jain lathering hair cleansing gel between his palms. The edges of my world fray, bits of black dance along the outermost regions of my consciousness. We're going to lose this war, and I can't bring myself to want to comprehend what it'll mean for us, for Rema, for everyone on our side.*

*I don't talk about it with anyone. I don't have close friends anymore. They were all soldiers, and most died in battle, the others are spread far and few. My brothers are... I close my eyes, breath choking in my lungs for an awful second before I let out a shaky exhale.*

*But Jain's here now. And he's talking. He's letting me in. Letting me see how upset he is. Caring for Corin like I thought no one else was. He's afraid. He's sad. And...*

*"There's a way out?" I ask.*

*Corin murmurs under his breath, and Jain shushes him before gazing at me. "Trust me."*

*The imploring light in his eyes sings of desperation, of something fragile and perilous and... "Jain, have you done something?"*

*Corin moans, and Jain kisses his forehead. "You're okay."*

*"Jain?" I ask, but his focus remains on Corin. "Did you do something?"*

*He pushes Corin's head under the water. "What makes you ask that?"*

I DROWN IN BLACK WATER. I can't see, can't breathe. Sound is muffled. And the water is... Shizz. It's not hot or cold, not heavy or light. I can't sense it against my body. So how do I even know it's water? I reach out. Phantom hydrogen and oxygen molecules flutter around a nucleus that I want to touch.

Sound breaks through the water barrier. Someone's screaming, voice breaking like a twelve-year-old's as they cry out, "Mom-mom-mom-mom-mom!" And fugnugget. *That's* me.

The blackness—the nightmare—drains, leaving me soaking wet. Sweat rests on top of me like a blanket. I kick out a leg. No sheet or cover hinders the movement. I roll onto my stomach, one arm flopping off the side of... of the bed, my fingers tracing what has to be a tangle of sheets on fuzzy carpet. Oxygen, hydrogen, carbon, nitrogen—cotton. And I can feel it all.

My nose tickles as I inhale the musty scent of my own body stink on the pillow.

Smell. Sound. Touch. Why is it weird to me that I can do these things? My brain's a mound of mush that bubbles like warming oatmeal. Each popping bubble is a shimmer of awareness—flashes of facts about things I should know, but I can't process them.

What time is it? Is it time to go to the clinic? Is this my last day to...?

No, no, I think I went to the clinic.

The procedure table was soft. And I counted backwards into nothingness. Terror spikes within me, shattering my ribcage and screaming in my ears until there's nothing but white noise. Wetness seeps from my nose, forming a puddle the size of my face on the sheets.

Fug. Fug. If I raise my head, open my eyes, and can't see, then what? It didn't work. And fug, do I really want to know right now?

The sound of feet pounding up the stairs breaks through the haze of white noise clouding my malfunctioning brain. Carbon dioxide molecules circled by nitrogen and water vapor rotate around a large body of carbon, hydrogen, oxygen... I sit up, back cracking, limbs heavy.

Evan?

Another body rushes behind him. Uncle Aeric.

They both smell like outside as they crash through the doorway.

"What happened? Are you okay?" My brother's voice is hard, like he's ordering me to speak. What'd I do to him?

And fug. When'd he get here?

Rough hands grab my face, tilting my head back. "Open your eyes." More orders.

And slowly. Carefully. I let it happen.

My lids part.

Tears spill down my cheeks as weak light pokes at my eyeballs. I squeeze them shut for a moment, bracing myself for more much desired pain, and open my eyes wide. Light attacks. I squint but won't shield my eyes, not while a blurry face is focusing. Messy curls, large, worried eyes, straight nose, deep brown skin. Evan's here. I *see* him.

"You're here." I clear my throat and try again. "How are you here?"

My brother pats my cheeks and lets me go, analyzing me. He traces his finger in the air in front of my face, nodding as I track it. Then, he grins and puts his hand down to hug me. I hold on for longer than I normally would, because he's here. He's here, and I can see him. He squeezes me and pulls back, looking directly into my eyes.

"I told you I'd come, *gak mopi*. Got here a few *cycles* ago."

Uncle Aeric's at my side, propping pillows behind my back. "You've been in and out of various stages of consciousness for weeks now."

I rub my eyes, wishing for better focus. The room, their faces, everything needs a darker filter. When I look at something too long, my vision trembles and my eyes water, but—

"The procedure worked." I sound so small.

"Seems it did," Uncle Aeric says with a bright smile. "The first few *cycles*, you weren't responding to any outside stimulus, but your healer said it was normal."

"Did they also say I'll keep getting better? What's the full recovery period?" I sniffle and wipe wetness off my face. Oh gross, I'm snot covered. It's all over my chin. And the bed. I felt a puddle under my face.

"About two weeks," Evan says. "Your vision might be a little blurry until then. You want to clean off?"

"Yeah, I want to clean off." I frown at him. Noticing something about him. It's subtle, not wrong, but different. If I delve a bit deeper, I sense it. The atoms that compose fire dance within him, as usual, but they have an odd feel to them.

I want to reach out and touch them. I *recognize* his atoms, but it's like labeling a color as blue only to have an artist get more specific and say it's turquoise.

"Ev, you're—"

"Let's get you cleaned up. We'll talk after."

THE WATER IS HOT AS it hits me at every angle, and I savor watching the steam rise. Seeing the glass cleansing chamber walls fog over. The daylight orb in the ceiling imitating sunlight filters into the room. I'm amazed at my hands in front of my face. At the mess of brown tangles that flops into my eyes.

"You all right in there?"

Evan perches on the gray marble sink counter. He's got his back to me, braid over one shoulder, head down. I stare, willing my focus to sharpen just a bit more. Because something's wrong with his neck. It's not weird or worrying, but it's different. Different like the feel of his magic.

"I'm good." But are you? I know he won't answer. Might even pretend not to hear me. When did I start being able to predict what this brother might do or say as well as I might guess Devon's next outburst, or Lyle's next sigh and rolling of the eyes?

Lyle. A tickling sensation circles beneath my ribcage. There's something off when I think about Lyle, but I can't grasp what. The tickle makes its way to base of my neck, teasing me.

"Did Lyle call at all?" I ask, grabbing a sponge from the holder behind me and starting to scrub clean. Gross. I was out of it for weeks, they say, and I believe them. Weeks' worth of yuck peels away with one stroke of the sponge.

I wait, still washing. Evan's quiet. The tickle reaches my ears.

I glance up at him. "Ev?"

"No, Lyle didn't call."

So distant. Defense mechanism. He's stressing about something. He did that on Lenore. But why is it coming out while talking about Lyle? The tickle touches my forehead. A flash—an image. Lyle sitting on the edge of tub, looking at me.

No, not Lyle. His hair's too long. Chin-length. And he's older, leaner. Seems wrung-out.

"Hurry up, Lawrie. We need to talk and… I don't want you to be naked. It's weird." His tone lightens, and I hear a smile. I like when he teases me or laughs at things. Means he's more comfortable with me.

I do a crappy job of washing my hair. Barely letting the soap touch it before rinsing it. I press a button to turn off the water. A human-sized hand dryer clicks on, sucking all the moisture off my body. The floor and walls of the cleansing pod are dry, as well. I pull on the jeans and t-shirt slung over the pod door.

"Done." The door opens, releasing a cloud of steam as I step onto the tile floor.

Evan's back is still to me as he straightens up. Before he tosses his braid over his shoulder and spins to face me, I see it again. And this time I know what's wrong.

I move to him as he hops off the counter and turn him around before he can push me off. I gape at the back of his neck. It's not there. "What happened to your Mark?"

He swats me. "Come on."

He leaves the bathroom. I trip over my feet, stumbling after him. I look down, marveling at being able to see my feet. I will never say I hate toes again. Well, maybe not for another month or so. My brother walks fast, and it's okay. His braid's over his shoulder, so I can stare at the back of his neck again.

What does it mean for the Mark to be gone? Is mine gone? I stop and turn to go back to the bathroom. I need to see—fingers grip my shirt collar.

"I said, 'come on.'"

I choke and grumble under my breath, following Evan to the stairs. He takes them by two as they wind downward and lead us to... I suck in a breath as mobs of carbon and nitrogen—bodies—bounce around downstairs. Voices carry, lots of heavy accents and foreign words.

"Did you bring a party with you?" Because Uncle Aeric doesn't have neighbors, and he hasn't invited any friends over on account of me being here.

Evan chuckles. "Maybe."

People in plain clothes, tunics, and pants like denim, along with soldiers in black, tan, red, and gray jumpsuits roam the first floor of Uncle Aeric's home. The stairs release us onto a marble stage that bleeds into a living room with extra chairs and tables that were not here before I went in for the procedure. I would know. I would have bumped into them.

I stare. "Bro, what's going on?"

Evan ignores me as he guides us through the crowded living room, only to run into more people in the carpeted den area. The kitchen is where it's quieter, more manageable. Sand-colored appliances hum and steam. Around the square, sandy stone island in several stools sit Uncle Aeric, Adonis, Jalee, Desiri, and an adult version of me—Devrik. My mouth goes dry as the man tries to catch my eye and smile.

I look away, to Adonis, Jalee, and Desiri, frowning. They feel as turquoise as Evan does. What happened?

Evan gestures for me to take a seat. I take a stool beside Adonis. It's like warring factions. Adonis, Jalee, Desiri, and I sit across from Uncle Aeric and Devrik. Were they arguing before? Uncle Aeric and Devrik seem tense, their faces long—and not as dissimilar as people let me believe. They're both as dark-skinned as I am with the same deep-set eyes—though Uncle Aeric's are blue—and square jaws. They have similar postures when they sit, and their worried expressions are mirror images.

"Okay, so...?" I wave my hand in a circle, studying it for a moment, appreciating the faint after-image motion-lines it leaves behind. "What's all this?"

Evan doesn't sit. He stands in front of the table like a guest professor with no whiteboard. He glances back at the slightly ajar kitchen door. Air particles stir, pushing the door closed. And now it really is just us in the cooking area, surrounded by walls and glass patio doors.

I can't help but glance behind me into the backyard, where green-blue pool water glistens, and water sprites—the monsters really do look like adorable fourth graders in grass togas—sing a variety of nineties classics. The din of the soldiers bustling about the house dulls in comparison.

"Lawrie?"

I snap back to attention. "Huh?"

"You want to know what's going on. Pay attention," Evan says. Patience is not his forte. But then again, it's not mine either.

"Dude, I was blind! I'm having eye-gasms over here." Everyone stares at me. My face burns. "Give me a second! Okay, had my second. What the hell is going on?"

A beat. Two beats. Then Evan lets out that cackle I didn't know I missed. Desiri, Jalee, and Uncle Aeric join him for a minute before they all seem to stop on a cue I didn't see or hear.

"What's going on, little brother, is a revolution."

"Come again?" But he really doesn't have to. My brain whirs and clicks. There are soldiers everywhere. Uncle Aeric's usually empty place is as busy as the Ievisara with people running to their battle stations. "Bro, what the fug did you do?"

Evan raises placating hands as a kettle, an egg-shell colored dome, glows a warm orange. "Have some kava first, and a biscuit."

I notice the glass bowl of fat brown biscuits on the counter beside the kettle as soon as Evan mentions them. Before I can move toward getting either, Devrik pops up and moves about the kitchen, getting down a cup, grabbing the huge kettle, and bringing over the biscuit bowl.

He pours my drink, then tops off the cups in front of everyone else. I hadn't realized those were there. I scan the table. A pocket computer—a compal, lays in the center.

"Project, please." Evan takes his cup of kava from the table as the compal hums and spits up a 4D construct of Greater Allegiance Space. "And you,"—he nods at me—"take a few swallows of that and I'll tell you how we got here."

Two and half cups of kava and four biscuits later, I want to kill my brother. I'm on my feet, and one long stride puts me in front of him. I'm physically taller—in fact, I'm pretty sure I'm even more so now—but he's still bigger than me somehow. We stare.

The urge to strangle him for being a suicidal, self-sacrificing idiot is strong. I remind myself to breathe and throw my arms around him. I see him giving himself up to an *ether* beast, standing in front of his court as a living shield. I see him drowning in a swimming pool.

His arms come up to return my hug, and I let him go, glaring. "Do you get off on crazy?"

"I could ask you the same." He smirks at me. "What's that Earth saying? Something about teapots."

"Why do you remember 'pot and kettle'?"

Evan shrugs. "Lyle said I remember odd things too." The grin slips, and he's serious again. He fiddles with his braid. One of his ticks.

I take my seat and bite into another biscuit as Evan moves on from his story of pledging fealty to another fugging goddess with an ulterior motive—fugging Order. Fugging us all over. I swore to Her. I accepted Her stupid rock, used it. Burned my own fugging retinas and for what? She let those planets die, because She doesn't care. She'll let Earth die. She lied, and hundreds of years ago, I paid for it, my brothers paid for it. History is repeating itself.

The hovering universal map is dotted with colors—green for us, yellow for enemies, blue for the unknown. My brother is raising an army under the Allegiances' noses, in their own territories and space. In less than a month, factions of soldiers flew his flag, ready to break from councils and governments that don't listen. The people here are generals, leaders, good friends. People Ev trusts.

And my body is numb; my court isn't here.

"Where are..." Evan glares at me as I cut him off. "Where's my court?"

Chasyn's my friend. Bhela and Tian, they tried to save me from the water sprites out back, but... Chasyn's my friend. Evan should trust him. Why doesn't he?

"Chasyn's picking up supplies in the city. Soldiers eat, a lot." Uncle Aeric taps the rim of his empty cup. "But um..."

"I sent Tian and Bhela on an off-planet retrieval mission," Evan says. "They won't return until we decide what you should tell them."

Relief floods me. Chasyn's still here. And with us. "Are they…?"

"Chasyn has proven he's loyal to you." The universal map disappears, and Evan reaches for a biscuit. He holds the fat, sweet mound as if he's discovered a rare element. 'Eureka, it's cinnamon and sugar flavored!'

He's stalling.

I wait.

In the backyard, the sprites launch into a rendition of Britney Spears's 'Hit Me Baby One More Time.' I don't even laugh that Evan hums along. Lyle's right. He remembers odd things. And forgets ever odder things, because in all this, he hasn't mentioned very important things in relation to his revolution.

"Ev? Where are Lyle and Devon in all this?"

He sets his biscuit down. "Lyle's on Lenore, with Order, and we received intel that Dev's joining him soon." He looks strangely relieved when he talks about Dev joining Lyle. But shouldn't Dev have already joined Lyle? Did he get sent off again and is just returning? What happened there?

"How will we get them here with us?" I don't like the way he avoids my eyes. A funny feeling flips the switch on the fuzzy dream I'd had. The one that might have had Lyle in it—Lyle as someone else who… I shake my head. "Evan, is something wrong with Lyle and Devon?" Or just Lyle?

Evan bites his lower lip and picks at the biscuit on the table, making crumbs. Mom would throw a roll of paper towels at his head. "I think Lyle is compromised."

And then he tells me the part of the story he left out. The part where Lyle is a snake in the grass that can't even be trusted by family, and how it isn't his fault. Order twisted him. But I wonder how hard, as I remember a brother who I'd once thought didn't care about anyone. I've changed my mind since, because of how he's shown he cares. How much he's done to help us. How hard he hugged

Devon when they separated, how he'd hugged me and was terrified to let me go. Blocks of ice plop into my stomach acid, and it fizzes like Dr. Pepper.

Evan cracks his knuckles. "We'll get them both off Lenore and away from Order, we just can't do it now. We're not ready to make a bid or flex our muscles yet. This movement is still undercover from the Allegiances and the Su and Nazflit."

I want to say something else about our brothers, about Lyle, but Evan's changing the subject. Moving on to talk more about supplies and training schedules for him and his friends to work on their upgrades, and for me, because I'm behind and will only have Chasyn with me. We talk about burying my Stone in a warded grave.

I watch with my restored eyes, listen with my sharper ears, and ignore the click-whir of my massive brain struggling to come to terms with everything going on around me. It's like I fell asleep and woke up in a new game where all the rules are different and all of the players have been upgraded or exchanged. Lyle might be on another team from us, a double agent even. Evan thinks he's being manipulated and might be unaware of Order's true intentions. He wants to give Lyle the benefit of the doubt.

I'm not as sure. The shimmery tendrils of the dream haunt me still. The person who looked like Lyle knew a lot more than he revealed. In that place, I didn't trust him.

Fugg, Lyle. You don't make anything easy, do you?

I grab another biscuit, shoving it in my mouth as I tune out my thoughts and lean into Evan's new plans. The dream/memory/warning is dismissed for now.

"IT'S *FIPPED* UP." CHASYN CREATES another fire plume. "But not far-fetched. I mean, if any one of you did anything underhanded, of course it'd be the psi. They…" he trails off.

I frown at him. "They what?" The combination of anger and hurt when I think about Lyle spirals like a thick, thorny vine around my vital organs.

"They're messed up by their powers," Chasyn says. "All the psis I've ever met are *cratchy* or jumpy or crazy as *fip*. And your brother, he's…" Chasyn grimaces and looks skyward, as if he'll find the words there.

The sprites splash around in the pool, launching into 'Wannabe' by the Spice Girls.

"Broken?" I supply. People call Lyle a cracked psi. A term for psychics with mental shields damaged beyond possible repair. Growing up on Earth wore him down too much. What would he even be like if he hadn't stayed with us? If Devrik had taken him to Rema too? According to Chasyn, he'd probably still be an ass, but maybe not an evil one. "Broken or not, he can't do things like that to us. It's…"

More than wrong. It's something that might make other people say it's okay to get rid of him. "Do you think the other soldiers might want to," —I swallow—"lock him up? I mean, if Evan even fills them in on what all happened. I don't think he's going to."

Chasyn shrugs. "I think if Leader One says Leader Three is off-limits, then no one will hurt him. They wouldn't dare."

"But should they, though?" I ask.

A pain in my chest radiates through my back. If Order's brainwashing Lyle like Evan believes, or if he just chose to do it, either way, he's dangerous. He got into Evan's head and screwed up his magic. The power Evan fights with. What if it got him killed? Did Lyle even think about that? Did he care?

My heart shudders as the thought resounds through my brain. Did he care?

Of course he did. He does. I rub my eyes.

Chasyn places a hand on my shoulder, and I like that he knows not to say anything else.

The sprites get to the 'Wannabe' rap and spit out a strange mixture of English and whatever it is sprites speak. Gibberish mostly, but does anyone really know what Random Spice is saying?

My ears perk at the sound of a door sliding open. It's not the main one that leads out onto the patio Chas and I sit on, but the one that leads into the garden. I don't think Chas noticed, but his ears aren't as sharp as mine have become through having to doubly rely on them for months.

Two voices, Uncle Aeric and Evan, drift from the garden.

"Only you could plot a mutiny, raise an interplanetary army, and *still* manage to pick up strays." Uncle Aeric.

"Well, you can't give me all the credit. They were gifts and... in my defense, only this guy is actually mine." Evan.

"The one that barks at everything and ate one of my garden shoes. How fitting."

Evan chuckles. "I'll train him."

"When will you ever have the time, *nancha*? You've taken on way too much." Uncle Aeric's voice thins. "And you've given yourself away."

"I was already given away, Uncle."

"But this time it was your choice." Uncle Aeric sounds like a terrified parent, like Mom and Dad when they kissed us goodbye.

"I know. I'm sorry it has to be this way. I know you were hoping that I'd go to school here after all this—"

"I wasn't hoping you'd do anything but find yourself. If you wanted to travel the sectors with a band, singing and banging on drums, I'd be fine with it. Good gods, *nancha*. You'll never have a life at all, will you?"

Their voices lower. Uncle Aeric's pain-soaked and Evan's apologetic.

"It's like your uncle is his dad."

I glance at Chasyn, who's looking toward the wooden gate the garden lies behind, and toy with the idea. Even when Devrik is around, Uncle Aeric plays the role of dad for Evan.

"I haven't seen Devrik since we met in the kitchen earlier today. You'd think he'd want to be the one talking to Evan alone."

"I saw him go out," Chasyn says with a grimace.

Irritation files a few of the thorns in the vine around my stomach, liver, and kidneys into finer points. It's better to think about Devrik and how much of a loser he is rather than trying to sort out how I should feel about Lyle. "I'm not surprised Devrik went out. He's so useless." Chasyn keeps quiet. I really do like that he knows when to hold his opinion. I don't want him to agree with me out loud. Devrik's a POS, but he's still my father. I can say shizz other people can't. As my grandpa would say, 'Them's the rules.'

The gate groans, and wood scrapes over grass. A high-pitched bark precedes the sound of pattering feet across the lawn. A tawny-furred puppy zigzags across the yard, rolling on its back and springing to its paws. It stops a few meters in front of the pool, yipping at the sprite choir.

I stand. I don't know if sprites eat puppies, but I don't think Evan would be crazy about the idea of me letting his dog be a snack.

"Relax." Footsteps crunch in the grass. "They won't bother him."

Evan joins Chasyn and me on the porch. Chasyn jumps up, saluting quickly. "Ah… uh… I'll go inside."

"You don't have to…" I stop at the look on Evan's face. He's smiling at Chasyn, but in a 'great idea' instead of a 'no, stay' manner.

Chasyn salutes me and goes through the patio's sliding door.

"What'd you do that for?" I ask.

"Do what?" Evan clicks his teeth together, and the puppy barks and spins in a circle before bounding to us.

"Scare him off. He probably thinks you hate him."

Evan shrugs, scooping up the puppy as it nibbles on his pants leg. "How are you?"

"How am I?" I stare at him as he kisses the pup's neck and puts it against his shoulder like he's going to burp it. "How are *you*?"

As if on cue, the sprites hum the opening riffs of 'Eye of the Tiger.'

"Shut up! Where's Uncle Aeric's pitch pipe?"

Evan snorts. "I don't need that." He whistles four high, detached notes better than Snow White's dwarfs, but the sprites hate it. They glare and sink below the surface of the water. "They're not gone, but they'll be quiet for a while."

He jumps off the patio, opting to lie in the grass with the puppy on his chest. I watch him stare up at the sky. Everybody's looking there today. It must hold infinite answers but doesn't seem to be sharing them.

I hop onto the grass as well and plop down next to my brother.

He likes to change the subject whenever it comes to him and feelings, but I didn't forget what I asked. "How are you?"

"Depends on what you need from me."

"What does that mean?" I reach over to scratch the puppy behind its ears. Its funky puffball tail wags.

"If you want to talk about being afraid of what happens next, then I need to be your big brother. If you want to talk strategy, then I'm a leader. If—"

"I need you to be you. I'm scared and I'm angry, but I want you to be too." Because it's not fair. "I heard you and Uncle Aeric just now."

Evan sighs and strokes the puppy's back. "He always thought that I'd get a lucky break. That most of the conflicts would calm down in a few more *revs*, and I'd get more time off. I told you I wanted to go to university here. Uncle really believed I would, and that after graduation, I could join the faculty."

And now he'll never be able to do it. "Why aren't you angry?" It's crazy how the guy can blow up about burned bread but be totally zen about signing the rest of his life and eternity away to another goddess.

The pool water gurgles, and insects chirp.

He laughs so hard it scares the dog. It jumps and then barks, eyes narrowed. Evan ruffles its furry head until the puppy nips his fingers. They play a game of catch-the-digit until I grab the dog in one hand and set it on the ground.

Is this what Evan's like when he's losing it? He sits up, smile gone, eyes assessing as they lock on my face. "Who says I'm not angry? I just want to be angry at the right thing."

"Which isn't Lyle?"

Evan shakes his head. "Which isn't Lyle."

"You really think Order made him do it?"

"I really think Order needs to die."

I recognize his deflection here as a work around for lying. So, he's not sure, but he wants to be. And him wanting to be sure triggers more flashes of Lyle. Lyle coming to visit me after physical therapy each day on Lenore, Lyle being with Devon at University of Houston—they'd both saved me. Lyle being so worn down at Galeo's house and on the Ievisara, dependent on psychic Tylenol that Devon gave him shizz for taking.

I close my eyes, making myself temporarily blind so I can listen harder to my heartbeat, the air moving in and out of my lungs, the click-whir of my brain processing input at high speed. *Click. Click.*

I open my eyes, the world coming into focus, internal noises quieter but not gone. *Whir.*

"Order needs to die," I echo.

And I decide—no, I choose—to believe in and save my asshole brother who could be plotting to screw us all.

I poke Evan's shoulder until he looks over at me. "Can I shadow you when you talk to the new recruits tomorrow?"

I need to learn how to co-lead a revolution.

# Chapter 19

# Devon

WE GAIN AN HONOR GUARD OF additional ships that travels with us into Sector Two as we enter Silver Allegiance Space. When Mineshka had deemed it safe enough to chance a transmission on a Silver Allegiance frequency, Xijure sent out a mayday, and from there, we were told where to fly and when we'd be joined. I want to call out to the other ships around us to let us board, because I'm tired of being inside a flying tomb.

Xijure and I wrapped the bodies and put them in cold storage, a morgue. There are morgues on battleships. We flew with a morgue full of bodies in a metal trap with poorly scrubbed walls and floors that reeked of cleaning fluid for weeks.

Mineshka pilots with tired eyes, putting the ship in autopilot but keeping a sharp eye on the controls and sensors. She took three-to-four-hour naps between flying eight-hour shifts, trusting Xijure and I to watch the controls for only so long. I couldn't be insulted, because I wasn't interested in crashing into any asteroids or planets, and Xijure admitted that Caea was the pilot in his family, not him.

I tap my fingers on the seat I'm strapped into as Mineshka shifts into landing mode. We enter the atmosphere of Lenore at what feels like a snail's pace as my mind races. Lyle's down there. And Lawrie and Evan. I'm going to see them. I'm going to hug Lyle until he punches me, and I'll laugh because his punches don't hurt. He's not that strong, and I don't injure easy. I look to Xijure and find the king grinning back at me.

"You thinking about Caea and Ramesis?" I ask.

Xijure nods. "Caea's going to kick my ass, but it's okay. I deserve it. And Ram... I don't know. Maybe he'll play whatever song he wrote about my death to me, and I'll be mad about how he described me."

"Song he wrote?" I laugh.

Xijure rolls his eyes. "Ram is a musician. Plays drums and string instruments in a band that screams and talks instead of sings. It's weird and loud and I just don't get it, but he's underground famous. Goes by a stage name and wears a wig when he performs."

"What the hell, man? You didn't tell me your bro is a rockstar!"

"Because I don't know what the hell that means." Xijure thwaps me in the back of the head. I don't dodge it and laugh as my head snaps forward. I catch Mineshka's eyes, but she looks away.

Damn.

When we touch ground, I'm going to hug my brothers and know that they're okay. Xijure will be with his siblings. Mineshka will be alone.

And holy crap, I'm going to have to report to the Allegiances that Loniad and Ilea are dead. Might have to talk to their families, Mineshka's parents, and Ilea's husband. Leader Two is back with one-third of his court after being kidnapped and turning traitor because he worked on a compromise with the enemy god whose Champion killed his court and crew.

And he's also empty-handed. He and King Xijure Harliel lost their Gifts from Order. No Stone, no Haribu. But it can't make us useless, because of the information we have. The fact that we shouldn't be fighting. We need to talk.

And talk we will, but only to people we know we can trust first. We'll kiss and hug our families and then pull them aside to tell them what we know and go from there. Xijure says Caea is brilliant, and Evan is amazing and Lawrie's a genius, and I'll have Lyle. We can do this, come up with something better with our families. Making a deal with Pan is probably off the table now, but maybe we can talk to Order. See what She offers, or there could be an even better way.

"We're going to talk to them as soon as we find a safe, secluded, warded place," Xijure says, as if reading my mind. "And we'll show them what we worked on for Pan and maybe we can use it with Order."

I nod. "Yeah."

"Brace yourself for landing." Mineshka's words are brisk.

I make sure I'm strapped in tight and ready myself for the nausea-inducing final drop onto the landing pad. I hate landings and take-offs. The ship drops like a theme park ride, and I hold in a yelp as my stomach jumps into my throat. I count backwards from one hundred, gritting my teeth until we touch down.

Landed.

We landed.

And I—Lyle!

A part of my brain clicks, like a puzzle piece snapping into place. That funny gap, like a space between my teeth I can wiggle my tongue in, closes. It's gone.

/Devon./

His voice in my head.

/Devon. I'm right outside. I'm outside./

He sounds giddy. I feel his bubbling emotions. He needs me to come outside. I need to go outside. I hurry to unstrap myself.

"Hold on," Mineshka says. "I need to do a few more things before it's safe for you to leave your seat."

So I wait, beaming at Xijure and the back of Mineshka's piloting seat, leg jittering, until Mineshka says I can release the harness. The ship hisses and huffs as it powers down and cools off. I rush to the dock, Xijure following, barely keeping up.

The doors open and I fly down the stairs, slamming into my brother.

It's a wonder we don't suffocate each other. He's not strong, but he squeezes so hard I can't breathe, and I'm sure I'm doing the same. Happiness floods through me and into him and rebounds. He's open to me, letting me sense what he's feeling in a way I haven't been comfortable with since we were little.

Oh, he missed me and needed me, and had been sick without me. The phantom echoes of the pain he'd suffered off Lenore and on it bombard me, along with his extreme joy and relief and then his anxiety.

God, Lyle. What's eating you up? He pulls away to inspect me, checking me for injuries while I look him over. He's thinner than he'd been when we separated, cheekbones more prominent, skin dusky, eyes hollow. His smile is genuine, though. I pull him to me again, and he wraps his arms around my back.

I sigh. This. All I want is this right now.

I feel whole. Complete.

And then I'm aware of a hard object poking me in the chest. Feel a warmth that chills me to the core. I pull away again, frowning at the blue glow I see through Lyle's white shirt. "Ly, what's that?" I point.

Lyle blinks and looks down. "My Stone." He frowns. "Do you have yours?"

I shake my head. "I'm sure Pan does. And He has Xijure's Gift too."

Lyle bites his lip and swallows. Fear?

"Ly?"

He shakes his head. "It's okay. Of course He'd take them. I just thought... but no. It's okay. You're here. It's all I asked for. You're here." He ruffles my hair and laughs, and I sling an arm over his shoulders.

Turning as a unit, we watch Xijure hugging both his siblings. They cry together.

I don't see Mineshka and wonder if she's still on the ship, running through post-landing procedures. She has no reason to rush out onto the landing pad. I sigh, then notice that we're missing two people.

"Where are Evan and Lawrie?"

LAWRIE'S STILL UNCONSCIOUS AFTER HIS procedure. His friggin' procedure. A lightning blast burned his retinas in a battle against one of Pan's dead Champions. My baby brother was in battle, fighting monsters, and could have died. He'd saved lots of people, Evan and his court included, with what he did, but now he's blind.

"Uncle Aeric says that the healer thinks he'll wake up soon," Lyle says. "I... I didn't call like I said I would. He was already under by the time I finally got up the nerve, and Uncle Aeric's been sending updates now that he knows I want them. He thought I didn't want them."

I nudge Lyle's shoulder. We sit side by side in his room. I hadn't wanted to go to mine. I showered here, and he brought in my clothes. Said I could sleep in here if I want, and I want to.

"Uncle Aeric doesn't know you. Just knows that you hadn't called before then. Maybe he thought you were too busy."

Lyle blinks and looks at me, eyes red-rimmed, exhausted.

"You *were* busy. Did you... how was it, getting your Stone? And how was it after? I felt pain and other things from you. Are you okay?" Because I don't think he is. He sits close to me, eyes following wherever I go if I get up to do something.

He serves me too. If I want water or food, instead of going to the dining hall or joining the others, he orders food to his room. When it comes on platters, he dishes out what he thinks I want and sets up his bedside table for me. Then he watches me eat and drink.

It's kind of creepy, kind of heart-warming.

"Ly? What's hurting you?"

He rubs his face, like he's got a massive headache and gives a weak smile. "You just got back."

"So? Tell me. I've been worried about you. And I... I wasn't okay when we split up. On the ship, going to—to that place,"—because I can't say Disiez without growling—"I was sick. Xijure said it was because you and I were too far apart. It was like something was ripped out of me."

"Yeah." Lyle bows his head. "That's my fault. I think my powers tethered us together on Earth. I always knew where you were, but I didn't think anything of it because it felt so normal to just know, until I didn't anymore. When you were gone..." He meets my eyes. "You can't ever be gone again. Promise that you'll never go that far away from me. I don't think I'd live through it."

He thinks he'll die without me nearby? I'm touched, but... "Lyle, you'll be okay if anything long-term happens to me. You just don't think so, because who wants to think about that? Definitely not me. And hey, I'm not planning on going anywhere. But geez, man. You can't go around saying you'll die—"

"I'll die," he says so simply my heart breaks. "I wanted to. Was fine with it."

I rein in panic. He wanted to die. "Are you still going to those mind healers?"

"There's a mind healer on my court," Lyle says. "Selected just to fix my broken bits, but it was only temporary patching." He strokes the blue Stone under his shirt. "This helps more."

That thing came from a god. Flashes of my red Stone talking to me, making me punch through walls and nearly kill my own team invade my mind. Ilea had made a magic pouch for me, like the one Evan has, to store the Stone and keep its influence to a minimum. Lyle should have one too. He shouldn't just be wearing that thing against his bare skin.

"Is it talking to you?" I ask.

Lyle cocks his head. "Is what talking to me?"

"That Stone. Mine said things in my head, like you do. Does yours do that too? Evan said his did."

Lyle blinks, then nods. "It just soothes me. Helps my head."

And makes you want to do things. "Take it off."

"No."

I reach for it and am repelled by an invisible force. Lyle's telekinesis. "Stop it."

"*You* stop it," he says.

I grunt in frustration and snarl, "That thing is bad for you. It made me do dumb shit that could have hurt people I cared about. I put it away and decided to only use it in a fight, like Evan wanted to."

Lyle shakes his head. "If you'd worn it the whole time, maybe it might have warned you about the ambush. It could have heightened your senses and you might have heard the enemy sooner."

"Shut up." It's not my fault. I couldn't have prevented what happened.

Could I?

"Shut up!" I get off his bed and pace the floor, guilt riding my shoulders.

"I shouldn't have said that." He lowers his voice, and I look at him. He sits with his legs folded under him in the center of his bed. "I'm sorry."

He is. From the slump of his shoulders and the lightness of his tone, I can tell that he is. The guilt wanes as worry takes its place. I return to the bed and sit beside him again. "You're not okay."

"No," he agrees with me. "But I'll get there, because you won't leave me again. Things are going to be fine. Lawrie will wake up and be able to see, and Evan will finish his mission and go out to get Lawrie and they'll come back here. We'll figure out how to get your Stone back and we'll... we'll end the war."

He's shaking.

I put my arm around him. "It's going to be okay. We'll be okay. But uh... we have to talk about something."

My middle feels like it's full of rocks. It's time to bring up everything that happened, time to mention that Xijure, Mineshka, and I met Pan, and that we were working on a deal. Time to tell him that Order and Pan are going to erase people and planets that fall on the wrong side of their war from existence.

Lyle's so fragile right now. I don't want him to fall apart, and he just might if I drop one more thing on him. I'll hold him, be whatever glue he needs, but my brother shouldn't be held together by glue and Band-Aids. He shouldn't be doing this, shouldn't be here.

Neither should I.

"Ly, Xijure, Mineshka, and I want to hold a meeting with just us, and Caea and Ramesis. We need to tell you all something important. Something that might make us seem crazy, but we're not, and we need your help."

Lyle's weary eyes lock on mine. "You want to fill me in now, so I'm not surprised in front of a room full of people?"

"Not full of people just... just people we trust."

His eyes narrow. "Tell me now."

I sigh, feeling his power tapping on my mind. Wanting to be let in, and as much as it used to freak me out in the past, I don't care as much now. If he can see what I know, instead of me having to talk, it'd be better. I'm not that great at words, and if he sees, he'll know it's true and I'm not nuts.

*Go ahead*, I think at him.

And I feel something pass through me. Lyle's eyes are glazed, pupils pinpricks. Meaning his consciousness is elsewhere. Inside me. Rooting around in my memories. Finding—

He gasps and rears back. He blinks rapidly, pupils dilating to normal size as he stares at me in horror. "D-D—y—you.... That was Kahine! You spoke to Kahine! You—you worked with Him."

The mounting terror in his voice scares me. "Lyle, calm down. I know it's freaky that I was in the same room with, what did you call him? Kahine? Some of His people called Him that too. But He... He didn't seem so bad. He was willing to let us come up with a compromise that could save some of our people. The gods, they want to rewrite existence by taking out all the creations that aren't Theirs. Order might erase us and Earth, if we win for Her. Pandemonium told his Champions the real deal, and all of them have agreements with Him. We don't have an agreement with Order, and—"

"We have an agreement with Order."

I stare at him. He still looks terrified, but for me. "What do you mean we have an agreement with Order?"

"We... me... I have an agreement with Order."

"What do you mean, Lyle? What does that mean? You... did you speak to Her somehow? Did She come here?"

Lyle wrings his hands together and looks away. "I spoke to Her, and no, She didn't come here."

"Then where—"

"I went to Her. Nialiah helped me. I asked Her to find you, save you. Bring you home."

Holy crap. The nymph comes to mind. Appearing in our camp, appearing on the flying morgue. Killing Shiham and his monsters. Telling us Order sent Her.

"You made a deal to rescue me?" My heart races. "Why—?"

"Because the Allegiances weren't going to. They wrote you off as dead, but I knew you weren't dead," Lyle says, words fast, breathing fast, "just lost, and She said She'd find you if I did some things for Her. And She found you."

"What'd you do for Her?" Morbid fascination joins growing fear.

Lyle takes a shaky breath. "Dev, I already had a deal. Before I knew you were gone. Had a deal to save you and Evan and Lawrie and Caea and her siblings, and our family on Earth... and I was going to add to it, I think. I was going to build a list. Because Kahanna has a list of people She's going to bring into Her new world. She's saving all of Lenore, and some of the Allegiance councilors and leaders. Everyone has deals.

"They know... They know what the gods want and will do. They've seen planets disappear. Lawrie and Evan saw it firsthand too. There's nothing we can do but watch. So, when She showed me the past, and told me what would happen, I... I chose. Devon. I'm pretty sure I made one of those prophesized choices. But get this. The prophecy? It's just a spell. A fortune spell She called it."

I stare at him. "You made a deal."

Just like I had been about to do with Pan. But he'd kept it to himself, or had he? "Does anyone else know about this deal? You said Nialiah helped you go to... Kahanna? Order?"

Lyle laughs, dull and flat. "Kahanna's inner circle knows about my first deal. The one to save who I want in exchange for being a part of Her elite group."

"Elite group? Inner circle?"

"Some of the councilors, Dev, and The Maidens. They've always known what Kahanna was up to. They're making this war move in Her favor. Staying on Her good side."

"Manipulating events." I lean in, nose to nose. "Have you been doing that? Manipulating people?" A strange feeling expands in my chest. I can't explain it. I don't know if it's anger, disappointment, or sadness.

Lyle shrugs. "Those people weren't going to be saved anyway. And… and I had to keep you all safe. And get you back."

"And getting me back was a second deal."

He nods.

"Did you do something different for that?"

He cringes. "Don't ask me about it."

"Lyle—"

"I can't talk about it. Please don't bring it up. Now, we need to talk about you and Kahine and why you need to forget that. In fact, let me help you forget that, because Kahanna can't know. Nobody can know."

"Lyle, I just told you Pandemonium is offering the same deals but is being more straight forward about it. More people on Pan's side know about the god game and He's going to spare more of His followers it sounds like."

"And you trust that, Him?"

"You trust Her?"

We stare at each other, nose to nose. Breathing each other's air.

"Shit." We speak in unison.

"Which is why I want to talk to a group we can trust," I say. "Lyle, let's talk to them. Xijure and Mineshka are expecting it. Xijure's probably already prepped Caea and Ramesis for the discussion. We have to."

"If She finds out, She might not forgive us. We might lose everything and so far, She's done what She promised. You're here."

I am here. He's right. But... something's still wrong. Wrong enough for us to continue the conversation with a group of new minds and perspectives.

"Lyle?"

His eyes are closed. The Stone around his neck glows.

Is it talking to him now? He has to take it off.

"Can we sleep on it?" he asks finally.

It's not that late. Dinner was only an hour ago, but I'm tired. Mineshka had turned down meals and gone directly to the quarters given to her to sleep in. Xijure is probably with Caea and Ramesis doing what Lyle and I are doing right now, and maybe he'd go to sleep early at his siblings' insistence. No one's calling me now. Which could mean—

"Mineshka's asleep. A deep sleep," Lyle says, eyes open and unfocused. "She won't wake up until morning. And Xijure—he's with Caea. He's..." A blink and his eyes are clear, present, and focused on me. "He won't knock on your door until morning either."

I almost ask him if he made Xijure decide not to come, and made Mineshka sleep harder, but I don't. Not when he's so broken. His hands tremble in his lap, and the dark circles under his eyes are starting to look like bruises. I push his shoulder, gently.

"Fine. I can sleep. I didn't sleep well on the ship. We can sleep and talk in the morning. But Lyle, we're going to talk, okay?"

He nods and flops back on the bed, unfolding his legs and stretching them out. Even with him lying spread eagle there's room for me to lie down on the bed as well. I let myself fall backward and inch my body across the soft bedding until we're side by side. Same length, though I take up more space because I'm bulkier. Our heads and feet are parallel, always have been, always will be.

We breathe together, and when I fall asleep, I'm pretty sure he does as well.

I hope we dream together because I don't want to be apart ever again.

## Chapter 20

# Lyle

CAEA WANTS TO TALK TO me alone.

I must look like I'm walking to the gallows, because Devon actually gets up to follow. I shake my head and motion for him to go back to Xijure, Mineshka, and Ramesis. Ramesis, who can't stop punching Xijure in the shoulders and smiling at him. Xijure, who can't get over the fact that Ramesis grew a little taller while he was gone.

Lawrie was taller when he came back from Nakshera. I need to check up on him. I'll do it after Caea breaks up with me. That's what this is about, and I expect and deserve it after how I left things. When we found out our brothers were alive, I'd gone into preparation mode and hadn't had time for her. Again.

We leave my office and head toward hers. Stepping through the door brings back memories of helping her make this place more comfortable. The couch in the corner is a great place for kissing. The desk a fun place to discover each other's birthmarks. The soft carpet is nice to roll around on.

There's art on the walls. Landscapes of places I've never been, done in oils and wax. Beautiful and bold, like the woman who sits on top of the desk that I swear has never been used for official business. I don't join her as I would have, before I learned Devon wasn't on his way back to me. Before everything I'd planned went to hell and never resurfaced.

I stop in front of her, not knowing what she wants me to do or say. She can lead. I meet her eyes, face a careful blank as I drink in the hurt on hers. Her brown eyes glimmer, her semi-full lips a thin line.

"Why didn't you tell me about Order and your deal?" She doesn't sound angry, just… disappointed.

My chest is tight. I didn't think she'd accept it, me. Didn't think she'd want to be with me anymore. Thought she might do something stupid and get hurt. Thought I could just handle it, save her, and step aside during the aftermath.

She shoves me when I don't answer.

"You stupid *cratch*. You walk around here half dead. Knowing our brothers are alive and killing yourself to find a way to get them back and keeping all that on your own shoulders. You… are supposed to trust me. We're in this together. That's what we said. And you…" She breaks off, musing her curls. "You saved me on Kupiku. The reason we all came out of that was because you made a deal with Her."

I nod.

She groans and tilts her head back to look heavenward. "You made a choice."

Wait.

"You were going to die in that cave. I saw it. Knew I couldn't save you. I actually thought that was how we were both going to die, but I didn't want you to know it, so I pretended like I knew what I was doing."

Wait.

She takes ones of my hands and turns over my palm, tracing the lines. Her touch tickles and I'm lost. What's she saying? Why isn't she yelling or telling me she hates me?

"You made the choice that I might have made in that moment." Caea stops her tracing and folds her hand over mine. "You chose your family and your court, and me and even added my family to that. What else could you have chosen? To die and have us all die with you?"

My eyes sting. Tears again? So sick of crying. But she... "You're not mad? You don't hate me or think I'm a sack of shit?"

"Oh, I think you're a lying sack of *pidge*." She squeezes my hand, gaze burning into my soul with its intensity and fury. "Not for that choice, but for joining in on that circle. For listening to Viveen, Theorne, and The Maidens screwing our people over, and not working against that. You should have brought me into it. We could have come up with ways to help more people. When you *fipping* met with Order on your own... you should have brought me. Instead. Instead, you..."

She breaks off to breathe, practically throws my hand back at me. "Instead, you trust that hag Nialiah. Over me. I mean, it's better than thinking that you were..." She has to breathe again. "You didn't, did you?"

"No." Never. I flirted to get what I wanted at first, but... "I never touched her. Not in that way."

Caea lowers her head, nods as if confirming something. She pats the area of the desk beside her. After a second of hesitation, I sit. Our shoulders touch.

"So, what now?" I ask. "Do you—do you want to stop being with me? I understand. I haven't really been here for you."

"Is that what you want? To end things?"

Her voice gives no hints as to what she wants me to say, and I don't dare try to read her mind. I'd never do that to her. So, I answer with what I know. It's all I have. "I don't want to end anything with you, ever. I… I had a lot of things to do. For Devon. And you. And I got lost in it all. It was…" I didn't really tell Devon how dark it got for me.

Caea rubs my back, like I'm some kid who just had a nightmare. "I knew that look in your eyes. Saw it in the cave. It scared me. If you had tried to run away from me while I was lighting that vigil, I would have tackled you to the ground. Ly, you can't do that. You can't let things get so bad, so heavy that you crash and can't take care of yourself. Not when you have people who are here to help you. Want to help you."

I press my lips together, not trusting myself to talk without my voice shaking. I feel a line of wetness itching over one cheek. Dammit.

"Let me help." She rubs away the tear.

She's too good for me. I should get up and leave. She can do better. She should talk to Devon, see how great he is, and switch. He'd be good for her. But I'd die more inside if she agreed with me.

I squeeze my eyes shut, head aching and searching for relief that I don't get. Can't depend on the Stone anymore. I took it off this morning after Devon asked again and haven't touched it since. Put it in a warded pouch, one Evan gave me before he left. It cancels out the worst of the Stone's calls.

I feel it tugging at me, offering peace and quiet, but it's muffled. I ignore it and reach for Caea's hand, bring it to my lips, and hope that's answer enough for her.

Her chuckle is breathy, and her kiss tastes like kava and a peach tart.

She maneuvers herself into my lap, straddling my waist and deepening that peach kiss. I shudder and sigh into her mouth, body releasing so much tension it almost hurts. I wrap my arms around her, pressing her closer. Caressing her hair, massaging her neck, back. My hands go lower as her hands run over my chest and shoulders, questing for buttons to undo.

High emotions seem to lead to cliché events that don't involve clothes or words that I can't complain about now that I've experienced the phenomena for myself. My body always went through the motions. They felt good, and the pleasure feedback that rolled through me and the other person was euphoric. But when it's love—a sensation I believed was a construct, a daydream, poetic nonsense—it's different. I think this is love.

The overhead lights go out at Caea's command. She pushes me back onto the desk. My back curves against the hard wood, and she straddles me.

For the next half hour, I forget about Kahanna, Stones, and apocalypses.

TIME PASSES. I SPEND IT with Devon and Caea and attend secret meetings with our new inner circle of Champions that includes Nialiah. I visit the palace's mind-healer who'd helped me before I knew Sensuen and discuss reestablishing my previous appointments. I put my Stone in its warded pouch for Devon and had him hide it from me.

He doesn't think I should give Order free access to my mind. It's easier to agree with him because his presence in my life makes me stronger.

The new circle of Champions shares meals outside of the palace. We walk to restaurants and places where we can eat outdoors, and Nialiah sets up silencing wards so we can talk. Devon, Xijure, and Mineshka show us the document they would have shared with Pan, and I see the influence Pan's Champions had over it. They don't seem like bad people from their suggestions, or from what Devon, Mineshka, and Xijure share with us about them.

My brother has grown so much. He speaks with more than just the confidence he used to have on Earth. He has a newfound competence. He had been hands-on while he was gone, earning respect from people who owed him nothing. Dev was always a good person, but now he glows, exuding an aura that others will want to follow. I'm proud to stand beside him, and that he'll still have me. That he looks at me like I belong in his light, and he won't abandon me. I can do this, be better, with him here, believing in me.

Nialiah and I still attend meetings with Order's Inner Circle, playing the parts of complacent followers, then bringing everything we learn to the Champion circle. Nialiah still wants to leave Lenore, but she wishes to take all of us with her. She thinks her husband Sayan on Nakshera will board us and that we can reconnect with Lawrie, who's still unconscious, and Evan, who's still on a mission, there.

The longer Evan's mission takes, the antsier Theorne and Viveen seem to get. Inner Circle meetings are less frequent, but the tingle of precognition that tells me something's going to happen flares up every time Nialiah and I are called to the dungeon for a briefing.

I push for us to move our plans to leave Lenore faster. It's time to go. We discuss preparations in a gathering we have in one of Nialiah's old workrooms. She spelled it for us to use when it's too suspicious for all of us to leave the castle grounds together.

Today, she told us to start without her, that she'd join later. She had business to attend to. The base of my neck tingled when she'd said it, and I almost warned her not to go. But that was stupid. Nothing would dare hurt Nialiah in her own castle. Caea touched my arm, I kept my mouth shut, and Nialiah left.

Everything is fine.

Even if the tingling won't stop.

Devon's talking when the light sequence that signals an emergency meeting for all military and government officials flashes in urgent patterns.

We look at each other.

It's the first time this has happened since everyone has been back. Dev stares at me. "Lyle, you've been sensing that something's up all day. Can you tell if this is going to be a good or bad meeting?"

I rub the prickle at the base of my skull. There's no physical pain. It's all psychosomatic, but I tremble all the same as I say, "I don't know."

Whatever happens next is going to affect something in a major way. Only I don't know what or for who, or if it's for better or worse.

Devon and the rest of the group frown at me, and disappointment in myself swells. I wish I could offer more than, "We'd better go, before someone comes looking for us."

After several seconds of silence, the room agrees with me, and we leave our safe space.

*HOLY SHIT BALLS, BIG BROTHER.* Devon barely hustles me out of the meeting hall before his thought busts into my head. I disguise a flinch with a raised brow.

*I told you that* gak mopi*'s scary.* Xijure's thought is gentler on my skull, but I'm still regretting the telepathic 'group chat' I opened between us all. Xijure walks beside Devon. Devon and Xijure make me think of Evan and Adonis and how they gravitated toward one another when in the same rooms.

Evan. Holy shit balls is right. *He's* the emergency. I want to fall over in relief, because not only is Evan unaffected by the seed I planted in his core, my precognitive inkling was about something positive. Evan's fighting against Kahanna, and we can join his movement instead of having to build our own. And when we fly out to meet him, I can apologize for what I did and hope he forgives me.

I take Caea's hand as she walks beside me, and she smiles without looking at me. The warmth radiating from her hand into mine and up my arm is intoxicating. I want to kiss her, but not here. I want to jump up and down, but not here. I'd have too much explaining to do to the soldiers walking around us.

*Evan's movement means we can leave here and have a better place to go than with Nialiah. And I bet wherever Evan is, Lawrie is with him.* Devon sounds giddy.

Lawrie. I smile. Lawrie who's awake, but there's no word on his condition. And I'm not sure if I care about that, so long as he's awake. We can—we can help him learn and live without sight. It's fine. He's Lawrie. He was already adapting before he left. Deluding himself, yes, but getting by. He'll be okay.

Just like I'm going to be okay. I daydream about leaving Lenore, who we'll meet and who we'll take with us. I'll have to talk to Orion and Falun. Not Sensuen. She's a zealot, but I like the other two on my court. The ones who don't think the suns of two planets beam out of my ass or bow and call me Leader Three, instead of my name. The ones who took me clubbing. It was terrible, and I'll never go again, but I remember they wanted to hang out with me when they had every reason to brand me useless and not try, because I certainly wasn't.

I'll invite them to lunch with the group, and we'll talk. If it turns out we can't trust Falun and Orion, I'll break my self-promise and erase the chat from their minds, but I don't think that'll be the case.

*We need to get ourselves assigned to a mission soon,* Caea thinks. *And we need to start speaking to our troops. The ones we know will follow us. I think all my aerial troops will join our team.*

*My ground units too,* Xijure thinks.

*Not so sure about mine.* Ramesis's thought is hesitant. *They're uh...*

*Too new to be completely loyal to you yet,* Caea assures. *You haven't fought enough with them,* bibi. *Don't worry about it. You did a good job training with them.*

I feel a trickle of gratitude from Ramesis and a hint of satisfaction that soothes a need for approval from his big sister. Sweet. I glance at him quickly and shrug as he sneers at me and my hand in Caea's. That one doesn't like me much. Can't say I blame him.

*Meeting in Lyle's office.* Devon puts his arm around my shoulders, then wiggles an eyebrow at my hand in Caea's. Dumbass. I shove him away with my other arm, and he laughs. *You two are cute.*

/Screw off./

*You also looked kind of... sweaty... when you two joined us for breakfast this morning. Just saying.*

I release Caea's hand to jump on him, something I haven't done in years. He staggers, almost losing his balance, then tries to get me in a headlock. I push him with telekinesis, making my wrestling moves stronger.

I hear Caea, Xijure, and a few new voices laughing. Soldiers and Lenorans traveling the halls chuckle at us. I pick up on their delight at seeing kids playing.

Kids.

They know we're Champions, but under the established veneer, they also know we're young. Some think we should play all the time and not be here. Others think: How sad.

And some think—

"Leader Two and Leader Three, you are in the corridor of a palace in front of your subordinates." Viveen's words cut through the amused thoughts and laughter of everyone else around us, and I let Devon go.

We turn as a unit to stare at the vulture woman.

"Leader Three, might I speak with you in private?"

*Is this going to be one of your underground meetings?* Devon asks.

I study her sour expression, and her mouth tightens.

/Yeah./

*I could come. Say I know and agree to everything. You shouldn't—*

/It'd be too suspicious. I'll be back./

I feel Caea and Devon's worry. Their thoughts and feelings tickle the back of my brain as I follow Viveen down another corridor that will eventually lead us beneath the palace.

The chamber is full today, with not only Theorne and Hellene, but also projections of three members of Golden Allegiance Councils and two from Silver Allegiance Councils. I don't know any of them by name or planetary affiliation. I've never gotten to meet Kahanna's other followers. I recognize some of them from larger meetings with the other Champions. They're usually stone-faced, presenting facts or nodding along when action is called for.

The dark-haired, purple-skinned woman was the one who briefed me on Isiphe Akitsa, telling me what she liked and the kind of people she preferred. I pretended to be all those things, though I didn't need to be close to rewire her brain for Kahanna. I'll have to find a way to make it right for her... and a few others. I'll atone in whatever way they want. Devon can help me find them all and go with me. I let out the breath I'd been holding, relaxing as I think about my confident, competent twin. I can do this.

I sit with my hands on the table I'd broken a month ago, staring at the new faces, then at the empty seat next to Hellene. Nialiah's.

Is she still finishing business? She's probably meeting with one of her off-planet buyers.

Hellene catches my eyes on Nialiah's seat. Her black eyes glisten, and she tilts her head, as if she's noticed something interesting. I look away from her. Creepy witch.

"The traitor Lauduethe should be killed on sight for his crimes," a Golden Allegiance councilor raves. Red eyes, red-haired and genderless, I believe. The voice is medium-deep. "The murder of another Champion is enough for execution without trial."

The murder of another Champion? "Evan wouldn't kill another—" I choke. I didn't mean to say that out loud. Don't want attention on myself, but... "Who do you think he killed?"

Because it's a lie. We're all accounted for.

"Maiden Imari." Theorne is icy as he stares at me.

Imari. No. Evan likes her, and besides... "She went to her estate. How could he—"

"Imari is *not* at her estate," Hellene says, voice clear and carrying. "She was last seen with Leader One and his court on that backwoods planet we stationed him upon. She abandoned her duties to follow him. A betrayal. The death of a traitorous Champion should not be avenged and should not count against Leader One, who is a useful Champion. We will extend an offer of forgiveness in exchange for his immediate return."

Clamors of outrage erupt from the virtual councilors. Theorne, Viveen, and Hellene remain cool.

Confusion warps my brain. Imari is dead and they think Evan did it? On what grounds? And if he did kill her, why? And finally, why does Hellene want to pardon Evan and bring him back into Order's fold without punishment? She doesn't like him.

What does she want from him?

"The spell still needs the Four."

"You were going to let Devon die. You didn't think of the spell then." I can't keep my mouth shut. Hearing her say that has my blood on fire. "You all said—""You got your precious brother back, did you not?" The evil gleam in Hellene's eyes keeps me talking, blood still boiling.

"Without help from you."

Hellene smiles, close-lipped. It reaches her eyes and turns them savage. "Not from me, no."

Warning vibes prickle up my spine. Something's wrong here. "Where's Nialiah?"

"Ill, I am afraid. She sends her regards."

Lie. I can't detect them like Evan can, but I don't need to. The tickle at the rear on my consciousness is enough for me to know.

I need to find her. My mouth doesn't reopen itself.

"Leader One, the Child of Magic, is key to a great many things and whose choices may be the ones we still need to achieve our end goal. It would seem that the choices of the Four are rather finite, and our Lady Kahanna knows how many each of you has left. She can also weigh just how much effect those finals choices will have on Her desired outcome. Some of you are more expendable than others." The sweetness in her tone is poisonous. "Leader Three, you will be the one to begin the mediation. Bring your brother back to us."

I planted a damn seed of discord directly into his brain and he still rejected Kahanna. Doubt there's anything else I can do, even if I was willing to do it. But I nod. "Tell me what to do."

"You are that quick to decide to do to your brother what you did to Isiphe Akitsa?" A Silver Allegiance councilor seems intrigued and slightly disgusted.

"He'll live." Should I add 'idiot?' I'm rude to Theorne, Viveen, and Hellene in these meetings. I should be rude to everyone, keep my attitude consistent. I'm Her cocky favorite.

They all watch me, even the ones in virtual seats, and I sit up straighter. Suppress the urge to shiver at the cold fingers of warning walking up and down my back. Something's about to happen.

"You choose to do this?" Viveen leans in.

"Yes, I choose to do it." The words echo. The fingers on my spine move faster, quivering with growing urgency. Did I say something wrong? I can't tremble, can't look away.

Viveen hums and sits back.

I'm silent for the rest of the meeting, listening to the others rant and argue about what's next, what other uprisings have to be quashed. What armies and people

Evan's already turned to his side. How did he manage to gain so much ground without it getting back to anyone? Does he really have that much sway?

What I gather from it all, without even trying to tap into their heads and emotions, is that they're terrified of my five-foot-six brother who can barely pass for fifteen in most crowds. I bite back a smirk.

The meeting ends, and I rise from my seat. It's not weird for me to be the first to leave. I walk quickly, mentally scanning for Devon and Caea on the upper levels. They're in a courtyard. Their thoughts are loud and vibrant. Enjoying themselves. Playing a game.

I reach out to poke Devon's mind, tell him I'm coming—

Intense pain, a dagger of fire and ice, slashes my spine. I can't breathe to scream, can't breathe to choke. I collapse, head slamming against the ground as my body spasms. My muscles feel as if they're being ripped apart with each involuntary jerk, and the roaring, fiery pain shooting through every nerve-ending I have doesn't stop.

I suck in tiny squeaks of air, but it's not enough. Black spots dance in my vision.

What's happening to me?

Make it stop.

Faces swim into view as something, someone, turns me on my back.

I arch but can't scream yet.

Fire eats me.

The faces looming above me smile.

I recognize them.

Hellene. Viveen.

And I know what this is.

The pain in my spine, lancing through every curve and straight line in the shape of Kahanna's Mark. The cursed Mark.

"I told Her that nothing descendant from a Peredil could be trusted. She finally listened." Hellene reaches down, fingers touching the tips of my eyelids, closing them.

Darkness fills every inch of my being.

# Evan

"HEY."

"Hey yourself." I hear the whistles of Lawrie pulling molecules from the air, combining atoms to create water in his palms. The droplets merge, becoming a ball of water that rotates on an imaginary axis between his hands.

I sit beside him, noting that his eyes are closed. He does that a lot. Keeps his eyes closed when opening himself to sensing elements, or just alone in a room. His other senses are sharper, his hearing and sense of smell more honed. He'd heard me walking up when usually only Adonis can tell I'm coming. I'm good at muting melodies that aggravate sensations which trigger the thresholds for acknowledging and interpreting sounds. In layman's terms, I can stalk with the best of them, but apparently not around someone who used to be blind.

"You're getting really good at that," I say.

Lawrie smiles. "Thanks. It's easier to feel things out with my power now. I kind of got used to it, you know."

"Yeah." I plant my hands in the grass behind me and take in Uncle Aeric's backyard.

It's really just a few leagues of a forest behind his house that he claims to own. Great to get lost for *jewels* in with cousins, Uncle Aeric's kids, who enjoyed running around barefoot.

Adonis didn't always come here with me when I spent seasons on Bruhje with this side of the family. The one he's not related to. The Amphoran side is more civilized, all about manicured gardens and landscapes. There was no running barefoot and coming indoors muddy with torn, bleeding knees and elbows. Uncle Rovn and Aunt Dahlia liked a clean, orderly home and family.

I love my uncles equally, but I've always felt more at peace here. In the wilds of Bruhje, with Uncle Aeric who understands what it's like to have crazy magic genes dancing around inside him, making him want to laugh too hard at things that aren't that funny. Or want to explore the woods for dangerous things and bring home creatures not meant to be pets.

I sigh, savoring the sweet scent of bread and honey. Sprite pee. Yum. "Uncle Aeric really needs to banish those things for good."

Lawrie chuckles. "They get on your nerves too?"

"Hm." It's not that they get on my nerves. They don't. Not really. They just... they call to that crazy, wild gene that makes me want to get lost in the woods and never find my way back. I could run barefoot and muddy forever, searching for dangerous things and making pets out of things that shouldn't be with no one to tell me to put them back.

I concentrate on Lawrie's ball of water, listening to the tinkling of bells in rapid arpeggios as the water moves. I pull on an arpeggio, marveling at seeing colors ripple through the water as it funnels into a thin straw, stretching upward.

"Hey," Lawrie murmurs, deconstructing the water I grabbed. My funnel snaps out of being.

"Not fair," I say.

He blows a raspberry. "Get your own water."

"The water in the pool's got sprite pee in it."

"Well, I'm not a sink, so—"

"If I get water out of the pool, I'm pouring it in your bed."

His eyes snap open. Gray-green, not the same color as before, and he doesn't have the same level of vision. He needs corrective lenses or surgery. He says he'll think about it later. He can see well enough, and what he can't make out, he can hear or smell or sense with his power. It works for him.

"You do *not* want to start a prank war with me." His grin is deranged, which sparks an unholy inner fire within me that makes me want to laugh too hard at something that doesn't deserve more than a chuckle.

"I think I might." I ruffle his hair, and he kicks me.

Moments like these are fun, and fleeting, between rigorous training sessions. He likes having solo sessions with me, and I can't disappoint him by not thrashing his ass every morning.

Yesterday, we got word that the Silver and Golden Allegiance Councils finally caught wind of our movement from somewhere, of the numbers we're massing. Turns out there are a whole lot of people who think all the councils are full of *pidge* and couldn't wait for a *gak mopi* like me to start uniting people under a '*fip* them all' banner.

My antics of being the badly behaved little leader of Rema with no filter won me votes where I needed them most. With soldiers and minor leaders sick of being told that every *pidgey* thing they got ordered to do was for the greater good. *Fip* greater good.

That's my motto now. I'll start the chant tonight, *Fip* greater good.

"You look like you're plotting a murder," Lawrie says, side-eyeing me.

"Just planning a motivational speech." My speeches are short and sweet.

Water splashes me in the face. I change the tune of the air around my brother, creating a cocoon around him so that he can't move, and hold him there. He fiddles with the atoms in the wind-net I built but can't alter them. Not like he could have before Niobe worked Her magic over mine.

I'm stronger. I see colors in magic now, the threads of The Tapestry, the essence of life, along with maintaining my ability to hear and shape The Movement, life's symphonies. I was never able to view the threads before now, and I still can't manipulate them, but Adonis always could, and now Desiri and Jalee can too. They've been working on learning to weave magic, to make something from nothing, with Adonis as their teacher.

"Dude, let me out." Lawrie fights my web as I adjust the tune to lift him off the ground.

He hovers a few *iuts* from the grass, and I urge the wind to move him further into the yard, closer to the pool full of bread and honey residue.

"No way!" Lawrie shrieks.

I bounce him higher in the air and feel currents of newly created wind pushing against mine. I'm stronger, but I let him win and guide himself back to the ground.

"Jerk."

"Maybe." I dimple.

The water sprites stare at us and croon a song I think I recognize… It's fast and… Oh. Disney. I loved that stuff as a kid. I sing a couple lines with the Water Children, and Lawrie makes a face.

"Seriously, dude? *The Lion King*?"

I shrug, not seeing the problem. Unless he's jealous of the notes I can hit and hold. Not everyone's as talented. As if he can hear my thoughts, he elbows me.

"You're so fuggin' weird." Said with love.

I feel it and reciprocate it with a burning urge to protect, teach, and encourage him. Uncle Aeric confirmed that it's a big brother thing, and it extends to Devon and Lyle. Intel confirmed when Devon and Xijure reached Lenore. We'll work out how to get them here, but right now, I'm just glad the twins are together. Hopefully Devon's taking care of Lyle, helping him. Making him take that damn Stone off, so that Order's not so loud in his head.

My Stone is a gray rock that doesn't transform when I near it. It doesn't acknowledge me as its owner anymore. Good riddance. No more voice in my head, no more temptation. We buried Lawrie's Stone deep in the earth and warded it with the strongest magic this side of Bruhje. He doesn't hear it anymore either, but it's still ready for him to reclaim it.

Which he won't, if I have anything to do with it. It's my mission to flush everything about Order and Pandemonium from this world, leaving it clean of godly influence and free to reshape itself in the image of whatever the *fip* it wants.

Lawrie grabs my shoulders and gives me a quick hug. "We're going to win, yeah?"

Every now and again, all the jokes leave his voice, and he sounds like he did when he was blind and not wanting to be alone. Scared, unsure.

I can't really answer him. Even with all the changes in my body, I still can't lie. So instead, I say, "If it doesn't work, it won't be because we didn't do everything in our power and beyond to make it happen."

"And if everything disappears because we didn't choose a side?"

I sigh. "Then we won't know about it for long, little brother." A cold, hard truth. If we fade from existence, then we can't care. We'll be gone. "But we'll be gone together."

"I hope that wasn't the motivational speech you were working on just now."

I snort. "My speech involved sparklers and sweets."

Loud yipping signals the entrance of four puppies bounding through the yard and tackling each other. Jalee comes out after them. I expect to see her smile, basking in puppy love. She likes things that are cute, but her face is grave. She catches sight of Lawrie and I and walks toward us with purpose.

Oh no.

"What is it?" I ask.

"You're being summoned." She sounds strange.

"By who?" I frown at her. Summoned? "Theorne's calling, or Viveen?" They were the ones who 'summoned' me, like a servant. Do they want to scold me or try to work the *rax* from this distance? Hah. It wouldn't work anyway. No Mark, no curse. Oh, will I love seeing Viveen's face when her trump card falls flat.

Jalee looks conflicted. "Come with me."

I reach to take her arm, but she starts walking back toward Uncle Aeric's back door before I can. We enter the kitchen, and she guides us past a few soldiers cooking lunch for us all. This house is our main base, but only a dozen or so people are here at time. They rotate, going to different planets and moons, creating and maintaining posts all over Bruhjen Space. This is our territory now.

Uncle's office is our conference room. I take calls from the leaders of my growing militia in here. Adonis and Desiri sit at the long table in front of the large screen that shows the inside of the meeting hall in The Maiden's palace. Around the round table sit Theorne, Viveen, Hellene... and Lyle.

The screen focuses on him. His eyes are cloudy, his face expressionless. I stop at the table, gripping it. Hear Lawrie gasp behind me.

"Lyle, what the—" he starts, but Lyle cuts him off.

"No binders. I assume your vision is restored?" His voice is robotic.

"Yeah," Lawrie says slowly. "Ly—"

"This connection was hard to achieve." His words are so formal, the speaking pattern foreign for him. "It will not last, so we will be brief."

'*We will be brief.*' "Are you—" I begin.

"Leader One, as Kahanna's favored Champion, She desires your return. All will be forgiven, and your place in Her new world will be guaranteed. She will even protect a select number of those you cherish. Be grateful for Her mercy."

I stare. We all do.

"If you elect to continue on your current path, your existence will be forfeit. What will you choose, Child of Magic?"

'*Child of Magic.*' I move closer to the screen, looking into the dead versions of my brother's eyes and falling into the depths of fathomless space. Images of sharp, jagged teeth and electric hair assault me as the sound of millions of fingernails screeching across glass makes my teeth grind.

Order's talking through my brother.

"What did You do to him?" I ask.

Silence behind me, laughter in front of me, from a humorless Lyle. His smile is pleasant and horrifying at the same time.

"I fixed him." She's not even pretending anymore.

"Bitch," Desiri murmurs.

"Get out of him."

"If you so choose, but that decision does require your return. Go on, Child of Magic. Say the words."

The words?

The ones that can save one brother—no, save two brothers, because Devon's there—from possession or maybe slaughter. Who knows what Order will do?

But their two lives against billions?

I shake my head. I can't choose that.

"Ev." Lawrie's behind me. His breaths are shaky. "You can't let Her hurt him."

I can. I just don't want to.

"Your choice?" Lyle presses.

"My choice..." I hesitate, studying him, memorizing the planes and angles of his face and forgetting those dead eyes. Then I lower mine and reach for the button that disconnects the screen, severing the connection.

It goes dark, the sound gone.

The room's quiet for all of seven heartbeats.

"Evan, what the hell?" Lawrie yells.

I dodge before he can hit me and turn to face the room. Adonis, Desiri, and Jalee stand at attention. They know the drill. They've seen the tough calls, the hard shots. Know what to do.

Lawrie's flushes with rage and an emotion that makes me want to hug him and tell him we're flying out after Lyle and Devon right now. We're getting our brothers. That's what I was going to do before. What I thought we could do before, when we might have been able to infiltrate the palace to take back brothers who weren't possessed by gods lying in wait to possess us too.

"Lawrie, I'm sorry."

"No, you're not!" His hands are still balled into fists.

"I couldn't say it if I wasn't." I keep my voice low, gentle. "But we can't negotiate on those terms. Can't trade two for hundreds of billions."

"You don't even know if we can save those hundreds of billions." His nostrils flare and he tenses like he's going to throw another punch.

"Or those two." I give a pointed look at his fists, then step away from him. "Stand down, Lawrie."

"You don't give me orders. I'm Leader Four. I'm your equal and co-leader of this revolution, and we're going to discuss this and make a joint decision." He uncurls his fists but his body remains tense, ready to fight.

The urge to hug him is so strong it hurts. I want to assure him everything will be fine. Anything to bring back what we had a few minutes ago.

"Leader Four is a Champion of Order. There are no Champions of Order in this army." I look him directly in the eyes and hold his furious gaze. Pity and sorrow bob in my chest at what I'm probably destroying between us. "The only Champions here… are Niobe's."

I don't break eye contact, as I hear and feel Adonis, Jalee, and Desiri getting up and coming to stand behind and beside me. Feel a thrum of power from each of them.

"We're the leaders now." I don't blink.

Lawrie's lower lip trembles, his eyes going wide and wet before he runs out of the room. Something inside me breaks. I want to chase after him. But I don't.

Without the ghost of a prophecy or fortune spell to haunt our steps, Adonis, Jalee, Desiri, and I are the first Champions to not have to play by any unspoken rules made by gods who didn't Create us.

I turn to my new fellow Champions. "Time to call our first war council."

## Chapter 22

# Devon

I HEAR HIM COMING. THE thing pretending to be my brother.

It stares at me through his eyes, talks with his mouth, but nothing that's my brother is controlling any of that. I search for glimpses of him, for fear or warnings, any signs that he's just playing along with Hellene, Viveen, and Theorne to get us all out of here later.

Mineshka's in the cell next to mine. She taps out rhythms in the wall, a song she and Loniad had sung on Disiez. It's how I know it's her, because I can't hear her voice, just make out the vibrations of her knocks. I never really thought about it before, but Mineshka probably hates being alone as much as I do. She was a twin too.

Was.

Because the thing that opens my cell door now and steps inside isn't my twin at all. I'm kept on a short leash, a ward that fans around my bed that keeps me from moving more than six feet on either side. There's a bathing column with a funky toilet inside, and I have a desk and a compal with no connection to the outside world.

Old sports videos and Earth shows play when I turn it on. Someone was thoughtful. There's even a fake window that lets in warm, false sunlight and shows me whatever sky I ask for. I request Earth, needing to see blue and white.

Not-Lyle doesn't move out of the doorway. Usually, he comes in and stops a foot from the desk, an inch out of my reach. I know because I made a grab for him once. He'd smiled without stepping back, knowing my hands would stop short at reaching the long sleeves of his uniform coat.

Not-Lyle wears ceremonial clothes inside the palace. Ornate silk shirts with silver trim in bold blues and greens. The slacks are tucked into silver-toed black boots. He looks weird, but good. No more dark circles under his eyes, no more hollow gazes like he's too tired to actually sleep. Bet that thing inside him sleeps like a baby. What would it have to worry about? Certainly not me, or family, or the people Order's going to kill on our side and Pan's.

Guilt. Regret. Should we have tried to stick it out with Pan after all? Sent out a mayday about Shiham and what he did? Pan hadn't liked the man. Maybe He'd have believed us. It's too late to know now, but maybe we would have been better off. I could have asked Pan to save Lyle, just like Lyle asked Order to save me. Bet Pan would have done a better job. I doubt I'd be in a cell again. But then again, trusting gods is what got everybody in this mess in the first place. So, who's to say I wouldn't be?

I sit on the bed, staring at Not-Lyle as he tilts his head at me.

"What do you want?" I ask.

"No pleas for me to let your brother talk?" His voice is pleasant, so un-Lyle. Lyle always sounded a bit exasperated or tired or bored. Like having to talk was a chore. I never really asked, but maybe speaking telepathically was easier for him.

I wish I'd asked him. Wish I cared to know when it mattered.

"Why bother? You won't let him," I say. "So, what do you want?"

The smile on Not-Lyle's lips is as pleasant as his voice and also completely alien on my brother's face. His smiles were either half-smirks or sarcastic. His real smiles were small and brief, unless he was charming a girl.

Emotionless eyes drink me in. I feel like a lab rat. At any moment, he'll pull a scalpel from his pocket and hack off some samples.

He folds his arms over his chest. "We require your service, as a Champion."

I snort-laugh. "I quit that job."

"One cannot quit a vocation for which one was bred." His proper tone irritates the shit out of me. I hate this imposter. Want to rip his face off and scowl at whatever's behind the mask.

I crack my knuckles and clench my fists, body tremoring with anger that I can't do anything with. I can rage and tear my limited space apart, but then what would I have? A wrecked prison that I'd still be stuck in.

Rage gives way to sadness, failure.

I'm sorry, Lyle. Lawrie. Evan.

A dull flicker of hope keeps me from lying on my back and giving up entirely. Lawrie and Evan are out there raising hell. Lawrie the genius and Evan the unbelievable. If any of us stand a chance, it's those two. But against gods…

"I don't have my Stone. Pandemonium's people took it, meaning it's probably with Him. Can't 'vocate' without that, can I?"

I don't look at the fake. He'll leave after a few minutes of not getting much from me. It's like this every day. He comes, asks me to be loyal to Order, to fight with him. Repeats the promise Order gave Lyle about being a part of Her new world.

It sounds pretty sometimes, but I think of all the people I met who aren't invited. Think about a squandered deal with Pan that might have offered us more. Think about how it all sucks and how we shouldn't have ever been fighting for a right to be without knowing it. And most of all, I wonder what it feels like to disappear and just not be. Because that's what all this is going to come to. So long as it doesn't hurt, maybe it'll be okay, and I won't have to fight anymore. Just fade.

I hear small footsteps.

The door's still open.

"Can I come in now? It's scary out here!"

I jump to my feet at that sound. That voice. That sweet, high-pitched voice that once asked me to fix her Barbie funhouse after Lawrie used it in a physics experiment. What the hell game is this?

"What the f—"

A little girl in blue jeans and a My Little Pony T-shirt peeks around Lyle's legs, little pink shoes lighting up. Hazel eyes grow wide when they see me. "Devon!"

She starts to skip to me. I drop to my knees, ready to catch her.

But Not-Lyle grabs her hand, jerking her back, holding her in place. She whimpers and scowls at him. "I'm telling Mommy that you're mean."

"I told you to stay put until I called for you. I will tell Mother that you were being disobedient in a dangerous place."

Nikki pokes out her lower lip. Her long brown hair is up in a ponytail with flower barrettes as decorations, and her little fingernails are painted pink and blue. She's so real and here, and the air around her seems brighter.

And that bastard's got her hand.

"Let her go." My words are strong, I stalk to the edge of the ward, touching the invisible wall. Staring down at my baby sister.

"Let me go," she echoes, tugging at Lyle's hand. "I want to play with Devon, not you. I have to show him what I brought! Devon! We're in a castle! There's a princess but she's all green and kind of mean-looking, and the flowers and stuff move around! Mommy and Daddy say we're going to live here with you for a while." She beams, smile taking over her face. She pulls at Lyle again. "Let go!"

Not-Lyle glances at her, and her body goes stiff, smile going slack, eyes going vacant.

The rage is back. I pound on the clear barrier that locks me in. "Stop it!" I'll... I want to scream that I'll rip him apart, but it's Lyle and not. I can't rip my brother apart, on the chance that he's still there.

Tears spill onto my cheeks as I scream for the monster to let both my little sister and brother go. Not-Lyle waits until I'm hoarse, until I'm quiet, then picks Nikki up, cradling her to his chest, eyes on me. I punch the invisible wall. I can't get to her. Can't get to him.

"Kahanna requires your service."

"What did you do?"

"I asked our family here, to keep them safe from the end of the world. Their travels were comfortable, and we have showed them every hospitality. It was a kindness, for you. For..." He smiles and taps the side of his head with his free hand. "Him."

Him.

"Let me talk to my brother."

The smile widens. "Kahanna requires your service. Will you choose to join Her?"

My heart skips as his words reverberate through my head. 'Will you choose…'

Choose.

Oh no. This is one of them, part of the spell. Was it planned to be this way?

"Leader Two?" Not-Lyle rubs Nikki's back, guiding her head to his shoulder. He turns so that I see her blank face and empty eyes.

I'm going to be sick.

Choose.

"I…"

He waits.

"I choose them. Him, her. My parents." Because he said they were all here. He brought them. She brought them.

"Say you choose Kahanna."

"I choose Kahanna, dammit."

The smile again. He adjusts Nikki on his hip. "You will need your Gift."

"Pandemonium has it." The words taste bitter as I press my palms against the clear barrier, wanting to take my sister from the monster in my brother's skin holding him hostage.

"There is a way around that." He kisses Nikki's cheek and sets her back on her feet. She sways but stands, hands at her sides, staring through me.

"What do I have to do?" I want to cry at how the brightness around my sister is gone. "What the hell do I have to do?"

Not-Lyle reaches through the barrier, hand gripping one of my arms. I yelp, stumbling back, surprised at the touch, and gape at his face. His eyes are black holes that remind me of shark-teeth and laughter like a zillion nails on chalkboards.

I'm pulled close, falling into those eyes, as the thing that isn't my brother breathes in my ear.

"You have to die."

# Order's Last Play

# Book Series

**Chronological Order:**

Book I, The Fourth Piece, November 2022

Book I, The Third Gambit, November 2022

Book III, The Second Endgame, January 2024

Book IV, The First Champions, TBA

**Join the mailing list or follow on social media through**

**EArdell.com**

Acknowledgements

# Author

First off, I want to say thank you to my family who may think I'm a little crazy, but who also support me: Mom (Teresa), Dad (Dale), and sister (Candice) Harris. I want to thank my godmother, Joyce, may she rest in peace, and her sister, Tommie, who have always believed I could do anything. Thank you to my best friend and fellow writer K. E. Andrea who keeps my science facts straight and whose pep talks keep my fingers on the keys. Thank you to my writing group friends: Janice Rocke, Jason Jurinsky, Brooke L. French, Spencer Lipori, Sarah Pruitt, Kelly Yarborough, Gaye Freeman and Andrew J. Stillman. I also want to thank Juanita Samborski, owner of the former 48Fourteen publishing company, who read my query for *The Fourth Piece*, and took a chance on publishing both *The Fourth Piece* and *The Third Gambit* in 2016 and 2021. When the publishing company closed its doors in the Summer of 2021, Juanita encouraged all of her authors to continue our writing journeys.

This series is my baby and without the people mentioned above my publishing dream would never have come to fruition. So, without exaggeration and with the utmost honesty, thank you to everyone mentioned and not mentioned, but you know who you are!

# E. Ardell

E. Ardell spent her childhood in Houston, Texas obsessed with anything science fiction, fantastic, paranormal or just plain weird. She loves to write stories that feature young people with extraordinary talents thrown into strange and dangerous situations. She took her obsession to the next level, earning a Master of Fine Arts from the University of Southern Maine where she specialized in young adult speculative fiction. She's a big kid at heart and loves her job as a teen services librarian. When she's not working, she's reading, writing, acting, playing The Sims, running writers critique groups, and even writing fan fiction as her guilty pleasure. Her first YA science fiction novel, *The Fourth Piece*, originally released by 48fourteen Publishing in 2016, went on to win the bronze medal for YA Science Fiction in The Readers' Favorite Book Awards 2017, Most Promising Series in the Red City Review Book Awards 2017, and to be a finalist for the 2017 RONE Awards for YA Science Fiction/Paranormal.

*The Second Endgame* is her third book, and a direct follow-up to *The Third Gambit* and *The Fourth Piece*. Get updates on the fourth book in the series, *The First Champions*, by visiting her website EArdell.com, and joining the mailing list!

Devon Lauduethe
Age: 17
Favorite Food: Seafood Enchiladas
Hobbies: Running, Baking sweets
Power: Enhanced strength, endurance, reflexes, and hearing
Fun Fact: Horror movies freak him out